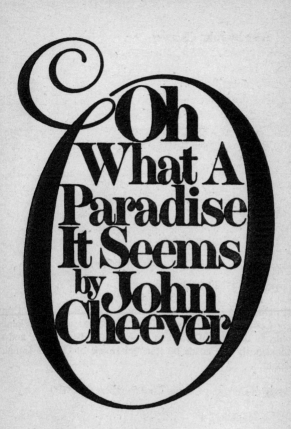

Oh What A Paradise It Seems by John Cheever

BALLANTINE BOOKS · NEW YORK

Library of Congress Catalog Card Number: 81-48109

ISBN 0-345-33832-4

This edition published by arrangement with
Alfred A. Knopf, Inc.

Printed in Canada

First Ballantine Books Edition: February 1983
Fifth Printing: January 1990

Back cover photograph by Nancy Crampton

1

THIS is a story to be read in bed in an old house on a rainy night. The dogs are asleep and the saddle horses—Dombey and Trey—can be heard in their stalls across the dirt road beyond the orchard. The rain is gentle and needed but not needed with any desperation. The water tables are equitable, the nearby river is plentiful, the gardens and orchards—it is at a turning of the season— are irrigated ideally. Almost all the lights are out in the little village by the waterfall where the mill, so many years ago, used to produce gingham.

The granite walls of the mill still stand on the banks of the broad river and the mill owner's house with its four Corinthian columns still crowns the only hill in town. You might think of it as a sleepy village, out of touch with a changing world, but in the weekly newspaper Unidentified Flying Objects are reported with great frequency. They are reported not only by housewives hanging out their clothes and by sportsmen hunting squirrels, but they have been seen by substantial members of the population, such as the vice-president of the bank and the wife of the chief of police.

Walking through the village, from north to south, you were bound to notice the number of

1

dogs and that they were all high-spirited and that they were without exception mongrels but mongrels with the marked characteristics of their mixed parentage and breeding. You might see a smooth-haired poodle, an Airedale with very short legs, or a dog that seemed to begin as a collie and ended as a Great Dane. These mixtures of blood—this newness of blood, you might say—had made them a highly spirited pack, and they hurried through the empty streets, late it seemed for some important meal, assignation or meeting, quite unfamiliar with the loneliness from which some of the population seemed to suffer. The town was named Janice after the mill owner's first wife.

One of the most extraordinary things about the village and its place in history was that it presented no fast-food franchises of any sort. This was very unusual at the time and would lead one to imagine that the village suffered from some sort of affliction, such as great poverty or a lack of adventure among its people; but it was simply an error on the part of those computers on whose authority the sites for fast-food franchises are chosen. Another historical peculiarity of the place was the fact that its large mansions, those relics of another time, had not been reconstructed to serve as nursing homes for that vast population of the comatose and the dying who were kept alive, unconscionably, through trailblazing medical invention.

At the north end of the town was Beasley's Pond—a deep body of water, shaped like a bent arm, with heavily forested shores. Here were water and greenery, and if one were a nineteenth-century painter one would put into the foreground a lovely woman on a mule, bent a little over the child she held and accompanied by a man with a staff. This would enable the artist to label the painting "Flight into Egypt," although all he had meant to commemorate was his bewildering pleasure in a fine landscape on a summer's day.

An aged man is but a paltry thing, a tattered coat upon a stick, unless he sees the bright plumage of the bird called courage—*Cardinalis virginius,* in this case—and oh how his heart leapt. But what was a cardinal bird doing on East 78th Street? He called his oldest daughter, who lived in Janice, and asked if there was any skating. Their friendship was a highly practical relationship, characterized principally by skepticism. She said that it had been very cold, there was no snow, and while she had seen no skaters on the big pond she guessed that it was frozen. His skates, she knew, were in the attic along with his Piranesi folio and his collection of mounted butterflies. This was on a Sunday morning in late January and he took a train, a local, to the province where his daughter lived.

His name was Lemuel Sears. He was, as I say, an old man but not yet infirm. One would not have to help him across the street. He was old enough to remember when the horizons of his country were dominated by the beautiful and lachrymose wine-glass elm tree and when most of the bathtubs one stepped into had lions' claws. He was old enough to remember the promise of dirigible travel, and he would never forget marching into one of the capital cities of the Holy Roman Empire. Turn and turn-about bombing had left nothing standing of this great crossroads that was higher than a man's shoulder. In the ruined cathedral lay the unburied dead. It was a lovely summer's day. He was armed with the earliest of the gas-recoil rifles (M-1), prepared to kill the enemy and defend with his life the freedoms of speech, religion and travel.

His daughter kissed him lightly. Their relationship was, as I say, skeptical but quite profound. She was the daughter of sainted Amelia, his first wife. She handed him his skates and offered to drive him to the pond but he chose to walk. It was around four miles and he wore a business suit with a vest and a fur hat bought in one of the Eastern European countries where he had frequently traveled on business for a computer-container manufacturer. He had white hair that grew like quack grass and a cat-boat tan. He was of that generation and class that regard overcoats as a desperate last measure. Of course he wore gloves. The pond he walked to was called Beasley's Pond but no one seemed to remember who the Beasleys had been. The pond was two and one half or three miles if one took the distance from end to end. It seemed to be frozen, although there were only four or five skaters on the ice and this was a clement Sunday afternoon.

Glancing at the scene Sears thought of how the eighteenth- and nineteenth-century Dutch painters had cornered the skating scene and that before the values of the art market had become chaotic there were usually, at the end of the art auction, half a dozen unsold Dutch skating scenes leaning against the unsold umbrella stand beside the unwanted harpsichord. Brueghel had done some skating scenes but Sears had seen a skating scene—

a drawing—from a much earlier period—the twelfth century he thought—and he always happily remembered Alan Gardener, the English paleontologist whose career was built on the thesis that the skate—or shate, since this came before any known language—had given *Homo sapiens,* as a hunter, the velocity that enabled him to outstrip Neanderthal man in the contest for supremacy. This was two hundred thousand years ago, much of the earth was covered with ice and the shate was made of the skull of the Judsas broadbill. That Alan Gardener's thesis was all a fabrication was revealed very late in his career, but Sears found the poetry of his ideas abiding because the fleetness he felt on skates seemed to have the depth of an ancient experience, and he had always been partial to any attempt to defraud the academic universe.

He put on his skates and moved off. This was quite as natural to him as swimming. He wondered why there were so few skaters on the ice and he asked a young woman. She was barely marriageable, with dark hair and gold rings in her ears, and she carried a hockey stick like a parasol. "I know, I know," she said, "but you see it hasn't been frozen over like this for over a century. It's been more than a century since it's been this cold without snow. Isn't it heavenly? I love it, I like it, I like it, I love it." He had heard exactly that exclamation from a lover so many years ago that he could not remember her name or the color of her hair or precisely what the erotic acrobatics were that they were performing.

He skated and skated. The pleasure of fleetness seemed, as she had said, divine. Swinging down a long stretch of black ice gave Sears a sense of homecoming. At long last, at the end of a cold, long journey, he was returning to a place where his name was known and loved and lamps burned in the rooms and fires in the hearth. It seemed to Sears that all the skaters moved over the ice with the happy conviction that they were on their way home. Home might be an empty room and an empty bed to many of them, including Sears, but swinging over the black ice convinced Sears that he was on his way home. Someone more skeptical might point out that this illuminated how ephemeral is our illusion of homecoming. There was a winter sunset and in this formidable show of light and color he unlaced his skates and returned to his apartment in the city.

But next Sunday he was back on the ice and this time there were more people. There were perhaps fifty—a small number for such a vast expanse of ice. A hockey rink had been improvised and somewhere to the left of this was an area where most of the skaters seemed to be accomplished at cutting figures; but most of the population, like Sears, simply went up and down, up and down, completely absorbed in the illusion that fleetness and grace were in their possession and had only to be revealed. Sears fell once or twice but then so did almost everyone else. Toward the end of the afternoon he maneuvered an accomplished brake-turn and stopped to listen to the voices of the skaters.

It was late. The shadow of a hill had darkened half the ice. The hockey game was in its last moments and the figure skaters had taken off their gear and gone home. The voices, considering the imminence of night, had an extraordinary lightness that reminded him of voices from a Mediterranean beach before, through the savagery of pollution, that coast was lost to us. He and his companions on the ice seemed to enjoy that extraordinary preoccupation with innocence that absorbs people on a beach before the fall of darkness. So he skated again until the sunset, kissed his skeptical but loving daughter goodbye and returned to his place in the city.

It was two weeks or more later when Sears returned with his skates to find that the ice had melted and Beasley's Pond was being used for a dump. It was a blow. Nearly a third of it had already been despoiled and on his right he saw the shell of a ten-year-old automobile and a little closer to him a dead dog. He thought his heart would break.

Why celebrate a dump, why endeavor to describe an aberration? Here was the discharge of a society that was inclined to nomadism without having lessened its passion for portables. Most wandering people evolve a culture of tents and saddles and migratory herds, but here was a wandering people with a passion for gigantic bedsteads and massive refrigerators. It was a clash between their mobility—their driftingness—and their love of permanence that had discharged its chaos into Beasley's Pond.

Why dwell on a disaster—and it was an absolute disaster that Sears saw, but a disaster with a power of melancholy. Most men have bought for their beloved an electric toaster or a vacuum cleaner and have been rewarded with transports of bliss. To see these souvenirs of our early loves spread-eagled, rusted and upended by the force with which they were cast off can be a profoundly melancholy experience. Thousands upon thousands of wire clothes hangers sounded the only homely and genuine note.

When he returned to the city Sears called his law firm and asked them to investigate the tragedy of Beasley's Pond. He also wrote a letter to the newspaper.

2

THE revolutionary discovery of the cerbical chip with its memory capacity infinitely greater than the silicon chip's had necessitated Sears's making several trips to the cerbical mines in the Carpathians and to the new deposits that had been discovered in the Danube Valley. At the time of which I'm writing both the silicon RAM and the ROM contained fewer than 16,000 facts, and while the silicon 64K contained 65,536 bits of information, the new VLSI circuit, introduced by the cerbical chip, contained more than a million pieces of information. A study completed by Thompson-Howard tended to support the superiority of cerbical chips. TH had tested 300,000 chips and found the cerbical freer of defects. The fact that the firm Sears worked for manufactured intrusion systems for computer containers kept him continuously exposed to the computer memory with its supernatural command of facts and its supernatural lack of discernment, and this may have heightened his concern with sentimental matters such as the end of his skating and the destruction of Beasley's Pond. Quite recently yet another sentimental encounter had become his concern.

The time of which I'm writing was a time in our

history when the line or queue had been seriously challenged by automation, particularly in banks. Customers were urged by newspaper advertisements, television and mailings to make their deposits and withdrawals by inserting cards into responsive machines, but there were still enough men and women who had mislaid their cards or who were so lonely that they liked to smile at a teller to form a friendly line at a bank window. They were of that generation who imagined there to be a line at the gates of heaven. Some force of change could be felt in the lines, but it was no more than the change one might notice in an airport a day or so after the fare to Rome or San Francisco had been increased. The air was filled with faint and random music.

She was two or three ahead of him—a remarkably good-looking woman who was an inch or so shorter than he although she wore high heels. She was small enough to be held—a consideration that he had come to think of as practical. Her figure was splendid and endearing. He thought that perhaps it was nostalgia that made her countenance such a forceful experience for him. It could have been that he was growing old and feared the end of love. The possibility of such a loss was much on his mind. When in the movies he saw a man and a woman kiss ardently he would wonder if this was a country which tomorrow or the day after he would be expected to leave. When he saw a couple in the street embrace with deep tenderness or walk delightedly shoulder to shoulder, he would be reminded, for no more than a moment, of his approaching age. This could have contributed to the fact that he thought her presence stunning. Her looks aroused the most forthright and robust memories: the flag being raised at the ballpark before the first pitch while a baritone sang the National Anthem. This was an exaggeration; but the memories her appearance summoned involved only brightness. Her hair was a modest yellow. Her eyes, when she took off her large dark glasses, would, he knew, be violet. In her rather small features he saw nothing at all like a mountain range and yet here was very definitely a declaration of paradise, either mountainous or maritime, depending upon one's tastes. He might have been regarding some great beach on another day of the week, but today he seemed to see the mountains, seemed disposed to raise his eyes, his head, and brace his shoulders as we do when, driving along some ghastly gambling-house strip, we see snow-covered mountains and feel how enduring is their challenge and their beauty. The components of his life seemed to present the need for a bridge and she and he seemed competent to build one that morning in the bank. She would, as a girl and a young woman, have been thought very pretty and this was an element—a grain—in the presence. She could have been the winsome girl on the oleo-margarine package or the Oriental dancer on his father's cigar box who used to stir his little prick when he was about nine.

The music that filled the air of the bank at that hour was a Brandenburg Concerto, played as rag-time. He imagined the smoothness of her naked back—its marked absence of declivity—so like a promised land. He wanted her as a lover, of course, and he felt that a profound and gratifying erotic consummation is a glimpse at another's immortal

soul as one's own immortal soul is shown. Our
lovers are always as tall as or taller than we. He
stepped out of line, tapped her lightly on the shoulder and said: "I wonder if you can tell me what
the music is that they're playing. You look to me
as if you understood music."

"You don't understand the first thing about
women," she said. She laughed sweetly and
dropped some papers she carried. Most of these
he saw, when he picked them up, were real-estate
advertisements, and when he passed them back to
her he asked if she was in the real-estate business.
She said yes and he said he was looking for an
apartment. She gave him a card with the name
Renée Herndon and they returned to their places
in line.

Sears was quite content with his apartment on
East 78th Street. He was not a dishonest man and
when he telephoned Renée Herndon a few days
later he fully intended to reward her generously
for any time she spent with him. He said he was
looking for a one- or two-room apartment, and
that he was prepared to pay a substantial rent and
sign at least a two-year lease. She agreed to show
him what was available the next afternoon.

The offices where she worked struck him as
being characterized by a kind of netherness. They
were on the nether floor of a nether building in a
nether neighborhood, and when he entered the
place he saw nothing that was not distinguished
by its portability. The reception room decorated
with a vast urn, filled with artificial grasses and
weeds, the receptionist's desk, the receptionist herself all seemed highly mobile as if they could be

moved, at short notice, to another building, another state or even another country. Renée Herndon, when she joined him, seemed quite permanent. Her hold on his attention, his senses and his intelligence was quite the most he knew of permanence, at that point in his life.

She was, he guessed, thirty-five or perhaps forty and would have been married once or maybe twice. Her past was, at this point, none of his business. She was the sunny side of the street. The uniformity with which women of her age then dressed—widowed or divorced, showing real estate or working in china shops—seemed nearly ordained. She wore a suit, a little good perfume and no hat. He would have liked to kiss her, as she well knew, and when they got to the street and he offered her his arm she took it warmly and smiled or laughed with pleasure. She said they could either walk or take a cab and he said that he would be delighted to walk.

They had walked for no more than half a block when she was attracted—magnetized was the word—to a display of embroidered scarves in a window. Still holding his arm she admired these. He offered to buy her one of the scarves and she politely refused, but her refusal was, he thought from his experience, genuine. He had known many women whose refusals were transparent. He felt that her distinct refusal to let a stranger buy her a present displayed a glimpse at the proportions of her self-respect. He thought this intimate and lovely. He was also delighted to see that in the three blocks they had to walk from her office to the apartment she was to show him she stopped to look at the display in absolutely every window with the exception of a window that displayed surgical appliances. They looked at shoes and hats and dresses and pottery animals and jewelry and china, and her interest in everything there was for sale charmed him and seemed to promise that she shared with him an undisciplined enthusiasm for men and women and circumstances and changes in the weather. The apartment she showed him was very different.

At about this time the high incidence of criminal rapes and robberies made it difficult to get into apartments in some neighborhoods, and though she had keys and credentials they had great difficulties with a doorman, whose uniform was unbuttoned and who cleaned his teeth, while he talked to them, with an old-fashioned kitchen match. When they finally got inside, the uniformity of the dim lights in the corridors, the sameness of the doors and the great difficulty she had in finding the place seemed to expose him to the loneliness of penance. The apartment that she showed him was a sort of nomadic hideout—it was still furnished with the chairs and tables of a divorcee whose lover or gigolo had abandoned her, although she still had photographs of him—many of them naked—hung on her bedroom wall. There was a narrow terrace from which you could see some blue sky, but the broad light of day could never reach the apartment.

She knew, of course, that he would not want it and said so. "I don't," she said, "know why I ever showed it to you. I detest the place myself." "It's given me an opportunity to ask you to dinner," he said. "I'd love to have dinner with you," she said, "if you don't mind having a late dinner. I'm busy early in the evening." "The time," he said, "makes no difference."

They walked back, now on the other side of the street, looking at the gloves, shoes, antiques, embroideries and paintings that were displayed. "When do we meet?" he asked when they reached the door to her office. "Thursday?" she asked. "Meet me in the parish house of St. Anselm's at about nine-fifteen on Thursday." Then she was gone.

St. Anselm's was Presbyterian and he wondered what she could be doing there on a weekday night. This was in Lent and the only church observations would be mournful. He didn't know but he thought the Presbyterians had a less exacting calendar than his own Episcopal Church, and he guessed that Thursday was not a church holiday and that she had not gone to church to pray. None of his wives or lovers had been enthusiastic church members and this might be the first time in his life that he had gone to church to meet a woman. St. Anselm's was on Park Avenue in a good neighborhood—that is a neighborhood where wealth was of the first importance. The main entrance to the church was dark and locked, but the parish-house door around the corner was lighted and unlocked. He let himself into a large vestibule. There was a second door—royal in its proportions. A sign was thumbtacked to this: MEMBERS ONLY. THIS IS A CLOSED MEETING. The sign was amateurish and he could imagine some woman—neither young nor beautiful but charmingly earnest—working on the sign at a kitchen table. Sears's

imagination was inclined to be optimistic and that
the gathering beyond the closed doors involved
membership—some vow or commitment or oath—
did not seem to him sinister. He thought perhaps
that dues were paid. He did not feel that to take
a look at the gathering would in any way involve
an intrusion and he opened the door a crack.

He saw an ecclesiastical meeting room or audi-
torium—one of those places where the rummage
sale would be held and the nativity play would be
performed. He looked into the faces of forty men
and women who were listening attentively to a
speaker at a podium. He was at once struck by his
incompetence at judging the gathering. Not even
in times of war, with which he was familiar, not
even in the evacuation of burning cities had he
seen so mixed a gathering. It was a group, he
thought, in which there was nowhere the force of
selection. Since the faces—young, old, haggard
and serene—conveyed nothing to him, he looked at
their clothing and found even fewer bearings.
They wore the clothes of the rich, the clothes of
the poor and a few cheap imitations of the rich.
Who were they: who in the world could they be?
Here were the plain, cheerful faces of the mixed
nationalities that distinguished his country.

He looked at the woman on the podium. She was
a black-haired woman, perhaps in her forties, wearing one of those long nondescript dresses known
as evening dresses although they are worn to weddings, christenings and barbecues. She was reading a list of names. Three men and two women
came to the platform as she called their names.
One of the women was bent with age, surely a

septuagenarian. One of the men was perhaps nineteen. He had three cowlicks and a high color and
wore a sweatshirt with Odium University printed
on it. Beside him was a blond young man in a
full suit and next was his beloved Renée, wearing
one of those very simple frocks that cost a little
less than a good used car. She looked as lovely—
as bright—as she had looked to him from the start.

"Turn out the lights, Charlie," said the woman
in the long dress. The lights went out and after a
minute or two of suspense a door opened and a
man came in carrying one of those flat, cheap
cakes with candles that are ordered to celebrate the
retirement of the building maintenance assistant
or the oldest member of the stenographic pool.
The lights went on and the gathering got to their
feet and sang in the customary genuinely sincere
and tuneless voices, "Happy anniversary to you,
Happy anniversary, dear celebrant . . ." Renée
smiled, laughed, and seemed truly happy with their
wishes, and he looked back at the congregation. It
seemed that he should be able to make some sense
of the variety in their faces, and then he found
himself, countenance by countenance, man and
woman, young and old, trying to imagine how
their faces would look contorted by the throes of
erotic love. He was chagrined at his willingness to
invade their lives—he was ashamed of himself
and he closed the door.

A workman was sweeping the vestibule. "What
is going on in there?" Sears asked. "I don't know,"
the workman said. "They're either trying to stop
smoking or drinking or eating but I don't remember which bunch is in there tonight. It's the no

smokers that give me a pain in the ass. I smoke a pack, maybe a pack and a half a day, I sweep up cigarette butts, that's my job, that's what I get paid for and it's nobody's business but my own. For instance I went to pay my state tax last week. This is in a government building, this is in a building I pay for and right on the wall there is this sign that says THANK YOU FOR NOT SMOKING. How the hell do they know that I'm not going to smoke? How do they know that I'm not going to piss or fart or get a hard-on? Thank you for not smoking. What the hell business is it of theirs? Thank you for not breathing. . . ." Then he went out a door.

A few minutes later Sears heard the group recite something in unison. He guessed from the eagerness and clarity in their voices that it could not be an occult mantra. It was difficult to imagine what it could be. The cadence had for Sears the familiarity of church scripture and might have been the Lord's Prayer or the Twenty-third Psalm, but there was some sameness to the cadence in the seventeenth-century translations of scripture and unless he was told he would never know what they were chanting.

Then the doors opened and they came out—not like a crowd discharged at the end of an entertainment or a lecture but gradually, like the crowd at the close of a social gathering, and he had, after all, seen them blow the candles out on a cake. He looked for her, he sought her brightness as he had for all his long life looked for lovely women in airports and railroad stations and ships' piers and now in a parish house. He saw her, as bright as ever, and he went to her and she took his arm as they went out the door and he hailed a cab on the avenue. "What in the world were you doing in there?" he asked, when they were in the cab. "Will you promise not to ask me that again?" she said. "I know this must sound unreasonable—I would think it unreasonable if I were you—but I spend quite a few nights in parish houses and I'd just as soon not tell anyone why. If you ever take me out on Friday you'll have to pick me up at the New School for Social Research. If you want to know what I'm doing there I'll tell you."

"What are you doing at the New School for Social Research?"

"I'm taking a course in accounting."

"Is this for business?"

"No. It's to help me understand my income tax."

"That's clever."

"You don't," she laughed, "understand the first thing about women."

He had booked a table at the most expensive restaurant where he was known. To his surprise, she was just as well known as he. The headwaiter greeted him warmly but he greeted her just as warmly. That she was intelligently aware of her attractiveness was apparent to Sears as he walked behind her to their table and saw how she carried herself. It was knowledgeable—so much so that he saw one waiter wink to another. This only increased the fun so far as he was concerned. For a first course he ordered some cold trout, most of which she ate. He ordered a '73 Montrachet but he noticed that she hardly drank her wine. She tasted his soup and said it was too salty but when he was served his duck *printanier* she ate as much of it as he did. She also enjoyed her own meal. Sears seldom ate sweets but she ate a *crème brûlée* while she told him what she pleased about herself.

She was divorced from a successful dentist named Arthur and had two children. Her son, who was eighteen, was absorbed in Eastern religions, but from what she said Sears wasn't sure whether or not he was in Tibet. Her daughter was in a ballet school in Des Moines, where Arthur lived. She said without sarcasm or laughter that she was at a turning point in her affairs. He felt that the time had not yet come for him to tell her that he was not really looking for an apartment although, considering the gait of her conversation, she might already know. "I hope we can go back to your place after dinner," he said. "My place is such a wreck that I would be ashamed to show it to you."

"But that's why I'm here," she said with a brightness that threatened to depress him for a moment but seemed then only a fair maneuver on her part. "I'm going to show you a new apartment. There is supposed to be a place in the eighties with two bedrooms and a marvelous view of the bridges. I thought we could see it after dinner."

He paid for the dinner with a credit card and when she saw the amount of the tip he wrote on the receipt she said, softly and sadly: "That's too much, that's really too much."

They took a cab to the apartment that was for rent. There was no difficulty with the doorman but the building seemed to Sears vast and labyrinthine. Forty or fifty stories in the air she unlocked the door on a tiny room that had a view of the river and its bridges and their lights. This was charming but distant. There were a very small bedroom and a kitchen and a locked door. She tried several keys in the door. "I know there's another bedroom with a view of the city," she said. "It says so here." She showed him some duplicated piece of paper that described two bedrooms, one spacious with a view of the city. But the door was locked. None of the keys she had would unlock it. She tried them all and so did Sears. "It doesn't really matter," he said. "I don't want to see the other bedroom. The living room is really too small. I mean I couldn't get any of my furniture into it. Don't worry about showing me the other room."

Worry was it; she was worried. When the keys wouldn't open the door she tried to force the lock with her hand. She kicked the door. Sears then remembered a scene with Estelle, his second wife. It was in some airport—London, he guessed. They had taken a night flight and it was three-thirty by their watches—an unholy hour. They were exhausted and deeply disoriented, and because of some strike or slowdown or some increase in passengers because of some historical catastrophe or celebration—an earthquake or a coronation—the whole process of claiming one's luggage and having its contents checked for contraband was unconscionably delayed. Before they were cleared there was dawn over London—a despairing light on this particular morning. He cleared the bags and was carrying them to the queue for cabs when Estelle stopped and tried to open a door on which NO ADMITTANCE was written in every known European language as well as in the Cyrillic alphabet. She tried to force the door's hardware as Renée

had done. She pounded on the EINTRITT IST VER-
BOTEN sign with her fists and then, as Renée was
doing now, she began to cry, to sob.

He felt then for his wife how much he loved her
and how absolutely ignorant he was of the com-
mandment that ruled her life. She seemed, pounding on the door in the London dawn, to have come
from a creation about which he knew nothing although they had slept in each other's arms for
years. His feeling for Renée was confused and
profound and when she began to cry he took her in
his arms, not to solace her for the locked door of
course but to comfort her for Arthur and every
other disappointment in her life. She wept on his
shoulder for a little while and then they locked
up the apartment and took a cab downtown. He
kissed her in the cab and her lips were as soft as
anything he had ever known and he thought that
he would never forget their softness; and he never
did. She wore a little more perfume than she wore
in business hours, and he loved the smell, but
when he touched her breasts she gently took his
hand away and said: "Not tonight, darling, some
other time." She lived in the fifties and he kissed
her goodbye in front of her apartment and asked
when he could see her again. "I'll be at the 83rd
Street Baptist Church on Monday night," she said.
"Sometime between nine-fifteen and nine-thirty.
You can't ever tell when the meeting will end."

On the next day Sears received a letter from a
junior member of his law firm—a man he had not
met—announcing the death, the murder, of the
lawyer Sears had asked to investigate the pollution
of Beasley's Pond. The lawyer had ascertained,

before his murder, that the Janice Planning Board had rezoned the pond for "fill" and given the property a tax-exempt status as a future war memorial. If Sears wanted to pursue the matter the young lawyer recommended an environmentalist named Horace Chisholm.

3

I wish this story I'm telling began with the fragrance of mint growing along a stream bed where I'm lying, concealed with my rifle, waiting to assassinate a pretender who is expected to come here, fishing for trout. What I can see of the sky is blue. The smell of mint is very strong and I hear the music of water. The pretender is a well-favored young man and thinks himself quite alone. There is, he seems to think, some blessedness in fishing trout with flies. He sings while he assembles his rod and looks up at the sky and around at the trees to reassure himself of the naturalness of this garden from which, unknown to him, he is about to be dismissed. My rifle is loaded and I put it to my shoulder and take the location of his heart in my cross-sights. The smell of mint seriously challenges the rightness of this or any other murder. . . . Yes, I would much sooner be occupied with such matters than with the death of the Salazzos' old dog Buster, but at the time of which I'm writing the purity of the water was of inexorable interest—far more important than dynasties—and the Salazzos are linked to the purity of Beasley's Pond.

Sammy Salazzo ran one of the three barbershops

in the village. He was a good man and a good barber but he never seemed to make ends meet. He lived in one of those little houses in Hitching Post Lane, a neighborhood that was once mentioned on Metropolitan television when it was swept by a plague of measles. The occupancy of a house there was signified by the fact that some sort of brazier for cooking meat over coals stood in the backyard. When the brazier went it meant that the family had gone and the house was for sale. The architecture was all happy ending—all greeting card—that is, it seemed to have been evolved by a people who were exiles or refugees and who thought obsessively of returning. The variety of these homesteads was international. They were English Tudor, they were Spanish, they were nostalgic for the recent past or the efficient simplicities of some future, but they all expressed, very powerfully, a sense of endings and returns. Anything about these houses that seemed artificial or vulgar was justified by the fact that they were meant to represent a serene retirement.

It had been a bad day at the tag end of winter. No one had come near the barbershop excepting the mailman and he had only delivered bills. Sam closed up the place at five and went home, coasting down the hills in his car to save gasoline. It is with the most genuine reluctance that I describe the house he returned to and the asininity of the game show that his wife and two daughters were watching on television. It was a show where a wheel was spun and when the winner was given merchandise, travel tickets and sometimes cash the award-giving was very noisy and demonstrative. Buster, the old dog, greeted him. "Where's my supper?"

Sammy asked. He had to shout to be heard over the television.

"There isn't any supper," his wife said, "there's nothing to eat in the house but dog food."

"I give you money to buy food," shouted Sammy. "What do you do with it? Throw it in the street?"

"With the money you give me I can't buy nothing but dog food," shouted his wife.

"Well, if we ain't going to eat, Buster ain't going to eat," shouted Sammy. "If I have to shoot Buster to get that through your dumb head that's what I'm going to do." His wife and his daughters either didn't believe him or were too absorbed in their television show to pay any attention to his announcement.

He got his rifle together and loaded the weapon. Then he went into the living room and turned off the TV. "You're all going to see this," he said. "It's about time somebody around here realized how serious life is. We can't go on welfare because I got this business but we got to make sacrifices and Buster is going to be the first sacrifice we make."

Both of the children began to cry, "Oh no, no, Daddy, no, no." In years to come, both of his daughters, lying naked in the arms of strangers, would say with as much intimacy as a declaration of love: "Did I ever tell you about the night Daddy shot the dog?" But now they were children, bewildered by the adult world and by a scene that would bewilder anyone in its grotesqueness. We know very little about the canine intelligence and nothing at all about the canine sense of eternity, but Buster seemed to understand what was expected of him and to welcome the chance to play

a useful role in the life of the family even if it
cost him his own life. The children were screaming. Maria's sobbing was profound and life appeared to her a chaos with no guiding lights of any
sort. Sammy led the old dog out into the backyard
and asked him to sit down a little to the right of
the charcoal brazier. He then backed away a few
yards and shot him through the heart.

As soon as she saw this, Maria went to the telephone and called Sam's Uncle Luigi and said she
had to see him. Sam came from one of those south
of Naples families whose bonds had been strength-
ened by their emigration to a new world. Luigi ran
the family restaurant out on the old post-road spur
that fed into the four-digit interstate. She didn't
ask to see Luigi, she simply told him that she was
on her way.

Luigi's was one of those Italian restaurants that
remind us all of how truly new is our settlement
on this continent and how many of us here are
still strangers. The rudiments of southern Italy—
its archways and masonry—were here, but like
some plant that has been transported thought-
lessly to alien soil the archways seemed to have
lost some of their ancient usefulness and beauty
and taken on new attributes. The place had passed
from one branch of the family to another and had
changed its name and its specialties again and
again. It had been Emilio's and Giovanni's; it had
had topless dancers and black singers and at one
time it had even advertised Chinese cooking. When
Maria came into the place that night a stranger in
a dirty tuxedo asked her what she wanted and
when she said that she wanted to see Luigi he said
Luigi was unavailable. She pushed past him and

opened a door beyond the bar, where she found Luigi watching a news show on television.

"Oh Lou, Lou," she said, and she was crying. "I know I'm not Italian and none of you think I can cook and most of the family treat me like a stranger but now you've got to try and help. Like about twenty minutes ago he took the dog out in the backyard and shot him where everybody could see. It's just that we don't have any money. We don't need very much. We don't need much at all. He doesn't have nobody but the family. He won't even join the volunteer fire department. I'm too old to work in fast-food places and I can't sew fast enough for that sweatshop in Lansville. You've got to help us."

"Sam's not sick?"

"No, he's not sick, he's not even sick in the head, he's just worried sick that's all."

"You live near the pond she's a called Beasley's?" Luigi asked.

"Yes. We live on Hitching Post Lane. It's about half a mile away."

"You tell him he comes here tomorrow afternoon."

The chain of energy in the Salazzo organization was exactingly familial and traditional. Their home in southern Italy had been along the sea before the Mediterranean had been bankrupted but they had none of the attributes of a maritime people with the exception of pirates. Nor were they like a mountain people. Perhaps all one could say was that they were a people who had been very poor. The exalted members of the family asked the governor to their weddings and two of them had had dinner in the White House. Sam knew this rank of

the Salazzos mostly from what he read in the
papers. He was one of a large number of barbers,
gas pumpers and masons who made up the Salazzo proletariat. All of this was true until the night
he shot the dog. The next night a large black car
stopped by the house and a young man—not a
member of the family—invited Sam to be vice-
chairman of the governor's committee for the impartial uses of Beasley's Pond. He would be paid
a salary three times what he made on a good day
in the barbershop. He was to avoid any sort of
show—he was not, for example, to buy a new
car—but the organization would help him to profit-
ably invest his savings. His only duties were to
collect cash payment for the dumping of fill in
Beasley's Pond.

Three days later Sam put a FOR RENT sign in
the barbershop window and at seven one morning
went out to Beasley's Pond where a five-axle, eigh-
teen-wheel dump truck was waiting. The rate was
eighty dollars a load and on his first day Sam took
in close to six thousand dollars. He kept a ledger to
record the dumping and had been given a leather
bag for the cash. He knew enough to be scrupu-
lously honest, and while the reputation of southern
Italians as murderers was highly exaggerated, he
had no disposition to steal. Each night at seven
with some punctuality, two men in a large black
car stopped at his house to collect the cash.

The collectors were not particularly sinister. The
older of them was one of those small, old Italians
who always wear their hats tipped forward over
their brows as if they were, even in the rain, enduring the glare of an equinoctial sun. These same
old men walk with their knees quite high in the air

as if they were forever climbing those hills on the summits of which so much of Italy stands. The younger man had a mustache and smiled a great deal. They both refused wine and coffee—they refused to sit down—and on Fridays they paid Sam his salary. It was a great deal more money than he had ever had before and he parceled this out to Maria although he was not ungenerous.

The only other witness to the assassination of Buster had been Betsy Logan, who lived in the house next to the Salazzos. She was a young woman with two small children whose husband worked in the post office. The Salazzos and the Logans were not friendly neighbors, perhaps because the Salazzos' daughters were too old to play with Betsy Logan's sons. The only closeness had been with Buster, who came over to the Logans for table scraps; and when Betsy saw Sam murder the old dog she felt nothing for her neighbor but hatred and contempt. She noticed the FOR RENT sign in the barbershop window and saw from her kitchen window the strangers who came to the house each night at dusk. From the rubbish that was dumped into the pond Sam had salvaged a broken over-stuffed chair and he sat in this while he collected his fees. Betsy had seen Sam reposing in this as she drove out toward Buy Brite on the interstate. He seemed to be supervising the death of Beasley's Pond, although Betsy would always think of him as the murderer of an old and friendly dog.

4

I N the next month or so Sears became familiar
with a great many parish houses and church
basements as well as with the vicinity of the New
School for Social Research, where she studied accounting on Friday nights. He was constitutionally
a traditional specimen with a traditional and at
times benighted concept of a woman's role in the
world, but her unchallengeable good looks seemed,
so far as he was concerned, to secure her place in
the stream of things. A good-looking woman study-
ing arithmetic seemed to him something of a lark,
and the people in her class in accounting presented an earnest, friendly and readily acceptable
appearance. However, the other gatherings where
she sometimes spent three nights a week continued to disturb him with their violent lack of
uniformity. Night after night they looked like the
crowd scattered by a thunderstorm on the evening
of some holiday in any park in the Western world.

The janitor had told him that these gatherings
aimed at abstinence in sex, food, alcohol and tobacco. He had suffered a good deal of embarrassment from carnal importunacy but he could not
imagine tempering this in a drafty parish house.
He had never smoked, his weight was constant

and he thoroughly enjoyed drinking. As I say, the authority of her good looks—she seemed too friendly to be thought a beauty—made her association with this weird crowd somewhat palatable. She let him kiss her goodnight and he would, for the softness of her lips and the fragrance of her breasts, have waited for her in a condemned mine shaft. She was, as women go, relatively punctual and Sears had come to believe that punctuality in engagements was an infallible gauge of sexual spontaneity. He had observed that, without exception, women who were tardy for dinner engagements were unconsciously delayed in their erotic transports and that women who were early for lunch or dinner would sometimes climax in the taxi on their way home.

Renée had nothing to do, of course, with the length of these sessions that she attended and Sears knew nothing but pleasure in waiting for her in parish houses and church basements, and watching the crowd with whom she chose to associate had begun to interest him, partly because they were her associates, partly because he was obliged by circumstances to regard them and because they so disconcertingly challenged his common sense. The traditional forces of selection—the clubs, the social register and the professional lists—were all obsolete, he knew, but some traces or hints of caste seemed necessary to him for the comprehension and enjoyment of the world. These people seemed not only to belong to no organized society, they seemed to confound any such possibility. They were a genuine cross-section—something he abhorred.

But since abstinence, continence, some intangible moral value was at the bottom of this group, how could he have expected anything but a disparate gathering? The life of the spirit had no part, it seemed, in the establishment of caste. Not, at least, in the Western World. Early Christianity cut the widest swath. So, coming from a generation that could, perhaps, be characterized by the vastness of its disposition to complain, he didn't suppose that he could scorn men and women who must be looking for something better. That things had been better was the music, the reprise of his days. It had been sung by his elders, by his associates, he had heard it sung in college by Toynbee and Spengler. Things had been better, things were getting worse, and the lengthening moral and intellectual shadows that one saw spreading over the Western world were final. What a bore it had been to live in this self-induced autumnal twilight! He supposed that these strangers—this queer congregation—would agree with him. However, he would not dream of abdicating his airs and pretenses for their company.

But she was always there—lightness and swiftness and the sense of an agility that flatteringly complemented his age. They dined and joked and she kissed him goodnight in the street by her house until one evening when she telephoned him and invited him to meet her, not in some church basement but in her apartment. "Don't bother to make a reservation," she said. "I'll cook the dinner here."

That was a rainy night. It would be very unlike Sears to ally the sound of rain to his limited knowledge of love but there was, in fact, some alliance. It seemed that the most he knew of love had been revealed to him while he heard the music of rain. Light showers, heavy rains, torrential rains, floods, in fact, seemed joined in his memory to loving although this did not cross his mind while he bathed, very carefully, and dressed that evening. The importance of rain is agricultural and plenty may have been involved, since plenteousness is one aspect of love. Darkness to some degree belongs to rain and darkness to some degree belongs to love. In countless beds he had numbered his blessings while he heard the rain on the roof, heard it drip from a faulty gutter, heard it fall into fields and gardens and on the roofs and backyards of many cities. He walked across the city that night in the rain.

At the time of which I'm writing jogging was very popular in every city of the world with which he was familiar. Toward the end of the day in Rotterdam or Moscow, in the brilliant winter afterglow that New York sometimes enjoys or in the early snows in Copenhagen you would find men and women of every imaginable age and specification going forth to enjoy a run. The only rewards for these exertions were small and worthless trophies. Commercialization would come, of course, but it would come later, and jogging was then one of the few taxing human endeavors that had absolutely nothing to do with the banks. One evening in Amsterdam or Leningrad—Sears couldn't remember the city but he must have known something of the language—Sears had stopped a dozen joggers and asked them why they ran. "I run to find myself," they said, "I run to lose weight, I run because I'm in love, I run to forget my debts, I run because I've had a stiff prick for the last

three weeks and I hope to cool it, I run to escape
my mother-in-law, I run for the glory of God." He
found all the answers gratifying and understandable, and now whenever at dusk in Bucharest or
Des Moines, in Venice or Calgary he saw the runners appear they seemed to him the salt of the
earth, they seemed to him stubborn and irreducible
proof of man's determination to excel. As he
crossed the city that rainy night he was passed by
many runners.

She met him at the door wearing a wrapper, a
shabby blue wrapper. He was out of his clothes in
a minute. "You were hardpacked," she said sweetly, sometime later. "You've burned the vegetables,"
he said. "I put everything on the back of the stove
when you telephoned from the lobby," said she. He
spent the night and left at around nine. Elevator
men, janitors, the whole service population play
an important role of approval or shock in our ex-
tracurricular appearances, and the elevator man
in Renée's apartment seemed surprised and bewildered by Sears's appearance. His look of bewilderment was followed by a look of solicitude as
if Sears aroused in him some concern. He asked if
he could get Sears a taxi. Sears thanked him and
said no. Sears thought him already a member of
the cast and wondered how the tip for Christmas
was arranged in that particular building, although
it was not yet Easter.

Oh the wind and the rain! Back in Janice Maria
Salazzo bought some wind chimes at Buy Brite
when she had some extra money after Sam shot
the dog.

Betsy first heard the chimes one night in early
spring when she was getting supper. Sam had

hung them from the ceiling of the Salazzos' back porch, which was very close to the Logans' kitchen, and even when Betsy closed the window she could hear the music of the wind chimes. That night their music woke her. It was three in the morning and she couldn't get back to sleep. The wind chimes seemed to speak to her although she wanted nothing to do with them. She blamed herself. She disliked the Salazzos because they had killed their dog and she disliked everything else about them including their wind chimes. It was her fault that she couldn't get back to sleep until dawn and when the alarm woke her the next thing she heard was the music of the wind chimes.

Betsy was working part time as a file clerk at the Scandinavian Lamp Factory, but when she came home from work and paid off the old lady who sat with Binxie she heard the wind chimes again. She closed the window. She still seemed to hear them and she went upstairs and closed all the windows on that side of the house. It was a warm evening for that time of year and when Henry came home and kissed her he asked why all the windows were shut. "The Salazzos' wind chimes are driving me crazy," Betsy said. "I may be neurotic or something but I hate the noise they make." "I'll turn up the TV so you can't hear it," said Henry, and he did, but when he turned off the TV and they went to bed at about eleven she could hear the wind chimes again, telling their dumb, continuous story in a language she could not understand. She imagined the Salazzos to be much less sensitive and refined than she and Henry and she guessed that their insensitivity involved an indifference to the sounds of the world around them, including the sounds of their wind chimes. However, they woke her again at three and kept her pretty much awake until dawn. She could not discern what she found so troubling in the noise they made but she thought they made a troublesome noise. When she came home the next night and was taking off her shoes she called her friend Liz Holland and told her about the problem.

"Well, ask her to take them down," Liz said. "Just tell her they're driving you crazy. Or maybe first ask her politely if she can hear them and if the noise doesn't bother her. Why don't you try that?"

At that time of year the Salazzos almost never came out of their house except to go to work. It was too cold for them to have filled their new stand-up swimming pool and there wasn't any grass to cut. Betsy didn't want to bring up the problem on the telephone but the next night when she was unwrapping some frozen vegetables she saw Maria Salazzo come down the back stairs with a garbage container. Betsy ran out of the house and crossed the yard. "Hasn't it been a nice day?" she asked.

"It depends on what you were doing," said Maria. She banged the garbage container against the pail. Betsy had been told that she sometimes drank a lot. She hoped she wasn't drunk. "I see you have new wind chimes," said Betsy.

"I got them at a sale at Buy Brite," said Maria, "but I think they're all gone. I got a friend in the Oriental Arts business who might be able to get you a set."

"Oh, I don't want any," Betsy said. "I just wondered if you can hear them as loudly as we can."

"Of course I can hear them," Maria said. "What do you think I bought them for?"

"Well, the thing is we can hear them too much," said Betsy. She was struggling. To say that they kept her awake would seem to state that she was an enfeebled sleeper. "I mean I wondered if you couldn't turn them off at night."

"You must be going crazy," said Maria. "You think I can turn off the wind?"

5

DURING the weeks that followed Renée refused
to take any presents from Sears. She gave
him a scarf, gloves and a pair of cuff links but
when he gave her a piece of jewelry she made him
return it. "You don't," she said, kissing him,
"understand the first thing about women." Sears's
sexual demands had given him a great deal of
pleasure, some embarrassment and a painful suspicion that the polarities in his constitution were
acutely incompatible and that the only myth that
suited his disposition was Dr. Jekyll and Mr. Hyde.
He'd never read the book but he had seen the
movie. Renée's understanding, her willingness to
accommodate him in taxis and hallways was of a
beauty that he could not remember ever having experienced before. There was an unspoken understanding between them. She had once said, over
her shoulder, that male discharges were in her
experience the most restorative face cream and
while he had heard this remark he had swiftly
forgotten it since the clinical aspects of carnality
were not what he sought. His importunacy and
her deep concern with youthfulness were facts
but facts that he would dismiss since in construct-
ing a useful paradigm for love there are various

39

organic needs that seem to contribute nothing to the pleasure we take in one another. They both had something the other wanted.

She was, in his long experience, the kind of woman whose front hall was always a mess. She was the kind of woman who always forgot to buy oranges and when you woke with her in your arms you would realize that the first thing you had to do was to put on your pants and go out and buy fruit. She was the kind of woman who, as soon as she entered her apartment, turned on first the lights and then the record player. Music had been playing when he first entered her apartment and it would be playing when he was long gone and forgotten. He knew from experience that silence— the absence of music—was for some men and women as suspect as darkness. It seemed a genuine need like protein or sugar but in his case continuous music presented a problem he had never before encountered. One night when they were making love the record player was performing a romantic piano concerto that closed with a long chain of percussive, false and volcanic climaxes. Every time the pianist seemed about to ascend his final peak he would fall away from the summit into a whole spectrum of lower octaves and start his ascent once more, as would Sears. Finally Renée asked, with great tenderness: "Aren't you ever going to come?" "Not until the pianist does," said Sears. This was quite true and they concluded their performances simultaneously. He never knew whether or not she had understood him.

He would have described her as a clever woman although from time to time she surprised and disappointed him. She knew absolutely nothing about radioactivity. When he came in one evening, very tired from a board meeting, and tried to explain what had tired him, she seemed bored and uncomprehending although he thought it simple enough. The conglomerate that owned his firm had, that afternoon, acquired an airline whose sales were three times as large as theirs. No conglomerate, he explained, should be overly committed. As she well knew, specialization of any sort could be very dangerous. Consider nuclear investedness: The cost of mining uranium had gone from ten to nearly forty dollars a pound while the price had dropped from forty dollars a pound to just under twenty-eight. The airline they'd bought only needed dynamic top executives to reverse their last year's losses of twenty million. When she whistled at this news she completely failed to understand that the superiority of his firm lay in the fact that they had lost thirty-seven million. However, he would have described her as a clever woman.

Her sister came to town and he was not to see Renée for a week or so. He missed her keenly. The physical deprivation was considerable and acute. On the day that her sister left she agreed to meet him for lunch and invited him to her place at one. He imagined that she would greet him in her old blue wrapper and that after they had made love he would send out for sandwiches. Dressing for the rendezvous he tried to remember what ties, shirts and suits she had said she liked, but then it occurred to him that he would be out of his clothes a minute or two after he entered her apartment and that there was no point in deliberating over his wardrobe. He even decided against underwear lest it delay his achieving nakedness. As we watch Sears put his genitals into his trousers it is worth observing the look on his face.

Sears was a thoughtful man and there was no effrontery or arrogance here, but he seemed to enjoy something very like authority, as if this most commonplace organ, possessed by absolutely every other man on the planet, were some singular treasure, such as the pen that was used for signing the Treaty of Versailles, robbing Bulgaria of Macedonia, giving her Aegean coast to Greece, creating several new quarrelsome nations in the Balkans, expatriating and leaving homeless large populations, giving Poland a corridor to the Baltic and sowing the seeds for future discord and war. Putting his genitals into his trousers Sears seemed to think he was handling history.

There were no cabs that day. He more or less ran to her apartment and was winded when he got into the elevator in her building. "Twelve B," he said to the elevator operator. It was the same man who had taken him down on his first morning. His face seemed to Sears to possess some innocence and so he could not attribute meanness to the exchange that followed.

"Are you her father?" the elevator man asked.

"No," said Sears. He could barely speak.

"Her grandfather?"

"I am her uncle," said Sears.

"Then you must have known her when she was a little girl," said the elevator man. "She must have been terribly pretty. She's beautiful now but I keep thinking about how she must have looked when she was a girl."

It was a blow to Sears, a stunning blow, although he should have been able to anticipate this in the way she wagged her ass around. Just following her to a table in a restaurant inaugurated an erotic competition that would leave the waiters, and any other players, obliged to dismiss Sears as an old man who, with his clothes off, would present nothing interesting but a costly wristwatch. He had been aware of the competition but he had always thought himself victorious. The blow was devastating.

When she opened the door she was not wearing her old blue wrapper. She was wearing the suit she had been wearing when she first showed him an apartment, and she also wore gloves and a hat. She was wearing the glasses she wore to read by and another pair of glasses—dark—either for cosmetic reasons or to screen the light.

"Oh, my darling," he groaned.

"I've made a reservation at the Tombeau de Couperin," she said.

"I've missed you terribly," he said. "I'm so hard-packed that I can't eat." He unbuckled his trousers and let them fall to his knees.

"I'm sorry," she said, "but I cannot help you."

"Don't you speak to me like that," he said. "Don't talk to me as if you were a department-store clerk talking to some customer about a discontinued line. You know perfectly well that you can help me."

"There is nothing between us," she said.

"I've fucked you a hundred times," he shouted, "and if that's nothing I think you highly immoral.

I've hoped all morning to see you in your blue wrapper and you've got everything on but the slip covers."

"Are you or are you not going to take me to lunch?" she said. "If you're too distracted I have a standing invitation from plenty of other men."

"I'll get some flowers," he said. He pulled up and fastened his trousers. "Wait here. I'll be right back."

She truly loved cut flowers, he thought. Cut flowers had for her a seductive force, and with cut flowers that sternness, so unlike her, would surely yield. He ran to the florist nearest her apartment but the place was closed. He hailed a cab and asked to be taken to a florist. It was a long search but they found one, where he bought two dozen yellow roses. Yellow was her color. He had often heard her say that she loved yellow. Back at her apartment he rang her bell for quite some time— a half hour, perhaps—before he would acknowledge the fact that she had gone out.

Now there are, it seemed to Sears, some Balkans of the spirit, where the villages are lit by fire and the bears weigh upwards of seven hundred pounds, and to which he now found himself quite helplessly being transported. Sears had taken many business trips to the Balkans and he was truly familiar with this world. He imagined some Monday morning—some Blue Monday—at the turn of the year, November probably, when snow was expected and his hotel room was cold. There was no hot water for shaving, there was no water of any sort and no way of procuring any. He dressed and went out to find that the elevator wasn't working. He walked

down five or six flights of malodorous and shabby
stairs to the café. The only person there was a
homely waitress in a very dirty uniform who was
wiping the dust off a rubber plant with a page of
an untruthful newspaper the tyrannical government published for propaganda purposes, distort-
ing all the facts including the weather and the
rainfall. When he asked for coffee—that most
international word—the waitress made an ugly
face and he realized that he was in one of those
provinces that had suffered the Turkish Occupa-
tion for centuries and that had seen no coffee since
its liberation by Alexander the Second in 1878.

He went out onto the street. The street was
named to commemorate the Plebescite of April the
Third. He turned right, looking for coffee, onto
Eleanor Markova Street. He didn't know it but
Eleanor Markova had, at some time in the forties,
been martyred by the Fascists. Markova Street led
to Liberation Street and he followed this to Freedom Avenue, Proletariat Boulevard and Victory
Square. He smelled coffee nowhere and saw no
smiles, no beauty of any sort, no brow even that
promised comprehension as brows will.

Sears had been raised by open-hearted and loving men and women, and why such a forlorn
mountain city should have established itself in his
consciousness was mysterious. He was truly a
stranger to hostility of any sort and yet, at the moment, hostility seemed to be his home. He had
loved his dear parents, he had loved and been
loved by his teachers and friends, love had illuminated even his military experience, and so why

then should he seem so susceptible to a hostility
that he had never known?

He seemed to have reached his Balkans by
plane. The plane was large and he traveled first
class, but he found himself in some airport where
no one could tell him when his plane would depart
and no one anyhow could speak any language that
he knew. His grief was more the grief of a traveler
than a lover. The grueling search for his baggage,
the ridiculous attempt to charm the customs police, the wish to send to college those venereal vagrants who haunt airport urinals had all contributed to his sense of abandonment and his gathering
fear.

The elevator door opened. It was not she. It
was the elevator operator. He was wearing
street clothes and a hat. He went directly to
where Sears stood and embraced him. Sears put
his head against the man's shoulder. The stranger's
embrace seemed to comprehend that newfound
province of loneliness that had frightened Sears.
He seemed to know all about that mountainous
city where there was no beauty and no coffee and
where a homely waitress wiped a rubber plant's
leaves with an untruthful newspaper. What the
elevator man then said came as a great surprise to
Sears. "I've worried about you ever since that first
morning," he said. What he then did came as an
even greater surprise to Sears. Sears had tried
genuinely to bring to his venereal drives something like the rectitude of Burke's *Peerage,* the
New York Social Register or the early days of the
Metropolitan Club. These congregations were, he
knew, not truly selective but they had the radiance,

the shine, of something chosen, an air of ordination that he unthinkingly admired. The stranger, whose name he hadn't learned, took him downstairs to a small room off the lobby, where he undressed Sears and undressed himself. Sears's next stop, of course, was a psychiatrist.

6

ONE of the several pleasures of Betsy's life was
visiting Buy Brite, a massive store in the
shopping mall on the four-digit interstate. She
liked—she loved—to push a cart with nice rubber-
tired wheels through a paradise of groceries, vegetables, meats, fishes, breads and cakes to the music
she danced to the year she fell in love with Henry.
Then when she paid for what she had chosen she
would be given a number that might name her the
winner of one hundred thousand dollars or a trip
to someplace like Honolulu. Betsy was not at all
interested in the paleontological history of barter
and marketing, but the purity and simplicity of
the bounty she saw at Buy Brite were like a re-
minder of the markets and festivals of our earlier
history.

It is because our fortresses were meant to be
impregnable that the fortresses of the ancient
world have outlasted the marketplaces of the past,
leaving the impression that fear and bellicosity
were the keystones of our earliest communities,
when in fact those crossroads where men met to
barter fish for baskets, greens for meat and gold
for brides were the places where we first grew to
know and communicate with one another. Some
part of Betsy's excitement at Buy Brite may have

been due to the fact that she was participating in one of the earliest rites of our civilization.

She had gone to Buy Brite that afternoon, leaving the children alone at home, in order to buy a bottle of soap that she had found efficient, sympathetic and cheap. This was called Flotilla. At Buy Brite there was a single entrance and exit. The corridor for soaps was a great distance from the entrance, and on her way there Betsy picked up a bag of potatoes (marked down), a jar of Teriyaki Sauce, a box of crackers, a dozen eggs and a pair of Argyle socks. She was careful to keep her purchases under ten so that she could use the express lane. Randy was an intelligent and obedient child but emergencies could always arise. There was the afternoon when he had gotten drunk on vanilla extract and been found playing with matches.

Now Betsy would have noticed the music that played while she looked for Flotilla only, perhaps, if it had been music that she had danced to or music that reminded her of the pleasures of dancing. Betsy was of that generation for whom the air was, oftener than not, filled with music. She heard music everywhere; she sometimes heard music on the telephone while she waited for her call to be completed. In some ways this had left her imperceptive. She would never have noticed that morning that the air of Buy Brite was filled with some of the greatest music of the eighteenth century.

This music had been chosen by a nephew of one of the majority stockholders, who seemed to think that there would be some enjoyable irony between eighteenth-century music and the tumult of a contemporary shopping center. He was, spiritually speaking, a frail young man who would amount to nothing, and the irony he so enjoyed would be discontinued and forgotten in a month or so. There is no irony, of course. The capital of Brandenburg was a market village and on a summer's day when the doors of the cathedral stood open the great concertos must have been heard by the grocers and merchants. Betsy pushed her cart toward the express lane to the music that has contributed more, perhaps, than any other voice to our concept of nobility. Betsy pushed her cart toward lane 9—the express lane.

Maria Salazzo was also there. Having, for as long as she could remember, examined the price of everything she bought, and tried not very successfully to cut their expenses by collecting coupons, to go to the store with a hundred dollars or more to spend was for her a new experience, a sense of freedom and power that was quite heady. It was because of this exciting sense of power perhaps that she headed for the express lane, in spite of the fact that her cart was heaped with groceries. She headed for the lane at the same time as Betsy. The scene with the wind chimes had left some enmity between them and they did not speak. They were neck and neck but Maria, moved perhaps by her sense of wealth, passed Betsy on her right. The queue was fairly long because at that time of day—twilight—shoppers were picking up what they had forgotten for dinner. First was a young man with two cans of cat food. Next was a black man with a bag of potato chips, a box of cheese, a can of apple juice and a novel about sex life in Las Vegas. After him was a woman with a dozen oranges in a bag, followed by Maria with a week's groceries. The clerk was too tired to send her away and began to check her groceries through on the register.

Betsy saw through the window that a light rain had begun to fall. She was worried about having left the children alone. Maybelle was the name of the checkout clerk and she wore a large pin that said so. "Maybelle," said Betsy, "would you kindly explain to this lady that this lane is the express lane for shoppers with nine items only."

"If she can't read I'm not going to teach her," said Maybelle. The twelve or so members in the line behind Betsy showed their approval. "It's about time somebody said something," said a black.

"You tell 'em, lady, you tell 'em," said an old man with a frozen dinner. "I just can't stand to see someone take advantage of other people's kindness. It's like fascism. It isn't that she's breaking the law. It's just that most of us are too nice to do anything about it. Why do you suppose they put up a sign that says nine items? It's to make the store more efficient for everyone. You're just like a shoplifter only you're not stealing groceries, you're stealing time, you're not stealing from the management, you're stealing from us. People like you cause wars."

"Will you shut up," said Maria. "Will you mind your own business!"

"It happens to be our business," said Betsy. "It's everybody's business. That sign up there says it's for nine items or less and it's for anybody who can read."

"They don't care," said Maria.

"What did they put the sign up for if they don't care?"

"Well, I know one thing," said Maria. "They didn't put the sign up so that troublemakers like you could interfere in other people's business."

"It is everybody's business," said Betsy. "It's just like driving on the right-hand side of the road. There are a few basic rules or the business of life comes to a standstill. I've left my two children at home alone because I counted on being able to check through the express lane without waiting for someone with a week's groceries."

"You tell her, lady, you tell her," called a man way back in the line. "You've got my vote."

"This line is for nine items or less," said Betsy, "and I'm going to see that we stick to the rule." She picked a dozen eggs off the counter and put them back into Maria's cart. Maria grabbed her hand and the eggs fell to the floor and broke.

"You keep your hands off my groceries," shouted Maria. "You keep your hands off my groceries or I'll call the police." She reached into Betsy's cart, took out a dozen eggs and threw them onto the floor.

Then Betsy, in an overwhelming paroxysm of anger, seized Maria's cart and, drawing it toward her, tipped all of the groceries onto the floor. Maria, quite as overwhelmed, and passionate as if she felt herself to be a figure in some ancient patriotic or religious contest, came at Betsy, swinging. Their raised voices, the screaming, drew a crowd, and perhaps a hundred shoppers, with their carts, gathered to watch these women fighting over groceries and precedents. The manager, helped by some members of the crowd, finally succeeded in parting the two women and sending them out on separate ways into the rainy dusk.

7

A^T the time of which I'm writing, vogues in healing were changing swiftly, and many of the old-line of yesterday's therapists were wiping windshields in carwashes. While the nomenclature "shrink" was long out of fashion and had been replaced by the old term "psychoanalyst," the conviction that one could master the mysteriousness of life through the interpretation of dreams and an exhaustive analysis of one's early life was perhaps the most prevalent form of belief in the Western World. This stood, of course, four-square upon the ruins of the legitimate confessional and the reformation of the roles played by parents in one's coming of age. The Freudian vocabulary had sunk well into the vulgate, and when the waitress at a truck drivers' diner spilled your beer she would say: "Oops. That was a Freudian slip." If you asked her what she meant she would say: "What's the matter with you? Born yesterday? Freudian means slippery. Get with it."

Sears, seeking counsel, thought of the word "alienist" because it had been in use when he was a young man and because it described that anguish that had racked him when he stood with his roses by the unanswered door. There had been nothing, absolutely nothing unfamiliar in the scene and yet he had felt himself more cruelly estranged than he had ever felt on an overcast Monday morning in some mountain village in the Carpathians. His doctor had given him a list of psychiatrists and he chose a doctor named Palmer because he had known a happy family of that name in the elm-tree-shaded lanes of his serene coming of age. Dr. Palmer answered the telephone himself and Sears made an appointment.

The doctor's office suffered that netherness that Sears had observed in Renée's office. He shared a waiting room, a toilet and some old magazines with a number of other practitioners. He was a tall man whom Sears would have described as ill-favored. Dr. Palmer was quite bald and the impression that he gave was mostly of bulk. He seemed to Sears mysteriously shabby, considering his East Side address, but Sears would blame this on his own parochialism. He was mistaken. Dr. Palmer was shabby because he was desperately in need of money. He was quite unsuccessful, plagued by the intensely internecine politics of his profession and worried about paying the rent. Considering the area in which Sears sought counsel, his choice of Dr. Palmer had been unlucky. Dr. Palmer was a homosexual spinster.

By "spinster" one means that Dr. Palmer, by a combination of ardent desire and pitiless repression, had exacerbated his feeling on the subject. He had, it seemed, from time to time endured random erections for a naked and anonymous male torso or the declivity of a male spine, and he had treated these arousals with vigilant repression. Indeed, he had crushed these random swellings as if they breached that paradigm that furnished his equilibrium. He was the victim of an erotic distress that in earlier and more traditional societies had characterized the unmarried woman who played out a role that was marked by bitterness, suspicion and loneliness.

While Sears told the doctor about the day he had bought the yellow roses for Renée and what he and the elevator operator had done the doctor squirmed in his chair. "You seem to think it neurotic of me," said Sears politely, "to be anxious about being homosexual, but in retrospect it seems to me probably the most sensible anxiety I have ever entertained. I've never really had any reason to be anxious about money or friends or position or health, but I did enjoy myself with the elevator man and if I should have to declare myself a homosexual it would be the end of my life.

"My sexual nature seems to contain some self-destructive elements and I've come to you to have these explained. There seem to be contrary polarities in my constitution. I think my sexual conduct moral only in that it reflects on my concept of love. This seems to be of the first importance. Renée had hanging, in one of her windows, a small crystal cut with many facets. When this filled with light it threw a spectrum on the wall, and one late afternoon I said to her, quite sincerely, that my love for her was quite as important, as iridescent and as insubstantial, as the beam of colored light. She said that I didn't understand the first thing about women but she always said that. She once took my cock out of her mouth only long enough to tell me that I didn't understand the first thing about women."

The doctor's offices were on the fourth floor of an old-fashioned building with windows that opened and shut, and through these windows Sears then heard the loud, cheerful voice of a man calling some other man to throw him a ball. It was a voice from the playing field but the depth of his longing and nostalgia was not only for his youth but for the robustness, simplicity and beauty that life could possess; and how far he had strayed from this! He was paying the doctor's rent in a sincere attempt to recapture this simplicity and usefulness, but the distance he had come seemed grievous.

"What are you thinking about," asked Dr. Palmer.

"I heard a voice from the street," said Sears. "It reminded me of summer days and happier times."

"Infantilism is obviously one of your greatest handicaps," said the doctor.

"I mean," said Sears, "that it reminded me of a fourth down with something like twenty to go. All you can do is to punt but how marvelous it is to punt, that feeling of booting a ball way down the field on a fourth down is such a hopeful feeling, such a feeling of beginning that I've often wondered why football never caught on in other countries."

"Did you ever make the first team?" asked Palmer.

"No, no," said Sears, quite sadly. "I was always second squad and a substitute some of the time."

"You're getting a little heavy," said the doctor.

Sears stood and said, "I'm wearing the belt I wore when I played football."

"Did you ever think of marrying?" asked the doctor.

"I was married twice," said Sears.

"Divorced?" asked the doctor.

"Both of my wives died," said Sears.

"Hmmmm," said Dr. Palmer.

Sears had met his first wife—beloved Amelia—at the intermission of a concert in Boston. Her hair was that light-brown hue that, early in life, turns a lovely yellow during a long summer spent sensibly on beaches, boat decks and tennis courts. This crowning with yellow passes swiftly—that may be one of its charms—and the gift is lost in one's early twenties. Their encounter came late in October; she was barely twenty and her hair was streaked with gold. This contrasted with her eyebrows. These were uncommonly heavy and dark and she carried her head in a lifted manner as if her eyebrows were something of a burden. Her figure was superb and she wore that afternoon a black velvet dress and carried a copy of *Paris Match,* folded to a page where there was a recipe for codfish served with cheese sauce. Sears felt at once that he had known her in some other life and he would never have any occasion to question the authority of this sensation of familiarity. When she lay dying in his arms, twenty years later, his grief was unassuageable but there was a sense that she was returning to some stratum of existence where they had first met and where they would meet again.

His second wife was not so much his choice as he was hers. She had ended an unhappy, childless marriage with a divorce, and when she proposed to Sears he simply accepted. She claimed to have

great insights into the future, and she assured
Sears that they would be very happy together.
After their marriage Sears discovered that Estelle,
his wife, considered herself a professional in occult matters. She defended her prescience compe-
titively as if supernatural insights were a field
sport. Sears's only other experience in this area
had been in Eastern Europe, where there was a
celebrated prophetess named Gallia. Sears had
heard of her mostly from American businessmen
who traveled to the cave where she lived and paid
large sums of money for her advice.

One evening, in Eastern Europe, a chance
American drinking companion had described Gallia's powers to Sears. She had prophesied an accident at their New Mexico mines, where millions of
gallons of radioactive mill tailings would have
been spilled. She had also, that year, prophesied
that uranium prices would fall. Sears had been
told that she had been blinded by lightning as a
child and that she lived in an extinct volcano, not
far from where one of the most famous oracles
of the ancient world had lived. The Minister of
Information had often offered to try and arrange
a meeting with Gallia, but Sears's lack of interest
in the occult was genuine. Returning one late
afternoon to his hotel after a tiring day, he found
an aide to the Minister of Information in the
lobby with the message that Gallia would see him.
He asked if there was time to change his shirt
and he was told there was not. He got into one of
those large cars that cabinet ministers enjoy in so-
cialist countries.

In the car he joined his interpreter, a middle-

aged woman whose language with him would be
French. The minister had furnished the car with
some ice and a bottle of whiskey. Sears was terribly tired. The car radio was on, very loud, and
Sears knew enough not to have it turned off; it
would be such a disappointment to the chauffeur.
There is some sameness to car radio music all
over the world and he would hear Hoagy Carmi-
chael's "Stardust" and the second Razumovsky
Quartet. In that part of the world there were regular reports on the water level of the Danube River.
It was a country where there were very few cars,
and they traveled through the farmland at a hundred miles an hour. This splendid rich country was
farmed still by hand. He was not that afternoon
to see a single piece of farm machinery, and although it was late in the day men and women
were still hoeing the rows. A few of these waved
happily to the limousine. The beauty of fertile,
well-irrigated and intelligently planted farmland
moved him and he was able to trace and admire
the fact that the variety of plantings reflected the
changed nature of the soil as they approached the
acid lava of the old volcanos he saw on the horizon.

He wondered what questions he might ask the
oracle. His business prospered, he loved his wife
and his children, his investments were insured
and his health was splendid. He couldn't think of
anything to ask her. He had been told by his
American friend that she was a terrifying presence, so frightening that it was sometimes difficult
to ask her your prepared questions. He tried to
imagine some traditional monster with a head

covered with adders and a mouth filled with fire,
but he was either too tired or too drunk or too
solaced by the beauty of the farmland to feel anxious about his interview with Gallia. His interpreter
was telling him about her beginnings. The story
was nearly as familiar as the radio music. Her
family had lost the houses and villas that most
families have lost at one time or another.

They arrived at the foot of the volcano a little
before dark. "Aren't you frightened?" the interpreter asked. "Oh yes, yes," said Sears politely. He
did not feel that he was giving the interview its
importance. There was a little garden at the entrance to the prophetess's cave and Sears noticed
that the soil was so acid it supported almost nothing but parsley. "Please let me take your arm,"
said the interpreter. "I'm so frightened I can hardly
speak."

There was a sort of room in the cave lighted by
a single electric bulb. Sears wondered where the
power came from. The prophetess sat at a plain
table covered with clean oilcloth. She was a mid-
dle-aged woman whose hair had begun to gray
and who held her head high with her blinded eyes
closed. She wore a clean cotton dress. Sears's feeling for her was one of absolute friendliness. This
wonder, who had prophesied the fall of uranium
prices, excited in him the broadest smile.

She asked to feel something of his and he gave
her his wallet. She fingered the wallet and began
to smile. Then she began to laugh. So did Sears.
She returned the wallet to him and said something
to his interpreter. "I have no idea what she means,"
said the interpreter, "but what she said was 'La

grande poésie de la vie.' " The prophetess stood
and so did Sears. They were both laughing. Then
she held out her arms and he embraced her. They
parted, laughing. Night had fallen and as soon as
he started the car the chauffeur turned on the
radio to very loud music and they returned to the
capital.

This cheerful brush with a prophet was no help
at all in Sears's understanding of Estelle. She
thought her prophetic attributes of the first importance. She seemed to think of them more as
an achievement than a gift. She felt that the world
we see—the world Sears adored—was superficial
and, in her case, transparent and that she could
see a more real world where love and death were
visibly ordained. It seemed to Sears that her fore-
sight was largely pessimistic. She most often
prophesied quarrels, poverty, divorce, madness and
suicide. Sears could not remember her having
prophesied any triumphs of the spirit. She dyed
her hair red and wore lime-green dresses, and
when you were introduced to her you would feel
that you had met her at cocktail parties. I don't
mean five or ten cocktail parties—I mean hundreds
and hundreds of cocktail parties before that social
ceremony vanished from the calendar and when
the cocktail party seemed as much as part of nightfall as the lengthening shadows. She seemed so
allied to the cocktail party that one wondered what
would become of her when that ritual had become
obsolete.

It would have been very unlike Sears to check
on the accuracy of her prophecies. When they returned home in the evening after a party she
would sit at her dressing table and say that it had

been revealed to her that the A's would divorce, B would lose all of his money, C would be arrested for fraud and Mrs. E would go mad. She considered prophecy to be her outstanding social gift, and the complex irony of claiming to know the future was revealed one night to Sears when they were entertaining. Estelle was a dreadful cook—indeed she was a dangerous cook and she had that night prepared a risotto that was particularly lethal. While she prophesied lengthily the misfortunes of a family in the neighborhood, Sears worried a little about what he knew of the immediate future. He knew that at three or four in the morning that was to come every one of their twelve guests, poisoned by the risotto, would spend an hour or more on the toilet, racked by excruciating diarrhea. While Estelle, with her eyes half-closed, sketched the future, Sears wondered why her prescience should overlook that violence in the immediate future that he was able to predict.

Her ending was rather like this. She had been to a matinee in Philadelphia and had returned by train to the suburb where they then lived. She could reach the lot where her car was parked by an underpass beneath the tracks or by an unsafe wooden walk that predated the underpass. It was a winter dusk. She had started across the walk when a young man shouted: "Hey, lady, that ain't safe. A train is coming." "Who *do* you think you are speaking to?" she exclaimed, believing in introductions and other courtesies. "I happen to *know* the future." She stepped straight into the path of the Trenton Express and nothing was found of her but a scrap of veiling and a high-heeled shoe.

"Your male lover is a traditional invention of the neurotic," said Dr. Palmer. "You have invented some ghostly surrogate of a lost school friend or a male relation from your early youth."

"I'm not sure what you mean by ghost," said Sears. "It may be that for a man of my age love is rather elusive. I seem these days to know love only briefly, but I honestly can't agree with you when you say that Eduardo is a surrogate. He seems to offer me an understanding of modes of loneliness that are quite new to me and new I expect to other men, since they mostly involve new places like airports."

"Of course you're afraid of flying," said the alienist.

"I am not afraid of flying," said Sears, "but I am afraid of airports."

"Do you really think you understand Renée?"

"Oh, no," exclaimed Sears, "but I never really cared about those parts of her life that she meant to keep private. I mean, I kept picking her up in these church basements where she was trying to stop smoking or drinking or eating too much. Sometimes I thought it was all three. Sometimes when we go out to a restaurant she eats most of my dinner, but she never gets fat. I think she wants to improve her ways, and I believe there are more people who feel like this than you might guess from looking at the faces in the street."

"Do you have any friends?" asked Dr. Palmer.

"I have loads of friends," said Sears.

"That is," said the doctor, "the classical reply of the neurotic, who constructs a carapace of friendliness and popularity to conceal his clinical aloneness. If you have so many friends you might send a few my way as patients. The politics in this profession are absolutely indescribable. Otherwise I wouldn't ask your help. I'd like to see you tomorrow at the same time."

8

THE telephone was ringing when Sears returned
to his apartment. It was Renée asking him over
for a drink. He was delighted. Considering their
last quarrel he expected her to be wearing the old
blue wrapper when she opened the door, or perhaps nothing at all. He was smiling at this possibility when he entered the lobby and saw Eduardo,
who laughed at the breadth of his smile. Here
seemed to be a union from which jealousy had
been leached. She opened the door as soon as he
rang. He was disappointed to see she was not wearing the old blue wrapper. She was wearing a dress
and some shoes and some perfume, but when she
kissed him her kisses were of such an inestimable
softness and variety that he didn't worry about
her clothing. She gave him a drink and sat on his
lap and unfastened both his shirt and his trousers.
While she fingered his trunk he remembered that
the gymnastics instructor at his school had lec-
tured them on the fact that the male torso, dis-
figured as it was by vestigial nipples, was totally
unresponsive sensually. He had, until very recently,
never doubted this statement. This was really
what one wanted, he thought. To have a lovely
woman on one's lap as darkness fell from the

wings of night was truly journey's end. She was kissing him when the telephone rang and she left his lap to answer it. "I'll be down in a few minutes," she said. "The doorman will let you double-park."

"What in hell was that?" said Sears.

"It was the man who's going to drive me to the airport."

She went into the hallway, where he heard her open a closet.

"Where are you going?" Sears demanded. "You haven't told me you were going anywhere and you certainly haven't behaved as if you were taking a plane."

"You might have noticed that my suitcase is in the hallway. You always notice that sort of thing."

"I've noticed that your hallway is always full of suitcases," Sears shouted. "I've been stumbling over the damned things for months."

"Well, would you like to help me to the elevator with my suitcase," she asked, "or shall I ring for Eduardo?"

She stood in the doorway wearing a hat and a coat and pulling on her gloves. He felt himself approaching those bewildering spiritual mountains where he doubted the reality of his person and his world. He went into the hallway and picked up her bag. "Where in hell are you going?" he asked.

"I'm going back to Des Moines to see my daughter," she said. "I must have told you but you've forgotten." Eduardo, rather more like a custodial relative than a lover, regarded the suitcase, Sears's face white with rage and Renée's airs of a traveler with great composure. Sears's only commitment was to wait for her on the sidewalk until the car

had its door opened and to accept her goodbye
kiss. "You don't know the first thing about women,"
she said. He did not look back in the lobby at
Eduardo and went to a movie. To scorn one's world
is despicable, he thought, and he would merely
observe that the theatre he chose was nearly empty,
that the film was about werewolves and that a
man in the row ahead of him had brought his
dinner to the theatre and ate it during the film.
When the movie ended Sears returned to Renée's
house and found Eduardo in the lobby. He was
pleased to see him as he would have been pleased
to see a dear friend. "We've got to find something
else we can do together," he said. "Do you like to
fish? Would you like to go fishing?"

"Sure I'd like to go fishing," said Eduardo. "I've
got some time coming, but I'll have to check with
the union about a replacement."

"I know of a good bass pond upstate," said
Sears. "There used to be a decent inn there. Do
you have any tackle?"

"I think I have a couple of bait-casting rods,"
said Eduardo. "I'll have to look. My sons may have
taken them."

"What do your sons do?" asked Sears.

"The youngest is a senior at Rutgers," said
Eduardo. "The oldest plays jazz piano in a place in
Aspen. That's in Colorado."

"Well, goodnight," said Sears. "We'll work out
something."

"Goodnight."

Ten days later in a rented car Sears and Eduardo
headed north for a pond near the Canadian
wilderness that Sears recalled having fished ten

years ago, although his memory was often mistaken and it might have been twenty years in the past or even longer. They left for the north on a rainy morning and this corresponded exactly to Sears's sense of the fitness of things. Eduardo drove until they stopped somewhere for lunch and Sears then said, "I'll drive." Eduardo tossed him the keys, and as soon as he started north in the rain Eduardo fell asleep. Sears was terribly happy.

He drove north on route 774, which had, like any main thoroughfare, changed greatly in the last ten years. Sears was not disenchanted but he did observe what there was to be seen. They traveled through what had been a neighborhood of small dairy farms, where the acre and half-acre fields had been divided by stone walls and light stands of timber. There were a few churches and farmhouses from the nineteenth century and even earlier that were completely unpretentious but that, in their charm and inventiveness, seemed outstandingly patrician. Seven seventy-four was now a length in that highway of merchandising that reaches across the continent. It would be absurd to regret the obsolescence of the small dairy farm, but the ruined villages were for Sears a melancholy spectacle, as if a truly adventurous people had made a wrong turning and stumbled into a gypsy culture. Here were the most fleeting commitments and the most massive household gods. Beside a porn drive-in movie were two furniture stores whose items needed the strength of two or three men to be moved. He thought it a landscape, a people—and he counted himself among them— who had lost the sense of a harvest.

While he drove he thought self-righteously of

what he had done to improve the scene; what he
had done for Beasley's Pond. He had employed the
environmentalist—Chisholm—and paid a laboratory at Cornell to specify the toxicity in the water.
The reports were not completed, but there was to
be a hearing in the town of Janice in the coming
week. Chisholm spoke of the people who were de-
stroying the pond as a huge and powerful criminal
organization, who were bribing small municipali-
ties and polluting water supplies to profit from the
high cost of fill sites. Sears was not completely
persuaded. Chisholm was one of those men whose
worthwhileness, it seemed to Sears, was more of
a genetic trait than a persuasion. One found them
all over the world. The size of Chisholm's teeth,
the thickness of his glasses, his stoop and the
spring with which he walked all marked him, Sears
thought, as a single-minded reformer. His marriage, Sears guessed, would have been unsuccessful and his children would have difficulty finding
themselves. Sears was not far from wrong. Seven
seventy-four seemed an extension of the destruction of Beasley's Pond.

It was late when they reached the inn. Sears
was disappointed but not surprised to find his inn
flanked by two fried-food shops. The inn had
changed ownership many, many times since he
had been there. They drank a lot at the bar but
whenever they mentioned fishing the barman
changed the subject. The kitchen was closed and
they ate sandwiches for supper. In their room they
watched a show on television and went together
to bed. Sears woke up. He had no idea of the hour
but it was that hour when one is given the illusion
of insight. He went to the window. The fried-food

places were closed but the window was open and the smell of fried food filled the room.

It was the smell of fried food that seemed to fill his consciousness. He thought, but only for a moment, of fried food as a new aberration like the strip with its cut-rate outlets and drive-in peep shows. He hastily amended this random thought with the knowledge that fried food had been one of the first things to be smelled on the planet. After the discovery of love, the importance of hunting and the constancy of the solar system came the smell of frying food. Even now, at the end of harvest in the most inaccessible of the Carpathians the shepherds come down from the mountains with their herds in the autumn to hear gypsy fiddlers and a snareless drum and smell sausages rotating over charcoal. It was barbarous—it disclaimed authority—and its magic was malnutrition, acne and grossness. It was indigestible and highly odorous and would be, if you were unlucky, the last thing you smelled on your way to the executioner's block. And it was portable. You had to be able to eat it as you sat in a saddle or rode on a Ferris wheel or walked the midways and alleys of some country fair. You had to be able to eat it with your fingers, picking it from a cornucopia of leaves or bark or human skin while you paddled your war canoe or marched into battle. They were eating fried food when they made the first human sacrifice. Eggplant was being fried in the Colosseum when they broke the philosopher on the wheel and fed the saints to the lions. They were eating fried food when they hung the witches, quartered the pretender and crucified the thieves. Public executions were our first celebrations and this was holiday food. It was also the food for lovers, gamblers, travelers and nomads. By celebrating and extolling fried food, all the great highways of the world kept alive our early memories of itinerant hunters and fishermen when we possessed no history and very little vision. It was the food for spiritual vagrants.

Eduardo was sleeping noisily when Sears returned to bed. Sears had been told that such lovers were always thieves, liars, felons, and sometimes murderers, but he thought he had never known anyone so honest. He felt then a surge of lewdness and with this some revelation that these caverns of his nature would never enjoy coherence. What he felt for Eduardo seemed more like nostalgia than the adventurousness of traditional love but it felt no less powerful. He saw then that if he was truly seeking purity he would never find it in himself.

In the morning they woke quite happily. Eduardo washed his hair with a shampoo that, Sears noticed, was advertised to make his head a glory of lustrous radiance. It reminded Sears of the happy and robust vanity of that time of life and—with no ruefulness at all—of the vast difference in their ages. How long it had been since Sears had ducked his head into a basin of water and combed his hair with the hope of appearing attractive.

After breakfast they rented an outboard. Fishing water was for Sears a creation with which he enjoyed a powerful rapport. He was enjoying this while tying a leader when the man who had rented them the boat came over and said: "I can't let you men go out without telling you that there hasn't been a fish here for about ten years. The last time

the water was tested—that was three years ago,
I think—it was a little more acid than commercial
vinegar."

"Are there any other ponds around here?" Sears
asked.

"Yeah, there're about a hundred ponds around
here," the stranger said, "maybe two hundred, but
they're all just as acid as this. Of course there's
nothing to stop you from trying. The fish may be
coming back."

They went out anyhow on the disqualified water
and cast for an hour or so. Eduardo, Sears noticed,
got his line out with commendable grace and ex-
pertise. When they brought the boat in Sears asked
his friend what he was going to do with the rest
of his ten days' vacation. "I'll take my wife to Key
West," he said. "The union has package tours that
you don't have to book in advance. I took her
down the year before last and she loved it." They
drove back down the strip again and it rained
again. The younger man's company helped Sears
to understand better the barbarity and nomadism
of 774. They parted at Sears's apartment. "I'll see
you when Renée gets back from Des Moines," said
Sears. "Get a great tan."

9

AFTER the fracas in the supermarket Henry saw
that Betsy needed a change. He got the day off
and they decided to go to Chelmsford Beach. It
wouldn't be as crowded as it always was on the
weekends and they didn't much enjoy it with a big
crowd. Betsy made a picnic, with lemonade for
herself and beer for Henry, and they took off at
about ten in the morning with little Randy and
Baby Binxie in the carrier. It was a nice summer's
day. They made the trip in less than two hours
and they both enjoyed reaching the beach on a
weekday when half the parking lots were closed
and privacy on the beach was just something you
walked into, which contrasted with their memories
of the weekends when privacy was something you
had to look for like a needle in a haystack. They
found a nice place and put a parasol up over
Binxie with his bottle. She and Henry had a nice
swim and then she went up and lay on the sand
and Henry gave Randy a swimming lesson. Henry
kept shouting: "That's the way, that's the way,
that's the way to do it!" He seemed very happy
and excited. A little way down the beach was a
group of very old people. They were so old that if

they went swimming they would sink. They sat on the sand wearing all their clothes, including vests and hats, and one of the women kept saying, "Oh what have we done to deserve such a beautiful day!" Betsy didn't know what she was talking about.

Then Randy came running up and said that he had learned to swim and so she went down to the edge of the water and watched him demonstrate his stroke. She was very happy to see how pleased both he and his father were and she did not mention the fact that the buoyancy of salt water made it easier to swim in the ocean than to swim in the pools where she had done most of her swimming. Then they ate their sandwiches and Henry drank his beer and kissed Betsy and felt very amorous, but there wasn't any place and they knew that when they made love or even thought about it it made little Randy feel lonely and left out and they didn't want to spoil his day at the beach and she understood when Henry stopped kissing her. She had thought to pack a softball and Randy and Henry were happy to throw this back and forth, and she was happy to lie on the beach and hear the waves and smell the salt water.

Her people were not fishermen or sailors and she had nothing at all to do with the sea so far as she knew, but the brine and the blue sky and the sand all seemed most natural to her as if this were her home, although she could not imagine what it must be like to live near the sea with its winter storms and tempests. She had never in her life seen the ocean but on a summer's day. She went swimming again and again. Then the old people left and the shadows began to fall toward the sea. They packed up their own things. They were the last people on the beach and Baby Binxie was sleeping. While she gathered up the towels and the sandwich papers and Binxie's diapers she remembered watching on TV when an astronaut went into space. After the countdown the camera had shown all the people along the beach packing up their sandwich baskets and their towels and their folding furniture and going back to the parking lot, and she remembered that this had moved her more deeply than the thought of a man walking around on the moon. Almost everybody else on the beach had gone home early, and it seemed to her that they had gone because they had received some urgent message to leave and that the beach was their home and that on leaving the beach they would be like the evacuees of war or much more recently like those people who lived near toxic dumps and who have to travel for years, perhaps for a lifetime, seeking a new home.

"That was a nice day at the beach, darling," she said to Henry when they got to the parking lot and she kissed him. "I've always liked to spend a day at the beach and that was a very nice one." He kissed her and said, "I thought it was a very nice day too, but I'm going to ask you to drive until we get to route 224 if you don't mind. I'm sunburned and my eyes are strained and I'd like to rest before I hit the heavy traffic on route 224." "I know what you mean," she said, "but I'd love to drive." And so he got in the back seat with Randy and they put Binxie's carrier in the front seat and off they went.

"That sun made me feel poleaxed," Henry said and that was the last she heard from him. Then little Randy fell asleep and Binxie was already gone and she found herself alone in the car like the captain of a ship but a pleasant feeling of aloneness. She knew what Henry meant feeling poleaxed, but she had the strength to drive to 224 in a car with three sleeping and beloved men. Two twenty-four was a convergence of six- and eight-lane highways that made her think with longing of the simplicity of their day on the beach, when there was nothing more difficult to comprehend than blue sky and salt water. All the converging highways and the gathering whiplike noise of traffic made her wonder—foolishly, she well knew—if modern life with its emphasis on highways had not robbed men and women of some intrinsic beauty that the world possessed. She well knew that they couldn't have got to Chelmsford Beach if it hadn't been for the highways that seemed so alien. She was tired, very tired, and while she hated to wake up Henry she felt when they approached the intersection that it wouldn't have been safe for her to continue driving. There was a wide, safe shoulder a mile or two before the intersection and she pulled off onto this and said: "Wake up everybody. Your captain wants to go to sleep."

Little Randy didn't wake up at all and as soon as Henry took the wheel Betsy fell asleep and slept until Henry woke her when they got back to Janice. "I don't ever remember the sun making me feel so sleepy," Henry said. "Maybe it has something to do with the solstice. I feel like going to bed."

"Me too," said Betsy. "Did you take Binxie into the house?"

"I didn't do anything with little Binxie," said Henry. Then he shouted: "Dear Jesus Christ, I must have left him on the road shoulder up by 224. I took him out of the car when we changed places and I must have left him there!"

She hurled herself into his arms and said nothing. Never had the importance of their love for one another seemed so clear. The cruel tragedy of the lost baby seemed endurable so long as they were in one another's arms. "You call the police," Henry said. "I'll go back to route 224. I'll have to go all the way to 427 to get it northbound."

"I don't know what to tell the police," Betsy said.

"Tell them we left a baby on the road shoulder of 336 near the junction of 224 northbound."

"What's the matter?" asked little Randy, who had just waked. "Why do you two look so funny?"

"We've lost little Binxie," said Henry.

"Is he dead?" asked little Randy with some concern and with some hopefulness.

"Of course not," said his mother gently. "But why don't you go in the house and see if there isn't something on TV." Then she kissed Henry and unlocked the door and went into the house with little Randy. She called the police and said: "I want to report a baby that was left on the road shoulder of route 336 about two miles before the junction of 224. The baby is in a blue bassinet."

"Is this a kidnaping?" the patrolman asked.

"Oh no, no, no," she said, "it was just stupidity, it was just stupidity."

"I'm afraid that's not our jurisdiction," said the patrolman. "You'll have to call the Department of

Transportation." When she started to cry he gave her that number.

Horace Chisholm, the environmentalist, was driving southeast on route 336 late on the same afternoon. Chisholm had been, until a year ago, a high school teacher of biochemistry but he had come to feel that the hazards to the environment around him summoned him imperatively to do what he could to correct this threat to life on the planet or at least to inform the potential victims. He was returning from a town planning board meeting, where a zoning change would involve paving a half square mile for a shopping center while poisoning and corrupting some wetlands that fed two brooks that in turn fed sources of drinking water. That it would take ten or maybe fifteen years before the damage was seriously felt by the community had been the deciding fact in the voting. The feeling clearly had been that they would all be living somewhere else when the drinking water became lethal.

This turn of thought troubled Chisholm. The diminished responsibilities of our society—its wanderings, its dependence on acceleration, its parasitic nature—deeply troubled him. He could see it all on route 336. That a hermetic society had comparable limitations had never been called to his attention. He was a truly honest and conscientious man, but his wife had found him immobile and had left him. In fact she had obliged him to leave her and she and their two daughters were living in the house in Queens while he was living alone in a small apartment in the city. It was he who had been ousted but it was she who made the spiritual departure.

Route 336 was a deadbeat to drive for anyone, but for an environmentalist who had just lost some wetlands it was perhaps worse. The vote for the shopping center had been determined first by a promise of reduced taxes and then by pure irresponsibility. Any display of venality is depressing. Chisholm felt quite lost. Nothing waited for him in his apartment. There was no woman, no man, no dog, no cat, and his answering tape would likely be empty and the neighborhood where he lived had become so anonymous and transient that there were no waiters or shopkeepers or bartenders who would greet him. He turned on the radio but all the music he seemed able to get was disco music, and disco music from those discos that had been closed the year before the year before last for drug pushing or nonpayment of income tax. He seemed to be searching for the memory of some place, some evidence of the fact that he had once been able to put himself into a supremely creative touch with his world and his kind. He longed for this as if it were some country which he had been forced to leave.

He passed a blue car and was passed by a red car. Then he passed two light-gray cars and one brown van. He had gas on the stomach and a slight erection. He felt so lonely that when the car ahead of him signaled for an exit he felt as if he had been touched tenderly on the shoulder by some stranger in some place like a crowded airport, and he wanted to put on his parking lights or signal back in some way as strangers who are traveling sometimes touch one another although they will never, ever meet again. In a lonely fantasy of nomadism he imagined a world where men and women communicated with one another mostly by signal lights and where he proposed marriage to some stranger because she turned on her parking lights an hour before dusk, disclosing a supple and romantic nature.

He passed a blue car and was passed by two black cars, a brown van and a convertible. His physical reality and the reality of the car he was driving were unassailable, but his spiritual reality seemed to be vanishing in a way that he had never before experienced. He even seemed to have lost the power to regret his past and its adventures. A pair of lovers in a car ahead of him—the girl was sticking her tongue into the driver's ear—failed even to arouse his jealousy. He seemed about to become a cipher. The pain, perhaps the most galling he had ever known, lacked any of the attributes of pain, any of its traditional bloodiness.

Then he seemed lost. He was lost. He had lost his crown, his kingdom, his heirs and armies, his court, his harem, his queen and his fleet. He had, of course, never possessed any of these. He was not in any way emotionally dishonest and so why should he feel as if he had been cruelly and physically stripped of what he had never claimed to possess? He seemed to have been hurled bodily from the sanctuary of some church, although he had never committed himself to anything that could be called serious prayer.

Then he saw blackberries in the scrub along the road shoulder. He could stop and eat some blackberries. That much would be real and true. His mother had liked to pick berries when they went for a drive. She had never forgotten the quiet lanes and roads of her youth and had never understood why her husband wouldn't stop on an expressway long enough for her to pick berries or violets. Chisholm was looking for blackberries, and blackberries that grew in a place where the road shoulder was commodious enough for him to stop safely and park his car. Then he saw the bright blue of the baby carrier. He didn't know what it was, but its brightness and blueness seemed to declare that it was worth his attention. It could have been some wrapping paper or a scarf or some other piece of clothing that had been thrown away by an ardent lover. There was no car behind him, and he pulled over onto the shoulder to see what the bright blue thing was. When he found a clean, happy baby waving its hands and feet he exclaimed: "You must be Moses, you must be King of the Jews."

Abandonment was the first thing that occurred to him, although it was hard to imagine such a clean and happy child having been abandoned. There might be a note, he thought, to explain the forsaken child, and he rooted around in the blankets but there was nothing but a half-empty bottle. The cleanliness of the baby's linen conveyed the fact that if the baby had been abandoned it had been a tragic abandonment—a cruelly enforced separation, a deprivation. He imagined a young, weeping mother. The sensible thing to do was to go on to the next exit and find a police station. The thought that the police might unfeelingly toss the baby into an orphanage aroused in him protective and paternal longings, although he was in no position to raise a child in his apartment.

He put the carrier into the front seat and, after

waiting his turn, joined the stream of traffic. He felt himself distinguished. He felt his to be one of the few cars on the road that was transporting a pleasant baby. The next exit said GAS, FOOD and Chisholm took this. His first stop was a garage, where he got directions to find the police. They were in a municipal building from the twenties with an image of blindfolded justice above the door. Holding the bassinet with both hands, Horace had some difficulty opening the door. No one offered to help him. In the vestibule an arrow directed him to a desk where people, he supposed, brought their troubles, but seldom a smiling infant.

"I found this baby on route 336," he said, "a little before the turnoff for 224."

"You ain't shitting me, are you?" said the patrolman at the desk. "I been in the service thirty-seven years and no one ever told me they found a baby on route 336."

"Hey, Charlie," someone called from the back. "We got a call out for a lost baby if somebody found one. We got this broad in a place called Janice who said she forgot her baby on 336. We got a number to call. She's hysterical."

Chisholm was terribly happy. The baby went on cooing and gurgling and most of the staff of the station came around to look at him. To return an infant to its mother seemed to please everyone and it was decided that Chisholm should call her. "Mrs. Logan?" he asked when he heard Betsy's voice. "I'm Horace Chisholm and you don't know me but I found your baby on route 336. The baby is well and happy and waiting for you at the police station near exit 37." Betsy was hysterical, but when she collected herself she explained that

Henry was on the road going south to pick up route 224 northbound and she gave them his license number. They agreed to call her as soon as Henry had been located, and the radio call for Henry hadn't been out for more than ten minutes when they picked him up. Then they called Betsy and waited around for Henry. The patrolmen had gotten possessive about the baby. "You can go now if you want," they said to Chisholm. "There's no point in your staying around. We'll give the baby to its father." "I'd like to see that the baby gets into the right hands," said Chisholm. To see the baby and his father reunited seemed to him some important part of the afternoon.

When Henry came rushing in and saw the baby in his blue bassinet he began to cry. He seized little Binxie in his arms and for the first time little Binxie began to cry. "I want to thank you," said Henry. "My wife and I want to thank you. We live in Janice and I wonder if you could have dinner with us tomorrow. My wife makes wonderful fettucini. That's green noodles. She makes them with spinach. We live in Janice, on Hitching Post Road. It's about an hour's drive from the city."

"I'd like to come for dinner," said Chisholm.

"We like to have dinner at around six," said Henry. "We like to eat early."

Late the next afternoon in his apartment Horace bathed and dressed, contented and secure in the memory of the fact that he had found a baby and restored it to its parents and would eat green noodles in their company that night. Continuity had seemed to be what he sought that afternoon when he had felt so painfully lost. Now he felt happy although he could not rig his hopes on the

repetition of such an unlikely chain of events. He
would settle for the evening. There wasn't much
else he could do. It was the second time he had
been to Janice and he knew the way. Hitching Post
Road was not far from Beasley's Pond. When he
rang the bell Henry let him in. "This is my wife,
Betsy," he said. "I know you've talked with her on
the telephone." Betsy looked at him shyly and
said, "I don't know whether or not I should do this
but I feel that I have to." Then she threw her arms
around him and kissed him on the mouth. "Did
you have any trouble finding the place?" asked
Henry. "I've been to Janice before," said Horace.
"One of the most difficult jobs I've ever had is
Beasley's Pond. We're trying to clear up the pollution there."

"Mr. Salazzo who lives next door supervises the
dumping," said Betsy.

"We'll have to cut the happy hour a little short,"
said Henry, "because Betsy doesn't like the fettucini to get overcooked. Her mother's Italian and
in Italy she says cooking pasta is a regular art."
They had some drinks and while Betsy was in the
kitchen Henry passed a box of crackers that the
label promised would stimulate conversation.
There was no need for any of this, for their excitement at having reclaimed their son made their
pleasure in Horace deep and spontaneous. The
fettucini was good, and the fact that the light of
the two candles on the table made it almost impossible for them to see one another made no
difference to the pleasures of the evening. After
dinner they settled down comfortably and watched
their particularly favorite shows on television. At
eleven o'clock when the entertainment ended

Horace said goodbye and goodnight and Betsy
shyly kissed him once again. It was agreed that he
would call them when he next came out to Beasley's Pond. "We don't know how to thank you for
saving Binxie's life," said Betsy. "Do whatever you
can to save Beasley's Pond," said Horace.

10

THE hearing that Sears's enemies had rigged was
held in the Janice town hall, a brick building
from the last century. Considering the power and
might of the organization Chisholm had described,
the building seemed very modest. In the lobby
there were posters urging passers-by to enroll in
classes in karate, ballet dance and remedial reading. These aroused in Sears those taxpayers' blues
that were so characteristic of his generation. There
was an elevator with an OUT OF ORDER sign and
he climbed a flight of uncommonly steep stairs to
the hearing room. Breathing deeply—puffing—he
became acutely aware of the fact that the air of
the building was permeated with a disinfectant.
It was pervasive and powerful and reminded him
of the loneliness and regimentation of Eastern
Europe, where even the grand-luxe hotel lobbies—
even the Kremlin Palace—smelled of disinfectant.
He was reminded again of Eastern Europe when
he reached the upstairs hallway. Everybody seemed
to be smoking and the hallway, filled with tobacco
smoke, seemed like a glimpse at the past. How
long it had been since he had seen so much cigarette smoke! He went on into the hearing room,

where perhaps fifty people had already gathered. Some of them looked to Sears as if they had come in to get out of the rain that was falling and because they were welcome nowhere else. Chisholm was at the back of the room, engaged in conversation with a young woman, and Sears waved to him and sat in one of the front rows.

The room was a little like an informal courtroom, with a raised table for the authorities. They were not yet seated but there were name signs at their places. If the power of their organization was rooted, as Chisholm claimed, in Eastern or Southern Europe, you could not tell this by their nomenclature. Their names were so conspicuously up-country that they would have served—Sears thought—for third basemen in minor-league baseball. They seemed names from that rural past when one shared one's family name with backroads, lakes, bogs and sometimes mountains. The mayor, who according to Chisholm was a puppet of the opposition, was named Chauncey Upjohn and his lieutenants were named Copley Townsend and Harrison Porter. On the walls of the room hung two large photographs of bearded elders. Then there was a large photograph of the village after the catastrophic fire of 1832. Nothing had been left standing but chimneys. Also on the wall was a sculptured copy of the town seal. This was a portrait of one of the Nock-Sink Indians who had settled the river banks. The brave had a hook nose, a headdress of game-bird feathers and was holding a tomahawk with which, considering the bloody history of his people, he might have mutilated a

Jesuit. Chisholm joined Sears a few minutes before
the meeting was called to order. The two men had
spent the afternoon in the wetlands around Beasley's Pond.

They had made the trip in waders. As they
struggled through the marsh Chisholm recited a
litany of the poisons the laboratory had promised
to find in the water. In the water of the pond Sears
saw islands of what appeared to be fermenting ex-
crement. Where the water was clear one saw trails
of vileness like the paraphernalia of witchcraft.
"Pollution has brought in the rat-tailed maggot,"
said Chisholm. "Two years ago you wouldn't have
found *Helobdella stagnalis* in a pond like this.
Another newcomer is the sludge worm. Tubifex.
Glossifonia complanata is also new." The only
things that cheered him were the cattails *(Typha
latifolia)* and *Phragmites communis*—the reed.

The wetlands drained into a stream that had for
Sears the appearance of a traditional trout brook.
It flowed over stones—glacial rubble—it formed
deep pools, its breadth was variable, one could not
quite anticipate its variety as it followed gravity
through the woods to some destination of its own.
The illusion of eternal purity the stream possessed,
its music and the greenery of its banks, reminded
Sears of pictures he had seen of paradise. The
sacred grove was no legitimate part of his thinking, but the whiteness of falling water, the variety
of its sounds, the serenity of the pools he saw
corresponded to a memory as deep as any he
possessed. He had on his knees in countless cavern-
ous and ill-ventilated Episcopal churches praised

the beginning of things. He had heard this described in Revelation as a sea of crystal and living creatures filled with eyes, but it seemed that he had never believed it to be anything but a fountainhead.

On and on went Chisholm's recitation of poisons. Polychlorinated biphenyls. Dioxin. Chloroform. Thoroviven. Clorestemy, Mustin and Thraxon. As they moved from the wetlands to the charming brook he recited the diseases these chemicals produced in men. Rickets. Blindness. Brain tumor. Impotence. Sterility. And these were all more desirable than what happened to the woman in Mitcheville who miscarried a child that looked more like a dog than a human.

Now and then the voice of the brook was louder than Chisholm's voice. A trout stream in a forest, a traverse of potable water, seemed for Sears to be the bridge that spans the mysterious abyss between our spiritual and our carnal selves. How contemptible this made his panic about his own contamination. When he was young, brooks had seemed to speak to him in the tongues of men and angels. Now that he was an old man who spoke five or six languages—all of them poorly— the sound of water seemed to be the language of his nativity, some tongue he had spoken before his birth. Soft and loud, high and low, the sound of water reminded him of eavesdropping in some other room than where the party was.

He remembered other voices he had overheard. One was at the end of some war in which he had been a soldier and was spending a day or two waiting reassignment or transportation, in a furnished room in some city where he was a stranger. He had been unable to sleep and had gone to the window to hear the strange city and had heard, instead, the voice of a woman from some nearby window. The voice was quite clear, weak with suffering and very appealing. "I don't feel like myself anymore, Charlie," the woman said. "I don't feel like myself anymore." The second voice that he remembered was very different. He had been a guest in a palace in Rome and had taken a bath in a room with a terrace. He had stepped out onto the terrace with a towel to dry himself and to see the view. It was a truly Roman view with clouds of swallows on the twilight and grass, weeds and flowers growing vigorously from every crack and orifice in the roofs and church spires that he saw. Then across the roofs he heard a man shouting. "I will not put my prick in your martini," he said and slammed a door. Sears then heard the laughter of a woman although whether or not her laughter was felicitous or bitter he had never decided. He felt like an eavesdropper that afternoon, hearing the voices of the brook.

"That's the mayor, the one in the gray suit," said Chisholm. "He's the worst of the lot, although the others will do anything he tells them to. What our enemies have is a great deal of money. They were taking twelve and fourteen thousand dollars a day out of Beasley's Pond until we got the hold order, and that expires at midnight." Sears regarded the mayor. He judged faces, it seemed, on their capacity to contain light. It was lightlessness in a face—the absence even of the promise of light—that reminded him unhappily of man's inhumanity to man. It was not, of course, in his power or his disposition to judge the faces of strangers, but walking down the streets of any city in the world he sought in the faces of strangers the quality of light. Sears looked for light in the faces of the mayor and his associates when the meeting was called to order. There was an unfurled American flag to the left of the table but the meeting did not begin with a pledge of allegiance but with their singing "The Star-Spangled Banner." The tape of an operatic soprano's voice led them on. Sears had never before seen a thing like this but then he had never before been to such a meeting.

Sears couldn't help noticing that the mayor was wearing a suit that looked expensive but was plainly a size too big. Had it been given to him by a friend? This seemed improbable since Sears felt sure he could have no friends. Sears also observed that the mayor was one of those liars who speak quite directly when they are truthful but who address their falsehoods to the fingernails of their left hands. It was a phenomenon that Sears had often noticed in bankers. "Beasley's Pond and the surrounding acreage," said the mayor, "were purchased a year and a half ago and declared a dump by the town planning board, with the approval of the governor's blue-ribbon committee on hazardous wastes. It was purchased by the Veterans' Committee for"—this was addressed to his fingernails—"the sole purpose of building a monument to the forgotten dead. The site has been chosen carefully. We used the exacting criteria we use for all hazardous-waste facilities. The population density is desirable. There is a suitable body of water. The soil is tight with good bedrock." Then he raised his left hand a little crooked, and said to his fingernails: "Exhaustive laboratory tests have proved that toxicity is no danger."

"May I ask to be recognized," said Chisholm, standing. "I have no objections to this meeting or to what you've said but may I propose a delay until our laboratory test results have been received?"

"Not until I've finished," said the mayor. "This meeting has been called," he said, "simply as a courtesy to placate a Communist-inspired conservationist, whose bread is buttered by an old man. Beasley's Pond is like the mainstream of American thought. It accords with human nature. To interfere in our improvements on Beasley's Pond is to interfere in the fruitful union between the energies of mankind and the energies of the planet. To try and regulate with government interference the spontaneity of this union will sap its natural energy and put it at the paralyzing mercy of a costly bureaucracy financed by the taxpayer. Our improvements to Beasley's Pond are a very good example of that free enterprise that distinguishes the economy and indeed the character of this great nation."

"The plans for the evacuation of Janice are known to us all," said a man who had not asked to be recognized but who stood and read from a paper. He was a tall man with gray hair and a face that, to Sears's taste, seemed intermittently lighted.

"I have described this meeting as a courtesy,"

said the mayor. "We have nothing to do with the evacuation plans."

"The urgency of the evacuation plans," said the stranger, "is a day-to-day matter but I only want to bring up the fallacy of a single point. As taxpayers we've been charged for these evacuation plans and as taxpayers gathered here together tonight we are entitled to discuss them."

"This has nothing to do with Beasley's Pond."

"The possibility of detonative contaminants in the water has been admitted by your commission on hazardous wastes, and since this would put Janice into a danger area with a B classification it most definitely concerns Beasley's Pond. But as I say my concern is over only one category in the plans. The Chamber of Commerce, the League of Women Voters and the Concerned Citizens of Janice have all expressed their objections to the abandonment of the imprisoned and the disabled and the general ignorance the evacuation plans display of the topography of Janice, its dead-end streets, inflammable buildings and high bluffs. All of this is on record. What I am here to protest is paragraph F in clause 18. This paragraph strictly forbids any congregating excepting at designated evacuation points upon designated summons. The idea here is that if a carcinogenic element is discharged into the air there will be fewer casualties if the population remains scattered. You are familiar with this clause?"

"Of course," said the mayor. He seemed defensive. "Of course."

"Under the best of circumstances the evacuation plans admit that no more than twenty percent of the population can be rescued. It seems to me that since so many of us must die we ought to be allowed to gather together in some house of worship and pray for life in the world to come."

"Who are you?" asked the mayor.

"I'm minister of the First Unitarian Church on Route 328. I speak for several other clergymen in the neighborhood."

"Do you realize," asked the mayor forcefully, "that the people of this great nation spend fourteen times as much money on breakfast food as they do in church contributions? The marketability of the church was exploded nearly six years ago when one of you clergymen endorsed a decaffeinated coffee and the firm went bankrupt in eight months. I can give you many more examples of how little of our national income goes into church contributions—pornographic appliances, for example—but I will confine myself to the fact that we spend fourteen times as much on breakfast food as we do in church contributions."

The churchman sat down. He seemed to be crying. Chisholm asked again to be recognized.

"I haven't finished," said the mayor. "I've described this meeting as a courtesy and I've encountered nothing but troublemakers. You, Mr. Chisholm, have, I happen to know, never served in the armed forces of your great country and you have no understanding, of course, of our wish to raise a memorial to our patriotic dead. You would like, I know, to prove that our fill in Beasley's Pond is comprised of leachates and contaminants. My father was an honest Yankee fisherman. He was a soldier. He was a patriot. He was a churchgoer. He was the husband of a contented, loving and happy wife and the father of seven healthy and successful children. If I spoke to him about leachates and contaminants he would tell me to speak English. 'This is the United States of America, my son,' he would say, 'and I want you to speak English.' 'Leachates' and 'contaminants' sound like a foreign language, and to bring governmental interference into our improvements of Beasley's Pond is like the work of a foreign government."

"I would like to request a postponement," Chisholm said, as politely as possible. "The Marston Laboratories are working on the specimens we gave them and they've promised a report by Thursday."

While Chisholm spoke the mayor conferred with the three members of the board and when Chisholm had finished he said, "Your request has been refused by a majority of the board, but before we close I would like to read a letter I have in my possession. This letter was written by your employer, Mr. Lemuel Sears, on the twenty-ninth of February last year and was published in the newspaper the following day. 'Is Nothing Sacred' was the heading of Mr. Sears's observations.

" 'I have been skating on weekends on Beasley's Pond,' he wrote, 'in the company of perhaps fifty men and women of all ages and for all I know all walks of life, who seemed to find themselves greatly refreshed for the complexities and problems of the modern world by a few hours spent happily on ice skates. The findings of the discredited paleontologist Gardener who claimed that the skate—or shate—was the turning point in the contest for supremacy between *Homo sapiens* and primordial man have been proven fraudulent—but isn't it true that we enjoy on ice skates a sense of fleetness that seems to be a primordial memory? Last Sunday, carrying my skates to the pond, I found that it had been rezoned as fill and had become a heap of rubbish, topped by a dead dog. There is little enough of innocence in the world but let us protect the innocence of ice skating.' That is your letter, isn't it, Mr. Sears?"

"Yes," said Sears.

"On one hand we have the grief of mature and thinking men and women who hope to commemorate the sacrifice of life made by their beloved sons and husbands in the cause of freedom. On the other hand we have this. The meeting is adjourned."

Almost everyone in the room, including the minister, looked at Sears with contempt. "I had forgotten about the letter," he said to Chisholm. "I wish they had," said Chisholm. Betsy Logan joined them and Chisholm introduced her to Sears. Her view of him was obviously prejudiced by the letter. "The town board may give us another hearing," said Chisholm, "if the laboratory reports are devastating. It is still too early to be hopeless. We can try the district attorney, although he'll refer us to the governor's commission and the governor's looking for campaign contributions." They were almost the last to leave the hall and go down the steep stairs. Betsy kissed Chisholm goodnight and started up the street. "I'll call you as soon as

I hear from the laboratory," said Chisholm. They shook hands on the sidewalk, but as Chisholm started to cross the street a car that had been double-parked and was without lights came down the street at a high speed and struck Chisholm with an impact that killed him dead.

11

SOME few hours later love music was playing at Buy Brite when Betsy chose a cart and pushed it past the fruits and vegetables that were the first things to be found on entering the place. It was well after midnight. The music was faint—too faint to be identified—but almost anyone would recognize it as a love song. The lingering ups and downs of the melody had never meant anything else. To the music of love Betsy pushed her cart through the vastness of a nearly empty market, although the place was flooded with light. She was sad and vengeful. Chisholm had saved the life of her son. She missed him painfully and felt that the world would miss this pure and helpful man. Her cart was empty and in her raincoat pocket she carried a bottle of Teriyaki Sauce to which she had added enough ant poison to kill a family. Pasted to this was a message that said: "Stop poisoning Beasley's Pond or I will poison the food in all 28 Buy Brites." She had made this of words cut from a newspaper while her sons and her husband slept.

Betsy headed for the aisle where spices and extracts were displayed. She couldn't clearly remember where she had found the Teriyaki Sauce on

that rainy afternoon when she and Maria Salazzo
had battled. She pushed her empty cart past the
shelves of spices and extracts again and again. The
search for anything, she knew, could be deceptive.
How often had she looked for labels, prices and
trade names in what was truly a crossroads of her
time. Whenever she couldn't find what she looked
for she always seemed to hear a chorus of elderly
women in her family asking for their eyeglasses,
their door keys, and lamenting the loss of telephone numbers, addresses and names. Oh where
was the Teriyaki Sauce? She was anxious at the
thought that they might have discontinued it or
exhausted their supply. That someone might seize
her, find the sauce in her pocket and sentence her
to jail for having threatened to poison the community was, of course, an absurd anxiety but it
remained very keen.

She went from the aisle for spices and extracts
to the aisle for sauces and condiments. She had
forgotten there were so many. She felt hopeful
when she saw some exotic sauces and then she
remembered that there was an Oriental corner
between the baked goods and the dairy products.
Here were the bottles of Teriyaki Sauce, and she
left her bottle of poison on its side where it would
be noticed. She left the store without anyone having
seen her face. She climbed into bed with Henry
but she felt too excited to sleep. It seemed to be
the fear of being apprehended that kept her awake;
but she felt that her bottle and its message would
be discovered in the morning. World press would
print the story since our supermarkets are such
an axial part of our way of life. The story would
appear everywhere including Russia and the Orient

and the dumping in Beasley's Pond would end at once.

Nothing of the sort happened. In the evening paper the principal story was about an unidentified flying object, seen by the wife of the chief of police, and some vandalism at the high school. Why Betsy should continue this project when there was so much in her life that contented her is a mystery. Her love for Henry and the children was quite complete, it seemed happily to transcend her mortality, and yet beyond this lay some unrequited melancholy or ardor. She was one of those women whose nostalgia for a destiny, a calling, would outlast all sorts of satiation. It seemed incurable. The next day she bought and poisoned some sauce and while Henry slept she made another sign and returned to Buy Brite. Her first jar had vanished but she put her second on the shelf, bought a box of Flotilla and came home. "Where were you, my darling?" Henry asked when she returned to bed. "Oh my darling, where were you?" "I couldn't sleep," she said. "I've been reading."

In the evening paper there was still nothing but news of the customary gains and losses and the next day she poisoned a third bottle and took it to the store when Henry fell asleep. When she returned Henry was aroused and angry. "Where were you, where in hell were you? You weren't downstairs reading. I've looked for you everywhere." She calmed him—he was a most amiable man—and they returned to bed but in the next night's paper she saw that she had been successful. POISONED FAMILY IN SATISFACTORY CONDITION, was the headline. "The Grimaldo family, disabled by a jar of poisoned Teriyaki Sauce, were reported to be satisfactorily recovering in the Janice Hospital. Whoever poisoned the sauce threatened to poison food in all the Buy Brite supermarkets until the pollution of Beasley's Pond is ended." This time the news went all the way around the world, and the dumping in Beasley's Pond ended at once.

Sears's business associates respected his success but those who knew him intimately—those who played bridge with him, for example—thought him not terribly intelligent. However, he was trusted and as soon as he learned that the dumping at Beasley's Pond had ended, he organized the Beasley Foundation. This took hours of tiring work with lawyers and was one of the most difficult projects he had ever accomplished or—he liked to think—that he had ever seen accomplished. The foundation was financed with assets taken from the Cleveland branch of the Computer Container Intrusion System. This subdivision then became a holding company with the status of a tax shelter and short-term bonds that enjoyed a triple-A rating.

Only a third of the pond had been filled, the despoiled end was dredged and an innovative aeration system was installed to cure the water of its toxicity. At the time of which I'm writing most of our great rivers and bodies of water were in serious danger, and when engineers from other countries came to assess the system, Sears sometimes joined them as a guide. His grasp of the language was rather like a tourist's grasp of another language. "After the dumping had ended," he could be heard to say, "we were faced with eutrophication. The end result of the eutrophication process is the development of a swamp or bog, which eventually dries into organic mulch, devoid of water. Historically the eutrophication and decay of a lake required tens and thousands of years, but with the increase of man-made contaminants and leachates it can be accomplished in no time at all." Sears liked to think that the resurrection of Beasley's Pond had taught him some humility, but his humility was not very apparent. When a visiting engineer offered to help him across a stream he said: "No thank you. I'm wearing the same belt I wore when I played football in college."

The loveliness of the landscape had been restored. It was in no way distinguished, but it could, a century earlier, have served as a background for Eden or even the fields of Eleusis if you added some naked goddesses and satyrs. "Our first approach to the problem was to pump bottom water to the surface, where it could absorb oxygen," said Sears. "As well as poisons, the dumping had brought nutrient chemicals into the water. These increased the algae and weeds. We had anaerobic conditions in the bottom water since it was completely devoid of oxygen. Hydrogen sulfide was released and manganese, iron and phosphates were dissolved from the underlying soil. Organic acids were produced and the pH of the water decreased. This destroyed all crustacea and other animals and ended the pond's life cycle.

"Bringing bottom water to the surface," he went on, "had worked well in small impoundments but this required considerable amounts of power per unit volume. We needed a new approach. We needed increased horsepower efficiency—we needed to move ten to one thousand times as much water per horsepower as provided by old techniques. We needed to reduce the bubble-rise rate—if the bubble-rise rate could be reduced to less than one fps, turbulent flow would be eliminated and a laminar uplift effect would be created. We needed to reduce bubble size. If the air were introduced in tiny bubbles at bottom level not only would oxygen be dissolved quickly and laminar uplift produced, but strata turnover would be continuous and the cold water of the bottom layer would be distributed into the surface. This would prevent water-quality deterioration.

"Our engineers developed a small-diameter plastic pipe with tiny apertures in a straight line. This can be seen in the office. The piping made for easy installation, reasonable cost and small-bubble formation. We put down 4,500 feet of this valved polyethylene tubing. The permanence of this was made possible by embedding a continuous lead line in a thickened portion of the pipe wall, opposite the line of apertures. The diameter of the tubing is 0.5 inch. The apertures—which are die-formed check valves—were sized and spaced to meet water depths and desired circulation rates. The weight of the lead keel embedded in the tubing was heavier than the water despite the advanced stagnation in Beasley's Pond. We then connected this piping to nine three-quarter-horsepower compressors with nine thousand feet of weighted feeder tubing. Air delivered by blowers at 4.4 cfm 30 psi continuously mix and turn over upward of three hundred million gallons of water. We have two auxiliary blower units in case of mechanical trouble. Fish kill has been cut by two-thirds and last month we ran tests at four water levels. These showed water temperatures of eighty-four degrees and dissolved oxygen of seven to nine mgl at all levels. A year ago the water was poison. Now it is quite potable." Sears spoke with an enthusiasm that sprang from the fact that he had found some sameness in the search for love and the search for potable water. The clearness of Beasley's Pond seemed to have scoured his consciousness of the belief that his own lewdness was a profound contamination.

The visitors drifted over to the office to see the compressors and the pipe diagrams. Sears walked around the edge of the pond to the beginnings of the brook. Some mint grew here and he broke a leaf in his fingers. It was in the early summer but the sun was hot. The sound of water and the broken leaf reminded him of waking one morning with Renée. It was early. It was the first of the light. She lay in his arms and smelled of last night's perfume and of her own mortality, her yesterday. Her eyelashes had been dyed black and these contrasted with her blondness. They seemed quite artificial. The beauty of her breasts was no longer the beauty of youth and he knew that she worried about their size. He thought this charming. Her hair was not long but it was long enough to need some restraint, and she had, the night before, pulled up her hair—he could easily imagine the gesture—and secured it with a gold buckle. He had not seen her do this but now he saw the gold buckle and the hair it contained and the strands that had escaped. He kissed the loveliness of her neck and caressed the smoothness of her back and seemed to lose himself in the utter delight of loving. It seemed, in his case, to involve some clumsiness, as if he carried a heavy trunk up a staircase with a turning.

The sky was clear that morning and there might still have been stars although he saw none. The thought of stars contributed to the power of his feeling. What moved him was a sense of those worlds around us, our knowledge however imperfect of their nature, our sense of their possessing some grain of our past and of our lives to come. It was that most powerful sense of our being alive on the planet. It was that most powerful sense of how singular, in the vastness of creation, is the richness of our opportunity. The sense of that hour was of an exquisite privilege, the great benefice of living here and renewing ourselves with love. What a paradise it seemed!

The Salazzos packed their charcoal broiler and their stand-up swimming pool and vanished. Betsy told no one but Henry that she had threatened to poison the community, and she did not tell Henry until some time later. But, you might ask, whatever became of the true criminals, the villains who had murdered a high-minded environmentalist and seduced, bribed and corrupted the custodians of municipal welfare? Not to prosecute these wretches might seem to incriminate oneself with the guilt of complicity by omission. But that is another tale, and as I said in the beginning, this is just a story meant to be read in bed in an old house on a rainy night.

JOHN CHEEVER was born in Quincy, Massachusetts, in 1912, and went to school at Thayer Academy in South Braintree. He is the author of seven collections of stories and five novels. His first novel, *The Wapshot Chronicle,* won the 1958 National Book Award. In 1965 he received the Howells Medal for Fiction from the National Academy of Arts and Letters and in 1978 *The Stories of John Cheever* won the National Book Critics Circle Award and the Pulitzer Prize. Shortly before his death in 1982 he was awarded the National Medal for Literature.

Praise for Clare Littleford's first novel, *Beholden*:

'A well-constructed mystery which explores the nature of obsession, building a real sense of foreboding as it moves inexorably to its chilling climax' *Big Issue*

'Clare Littleford's intriguing debut novel draws the reader into a world where loyalty becomes obsession . . . The twist in the tale leaves the reader wondering whose version of events is closest to the truth' *Good Housekeeping*

'An unstoppable and perturbing mystery by a brilliant new author' Graham Joyce

'A classically wrought, tight-as-a-drum thriller . . . Clare Littleford goes straight for the jugular' *Nottingham Evening Post*

Also by Clare Littleford

Beholden

Born in Bedford in 1973, Clare Littleford worked in the housing department at Nottingham City Council before taking an MA in creative writing at Nottingham Trent University. Still based in Nottingham, she now works in community development in the voluntary sector. *Death Duty* is her second novel.

Visit *www.clarelittleford.net*

Death Duty

Clare Littleford

POCKET
BOOKS

LONDON · SYDNEY · NEW YORK · TORONTO

First published in Great Britain by Simon & Schuster UK
Ltd, 2004
This edition published by Pocket Books, 2004
An imprint of Simon & Schuster UK Ltd
A Viacom company

3 5 7 9 10 8 6 4 2

Simon & Schuster UK Ltd
Africa House
64–78 Kingsway
London WC2B 6AH

www.simonsays.co.uk

Simon & Schuster Australia
Sydney

A CIP catalogue record for this book is available
from the British Library

ISBN 0–7434–4106–0

Typeset by Palimpsest Book Production Limited,
Polmont, Stirlingshire
Printed and bound in Great Britain by
Cox & Wyman Ltd, Reading, Berkshire

To Brian and Kath

Acknowledgements

Many thanks to Luigi Bonomi, Kate Lyall Grant, Helen Jayne Price, Stephan Collishaw, Taymar Ingram.

One

I didn't know what he hit me with. Something hard, that's all, something hard against the back of my head and then lights out, I hit the floor. I felt myself hit the floor, felt the ridged cord carpet stinging my hands, and my cheekbone hitting the ridges, and the sharp rebound of my head. It was dark, as if I'd gone blind in that instant, but I knew he was still standing over me, I knew he was still hitting me, even though I couldn't feel it.

I opened my eyes. A thin, angular face leaning over me, young, Asian, wearing dark lipstick. He was gone – she leaned over me and I smelled her perfume, flowery, sweet. I realized that I was screaming; I tried to stop, tried to suck in breath, but the air caught in my throat and I couldn't get it into my lungs and it hurt from the effort and I had to be able to breathe, I needed air.

'It's okay,' the woman said. 'Shh, shh, it's okay.'

She was holding a roll of kitchen towel against my head, and there was blood spattered on her lilac blouse. I was lying on the floor in her shop,

1

in the narrow aisle between the shelves, and there was my blood on her blouse. I tried to stand, tried to apologize, but I couldn't get beyond sitting up, and she was holding me down, one hand anchoring my shoulder, repeating, 'Shh, it's okay.'

My skirt was rucked up over my knees. There was a big hole in my tights, and slight grazes on my knees, and one of my shoes was lying near the door, just out of my reach.

The woman bending over me said, 'What happened?'

I tried to think back, but then I couldn't breathe, the air caught in my throat again, and I couldn't swallow it down. 'He hit me,' I managed to say, and then I was so surprised by my words that I didn't know what else to say.

There were other people in the shop. An older Asian man with a heavy moustache coming round from behind the counter, a young black woman in a yellow sweatshirt framed in the open doorway with the sunlight so bright behind her. The woman kneeling over me said, 'We've called an ambulance.'

'No, no,' I said, and tried to stand up again, but I seemed to be attached magnetically to the floor. 'I'll be fine. I've got to get back to work, they're expecting me back.'

The black woman in the doorway brought me my shoe and said, 'Where do you work?'

A dark hole in my mind where the automatic knowledge should have been. I panicked for a moment, then remembered. 'Social Services. Round the corner.'

She had knelt down to help me put the shoe back on. 'I'll go and tell them. What's your name?'

'Jo,' I said. 'Joanne Elliott.'

She left. I should have said thank you, but I didn't think of it in time. I should have told her to tell them not to worry, I'd be fine once I'd managed to stand up, once my head had stopped bleeding. But as soon as I thought that, I could feel the pounding in my head, pulsing deep inside, and I was thirsty, my mouth seemed to be swelling with dryness, and it was cold sitting there on the floor, so very cold. I closed my eyes.

Someone was speaking to me. For a moment I thought it was him, repeating the same words again, but I opened my eyes and there was Colin leaning over me, sweet Colin, such a nice guy, and he put his arm around me, and I understood that the ambulance was coming, I shouldn't worry, everything was going to be fine. And Colin had come out of the office without his jacket, and he must have been cold just in his shirtsleeves, and he was smiling at me then. I wondered whether maybe I'd asked aloud if he was cold, but I couldn't tell.

Two

I was in a small room with the door open. The room was lined with shelves stacked with bandages and sterile dressings in paper packets. I wondered if they'd put me in a store room by mistake, but Colin was still there and he was smiling although the smile wasn't so strong now. I tried to tell him to go but he just shook his head and said no, and I must have told him again how sweet and kind he was because he looked away and seemed embarrassed by something.

And then Alex was there, and Colin made his excuses and left, and I couldn't believe that the office had phoned Alex, I couldn't believe that someone had thought that was a good idea, but there he was. Alex standing over me while I sat back on that bed like an invalid, an imbecile, and he was so tall standing over me with a frown that hid his black eyes in shadow.

'How are you?' he asked.

'Fine,' I said. 'Well, I've got a headache.'

'Surely an understatement,' he said, and gave a

softened-down, sick-person-nearby version of his laugh, and unfurled himself into the chair next to the bed.

'You didn't have to come,' I said.

'I couldn't leave you alone.'

'Colin was here.'

He ignored that. 'Anyway, of course I was going to come.'

'Well, thank you,' I said, because I didn't want to appear ungrateful.

We waited. When the doctor arrived he was young, thin, tired-looking. I wondered how long he'd been on duty, when he last had a meal or some sleep or a cigarette break. I needed a cigarette. I needed a glass of water, too, but I didn't like to ask, and anyway, the triage nurse had told me not to eat or drink anything, just in case.

I sat up and allowed the doctor to shine a torch in my eyes, and told him no, no blurred vision, no dizziness, no numbness, I wasn't tired really, I just had a thumping headache, I'd only been out cold for a few seconds tops, and when could I go?

The doctor gave a patient smile – a patient smile for a smiling patient – and said, 'We need to do an X-ray, just to be sure there's no serious injury. And you need a couple of stitches on that cut.'

I wanted to say that it wasn't necessary, but I was aware of Alex next to me, so I said nothing.

When the doctor had gone, Alex said, 'Are you going to tell me what happened?'

'You know what happened. I was mugged. He took my purse.'

'Yes, but what actually happened?'

'You mean blow by blow?' I said, and he started to say yes, then frowned at me. I forced a smile, but it didn't feel convincing. 'Later,' I said. I was feeling tired, now that the initial shock was starting to wear off, and the last thing I wanted to do was go through the entire experience again just to satisfy Alex's curiosity.

Alex said, 'But it wasn't a client, was it?'

'No, nothing like that.'

He nodded, as if that made it better, as if it was better to be knocked unconscious by a complete stranger than by someone who thought they had a reason for attacking me. I didn't find that comforting, and I would have said as much, but I wasn't sure why I had given such a definite reply. After all, I didn't know who my attacker was – how did I know why he had picked on me?

I wanted a cigarette more than ever now. I was about to ask Alex whether he thought there was time to nip outside before the nurse came to stitch the cut on my head, but as I opened my mouth to speak two policemen in uniform came into the room.

'Joanne Elliott?' one of them asked.

'Yes,' I said.

The policemen approached the bed.

'I understand you want to report an incident?'

It was the younger of the two PCs who spoke, using a tone that suggested he'd been on a training course on how to speak to victims of crime. He looked young enough to be a schoolboy wearing the uniform for a dare.

I hesitated, and Alex said quickly, 'She was mugged. At lunchtime. He took her purse.'

The young PC glanced at Alex then looked back at me, as if waiting for me to confirm. I didn't want to speak – I didn't know what to say. I didn't want to say anything, but they were waiting. I said, 'He came up from behind. I heard him say something.' I put my hand up to my head, as if touching my head was going to clear my thoughts, but I couldn't remember, I didn't know what he'd said to me. 'I tried to walk away – I went into a shop, I thought I'd be safe, but then he hit me across the back of the head and took my purse.'

The young PC said, 'Can you remember what he looked like?'

I wanted to. I imagined myself giving a clear, concise, detailed description, and them producing knowing grins and heading off to arrest a familiar face, up to his usual tricks. I tried to form a picture of him in my mind, locate the details of that face. I had a misty impression of dark hair, pale skin, and the way he had twisted his whole face up as he spoke to me. What had he said? He had spoken to me; I had heard his words, through the pumping of my heart and the rush, the roar of the moment. What was it? I saw the disappointment on the PC's face – he must have thought a smart, professional woman like myself would have made a good witness.

7

Eventually, the PC took pity on me and said, 'We can do this tomorrow if you'd prefer.'

'Yes,' I said, breathing freely at last. 'That would be better. I'm sorry, I just can't think—'

He cut off my apologies. 'Don't worry. He'll be long gone by now, anyway. We'll send someone round in the morning.'

I nodded, and then they were gone.

Alex looked at me with a strange, almost disappointed expression, but didn't say anything. I turned away from him – I didn't want to confirm that I knew what he was thinking. And why should I have all of the answers right away? Alex might think he knew it all, Alex might think he was a cool-headed professional who could handle anything, but that didn't mean I had to be the same as him. I couldn't avoid his gaze for ever – I didn't want to. I wanted to explain, but I didn't know what there was to explain. I wanted to make Alex see, get him to understand how determined the attacker had been, get him to understand the expression on the boy's – man's – face. Even as I thought about that determination, his concentration, I had the strangest feeling that I could have prevented it, if I had only come up with the right words at the time. I could remember him coming up beside me – I could remember that I didn't see him come, I was just suddenly aware of his presence at my elbow as I walked along the street. And then I could picture his face, and his anorak with the rip in the sleeve, showing the white stuffing under the black outer material, and his blue tracksuit bottoms, dirty around the knees. I saw his dark eyes, and his dark hair brushed forwards over the top of his forehead, the traces of acne around his mouth, his slightly crooked front teeth. The anorak was too big for him and the sleeves hung down over his hands, I could remember that. He had tried to speak to me, but I had kept walking, towards the shop doorway. What had he been trying to say? But I couldn't answer, I didn't know.

Three

Alex drove me home. I sat in the passenger seat, resting the side of my head against the window. The glass was cool to my skin, and I felt the throb of the engine vibrating as he moved through the gears.

I looked out. Night was falling; the street lights cast an orange glow that glinted off chrome and glass. Most of the traffic was heading in the opposite direction, out of Nottingham, and I imagined us turning and following, leaving the city behind. I didn't want to be surrounded by all the red brick, by the tall terraced houses sagging against their age, and all the warehouses and factories, and the boarded and shuttered shops. I could see youths hanging around on street corners, smoking and drinking, laughing to each other, and any one of them could have attacked me. I wanted to be a long way away, somewhere where Nottingham was a distant memory, somewhere green and wild with a great expanse of sky.

But I didn't say anything, and Alex kept driving. Soon, we were turning into my road, and parking outside my house, and I was tired, so very tired. I let Alex take my arm and walk me up the front path. I leaned against the wall while he searched for his key. My keys were in my handbag in my desk drawer at work, and I nearly joked that it was lucky I hadn't taken his set back when he moved out, but I said nothing instead.

The house was cold. I flicked on the lights in the front room, drew the curtains and then lit the gas fire. Alex shrugged off his coat and sat down on the sofa.

I said, 'You don't have to stay, you know.'

'Someone's got to,' he said. 'They wouldn't have let you come home alone. Anyway, I don't mind.'

I looked at him, trying to judge whether he really meant that, but he had bent down to unlace his shoes and I couldn't see his face. I said, 'I'll make up the spare bed for you.'

'No,' Alex said. 'Leave it. I'm supposed to be looking after you. I'll do it later.'

He pulled off his shoes, then examined a hole in the toe of one of his socks. I lit myself a cigarette and sat back as the nicotine rush from half a day without a smoke flooded into my brain. It made me feel slightly nauseous, but I persevered.

Alex had taken his mobile phone from his pocket and was pressing his way through the menu. The sound of the beeps cut right into the centre of my brain. He said, 'I've got to make a phone call.'

He looked at me pointedly, so I said, 'I'll put the kettle on,' and went into the kitchen. As I filled the kettle from the tap, I looked down through the dining room and the archway into the front room and saw him huddled over his mobile, talking. He had half-turned away from me and I couldn't hear what was being said, but I assumed he was phoning Simon to say he wouldn't be back that night.

I made a couple of mugs of coffee and carried them through into the front room. Alex put his mobile away and smiled at me as he took the mug from me. 'How do you feel now?' he asked.

'Okay,' I said. 'Headache.' I had a couple of paracetamol in my hand and I broke them in half and swallowed them quickly with my coffee. I lit myself another cigarette. 'I hope you didn't have to rearrange anything to stay here.'

'Oh, just some friends,' he said. 'It's okay, I can see them another time.'

I forced a smile. I wanted to ask which friends – there was a time when I would have had automatic knowledge of his social calendar. It was strange to think of him with a life I knew nothing about. I was very aware that I didn't have any plans for that night, there was nobody worrying about me – and Alex knew that, Alex was acting as stand-in, Alex was taking his responsibilities seriously even when they were no longer his, Alex was being so bloody kind to me.

We sat drinking our coffee. I stubbed out my cigarette in the ashtray. I thought about asking him about work, or whether he liked lodging with Simon, or about what he'd been up to, but my head still hurt and I couldn't bring myself to form a sentence.

Finally, he said, 'I'll fetch your stuff from the office tomorrow.'

I wanted to say that it was fine, he'd done enough; instead, I closed my eyes and said, 'Thanks.' I felt very sleepy but I could sense his presence even with my eyes closed.

After a minute or two he said, 'How come you couldn't tell the police more?'

I opened my eyes. He was slumped on the sofa with his arms stretched back over his head and his socked feet crossed. 'I just can't remember,' I said.

'Really?' He looked doubtful. 'The doctor said—'

'I know, I know. My head hurts. I'm tired. I don't want to think about it right now.'

'Well, you've got to at some point.'

'But not now,' I said.

'But you have to tell the police.'

'I know,' I said, and couldn't keep the irritation out of my voice. 'Don't you think I know that?'

He raised his eyebrows. 'There's no need to get like that about it.'

He sounded hurt, but I thought he might be putting that on. I sighed. 'I just got knocked unconscious in the street in broad daylight – how d'you expect me to be about it?'

'But it's over now,' he said. 'I mean, c'mon, statistically you're unlikely to get mugged twice, so you don't have to worry about that any more, eh? It's all out of the way.'

He was searching out eye contact, searching out a smile. I fought back the tears that had been threatening and forced myself to laugh. 'So I'm statistically mugger-proof now, then?'

He nodded and grinned. 'Exactly,' he said.

I knew he wanted me to continue smiling, to show him that I was my usual self, but I felt slightly sick from the effort. I wanted him to be quiet, to leave me alone, but I realized he had no intentions of doing that. I didn't trust myself to speak.

He said, 'C'mon, smile. At least you've got a week off work out of it.'

'Huh,' I said. I put my hand up to my head and touched the sore patch around the stitches on my scalp. 'I'd rather be at work.'

'You would,' he said, shaking his head slightly as though I'd said something he disapproved of. I wasn't sure if he was still joking or not. Then he said, 'You've got to tell me about it at some point.'

I wanted to demand why, but my head hurt too much; the sound of his voice hurt. I said, 'Not now. Maybe I just want to forget about it?'

'But you can't,' he said. 'You've got to tell the police.'

I just shrugged.

'But this bloke could do the same to someone else. Or worse.'

I stood up. 'I'm going to have a bath.'

He didn't say anything for a moment, but when I had reached the door, he said, 'Well, don't drown yourself.'

I just flashed him a grin and went into the hall. As I climbed the stairs I heard the TV come on, and snatches of programmes as he flicked through the channels. I wasn't sure what he expected me to say, why he thought I should be able to tell him exactly what had happened. I realized that I didn't want him here at all.

I went into the bathroom, closed the door and started to run the bath. It felt strange to finally be alone. I stood there, fingers on the buttons of my blouse, and after a moment I went back and bolted the bathroom door. I took my clothes off slowly. There was a small amount of blood on the collar of my blouse, dried onto the fibres. I looked down at myself, at the grazes on my legs and the bruise on my hip that I hadn't felt until now, and finally I looked at my face in the mirror. My hair was dishevelled, but I had expected that; it was matted with blood at the back. There was a brown streak of blood on my forehead that Alex hadn't mentioned, and my eyes were reddened and the rest of my skin was very pale. I watched myself in the mirror, this woman who looked as if she'd been through an ordeal, and I felt that I should cry, I should show some sort of emotion, but I couldn't, I couldn't bring myself to react that way.

I shut off the bathwater and climbed in. I cupped my hands and started to wash my knees, rinsing off the grime I had picked up from the shop floor, washing away the little flecks of blood in the grazes. Lying back, I felt the edge of the bath pressing against the stitches in my scalp. I touched them and the pressure of my fingertips stung in the cut, and I felt the bruise that had swollen around it, hardened by the skull underneath. Then I ran my fingers through the rest of my hair, and felt the softness of the other bruises. Touching them hurt but I had to do it. Four in total. Did that mean he had hit me four times? Did I hit my head on a shelf or on the floor as I went down? I remembered the feel of the cord carpet against my face and the rebound of my head, but I couldn't remember any more.

And that frightened me, more than when he had appeared beside me, more than when I had realized that something was about to happen, more than the blow that had knocked me down, and the X-ray, and the stitches, and the police asking questions. I hadn't seen it coming. He had stood over me, hitting me, and I hadn't known, there was nothing I could do to protect myself. Whatever Alex said about statistics, whatever I knew about the likelihood of being attacked or robbed, it made no difference; it had happened, and what was there to stop it happening again? And what if he hadn't stopped, what if he'd had a knife, what if he'd decided he was going to kill me?

I wanted to think that my scream had chased him off, but I didn't know; I had the horrible feeling that I had only started to scream later, after he had gone, when the shopkeeper was already bending over me, when I was already safe.

I closed my eyes and held my breath and dipped my head back until I was under the surface of the bathwater. I pinched my nose between thumb and forefinger and let the water rush right over my face, and I felt myself floating free, weightless under the water, deafened. The water was warm but my skin felt cold against it. I imagined coming up out of the water, remembered that feeling of return as I came back from the darkness; the return of sound and sensation. The floor had been cold against my skin, too. I should have been safe; in a street, in a shop, in the middle of the day. Nothing should have happened, and if I hadn't been safe then . . . I imagined someone bending over me, and it was him I saw, my attacker, reaching his hands down towards me in the bathwater.

I sat up quickly, too quickly, swallowing water, slopping water over the side of the bath, opening my eyes, but there was nobody there. I was alone, and I had locked the bathroom door. I heard muffled voices and canned laughter from the TV downstairs.

I could picture the youth's face, the way he had looked at me, with a slight smile that I had thought meant he knew me. He had smiled at me, and I had smiled back, trying to place his face, trying to remember where he knew me from, where I knew him from. And then it had happened, but I couldn't remember his words, just that slow certainty saturating me, and trying to think, trying to see how I could get away, and stepping towards the shop doorway. I could remember pushing open the door, and then I was falling, before I even felt the blow I was falling, and I didn't see the floor, I didn't see myself hit the floor.

Four

I woke early and lay trying to doze for a long time. Outside, I could hear the traffic building up on Sherwood Rise, heading into the city centre. I didn't want to acknowledge that it was morning, but my brain was too alert to allow me to sleep again. My head ached and the cut on my scalp felt sore and swollen; I didn't want to sit up and feel the full effect of the pain. I heard Alex get up and go to the bathroom, and then the toilet flush and his footsteps going lightly down the stairs. I didn't want to face him just then, so I lay where I was until I could no longer deny being awake, then I put on my dressing gown and went down to the front room.

The TV was tuned to the breakfast news and Alex was sitting on the sofa eating toast, with a mug of tea on the carpet by his feet. He was already dressed; even his tie was in place.

'Sleep well?' he asked, glancing up at me. I nodded. 'How are you feeling?'

'Fine,' I said. 'It's a bit sore round the stitches, but no major damage.'

'Oh, you'll be right as rain in no time,' he said.

I just smiled and didn't say anything. He looked at me for a moment, then sipped his tea and looked back at the TV screen. I stifled another yawn and tried to think about what I was going to do today, but I had no ideas. All those times I had wished I could just take a day off and do nothing – the situation would have been funny if it wasn't for the dull pain in my head.

'When are the police coming round?' he asked.

'Not sure,' I said. 'Later.'

I had wanted to forget about their visit until it happened, but now that he had mentioned it I knew the thought would stay with me. I had dreamed about the attack, I remembered that now – the familiarity of that feeling, that slight edge of sickness, and seeing the attacker's face close to mine. I had dreamed that he had pushed his face into mine, that I had felt the damp warmth of his breath, and looked into those eyes, and felt the pressure of his hand against my skin. But that hadn't happened, I was certain of that – I had hardly seen his face at all, and the impact of the first blow had been so hard, so sudden. I wanted to tell Alex, to explain that feeling of familiarity, to tell him that maybe I had recognized the attacker, but I wasn't sure. I didn't know if that was just the immediacy of the dream, and I didn't want to fix the idea in my mind by vocalizing it, not when I could have been wrong.

Alex had started to lace up his shoes. He said, 'I'll pop into your office later, pick up your stuff.'

Then he hesitated, and added, 'Why don't you come round tonight? About seven? I'll cook. You need a day off, yeah?'

'Thanks,' I said, surprised by his thoughtfulness and then ashamed of my surprise.

'You'll be okay?' he said. 'To drive round, I mean?'

'Oh yes,' I said, because I didn't see why I wouldn't be. I was glad I hadn't taken the car to work the previous day – I couldn't imagine going to pick it up, past the place where he had –, past that shop.

Alex had stood up and was pulling on his jacket. I got to my feet, feeling slightly dizzy, but Alex didn't notice that anything was wrong. I saw him to the front door and then shut it and stood listening to his car start and pull away up the street. When the sound of his engine faded I went back into the front room and turned the TV off. The house was very quiet. I had intended to have a bath before getting dressed, but I didn't want to any more.

When I was dressed and had brushed my teeth, I phoned work. My supervisor, Douglas, wasn't in, so I had to talk to Colin. He was a gush of questions, about how I was and whether the police had caught my attacker. 'You'll be back in no time,' Colin said. 'Nothing'll keep Jo Elliott away from her caseload, eh?'

I gave a tentative laugh. Behind him in the office I could hear the usual noise of conversations and phones ringing. 'I'll let you get back to it,' I said. 'Tell Douglas I'll send my sicknote in.'

'Sure,' Colin said. 'Get well soon.'

I hung up, and stood there for a moment. Get well soon. I was hardly ill, it wasn't that sort of thing. I'd be fine within a couple of days, I was sure of that.

And I had nothing to do. I didn't even have any case files to review – I'd left everything at the office, even my filofax with all my contact numbers in it. I felt oddly dislocated. I moved around the house, trying to decide how to fill the day. I went into the spare room and opened the curtains. The room smelled of Alex, the warm air stale with his presence. He hadn't made the bed and I stood looking at the slight indentation in the pillow where his head had been, and the way the sheet had pulled free of the mattress and the duvet had been pulled back but still held the shape of his body underneath. I could imagine him curled up there, warm, comfortable, safe. I didn't want to disturb that shape, that shell, so I left the room as it was.

I wandered downstairs and made myself another cup of tea and smoked my first cigarette of the day. I would have to go out for cigarettes and milk later, but I put off thinking about that. Daytime TV had started in earnest, so I watched housewives getting makeovers and a report about prostate cancer and tried not to think about what I would do with the time that was yawning out in front of me.

At about eleven-thirty, the doorbell rang. I got up and went into the hall. The spy-hole in the door was too high for me, designed for someone several inches taller than my five foot two; if I stood on tiptoe and peered I could just about make out a scrap of sky, but never the person on the other side of the door. I put the chain across, took a deep breath and opened the door as far as the chain allowed.

Two police constables, different from the ones I had seen at the hospital.

'Joanne Elliott?' one of them asked. The man. He was smiling kindly at me. His female partner hung back behind him and looked up and down the street, as if she was bored, or was covering his back.

'Yes,' I said.

'You reported an incident?'

'Yes,' I said. Then I realized that I was still talking to them through the crack in the door. I undid the chain, opened the door and signalled for them to follow me into the front room. I switched off the TV.

'I'm PC Short, this is PC Andrews,' the man said, and the woman managed something approaching a smile as she scanned the room.

'Nice house,' PC Short said, and sat himself on the edge of the sofa, adjusting the radio pack in his belt to make himself more comfortable.

I nodded thanks and sank down into the armchair. PC Andrews continued her examination of the room and I caught myself wondering whether she would find something she shouldn't. But she was nosing, that was all, snooping around looking at everything just because she could.

PC Short said, 'So, you wanted to report a robbery?'

I looked back at him. He had short dark hair and chocolate-brown eyes; like Alex, I thought. He wore heavy boots that laced right up his ankles and disappeared under his trouser legs. He had taken his notebook out of his pocket and was leafing through the pages. PC Andrews suddenly seemed to feel that she was needed at his side and sat down next to him on the sofa.

I said, 'Yes. I was mugged.'

'And where was this?'

So I ran through the details once more, a condensed version because I was starting to get the hang of this. Young man appears, threatens me, I try to get away, he bashes me on the head and takes my purse, I wake up with a sore head. Even as I told them the story I felt how ridiculous all of this fuss was, how little anybody could do to prevent this sort of thing. I told them that he'd hit me in broad daylight, in a busy street, in the doorway to a busy shop, and I'd done nothing to provoke him. But as I said those words, I thought again of the dream I'd had. Maybe I had seen him somewhere before? I opened my mouth to suggest it, looking towards PC Andrews as if she was going to offer me some kind of sympathy, or encouragement. But PC Andrews looked slightly bored, almost impatiently so. Alex would have been angry with me if he had known I wasn't telling the police everything – I could imagine him, telling me I had a responsibility towards the attacker's next victims – but I didn't know what I could say that would make any sense. I couldn't imagine PC Andrews regaining her interest in my story if I told her that he had said something I hadn't heard, or looked at me as if he recognized me. And how could I be sure, when I had barely even caught a glimpse of his face?

PC Short said, 'So, you were on your lunch break. Where do you work?'

'Social Services,' I said. 'I'm a social worker.'

He gave a low little laugh. 'You're as popular as we are, then. On the streets, I mean. You're sure it wasn't a client having a pop?'

'Yes,' I said. But he had tried to speak to me, I was fairly sure of that – if I had only heard what he was saying to me, if I could only piece it together, then I would know. What if it had been a client? Maybe there was something I could have done to prevent it? I kept my voice even and said, 'I'm pretty sure, anyway. I didn't get that good a look at him.'

PC Andrews was looking around the room again, and I tried to see what she could possibly find so interesting in a plain old through-lounge with a few books on shelves and green plants in pots on the varnished floorboards and a couple of Kandinsky prints in clip-frames on the walls. I fought down the irritation, and the urge to tell her to stop, but I recognized the kind of look she was giving the place, the kind of assessment. It was what I did on a first home visit; deconstructing the home environment, trying to work out what the choice of ornaments or the lack of them meant, trying to figure out something about the character of the household from the kinds of objects and furniture and wallpaper they chose. I followed the policewoman's gaze and wondered what she made of me, and whether she would like the same assessment to be done in her own front room.

PC Short said, 'We'd like you to come down to the station tomorrow and look through our photos, see if this chap's known to us. We'll pick you up. You can make a proper statement then, too.'

'Okay,' I said, but I felt a little weak, a little dizzy at the thought. I walked the police back to the front door and once they had gone I shut it and leaned against it and tried to get my breath back. I didn't want to go to the police station. I didn't want to get in a police car. What if he saw me in the back of the car and decided he was going to come after me and shut me up? He had my purse, there had to be something with my address in that purse, and he could come back, he could come and find me. I imagined a knock at the door, opening the door, seeing his face pressed against the crack, grinning at me, the way he had grinned at me in the street, and a little chain wouldn't keep him out, he could force his way in and there wouldn't be anyone to stop him, and screaming wouldn't scare him away, not if he was determined.

Five

By the time I was due to drive over to Alex and Simon's place, I was starting to think that agreeing to go hadn't been such a good idea. It was dark outside. The street looked empty from the front window, but there were plenty of places where a person could stand unseen, if they really wanted to. An empty street meant nobody to rescue me – and there were such terrible stories in the newspapers and on the TV – mobile phone thefts at knifepoint, people taken to cashpoints with a gun in their back, car-jackings. People attacked as they unlocked their cars, or as they waited at traffic lights, or blocked-in when they pulled up to park. And there were the other crimes, too, the ones I didn't want to contemplate, because I could imagine the hand over my mouth, the press of someone's body against mine, the sound of their breath and its moist warmth against my ear.

I stood there by the front window for a long time, my shoes and coat on. The house was quiet behind me, and there wasn't much traffic on the main road. A stereo played pop hits somewhere nearby; the music was softened by distance, a lazy background sound.

I had thought about not going to Alex and Simon's at all. I could make an excuse; they would accept that. I could tell them I had a headache, that I was tired. I could sit in front of the TV instead – I had a bottle of wine, and something to smoke. I could relax; it would be nice just to relax.

But something rebelled against that idea. If I started lying about it, if I hid behind a headache, didn't that say that the attacker had won? I could imagine what Alex and Simon would say if they guessed the truth. Alex would make some joke about being surprised that anything could scare me; Simon would tell me that I shouldn't let the boggers win, I should stand up to them, show them that I wasn't afraid. I could imagine their disappointment, and how that would make me feel, and how angry I would be with them for making me feel that way. Why should I be brave about it? Why shouldn't I allow myself to hide, just for a while?

But I didn't want to feel angry with them. There was only one person I felt angry with – that face, so close to mine. And why should he win, anyway? I was stronger than that; I had to be stronger than that.

So, eventually, I opened the front door and stood there on the step, getting a better look at the street. It wasn't far to my car, and there was nobody around, and I had done this a thousand times before without even thinking about it.

I went quickly to my car and put my key in the lock. The street was still clear. I turned the key and the click of the lock sounded unnaturally loud. I looked around again, but there were no shadows stepping towards me, taking the form of people, stretching their hands out. I got into the driver's seat, locked my door, fastened my seatbelt. I started the engine and the vibrations set against the sickness in my stomach. I needed air but I wasn't going to open a window, not when somebody could reach their hand through.

I drove too quickly to Simon and Alex's place. I had expected something to happen on the journey – it seemed impossible that I could pass along the narrow streets, so close to all the people, all the lives, and come out unscathed. Even if it was just the police pulling me over for speeding, I felt that something was bound to happen – but nothing did. I parked outside the house and sat taking deep breaths for a long moment before I looked up and down the street. Dusk deepened the shadows in the cul-de-sac. Further up, outside one of the big Victorian houses sub-divided into bedsits, I could see a group of young men sitting on the front wall, drinking from cans. I avoided looking at them as I locked the car and hurried to Simon and Alex's front door. By the time Simon opened the door, the shadows seemed to have lengthened, drawing closer to me, bringing the cold night in.

I followed Simon down the narrow hall, squeezing past the bikes stored there, and out into the kitchen-diner at the back of the house. Alex was standing at the cooker, stirring something that smelled like curry. Simon and I sat at the table against the opposite wall, and I felt how hot I was, how sweaty, and how humid the kitchen was even with the back door open.

Alex turned from the cooker and said, 'You like your curries hot, don't you, Jo?'

'Yeah, sure,' I said, then saw Simon's expression and added, 'But not too hot, I like to feel my tongue afterwards.'

Simon giggled as if I'd said something genuinely funny. He had a spliff resting, half-smoked, in the ashtray and picked it up and re-lit it.

'How'd the thing go with the police?' Alex asked.

'Fine. They want me to look at mug-shots tomorrow.'

Alex turned and looked at me, as if he'd picked up something from my tone, but he said, 'Well, at least they're taking it seriously.'

I just smiled. Simon handed me the spliff and I took a couple of drags. Simon said, 'How's the head?'

'Okay,' I said.

'You've not been feeling dizzy?' Alex asked. 'Or unusually tired? The doctor said—'

'I know,' I said. 'No, I'm fine, honestly.'

'And you'll call if you need anything?'

'Yes. Stop fussing, will you?'

Alex turned back to the cooker, but I could tell he wasn't irritated.

I said to Simon, 'How's work?'

He rolled his eyes and took the end of the spliff back as I offered it to him. He didn't ask Alex if he wanted it, but nipped the roach between thumb and forefinger and sucked in carefully. Then he said, 'The union's all over the place with this Chantelle Wade thing. All the full-timers are getting pulled into it.'

'So, you're working on it, too, then?'

'Working on it? The union've practically dumped it on me, being the only full-timer in the region who used to work for Social Services. Talk about stress.'

Alex laughed. 'End of the union being a cushy little number for you, then?'

'Yeah, yeah,' Simon said, squashing the end of the spliff into the ashtray. 'Very funny. It's not exactly been a barrel of laughs since the kid died, I'll say that much.'

'Nor's Social Services,' I said. 'You should hear the rumours. Everyone's convinced they're going to drop the workers in it to save the department. It's not like we can be with the clients twenty-four hours a day in case something happens.' I hesitated, but went on, 'Unless it's true that they screwed up big time?'

Simon smiled. 'You know I can't talk about it, Jo. It's confidential.'

'I know, I know,' I said. I could see that Alex was listening carefully now, and that probably meant that

31

he'd asked, too, and got nowhere. 'It's just the whole department's so jumpy about it. Not to mention the clients.'

'Oh, tell me about it,' Alex said. 'All I get is bloody clients making comments.' He turned to face us, holding out the wooden spoon to emphasize his point. 'You should hear them, Simon, it's a nightmare.' He screwed up his face and imitated a whiny voice. '"You lot don't know nothing. You lot get things wrong all the time. You lot let that little girl die."' The spoon bobbed in his hand as he spoke. 'You can understand it, really, the way everyone's going on about the investigation, but it's still a complete nightmare.'

'Everyone always blames the social workers,' I said.

'I know, I know, but I still can't talk about it.' Then Simon relented a little. 'It's not as cut-and-dried as the media'll have you believe. That's all I can say.'

I would have pushed for more, but Simon had clamped his jaw firmly shut. I was trying to think of a way to change the subject when Alex announced that the curry was ready. I watched him slopping some sticky-looking rice onto three plates.

'Oh, c'mon,' Simon said. 'Cheer up, you two, for Christ's sake.'

I forced a smile onto my lips. Alex was spooning curry out over the rice and didn't reply.

Simon went to the fridge and returned with three bottles of lager, then opened one with a flourish. 'For you, madam,' he said, presenting the bottle to me label-first. 'A fine vintage, madam, from the Asda victuallers of the Alsace region.' He poured a little into a glass.

I laughed, then took a sip and swilled it around in my mouth before swallowing. 'Mmm,' I said. 'A fine body, a cheeky little nose. I sense hops and fruit and autumn leaves on bonfires, a heady concoction.'

Simon giggled and Alex said, 'Heady's right, the way he pours the stuff. Froth all over the table if you don't watch him.'

Simon pretended to be indignant, but then Alex put the plates of curry in front of each of us and sat down, so we all shut up to eat. Alex hadn't overdone the curry paste this time but the cauliflower had almost dissolved into the sauce.

When we'd eaten and the dishes were stacked up in the sink, we went into the front room. Simon rolled another spliff and I saw Alex's not-on-a-weeknight frown, but he didn't say anything. Simon and I shared the spliff while Alex played CDs on Simon's stereo. I could tell by the way he held his shoulders hunched that he was angry with us for smoking, but I didn't really care. I was sliding into the warm, drowsy feeling of being half-stoned, and my face was starting to ache from the effort of smiling; I knew that another spliff would take away my powers of speech altogether.

Eventually, Simon announced that he was going to the pub to meet some union buddies. I made

another attempt to get him to tell us about the
Chantelle Wade enquiry, but he just laughed that
off and started to lace up his boots. Alex changed
the CD again, this time for some Velvet Under-
ground, and I closed my eyes and felt myself sinking
back into the music. I heard the click of the front
door as Simon left the house, and I allowed myself
to drift.

Alex said, 'The Chantelle Wade case seems like
a mess.'

I opened my eyes. He was sitting in the armchair,
one leg crossed over the other, very upright. His
voice sounded far away. It felt like a long time
before I answered, but then I heard myself say,
'The media's got hold of it. That'll screw anything up.'

He gave a little grunt. 'I'm glad I wasn't involved.'

'Me too,' I said, and, after a pause, 'I think
everyone feels that way.'

I was having to concentrate very hard on each
word as I spoke. I lit myself a straight cigarette and
that cleared the fog a little. Alex was talking again,
rattling on about stress levels in his office and how
everyone in the department was on edge, waiting for
the next accusation about missed procedures and
neglect of duty. Journalists sniffing around buying
people drinks, clients making waspish comments,
that whole atmosphere of bad news about to come
out. I forced back a yawn.

'Am I boring you?' He sounded hurt.

I jerked awake again. 'Course not.'

'Just you're stoned,' he said. 'Christ, I try to have a conversation with you and you're wasted.'

'I'm not wasted.'

'This is important,' he went on. 'They're looking for any excuse, you know.'

I had to laugh at that. 'I don't think the journalists are looking for a great exposé on dope-smoking social workers, do you?'

'Not them,' Alex said. 'Management.'

He was looking gloomy. I said, 'Oh, get real. I'm off work this week, remember?' He didn't respond to that, and I was irritated to find that he'd punctured my feeling of well-being. 'Anyway, the last couple of days have been a nightmare. I think I'm entitled.'

'It doesn't solve anything,' he said.

'Oh, for fuck's sake,' I said. 'Spare me the drugs education speech, will you? I'm not one of your clients. You're drinking beer, and what's the difference?'

He frowned, but didn't respond. I could tell he was building up to saying something else and I couldn't face one of his meandering arguments, trying to score points, trying to make an issue out of nothing at all. After a pause, he said, 'It's probably just as well you've got some time off.'

That pricked me. 'What's that supposed to mean?'

'Nothing,' he said, sounding irritated. 'Just that everyone's on edge. Stressed out.'

I wanted to demand if he meant that I couldn't handle it, but I knew what he'd say to that. Taking things to heart – well, why shouldn't I? He might think of himself as perfect, never putting a foot wrong, all 'professional distance', but what did that prove? Sure, people could get support from him, maybe even some advice, but actually rely on him? No way. It would be like asking the book of guidelines for a hug.

So I let out a long breath and said, 'We're not at work now. Let's not talk about it, eh?'

He nodded, but I could see he was still brooding. And that was his great example of professional distance, of not taking things to heart? I could feel that the argument was still in the air and I didn't want my mood to be ruined any further, so I forced myself out of the chair and onto my feet.

'I'm going home,' I said. He looked at me in surprise. 'Thanks for the curry, but I'm really tired.'

He said, 'Don't go because of that. I don't care if you smoke a spliff, honestly, why would I? And we don't have to talk about work. We can have a nice evening still, can't we?'

'It's not because of that,' I said. 'My head's aching. I really just want an early night.'

He considered that. 'Fair enough. The stuff I got from your office is in the hall.'

I collected everything together and thanked him and he saw me to the door. Then he said, 'You will be okay to drive, won't you?'

'Of course,' I said. I felt bright and alert again. I gave him a quick peck on the cheek and, to my surprise, he put his arms around me and squeezed me into a hug.

'Take care,' he said.

I nodded and smiled and went to my car. He stood in the doorway, watching me. I wasn't sure what he had to be concerned about, and I tried to remind myself that it was really rather sweet.

Six

PC Short came alone to fetch me the following morning. I didn't ask what had happened to PC Andrews and he didn't volunteer the information, just smiled at me as if he felt I needed my confidence boosting. His car was parked next to the kerb. The street was very quiet, as it usually was – inner city pretending to be suburbia. PC Short opened the back door of the police car and I climbed inside.

I watched the policeman walk slowly around to the driver's side, his footsteps muffled. The inside of the car smelled slightly of warm plastic and pot-pourri air freshener. PC Short got into the driver's seat, started the engine and then put his seatbelt on. I looked at the back of his head; he must have had a haircut recently, because I could see the slightly paler skin like a rim around his hairline where it had been shaved into the nape of his neck. I thought about my attacker, about striking a stranger on the back of the head, about feeling the impact and seeing someone stumble and fall. He had screwed his face up into an ugly expression when he confronted me, and I couldn't imagine what he had been thinking, or how he had been feeling, or how he could have done something like that.

And he was out there somewhere, and I was in this car, surrounded by metal and glass, visible to everyone. I took a deep breath; I wanted to get out of the car, get out and run back to my house, shut myself in with the door deadlocked and the curtains drawn, where nobody would be able to see me or talk to me or get at me.

PC Short turned in his seat and said, 'Are you okay?'

For a moment, I thought that he must have been possessed of a sixth sense, an intuition, but I realized it was just a routine enquiry. I forced myself to nod, and he turned back and we moved off up the street.

I was hardly breathing as we came out onto Sherwood Rise. There were people on the pavements; women pushing pushchairs and dragging small children along, pensioners walking slowly up the hill, and small clusters of students. I closed my eyes and forced myself to draw air into my lungs. He wasn't out there, he wouldn't be, I knew it, but still I didn't want to look. PC Short must have glanced at me in the rear-view mirror, because he said, 'Are you sure you're okay?'

'Yes,' I said. 'Just a slight headache.'

'Have you taken anything for it?'

'Yes,' I said, even though I hadn't since first thing, because I wanted him to stop talking. He seemed to take the hint; at any rate, he didn't speak again until we were pulling into a yard at the side of the police station.

He said, 'I'll have to let you out,' as he parked the car up hard against the handbrake, then slammed the driver's door and ambled round to let me out of the back. I climbed out and followed him into the police station. We passed through a reception area with a handful of people waiting, their expressions fixed with the kind of boredom I associated with the dole office or the doctor's surgery. Through a security door and down a tiled corridor, me trotting after PC Short and wishing I could stop, sit down, catch my breath.

'We'll take your statement after you've seen the photo books,' he said. We swept up some tiled stairs with fake mahogany banisters. Plastic ivy dripped down the stairwell from ceramic pots on the landing and there were prints in wooden frames screwed to the walls, but it didn't feel welcoming.

I followed PC Short down a narrow corridor and into a small room. My first impression was that it was a store room; every available space on the walls was filled with shelves of lever-arch folders and bound reports, below which were melamine units sagging under the weight of stacks of paper and more reports. There was a table at the centre of the room; the kind of veneer-topped metal-legged table that reminded me of school. I sat down on the grey plastic chair PC Short indicated.

He fetched a heavy lever-arch folder from one of

the shelves and set it down in front of me. 'Have a good look through,' he said. 'Take your time. Would you like a coffee?'

'Yes, please,' I said, more so he would leave me, so I wouldn't have to feel the concern through his gaze as he waited for me to find the right face in the book.

He went over to the far end of the room, behind me, out of my line of sight. I took a deep breath and looked down at the first page of photos. There were twelve to a page, playing-card size images, youths looking straight into the camera. Twelve pairs of eyes. I think I had expected my attacker to be looking up at me from the centre of the first page, maybe even laughing, looking up at me with a challenge that I would recognize was aimed straight at me. But the first page were all strangers, some looking back at me with bewilderment, as if they couldn't understand how they had ended up in this situation. Kids. I turned over to the next page. There were lines and lines of the images.

PC Short returned to the table and placed a plastic cup of coffee down for me. 'Sugar?' he asked.

'No, thanks,' I said, and turned over to the next page.

'It's not real milk, I'm afraid,' he said. 'It's only that powdered stuff. Coffeemate.'

There was something in his tone that made me glance up at him. He had run his hand through his hair and now a small clump was sticking out at an odd angle near the crown of his head. It gave him an oddly boyish look, and I realized with a shock that he was about my age, and had a nice face – the kind of bland, inoffensive face that was rarely remarked upon, the nose and mouth an average size, the chin tapered to an average angle. The only remarkable thing about his face was the fluid brown of his eyes. He ran his hand over his hair again, smoothed down the offending clump and smiled slightly. I realized that I must have been looking at him a moment too long, so I took a sip of the coffee and said quickly, 'It's fine, thanks.'

'Any luck so far?' he asked.

'No.'

'Well, take your time.' But there was a slight hint of disappointment, a drop in the enthusiasm in his tone.

I turned another page. The thickness of the book daunted me. And they were mostly so very young, too – barely out of school, bad skin, ragged haircuts, their flesh taut over their cheekbones where they'd grown too fast for their metabolisms to keep up, or flabby where the puppy fat still lingered. They were the sorts of kids I had to deal with at work, and as I progressed through the folder a few faces made me stop – the ghost of a similarity in the turn of the lips or the way the eyes looked at me. Each time I stopped, I tried to refocus the image in my mind, wanting to define the features I was searching for, but those features blurred and smoothed even as I searched my memory for them. It could have been any one of a dozen – or none of them. But that sense of familiarity I had had – I found myself wondering whether I did know him, whether he was a client I had forgotten. The thought sat uneasily in my mind as I closed the folder.

'Didn't spot him, then?' PC Short asked.

'No,' I said.

He sighed. 'Well, it was worth a shot. Shall we go and sort out your statement?'

We went back down the stairs and into a small interview room with a hexagonal table at its centre. As he readied himself with forms, I wondered whether I should tell him what I was thinking. It would be crazy not to – but what could I say? I didn't know who my attacker was – what kind of a social worker was I if I couldn't remember one of my own clients? And I could be wrong – he had taken my purse, so maybe it was just a robbery after all? I didn't want the police to go trampling through my case files on a wild-goose chase.

'Ready?' PC Short asked.

I nodded, putting those thoughts out of my head.

Seven

When I got home from the police station, I couldn't relax. I tried sitting down with a mug of tea and a cigarette, but even the nicotine couldn't block out the pages and pages of faces in that folder, and the fact that my attacker hadn't been among them. I watched daytime TV for a short while, but I couldn't be bothered with quiz shows and the schools programmes were covering basic maths, so I switched the TV off and fetched my filofax from the bag Alex had collected from the office for me.

I hadn't missed anything important so far that week, but there was a case conference to prepare for and a couple of reports to write and case files to update. I made a list of the outstanding work, but my head started to throb and I couldn't bring myself to complete any of the tasks. I lit another cigarette.

My attacker's face. I had been so sure I would recognize him, but I hadn't. The police didn't know who he was, and neither did I, and what if he was never caught? I wanted to forget about him, but my head hurt and he was still out there somewhere. I had a clear idea of the shape of his nose, the contour of his chin, the peculiarly pale hue to his skin, but it was possible that my memory was just playing tricks, filling in the gaps, and the face I saw in my dreams wasn't the right face at all. He was still out there in the streets; I could imagine him pacing the pavements, walking around knowing what he had done to me, and that he had got away with it. I didn't want to know whether he was still angry, whether he was hoping to see me again so he could do something more to me. I tried to remind myself that it had just been a mugging, nothing more than street robbery – it happened every day, it wasn't even significant. But still, there was that stab of doubt, that moment when I had thought I recognized him, and what if I was right?

But there was nothing I could do about it. I lit another cigarette and realized I had only just put one out, but I smoked on anyway. I couldn't allow this one little incident to affect my life. I had a job, I had responsibility for other people's lives, people were relying on me.

I decided to phone work. I had my diary open at that week's appointments and the list of tasks set next to it. I phoned my supervisor.

Douglas came on the line very quickly, said, 'How're you feeling, Jo?'

'Fine,' I said. 'I just wanted to check my workload was being covered.'

'You're off sick. Don't worry about it.'

'I have to worry about it,' I said. 'I'm the one

who'll have to pick up the pieces when I come back.'

'You're not going to be off for that long,' he said. 'Their worlds won't collapse in the next week, will they?' But he allowed me to read out the appointments I had that needed to be kept, and I knew by the way he hummed and hawed that most of them would be cancelled anyway. 'I can't get anyone out to Mrs Adams this afternoon,' he said. 'Too short notice. We're snowed under.' Before I could object that Mrs Adams would worry, he continued, 'She's too dependent on you, anyway. Shouldn't even be an active case by rights.'

I tried to argue with him, but he was adamant and my head was pounding too hard to form a coherent case, so I gave up. I rang off and took three paracetamol with some water. I could imagine what was going on in the office; talk always turned to the Chantelle Wade enquiry these days, and the tension would rise throughout the office like a communal palpitation at the mention of that name. The bogey case, the nightmare we all wanted to avoid, the scenario that sat in the back of our minds every time we made a judgement call, or skipped an appointment, or rushed writing up the case notes. I thought about all the appointments Douglas would be cancelling, and Katie Adams waiting in her house, her whole day, her whole week a build-up to my visit. It was too easy to let things slide or lose a client's confidence or miss the signs of trouble. Douglas never seemed to understand that, and nobody else would point this out and volunteer to cover my caseload for me, not when they had so many cases of their own.

My headache was fading under the influence of the paracetamol, so I took a pad of paper and began to make notes about each of the clients I was due to see that week. Douglas would probably be irritated by my presumption, but I could imagine that whoever had to actually deal with my clients would be grateful for the insights. I started to make a few notes about Katie Adams, but stopped after a couple of lines. Douglas wasn't going to send anyone round to see her, I knew that – and even if he did, I could imagine her reaction to a stranger on her doorstep. I thought about Douglas's words – that she was too dependent on me, and I pictured Katie Adams with a stranger, faltering, stammering as she tried to make herself understood. What was wrong with her wanting to see me? What was wrong with her feeling that she could rely on me, and that trust, that bond we'd built up? I thought of some of my other clients; their hostility, their refusal to listen, the way they always held back, as if it was inconceivable that they could actually trust me. Why should I give up seeing the client who was always friendly, always grateful, always so pleased that I was there? Other people – Douglas, Alex, even Colin – might think she was a waste of my time, but I didn't. And what if I did stop seeing her, and something happened, and the accusations started to fly – incompetence, neglect of duty, ignoring the warning signs – what then?

I could imagine how Douglas would react if he

found out that I had decided to visit her, but he didn't need to know. She was my responsibility. I put the other notes into an envelope and addressed it to Douglas, then loaded the envelope and my filofax into my bag.

It was a bright, sunny day, a false start at spring. The street was quiet when I went out to the car; even the sound of traffic seemed muted. It seemed impossible that I had been afraid of being seen by my attacker, and I deliberately put the thought out of my mind as I started the car up.

Katie Adams lived a couple of miles away, just off Canning Circus, a narrow section of streets hemmed in by the traffic along the Alfreton Road, the edge of the cemetery and the steep hill leading up to Forest Road and the recreation ground where Goose Fair was held each October. The area consisted mainly of big Victorian houses sub-divided into bedsits, with scatterings of red-brick seventies semis, but there were new buildings pushing their way in; student halls of residence with stolen traffic cones and empty beer bottles in the windows, and newly built city living apartments with security doors and high fences. Katie lived in one of the box-like Housing Association semis. When I pulled up outside her house and went to her front door, I could hear the television playing and one of her children crying.

I knocked and waited. I made out the shape of Katie Adams approaching through the nets that covered the wired glass panels in the door, and then I heard bolts being pulled back and the key turning in the lock. Finally the door opened and I was assaulted by that sickly sour smell of warm milk and babies.

'I phoned you,' Katie said. 'They said you were off sick.'

'I was,' I said.

I followed her through into the living room. Her mousy hair hung like limp twine, straggling over thin shoulders as she hunched herself into the nightdress of a T-shirt she was wearing. She sat on the sofa and wrapped her thin arms around her knees, knotting her fingers together and fixing her large blue eyes on a point somewhere just over my shoulder.

I sat down in my usual armchair and said, 'So, how are things this week?'

Jack, her three-year-old, was sitting on the floor watching the *Tweenies* on TV. The baby was in the carry-cot on the sofa next to Katie. 'Okay,' she said, and huddled herself further, as if she was cold.

'Did the health visitor come?'

She nodded, then turned to fuss over the baby, adjusting its clothing, as if I'd reminded her of what she needed to do.

'And everything's okay with your husband?'

'Yes,' she said quietly, and for a moment managed to make eye contact with me, then looked away again. A slight flush had come into her cheeks. 'He's away working,' she said. 'Down south. Three days.'

'And you're okay while he's gone?'

'Yes.' I thought she was going to say more, but she stopped herself.

I forced my gentlest smile onto my face, preparing to probe for the answer I wanted to hear, but Jack had been distracted from the *Tweenies* by a group of boys cycling past the window, calling to each other. He leaned against the low windowsill to look out at them. Katie Adams was out of her chair and pulling him away from the window faster than I'd seen her move before. 'Should call the police on them, I should,' she said, watching the boys circle lazily in the street. 'Bleddy monsters. Should be at school.'

I thought she was about to rap on the window and draw attention to herself, so I got up and went to her side and said quickly, 'Are they the lads who've been causing you trouble?'

The boys were still circling on their bikes, laughing about something. There were five of them, all about twelve or thirteen years old. I watched one skinny dark-haired lad saying something to the others, balancing on the bike even as he used his hands to gesticulate. I couldn't hear what he was saying, but there was something familiar about the way he moved.

'They throw things at my window,' Katie was saying. 'They threw fireworks at Bonfire Night, I know it was them. Could've hurt someone, that could've. Last time Gary was back he chased them, but it didn't do no good. Get the truant officers round, I reckon. It's all that Metcalfe kid's fault, he's always behind it.'

It was the longest speech I'd heard from her in recent weeks. I started to say that responding in anger would probably make them do it even more, but the name she mentioned had jarred in my memory. I said, 'Did you say Metcalfe?'

'Little monsters,' Katie said. 'They think I don't know it's them, but I know who they are.' I thought she hadn't heard my question, but then she said, 'Yeah, Metcalfe, that Mrs Metcalfe, she's as bad, out all hours with all kinds, it's no wonder her kids've turned out bad. I told her to her face what Danny's been up to, but she don't care. Told me to do something I wouldn't repeat in company.'

I watched the skinny dark-haired boy in the street. He had been facing away from me but now turned, and as he turned I caught a glimpse of a familiar face, an older face, one I'd seen close up. But it was gone in an instant; he was just a kid, a young lad, and I wasn't sure if my eyes had been deceived by the light, or Katie Adams's words, or whether I was looking too hard for something where it didn't exist. But 'Metcalfe'? I said, 'Is Danny Metcalfe the dark-haired kid with the denim jacket?'

'Yeah,' she said. 'That woman's the problem, you mark my words. Get someone to see what she's up to.'

I wasn't really listening to her – I'd heard these theories before – but asked, 'Does she live in this street, then?'

'Number five. Been there a coupla years. You going to sort her out, then?'

I forced myself to smile, but I felt slightly sick.

'Leave it with me,' I said. 'Don't you say anything, okay?'

'Oh, sure,' she said. I wasn't sure if I'd imagined the malicious glint in her eye, but I said nothing. Katie Adams wouldn't do anything anyway – she was like a child, really, an overgrown kid with a baby and a toddler for toys.

As I said goodbye to her at the door, I knew I wasn't thinking about the right things. I should have been contemplating the strain she had been under, and the way the boys on the bikes had been tormenting her. I should have been worrying that her husband was a useless lump who never lifted a finger to help her but was quick to raise his hand to her, and yet, going down the path to my car, it was the Metcalfe boy I was thinking about. That name – that glimpse of a face when he had turned on his bike. I wasn't sure why it all seemed so familiar to me, but seeing the boy on the bike and hearing that name had flashed an image into my mind – a skinny dark-haired boy, a sneering sort of a grin, that face – had that been him? I tried to recall the face – it had been, what, seven, eight years ago? I tried mentally to age the face, a young man rather than a boy, approaching me in the street, but I couldn't be sure.

The boys were still circling on their bikes. I walked over to them. 'Shouldn't you be at school?' I asked.

They looked at one another, and then the boy I recognized, the Metcalfe boy, said, 'It's teacher training today, intit?' The others all laughed, as though this was the height of wit. He caught me looking at him and glared back at me.

'I know you,' I said. 'You're Danny Metcalfe, aren't you?'

He looked slightly surprised, then regained his composure and said, 'So?'

I kept my tone light. 'How's your mother?' He didn't respond to that, so I took a gamble on my memory and said, 'And your brother?'

He didn't reply to either question, but just looked at me. I wondered whether he had been expecting me to ask, but I knew I was probably wrong – after all, I could barely remember if he had a brother, and a passing likeness to the images that played through my mind was nothing to rely on.

He said, 'You're always round at her house,' indicating Katie Adams's with a contemptuous jerk of his head. 'I've seen you,' he added, as if I was going to deny it.

One of the others circled closer on his bike, standing on his pedals as he looked at me. 'You a head-doctor then?' he demanded. ''Cos she's a nutter. She's always raving on at people.'

'That's enough,' I said, seeing Katie Adams's net curtains move, but I knew I wouldn't have any impact on the boys.

They were all giggling to each other again now, apart from Danny Metcalfe, who looked at me with a frown. He said, 'My mum says you're a social worker.'

This was not going as I had planned. I said, 'And

does your mum always gossip about other people's visitors?'

'She just knows,' he said. A sudden seriousness had come over his expression. The others hadn't heard our brief conversation, and now he turned his bike to face up the street and said loudly, 'C'mon, let's go to mine.'

As they prepared to move off, I said, 'I know who you are. You should think again before causing trouble around here.'

Danny Metcalfe was holding one finger up to me in a salute as he cycled away, and the others laughed as they followed him. I glanced over towards Katie Adams's house and saw her net curtain drop back into place. I went to my car and got in.

I did a slow three-point turn to avoid hitting any of the boys, who made no attempt to get out of the way, and drove back towards Canning Circus. As I passed number five, I glanced over. A house just like the one Katie Adams had. The grass on the strip of front lawn needed cutting, and the windows looked dirty, but that didn't prove anything. I headed back up Alfreton Road and onto Radford Road, still thinking. That name was so familiar, and it had brought a sharp image into mind. If it was a Metcalfe who had attacked me . . . but how could I be sure? I had only a vague idea of what my attacker had looked like – and it was clutching at straws to think I could spot a family resemblance in the boy on the bike. I remembered the family, they had definitely been one of my cases, but I couldn't remember any details

– surely anything that could cause a long-standing grudge would be difficult to forget? Unless it hadn't been a grudge at all – unless it was a straightforward mugging, and I just happened to be in the wrong place at the wrong time. The police didn't seem to think there was anything more to it – but then, I hadn't voiced my suspicions, so why would they?

I was coming up towards Asda, and on impulse I pulled off the road and into the car park. I had a sudden desire for pizza and wine, plenty of wine, to take my mind off the events of today. I found a parking space and then cut the engine.

It was starting to get dark, and I sat there for a moment, looking out at the lines of parked cars, strangely uniform with the dusk and the yellow street lights washing out the colours. There were a few people wandering through the car park – people popping in on their way home from work, schoolkids in varying degrees of uniform (so much for teacher training day, I thought), and a gang of youths with hoods pulled down over their faces, the way the kids thought was cool, walking with a slouch and playing at being gangsters. Some of them could even be gangsters, for all I knew. The local news was full of it – shoot-outs, armed robberies, drugs raids, gang warfare – but I'd never believed things were really that bad. I lived in the inner city; I had thought I understood what was going on. I had thought that not being involved in that world was enough to keep me safe, but now I wasn't so sure. I watched the gang of youths meander across the car park. A few days ago, I wouldn't have given them a second thought, but so much had changed. I felt a little dizzy. My attacker was about their age; he probably dressed that way, too, and how would I ever spot him if I couldn't see his face?

I forced myself to slow my breathing. I concentrated on sucking cool air down into my lungs. My hands were shaking slightly and I gripped the steering wheel hard. He wouldn't be here, I knew that; I was half a mile from my office so why would he be here? And even if he was – it was so unlikely, but even if he was he wouldn't approach me. He was more likely to avoid me, in case I identified him.

So I took a deep breath and got out of the car and shouldered my handbag. Now that I was out of the car I could hear the traffic, and engines starting up elsewhere in the car park, and the tinny sound of trolleys being stacked and pushed together.

It was stupid to be so nervous. I had nothing to fear. I went towards the supermarket entrance. But I could imagine him coming up beside me, appearing at my elbow the way he had the other day, demanding that I stop, that I stop walking and turn and face him and talk to him about whatever his problem was, whatever he had been so angry about.

But he hadn't been angry at me, I reminded myself. He was a mugger, that was all; he had just wanted to take my money and get away as fast as he could. Even if he was a Metcalfe, that didn't mean there was anything personal about it.

I went through the revolving door and into the

supermarket, into the bright lights, past the displays of special offers, past the pharmacy counter and the cigarette and lottery ticket kiosk. There, I was handed a basket by an elderly man with a 'Can I Help You?' badge on his overalls who should have been at home with his feet in slippers and a pipe in his mouth.

I moved numbly through the aisles in a daze of artificial light. Tinned music muttered over the loudspeakers, distorted by the vast space, sometimes muffled behind the hum of the refrigerators and the regular pulse-beat of goods being scanned through the checkouts. I had expected the familiar, ordered calm to reassure me, but it didn't seem to be working. Looking around at the shelves, at row upon row of jars and tins and packets, dizzying in their uniformity, I didn't feel reassured. I watched the people gliding past as they filled their trolleys, and the workers scurrying to re-stock the shelves, and I realized that none of them knew that the world outside had changed. I was dizzy with the revelation – the world had changed, but I was the only one who had noticed that it wasn't safe and secure and familiar any more.

I stopped still, stood there in the centre of the aisle, watching the people stream past me. I felt slightly sick. I wanted fresh air, not the controlled chill of the store. I wanted to feel sunlight on my face instead of the cold glare of fluorescence. I tried to think what I had come in for, hoping that would numb the pain swelling inside my skull.

In front of the wine, I gazed at all the different bottles. I had to make a choice but the thought caught my breath inside my chest. I closed my eyes, steadied myself and opened them again. I saw a couple of Chilean reds on special and put them into my basket. As I walked back towards the entrance I wanted to laugh.

The old man was still handing out baskets. There was a queue at the kiosk buying lottery tickets. Beyond the kiosk and the revolving doors it had grown very dark outside. I was surprised at how much time had passed, and then a face caught my eye, a face pressed against the great expanse of glass frontage, looking into the store with a surprised expression, looking in from the outside, looking at me. My eyes connected with his, just for an instant, and my heart started to pound. I moved towards him, towards the glass, and he seemed to hesitate, and then I knew he was going to walk away. It seemed so absurd, that he could attack me and then simply walk away. It seemed absurd that he was right there, on the other side of that glass, and what could I do?

I started to run. I ran past the old man handing out baskets, past the queue at the lottery kiosk, out through the revolving door, out into the cold air under the covered walkway that fringed the building. I stood there, looking around, looking for him, but I couldn't see him. I went to where he had been standing, looked in at the brightly lit interior, looked around at the cars lined up in the car park, looked at the people walking across the car park. He wasn't there.

And then I felt a hand on my arm, and I tried to jerk free of the grip. I remembered him appearing at my elbow, trying to talk to me, and I tried to pull away, but the hand gripped me harder. I turned, ready to face him, ready to challenge him, but it was a security guard. It took me a moment to realize that he was reaching for my other hand, and that I was still holding the basket containing the two bottles of wine. I tried to speak, wanting to explain, but I couldn't find any words and the security guard guided me back into the store.

In the manager's office, I sat on a plastic chair while the security guard wrote something down on a clipboard and the manager looked at me. The security guard was a big man squeezed into a blue ribbed jumper with 'security' stitched in gold thread on the epaulettes. The manager was younger than me, thin, with his hair gelled into a fashionable style at odds with his corporate green polyester suit.

I said again that I hadn't meant to walk out without paying. The basket and the wine sat on his desk, on top of a pile of papers, the irrefutable evidence there for me to contemplate. I said, 'I told you, ask PC Short, he'll tell you.' I had the impression that my story was having no impact on the manager. 'For Christ's sake, the wine's on special offer. Why would I choose a special offer if

I was going to nick it? I'd have gone for something decent if I wasn't intending to pay.'

The manager wrinkled up his mouth a little and glanced at the security guard. I realized I probably hadn't helped my case much. The radio on the security guard's belt gave a little cough of static, as if in comment. The guard looked at the radio then said, 'Police are here.'

The manager gave a slow nod and the security guard went out. The manager rocked gently backwards and forwards in his chair, steepling his fingers and touching his lips to his fingertips. It was a small office, windowless, with bits of paper tacked to every available space on the wall, and when the security guard returned, the sudden breeze set all the papers flapping.

I had been feeling very distant, as if this scene didn't connect to my life, but when I turned in my seat I saw that, whatever I had thought, the manager had been listening to me, because PC Short was standing there.

'Hello, Jo,' PC Short said, and I wondered when we had become familiar enough for him to use my first name, or whether this was what happened when a victim became a perpetrator.

'Hi,' I said, trying not to look too embarrassed.

PC Short pulled up a chair, sat down and looked at me. 'So, what's been going on?'

The manager opened his mouth to speak, but PC Short glanced at him – that was enough to close his mouth. I wondered how PC Short had learned to throw a look like that, whether it was part of police training, whether the technique could be adapted to social work.

I said, 'I saw my attacker. The mugger. He was looking at me through the window. I followed him out but he'd gone by the time I got there.'

'Okay, don't worry.' PC Short sighed and looked at the manager. 'Can I have a word with you outside, sir?'

I was left there while they went outside. The security guard was still standing behind me – I had the feeling that he would have jumped on top of me and pinned me to the ground if I had so much as stood up, so I stayed where I was, staring at the multi-dotted year planner and the stock rotation procedures and the health and safety notices on the wall.

After a couple of minutes, the manager led PC Short back into the room. PC Short said, 'Come on, Jo, I'll drive you home.'

The manager didn't look at me. The security guard seemed to deflate at the news that I wasn't going to be prosecuted. I stumbled out of the office and followed PC Short out through the revolving doors to where the police car was parked in the taxi rank.

I felt that I had to say something, offer an explanation, show him that I wasn't losing my grip. I blurted out, 'I don't know what happened. It doesn't make any sense.'

'Don't worry about it,' he said.

He was guiding me towards the police car. I said, 'I've got my car here.'

He held open the back door of the car. 'Come back for it another time,' he said. 'You look all-in.'

I wanted to explain that I was just confused, I had been thrown off balance, that was all. I wanted him to understand that everything had changed – all the rules, the way things were meant to be; was it any wonder I was confused? But I didn't know how to make him understand me, so I just got into the back of the car. When he got into the driver's seat and started the engine, I managed to say, 'Thank you.'

He just shrugged. 'No problem. But I think you should stay at home for a few days, don't you? Get a bit of kip, relax a little.'

I nodded. I needed cigarettes, I remembered, I was almost out. And I'd left the wine behind, although I couldn't have brought myself to drink it after the humiliation it had caused.

PC Short said, 'So, you saw your attacker?'

'Yes,' I said, but I was less sure now. 'At least, I think I did.'

I could tell that he was smiling even though I could only see the side of his face from where I was sitting. 'It happens all the time,' he said. 'People thinking they see a perpetrator. Something to do with the shock of it all, and nerves, I expect.'

I wanted to protest that it wasn't like that, I wasn't being controlled by these events, but I couldn't bring myself to speak. He didn't seem to be aware that I was different to most victims – I was a professional,

I was used to having distance, I was used to stopping these sorts of things from affecting me.

PC Short said, 'It'll probably take a while to get over it, but that's normal, too. You can get help from Victim Support if you feel you need it.'

That stung me. 'I'll be fine, thanks,' I said.

We drove in silence the rest of the way until he parked outside my house. I was looking in my handbag for my house keys as he came round to let me out of the car, and I realized I still had the envelope of case notes in my bag. I pulled it out as PC Short opened the back door. I had been going to say thank you, but instead I heard myself say, 'Oh, I meant to post this.'

He glanced at it. 'I'll do that for you, don't you worry about it.'

'Thanks,' I said, and gave it to him as I got out.

He looked at the address. 'What is it, your resignation?'

'No,' I said, and I was about to explain when I realized he was joking.

He just smiled at my confusion. 'Now, don't go doing anything stupid again, will you? Stay at home.'

'Okay,' I said, and made myself smile for him. 'Thanks.'

I went up to the front door and unlocked it. He watched me until I closed the door. Then I heard his engine start and the car pull away from the kerb. As I stood in the hall, I realized that I hadn't told him

Clare Littleford

about my suspicion that my attacker was a Metcalfe, and he hadn't said anything about catching him. But it had been a long afternoon, so I tried to put it out of my mind.

Eight

I slept badly that night. I woke frequently to the sound of rain against the bedroom window, and cars in the street, and the wind skittling stones and rubbish along the tarmac. Once, in the early hours, I heard someone shouting – I lay there, eyes wide in the dark, tensed, listening, until I heard the drunken stagger in the half-remembered lyrics of a chart song and I knew there was nothing to worry about.

At four a.m. I rolled myself a spliff and smoked it in bed. The bedroom filled with the fumes and the back of my throat burned, but the dull ache in my head faded away and I relaxed enough to sleep.

I didn't wake again until after ten the next morning. I wouldn't even have woken then if someone hadn't been ringing my doorbell. I pulled on my dressing gown and went downstairs. I entertained a brief notion that it might be PC Short being gentlemanly, calling round to check I was okay, but it wasn't him at the door. It was the thin young Asian woman from the shop.

She gave me an apologetic smile and I realized that

I still had the chain across, so I said, 'Hang on,' and closed the door, unchained it and opened it again. I had half-expected her to have disappeared, but she was still there, smiling.

'I'm sorry,' she said. 'I didn't mean to wake you.'

'No, it's fine, I was just dozing. Come in,' I said. 'Please, come in.'

I led her through into the front room. She sat down on the edge of the sofa. She was carrying a plain white plastic bag, the top rolled down and clutched in her hands. I couldn't see what was inside. She offered it to me, saying, 'We found this.'

I took the bag and opened it. My purse, fat and heavy with cards and coins. I took the purse out of the bag and looked inside – credit cards, library ticket, my Social Services ID card, forty-something quid in cash. I looked at her, surprised.

'It was under the shelves,' she said. 'It must have fallen there when you fell. We only opened it to check whose it was. It's got your address inside, that's how I knew where to come.'

'Wow,' I said, because I didn't know what else to say. The full significance of this had not yet permeated into my thoughts. 'Well, thank you, thanks for bringing it round.' I glanced at her, and then I realized how much I owed her, I remembered how kind she had been to me, what a comfort it had been to find her bending over me. I said, 'Would you like a cup of tea or something?'

'If it's no bother.'

'No, not at all,' I said, and headed off to the kitchen to put the kettle on. While I waited for it to boil I went back to her and added, 'I wanted to thank you, anyway, for being so nice to me, looking after me like that.'

She just smiled. I felt slightly embarrassed. It was difficult to know what to say to her, how to express what had happened to me, and how much I did owe her. I thought it would sound silly if I told her.

I said, 'I don't know your name.'

'Davinder,' she replied. I was about to introduce myself, but she stopped me. 'I know yours, of course, from your purse.' I just nodded, and we fell silent. Then she said, 'How is your head now?'

'Oh, not so bad. I had a couple of stitches but it's fine now.'

I went into the kitchen and made the tea, and then we sat at the table. I wasn't sure what to say to her. I had so much to ask – about what she'd seen, and what exactly had happened.

She seemed to know what I was thinking, because she said, 'The police came round, asking us what we saw.'

I sipped my drink. 'And what did you say?'

'We didn't see anything.' She seemed slightly defensive about it. She flushed again and said, 'I'm not sure if they believed us, but why would we lie about it?'

'I'm sure they do believe you. Anyway, it all happened so quickly.'

'That's right,' she said. 'One minute there was

nothing happening, the next you were lying on the floor. I mean, how could we have seen?'

'Precisely,' I said. 'You were busy working. Why would you have been looking at the street?'

She inclined her head in agreement, but it wasn't a very definite movement. Then she said, 'Telling the police stuff makes it all so – so final, you know what I mean?'

I thought of the things I hadn't mentioned, that moment of recognition. 'Oh yes,' I said. 'It's hard to be vague with them, but sometimes things are vague.'

'Exactly,' she said, then hesitated and smiled at me.

'What is it?' I asked.

She sighed, as if she was wrestling with whether she should say this at all. I tried to urge her on with my expression, and she smiled again. 'Well, I don't know if it was anything at all, it was probably nothing, but I did hear someone, just before you were – well, just before. I was in the store room at the back. There's a barred window, high up, opens onto the alley next to the shop. I heard someone. Sounded like he was talking to himself. Youngish lad, sounded like. Local accent. He was saying the same thing over and over, like he was building up to something.' She looked embarrassed again. 'I ignored him. People like that, it's best not to take any notice of them, you know what I mean?'

'Yes,' I said. 'I know. What was he saying?'

'Sounded like "she's going to apologize". That

was all. Just "she's going to apologise", over and over. It didn't make any sense.'

But she was looking at me with the same curious expression, as if she was hoping I could give her an explanation. I wondered how long she had been thinking about all of this, trying to work it out. 'No,' I said. 'It doesn't.' I was slightly disappointed. I had hoped that she might have caught a glimpse of the young man, been able to fill in some more of the details, because I wasn't sure any more. But 'she's going to apologize'? He had been saying something to me – something I hadn't been able to make much sense of – was that it? But what did I have to apologize for? What had I done to him?

Davinder said, 'The police described it as a robbery. Did he actually take anything?'

I opened my mouth to say yes, but then I realized that he hadn't, I had dropped my purse, she had brought it back to me with nothing missing. So I said, 'No. I thought he had my purse. I wasn't carrying anything else.'

She nodded, but didn't comment. I wondered whether I should tell the police, whether PC Short would need to know – would they downgrade the incident if they knew that nothing had actually been taken? I could imagine PC Short explaining it to me, explaining that they couldn't do a lot and had little chance of catching him and had so little manpower. And my attacker would be left to roam the streets, he would be able to approach me any time he wanted to, and there would be nothing much I could do about it. I remembered the Metcalfe family, suddenly, but I still couldn't make any sense of it.

Davinder said, 'Well, I'd better get back to the shop.'

She had stood up and was rearranging her clothing. I wondered how long I had been silent. I said, 'Thank you so much. For bringing the purse round. And for helping the other day.'

She shrugged that away and went out into the hall. I thanked her again as she went into the front garden and I watched her walk down to the gate. She glanced back at me with another embarrassed smile, and I nodded at her and shut the door.

I felt almost weak as I found my way back onto the sofa. I sat down and looked through my purse, but everything seemed to be there. My head was aching with the effort of thinking this through. If he hadn't taken my purse, then had it been a robbery at all? Had he been intending to steal but couldn't take the purse after I fell, or had he only ever intended to hit me? I thought again about how familiar his face had seemed to me, how like a Metcalfe, and that he had spoken to me – why couldn't I remember what he had said? When I thought back and tried to reassemble his words, I had the sensation of being underwater, of hearing the words from a great distance, and I couldn't make out his meaning. But if Davinder was right, if he had been demanding an apology from me, then what did it mean?

Focusing my mind, I tried to think back, trawl up any detail I could remember about the Metcalfes from all those years ago. I had a vague impression of a thin woman crying, sitting on a sofa with one hand hiding her face from me, crying and trying hard not to. But what had I ever done that I needed to apologize for? My head was still fuzzy from sleep and I couldn't think. There was nobody I could ask.

A shiver ran through me. Maybe this was the ghost of caseloads past come back to haunt me? Or maybe it was the department he wanted an apology from, not me at all? Maybe he had seen me coming out of the office and had decided I was as good a target as anyone else? I wasn't sure which scenario was more unsettling.

The TV was showing repeats of some medical drama, and I allowed it to numb my brain while I thought about PC Short's reactions the evening before. He hadn't asked me any questions really, and that was nice, I hadn't wanted to talk about it, but now I had the feeling that maybe I should have done. He probably thought I was just seeing things, he probably didn't believe I had actually seen my attacker. And I wasn't one hundred per cent sure myself – it could have been someone else, someone who just looked a little like him, someone waiting for their family to come out through the checkouts. I couldn't lose my detachment; I had to remain focused. It probably all amounted to nothing anyway.

I thought of all the times I'd talked to women about the issues they faced, about the action they had to take to improve their lives, all the times they had looked up at me with those big scared eyes and told me they couldn't, they just couldn't do what I suggested. I'd acted all sympathetic, told them I understood, it must be hard, they should take their time, but inside I'd hardened against them, I'd dismissed them as flakes, the victims who deserved everything they got if they weren't prepared to stand up or, at the very least, walk away. And what was I doing now? One minor little incident and I was all over the place.

Being in the house for so long was starting to get to me; I'd develop cabin fever if I wasn't careful. I needed to build up the courage to walk to Asda and fetch the car back. It wasn't that far to walk – twenty minutes tops – but if I had been right, if I had seen him at Asda, wasn't it possible, even likely, that I would see him again? Sure, it was now broad daylight, but that hadn't stopped him from attacking me on Tuesday, that hadn't offered me any protection.

I would have left the car where it was for another day, but I suspected that Alex might call in on his way home from work, and he was certain to notice that my car was missing and ask where it was. I didn't want to have to explain what had happened at the supermarket – Alex would probably just laugh, but I knew he'd be thinking I was losing my grip.

Burying myself deep inside my coat, I headed out to walk to the car park. The wind gusted around me, playing with the litter on the pavements, tugging at my coat, and I folded my arms to hug the material to me even though I wasn't cold. The route to

Asda cut through the housing estate and into the narrower terraced streets of Forest Fields; the real inner city, unlike the almost-suburban tree-lined streets around my house. I walked quickly along Berridge Road, past Victorian terraces with ugly tiled doorways opening directly onto the pavements, past streets where neatly kept houses were crowded in on all sides by the dishevelled façades of giro-drop addresses and damp student digs. Places I had lived in when I first moved into the city; places that had made me feel adventurous, and brave, for calling the inner city my home. I had laughed at other people's concerns – Nottingham was not that dangerous, the inner city was not that alien if you understood the place and played by its rules.

And what had happened to me? I realized that I was walking very fast, almost running. I realized that it didn't seem friendly any more, but I wasn't sure whether the safety had been the illusion or whether it was the fear pumping through my veins that had no place.

Alex had always talked of 'getting out' – swapping the inner city for a nicer area, with trees in the front gardens and room for decking out the back, with Neighbourhood Watch and off-street parking. I had laughed at that whole semi-detached thing; I had laughed and told him he was kidding himself, we were inner city people, we needed to be right in the heart of things. So close to the city's pulse that I now heard it hammering in my ears.

I forced myself to stop. My legs ached from the

strides I had been taking. I was a little out of breath. Unfit, I told myself, too many cigarettes; and I forced myself to laugh. I was outside the first of the sari shops; I heard my laugh, high, unnatural, but the mannequins in the window looked impassively at me from painted eyes in painted faces. I sniffed the air, hoping for the spicy sweet scent I sometimes caught, but it smelled damp, fetid, like bricks after hard rain. All the energy had seeped from my body; my limbs felt heavy, but I had to press on. Past the grocers' stores and Halal butchers, past the shop with slabs of pink and green and yellow sweets in the window. I picked up my pace as I came past the last of the shops and plunged back into bedsitland. There were more boarded-up windows than the last time I had walked this way, and scatterings of drunks of various ages camped out on low walls with plastic bottles of cider. In a side street, next to a car with its stereo pulsing, two young men argued loudly, using their arms to exaggerate their points.

I looked directly ahead, not acknowledging anyone, and finally I reached my car. I got in and locked all the doors. I lay my arms across the steering wheel and pressed my forehead into my wrists. With my eyes closed, the thumping in my head grew louder, and I had to wait for my strength to return before I could fit the key into the ignition and start for home.

Nine

My week off had stretched itself out to elastic proportions, but finally it was time to return to work. I woke with a fuzzy head from the sleeping pill I'd taken but coaxed myself alert in the shower. By the time I got past all of the roadworks and reached the office, most people were already in. I negotiated a couple of enquiries about my head and went straight to my desk. It was exactly as I'd left it a long week before – my action book with the list of ticks only going halfway down the page, the bundle of opened mail still waiting to be dealt with, the most recent case file still stacked on top of my reference books with its curling buff corners accusing me for not having locked it away in the filing cabinets. True, the hoard of biros in my top drawer had gone missing, and there was a hefty wedge of mail on top of my in-tray, but otherwise, time could have stopped in a bubble around my desk the moment I last left it. I flicked through the pile of mail but none of the envelopes looked particularly urgent or even interesting, so I didn't open any of it.

The others in the office were all doing the usual Monday morning things, yawning their way through the work they'd abandoned on Friday afternoon. They chatted to each other and down telephones and the low hum of their voices was familiar, almost a comfort. The whole scene was familiar; even the slightly dry smell of dusty air was familiar, and yet, everything seemed slightly different, that odd sense of unreality, as if the world had shifted slightly on its axis. I wasn't sure if it was me or them who was off-kilter. I waited for the feeling to pass.

From my desk, I could turn my head and look across the office to the window with the broken venetian blinds sagging against one side of their strings, out at the grey sky. I could see a corner of the street; a flash of traffic passing through the angle between the window frame and the edge of the next building. Occasionally, I saw people walking through the gap, striding along towards their business or dawdling the morning away. I knew I should get on with my work but I couldn't find the energy to get started.

Finally, when I had failed to prioritize any of my workload, I took the file that had been lying on my desk for a week and went down the corridor to the tiny room that held the filing cabinets. There was nobody else in the room. Somebody had Blu-Tacked new notices to the walls reminding us to update case notes regularly, and file things carefully and remember to lock the cabinets after use. Part of the response to the Chantelle Wade enquiry, I supposed.

I put the file I had brought with me back into its correct slot and relocked the cabinet. I glanced towards the door but I didn't expect anyone to venture into the file room this early on a Monday, so I took a deep breath and opened up the drawer labelled 'M'. I ran my fingers through the folders until I found the Metcalfe file. I knew it was wrong to do this – they weren't my case, after all, and a slight resemblance I might have seen in the younger brother was hardly a solid basis for suspicion.

Kneeling on the carpet, I was about to open the file when Douglas came in. He was wearing his usual frown, designed to remind us that all the blame for our mistakes would fall onto him before he let it cascade down to us. He said, 'Ah, Jo, here you are,' in the kind of tone that suggested I should have been at my desk just waiting for him to drop by. 'I need to see you, my office, as soon as you're done.'

'Right,' I said.

He hesitated there for a moment, then seemed to decide. 'How is your head now?'

'Fine,' I said. 'Slight headache, that's all.'

He gave a stiff nod and hesitated a moment longer before saying, 'Okay, well, we'll talk in a few minutes, then.'

'Okay,' I said, still kneeling there.

He turned and went out, letting the file-room door slam heavily against its fire hinges. I looked down at the file. It was thick, with recent additions initialled by CF – Colin Fuller. Maybe Colin would be able to help me? But he would probably be angry if he found me looking through one of his case files, and I didn't want to make him angry. I took the file back to my desk and put it in my in-tray, under the pile of unopened mail. It looked innocuous there, even ordinary.

I collected my filofax and went down the corridor to Douglas's office. I knocked, heard him call, 'Come in,' and pushed the door open. He was on the phone, sitting in his swivel chair with his legs stretched out, tapping a Biro against the desktop as he listened to someone on the other end of the line.

'I'm telling you, Phil, the Laming recommendations were being implemented at the time,' he said.

He glanced at me; I realized he was talking about the Chantelle Wade enquiry, so I averted my gaze, sat down in the low chair he kept positioned in front of his desk and pretended to be engrossed in my filofax.

'They were following current practice,' he said into the receiver. 'But we'll talk about this later. All I'm saying is, you can't expect these changes to happen overnight. It's not obstructing change, it's being human.'

I flicked through a few pages of notes, frowning as if concentrating on reading.

He laughed loudly, his power-laugh, his I'm-in-control laugh. 'Exactly. I'll speak to you soon.'

As he replaced the receiver, I looked up. Coming into his office always made me think of school.

I'd been scared of him when I was still green and passionate. It seemed like a very long time ago.

'I'd appreciate it if you didn't mention whatever you just overheard to anyone,' he said.

I inclined my head as if it would never have occurred to me.

'Good. So, how's the head?'

He seemed to have forgotten that we had already done that bit. I said, 'Oh, fine, really. A bit of a headache still, but nothing too serious.'

'Good, good,' he said absently. He was fishing around on his desk and produced a flimsy stack of notes. 'Updates on your cases from last week,' he said, and passed me the papers.

I nodded. 'Did everything get covered?'

'Well, we prioritized a bit,' he said. 'There's notes on there, and you can ask the others in a minute.'

I waited, because he obviously had something else to say.

He seemed to be finding it hard to put into words. Finally, he said, 'Did you go and visit Mrs Adams last week?'

'Yes,' I said. 'I told you, she needed—'

'But I told you not to. You were signed off sick, you shouldn't have been visiting anyone. She shouldn't even be a current case.'

'She needs our support,' I said.

'She should be NFA'd. The kids aren't in any danger, are they?'

'No, but—'

'So it's a No Further Action, isn't it?'

I took a deep breath. 'Under section seventeen—'

'I know all about section seventeen,' he snapped. 'Don't try quoting the Children Act at me, Jo. It's section forty-seven that concerns me. Our priority is with children in need of protection, you know that.'

I kept my breath steady. 'They are children in need,' I said. 'We can prevent things getting to that stage by supporting the family now.'

He brushed that aside with a flick of his hand. 'You're not supporting them, you're making the situation worse.'

'Not really,' I started to say.

'You're supposed to be making sure she can cope, not taking on her responsibilities for her. How's she going to learn if you do everything for her? It'll cause problems for you, and that means it'll cause problems for the whole department.'

'You're overstating the case,' I said. 'I just popped in to check on her.'

'She doesn't need that level of intervention. She'll use you, just like she always does. You know her history. She'll use you and play the department just to get what she wants.'

'No,' I said. 'I know how she works. She doesn't get away with anything with me. And she just needs to feel there's someone she can turn to if she gets stuck, that's all. She's lonely, in that house on her own.'

'She's just playing you for sympathy. I've talked to you about this before, you have to stick to the guidelines if—'

'I do stick to the guidelines,' I said. 'Sometimes you have to use discretion, that's all.'

'Discretion doesn't mean doing whatever you feel like. Whatever you may think, you don't always know best.' I opened my mouth to speak, but he cut me off. 'You'll end up having problems if you don't listen to what you're told, and we don't want to go through that again, do we?' I wanted to protest that I was experienced, I didn't need my hand held, but he wasn't going to let me speak just yet. 'We've talked about this before, haven't we? About getting too involved? You just need to step back a little, stop getting so personally bound up in things, then maybe you'll see you're doing Katie Adams no favours.'

'I can't just abandon her,' I said.

'Her problem is dependency.'

'No,' I said. 'Her problem is she's stuck on her own and can't cope, and the people who should be looking out for her don't give a damn about her, and her bloody neighbours are scaring the life out of her.'

He let out another sigh and looked at me as if I had just proved his case. 'You have to get some distance,' he said. 'I want you to see her less often.'

It was clear that any objection would just make his case stronger. I said, 'I've already told her I'll see her this week.'

'So, see her and explain the situation. I'm saying this for your own good, Jo. You need to be sure you've followed procedure. You don't want to lay yourself open, do you?'

He was talking about the Chantelle Wade enquiry, I realized. I'd heard that he was friends with two of the social workers who were being blamed for her death. Even the thought of their situation made me shudder. I gave Douglas a jaunty smile and said, 'I have been following procedure. And writing up my notes. And filing everything properly.'

I had hoped he would see the joke and smile back, but he didn't. 'I know,' he said. 'You're very thorough. But you've got to step back. You can't allow this woman to rely on you. You're not her friend.'

'I know that.'

'Of course you do. But does she?' He sighed again, kneading his forehead briefly with one hand. 'Some people,' he said, 'some clients, they can be like vultures, or vampires. Most are okay, but some of them, they suck the blood out of you. You have to protect yourself.' He looked tired, and I knew his mind was back with Chantelle Wade. I wanted to ask him how the enquiry was going, but I held back. He said, 'Oh, go on, get back to work. But listen to me, okay?'

'Sure,' I said, and gave him my most encouraging smile before leaving him to whatever he was doing.

I wanted to start reading the Metcalfe file straight away, but when I went back into the main office there were two police officers standing in the room, and I recognized them immediately as PC Short and PC Andrews.

'Hi,' I said, surprised to see them.

PC Andrews gave a friendly sort of smile, but PC Short seemed as surprised as I was to be meeting again. He said, 'I'd forgotten this was your office. How are you?'

'Fine,' I said. I was wondering why they were here, but it clearly wasn't to see me. 'Are you waiting for someone?'

'Colin Fuller. Someone's fetching him.'

I wanted to ask whether he had got any further with my case. I wanted to tell him about having my purse returned to me as well, but before I could say anything more, Colin had appeared in the doorway and they smiled at me and moved towards him. I heard the low rumble of their voices as they went up the corridor towards the interview rooms, but I couldn't make out their words.

I sat at my desk for a moment, trying to figure out whether this could be connected. It seemed like quite a coincidence that they were here to see Colin, when he was the one in charge of the Metcalfe case. But I knew there was probably no connection – Colin probably dealt with a dozen cases that might need the involvement of the police. But still, it occurred to me that I had to be careful, and I didn't dare open the Metcalfe file while the police were in the building.

When I saw them leave, however, I was deep into a frustrating phone call to a client's GP, and after that I needed a cigarette before I tackled anything else. I went out into the little yard at the back of the office and found Colin already there, halfway down a cigarette. He greeted me with a weary smile.

'Looks like you've had a fun morning,' I said.

He looked confused for a moment, then said, 'Oh,

the police? It's nothing really. Checking up on one of my families. Couldn't tell them much, of course.'

I wanted to ask which family, but I knew that was going too far. Instead, I said, 'PC Short's the one looking for my attacker.'

'I know, he told me. Nice guy, Dave Short. Dealt with him before.'

I pretended to be interested in the burning end of my cigarette. 'Yeah? Any cases I know?'

He gave a slight laugh. 'Why're you so interested in Dave Short? Taken a shine to him, have you?'

I laughed, too. 'Course not. Just seem to bump into him everywhere I go these days, that's all.' Colin was grinding out his cigarette on the ground, preparing to go back inside, so I said quickly, 'You're dealing with the Metcalfes, aren't you?'

He stopped mid-step towards the door. 'Yeah, they're one of mine. Why?'

'They're neighbours of one of my cases,' and I told him briefly about Katie Adams.

'And young Danny's been giving her hassle?'

'Not just him,' I said. 'All his friends as well, by the looks of it.'

'I haven't been to see them for a while,' he said. 'Behind on my Statutories, you know how it is. God, that's all I need. I suppose I'll have to find time to go round there now.'

He was suddenly looking tired. Monday morning and too much already. I said lightly, 'It's not that big a deal, just leave it. Going round'll only cause trouble for my case, anyway.' He raised his eyebrows slightly but didn't comment. 'There's another brother, isn't there?' I asked, and he was still thinking about what I'd told him, so he just nodded.

'Sean,' he said. 'He's a bogger, that one, but he's away at the moment. Glen Parva.'

'Yeah? What'd he do?' He looked at me sharply, and I knew I'd strayed too far into his case. 'Not that it matters,' I said, and it didn't, because if he was locked away in a Young Offenders' Institution, he couldn't have attacked me. I flicked the end of my cigarette away and flashed Colin a smile to show that I wasn't really interested. 'Better get back to it,' I said.

When I returned to my desk, I sat there looking at the unopened Metcalfe file for a long time. I had convinced myself that I was right about recognizing my attacker, about it being Sean Metcalfe, but now that I knew it couldn't have been him I wasn't sure what to do. All the certainty I had felt was evaporating. If it wasn't Sean, then my attacker was still out there, and I didn't know who he was, or why he had chosen me. I didn't want to think that it had just been random – it seemed so arbitrary, so meaningless. But if it had been random – what then? Did that mean it could happen again? Did that mean I would never be safe, never feel safe, as I waited for it to happen again? I didn't know how I should act, what I could do to stop it.

But then, almost suddenly, I felt calm. I was a strong person, after all; I wasn't like my clients, jumping at every knock at the door – the pensioners seeing muggers at every turn, the women hiding in refuges, the school-phobic kids seeking comfort from the TV set. They might allow something like this to scare them, but I wasn't like that. I thought of the young man, the boy, appearing at my elbow, and I was ashamed of my reaction to him. He was nothing more than a boy and I had allowed myself to be scared by him, hurt by him. I thought about the police, about PC Short being so kind and mentioning Victim Support and talking as if it was normal to start seeing things, to be paranoid, to think of nothing but the attack and its consequences and whether it was going to happen again. I didn't want it to be that way.

So I took the Metcalfe file back to the file room without opening it, and then I sat at my desk and prioritized my workload and started on the list of actions. I was stronger than PC Short thought I was; more in control than Douglas thought I was. By the end of the day I had made a satisfying dent in my backlog and had even started to write up some case notes. I was back, on top of things, in charge of things, and I didn't have to think about the attack at all.

And as the week passed, I thought about it less and less. I was back in the rhythm of the job, back in the team, and there wasn't time for thoughts, for memories to intrude. I had a job to do; clients to see, a backlog to clear, and that was all that mattered. Besides, I was strong. By the time Friday finally crawled into view, I only thought about the attack at all when I started to get a headache and the cut on my scalp began to throb.

Ten

It was Alex's birthday that Saturday. He and Simon had been planning the party for weeks, casually dropping invitations into every conversation, checking and re-checking that key people would be there. Alex had told me that they wanted it to be 'like the old times'. I knew what he meant by that – hell, he'd told me often enough before he finally moved out that he missed having fun.

I did briefly consider not going to the party. I had a slight headache and there was some decent TV on for once, but whether or not Alex would appreciate my presence, he would certainly notice my absence. Far better to go along with it – and besides, it had been a long, hard week at work; I probably deserved to let my hair down a little.

I smoked a spliff while I got ready, and I was already feeling warmly half-stoned as I walked to Alex's house with a bottle of wine in my jacket pocket. It did occur to me that only a week before I would have been terrified to step outside the door once it was dark, seeing muggers and attackers in every shadow, but it was proof of mind over matter, of logic over emotion, that I felt fine now as I strolled towards the party.

I had timed my arrival to perfection – Colin and a couple of people from Alex's office, Selima and Milton, were just pulling up in a taxi, so I went in with them and avoided the embarrassment of arriving alone at a party at my ex's house.

The place was already crowded. The stereo in the front room had been turned up loud and people were dancing to a pop compilation that would never have been allowed into Simon's or Alex's music collections. We went down the hall into the kitchen-diner, where Simon and a couple of other lads were gathered around the Playstation, attempting to get a Lara Croft clone through a cave system with the help of a cheat one of them had got off the Internet. Colin poured out the drinks into plastic cups and we insinuated ourselves into a space near the back door.

'Wonder where the birthday boy is,' Selima said.

'Hiding.' Milton laughed, and proceeded to tell a convoluted story about locking Alex out of the main office until he stopped being so cheerful.

'He's been driving us crazy all week,' Selima said. 'Everyone else is stressed to fuck about the Chantelle Wade thing, and he's wandering around like the cat that got the cream.'

'Why?' I asked. 'What's got into him?'

They were all grinning – I wasn't sure if I had imagined the awkwardness, or the stiff way those grins gripped their faces. Milton nudged my arm and said, 'Maybe it's turning thirty-five, eh? Dementia must be getting to the old git.'

We all laughed at that. I dismissed whatever suspicions had started forming in my brain – I was imagining things, that was all. I looked around for Alex but there was still no sign of him. Simon and his mates were talking loudly about whether to use a super-booster power-pack to get across a chasm. Colin, Selima and Milton had started on the usual Chantelle Wade conversation, so I made my excuses and headed upstairs to see if Alex was there. I had the present I'd bought him in my jacket pocket – a CD he'd been going on about.

There was a circle of people in Alex's bedroom, sitting on the floor smoking dope, the room lit only by a larva lamp that looked new. Alex was among the group and smiled at me as I came in. I recognized most of the people as Simon's friends – shop stewards from Housing and from the City Treasurer's whom I'd got to know through various functions and benefit gigs that Simon had dragged us along to in the past. They made space for me, and I sat down cross-legged and took the joint I was offered. It turned out to be some pretty powerful skunk, so I took a couple of drags and passed it on and sat there in a blue haze for a few minutes, leaning back against my hands, waiting for my brain to settle down again.

When I felt able to listen to the conversation, one of the guys from Housing was telling a story about a client whose flat had been raided by the police. 'When he got home from the station after six hours of questioning,' the Housing guy said, 'he found more police waiting for him, because CID hadn't bothered to secure his door after kicking it in, and some bogger had got in and cleaned the place out. I mean, they took everything, furniture, clothes, the lot. They even took the bleeding radiators, only, being burglars, they didn't bother to drain them first, so the whole flat got flooded out with filthy black water, and he'd only just had new carpets laid.' The Housing guy gave an appalled sort of laugh. 'This poor lad, he comes into the office to report what's happened, and this policeman's come with him, and the lad looks like he's been through hell, and every ten seconds this policeman's apologizing to the lad, and I can see him getting whiter and whiter as he tries to hold himself together.' He shook his head, laughing, but not really finding it funny. 'The worst bit was, he wasn't even the guy that CID were after. They bashed the wrong door down, it was the place upstairs that they meant to raid.'

I found myself laughing the same half-appalled laugh, and glanced over at Alex to see his reaction. He was laughing too, but he didn't seem to be concentrating on the story. He was sitting next to a blonde woman encased in black Lycra, and as I watched he leaned in towards her and said something into her ear. Her face creased in concentration as she listened, and when he had finished she turned to look at him, touched him lightly on the arm, and said something that made him laugh.

Someone else was telling another story now, but I found I couldn't concentrate on what was being said. The blonde woman in black Lycra was holding out her hands and looking at them, talking as she did so, turning her hands and inclining her head towards Alex. I watched Alex take hold of one of her hands and examine it, then he leaned in towards her again and said something, and she laughed and pulled her hands away and looked around the room. I turned away quickly, but not before I saw the frown that flashed onto her face.

The spliff had reached me again so I took a couple more drags and passed it on, trying to look unconcerned. It didn't matter, anyway – Alex was a grown man, he could do what he wanted, he didn't have to ask my permission before he flirted with someone else.

Someone had come into the room. I looked up and realized it was Colin and made space for him next to me. He sat down. 'Thought I'd come and see what you were up to,' he said. 'They're still talking about fucking Chantelle Wade down there.'

'Oh Christ,' I said. 'Don't they ever shut up about that? We're not at work now. They should give it a rest.'

'Yeah, but you know how stressed everyone is.'

He had brought two small bottles of lager with him. He passed one to me, then took a sip from his.

I nodded thanks, then said, 'But this is a party, not a staff meeting.'

'True. But not everyone's as self-contained as you, you know.'

I glanced at him, trying to figure out what he meant by that, but I didn't really want to pursue it. Instead, I said, 'Who's the blonde Lycra woman?'

He followed my nod and looked across at the woman. Alex was talking to her, coolly, as if they were just friends.

'I've seen her around,' Colin said. 'Works in Policy, Chief Exec's Department. Must be a friend of Simon's.'

I looked back at her. It didn't seem to be Simon who was fascinated by her company. I tried to put it out of my mind, but I couldn't help watching her. Her Lycra top was tight over her flat stomach and tiny breasts. She was so thin that I could see her hip bones outlined beneath the Lycra, and the material hung loose around her knees and ankles. She was wearing flip-flop style sandals with a cartoonish yellow flower sewn onto the grip between her toes, and her toenails were painted a lurid red to match her lipstick.

'That's a fake tan, too,' I said. 'Out of a bottle.'

'You think?' Colin looked over, as if he doubted me.

'She likes herself a bit, doesn't she?' I said.

She had stretched out her legs and was leaning back on her arms, twisting herself to listen to Alex, her whole body arched ready for his next joke. Colin gave a half-shrug and said, 'She seems all right to me. I want some air. Come outside with me.'

I was happy where I was, watching the floorshow, but Colin persuaded me to follow him downstairs and out through the kitchen to the little garden out back. We sat down on the low wall that divided the concrete yard from the scrap of lawn.

'D'you think she has to spray that Lycra on?' I asked.

He said, 'Why the interest?'

'Just curious.' I took two cigarettes from my packet and passed one to Colin along with my lighter. 'Just wondering what Alex sees that makes his tongue hang out, that's all.'

I had expected Colin to make some sort of joke about me being jealous, but he just said, 'Shut up about fucking Louise, would you?'

I said, 'Oooh,' and nudged him. 'Who's feeling sore, eh?'

He just shook his head, not rising to it.

I said, 'So, her name's Louise, is it? Thought you'd only seen her around?'

'Yeah, well.' He seemed uncomfortable. 'Alex introduced me.'

Something clicked. 'Wait a minute, are you say-ing—'

'I'm not saying anything,' Colin said. He sounded angry. 'Christ, Jo, can't you ever leave anything alone?'

'Sorry.' We smoked in silence for a moment, but I couldn't stop myself from asking, 'But Alex and her, they're an item, right?'

'How the hell would I know?'

'Okay, okay,' I said. 'Sorry.'

Colin relented. 'No, I'm sorry, I'm just stressed, you know?'

'Sure.' I waited for him to say more but he didn't, so I said, 'Anything I can do?'

He glanced at me. 'We've been friends for a long time—' he started.

He didn't get any further. Alex had come out into the yard. He was alone. He said, 'Jo, can I talk to you?'

I looked at Colin, who threw up his hands and stood. 'I'll see you later,' he said, and slumped off back into the house.

Alex took his place on the wall. 'What's up with him?'

'Don't know,' I said. 'Who's this Louise, then?'

I had tried to keep my tone light, but a crack had crept into my voice. Alex frowned a little. 'I wanted to talk to you about that. I wanted to tell you before you met her but – well, I wasn't expecting to see you tonight. I thought – you know, your head – I didn't think you'd come.'

'You didn't want me here?'

'Oh, I don't mean that.' He was stumbling over his words. 'Just – well, I haven't seen you all week, you've been like a hermit. If I'd thought – I'm sorry, I should've thought.'

I looked down at the end of my cigarette. I smoked a little but I couldn't taste anything. I said, 'You should've told me you're seeing someone else. Christ, everyone's been tiptoeing around me. They must think I'm an idiot.'

'No, no,' Alex said. 'I'm the idiot.'

I felt a lump rising in my throat. I felt slightly sick. 'Why didn't you call me?'

'You never called me either,' he said.

'Oh, right. Tit for tat, is it?'

He rubbed his hand through his hair and squinted at me. His eyes looked darker than ever in the gloom. 'You're right. I should've called. I'm a bastard. I should've told you before you came here tonight.'

'Yes,' I said.

'But.' He hesitated before starting again. 'I knew what you'd be like.'

'How d'you mean?'

'This. Fractious. Irritated. I hate it when you're like this.'

'That's it,' I said. 'Turn it around, it's all my fault really.'

'No,' he said. 'No. But you're not always that easy to talk to.'

'I'm fine to talk to.'

'There you go again, you see?'

I didn't see. 'It's just you twisting everything, as usual.' He was about to reply but I added quickly, 'Oh, just go back to the Lycra maiden. You deserve her. She seems very – available.'

That angered him, but I was in no mood to back down. Alex said, 'You keep those sorts of comments to yourself.'

'Well,' I said. 'Just look at her. It's plain as—'

He grabbed my arm, hard; his grip twisted my flesh, pressed against my wrist. I gave a little cry and tried to pull away. He said, 'You can be a bitch sometimes.'

I didn't respond. I didn't think I could trust myself to speak. The sudden violence in his voice, the swiftness of his actions, the strength in his grip – I felt bile rising in my throat, felt the sudden sharp pounding of my heartbeat. He was so much stronger than me – I was weak, there was no power in my body. I could barely breathe. He looked down at his hand gripped around my arm, then released me. He seemed to be about to speak, but then he stood up and went back into the house, slamming the kitchen door shut behind him. I was submerged in sudden darkness. I closed my eyes, put my hand over my face. I didn't want to cry but I could feel myself shaking.

'Are you okay?'

It was Colin, standing in front of me. I hadn't heard him come back out. I looked up at him and nodded.

'Disagreement?' he asked. 'Alex just stormed up to his room like he was going to kill somebody.'

I forced myself to smile but didn't trust myself to speak. Colin came and sat next to me. He had a full beer in his hand and offered it to me. I took a sip but didn't want any more than that, so I gave the bottle back to him.

He said, 'You want to talk about it?'

'No.' My voice was stronger now. 'It's nothing. Ex shit, you know.'

'Sure,' he said. After a moment he added, 'You want me to go?'

'No.'

I sensed rather than saw him nod in the darkness, and then lift the bottle to his lips again. From the house, I heard laughter, and then the music changed. Two-tone ska. Simon was at the stereo controls, I guessed.

Colin said, 'So,' and then stopped. He brightened his tone. 'Did I tell you I'm going to Barcelona for the weekend?'

'No,' I said, and then, because he was making an effort, 'When?'

'Next month.' And he rattled on about Gaudi and tapas bars and Catalonia during the Spanish Civil War. Then he started talking about work, about one of his clients, a heroin user whose flat was being taken over by his drug-dealing neighbours, and how difficult it was to help when the client wouldn't face up to his problems. I thought about Katie Adams and the neighbours she put up with, and all the other clients who would have been fine if they didn't have their neighbours, if they didn't live on such shitty little estates. So much going on, so much going wrong, and how were we ever supposed to solve any of it? It weighed against me. I found I couldn't respond to Colin, I couldn't give him the reassurance he was looking for, because maybe there wasn't any point to it?

Colin said, 'You know, I've got this client who just upped and went one day. Didn't take anything with him, not even a change of clothes or a toothbrush. Left a note stuck to the fridge for his girlfriend to find. Know what the note said? "Everything I own belongs to you." That was it. Nothing else. No saying he loved her, or didn't love her, or was sorry, or anything like that.' He let out a long sigh, as if he was thinking about this. I waited, and he continued in a level tone, 'I thought he'd topped himself when I read that. I think she did, too. Sat back and waited for someone to find his body. But he didn't top himself. He's just one of those people who decide to disappear. It's kind of a romantic notion, just leaving everything behind and starting again from scratch.'

'Yeah,' I said. 'Except we know it doesn't turn out like that.'

He glanced at me, quickly, but it was too dark to read his expression. 'Yeah.' His voice held no emotion. 'We know it doesn't work. We know they're just throwing away their life and they won't end up free, they'll end up alone and depressed and skint in a shitty bedsit in Blackpool.'

Something almost angry had crept into his tone. I said, 'Why Blackpool?'

'Well, why not?' he said. 'It's got to be somewhere. He chose Blackpool.'

I tried to think about that.

He said, 'Anyway, the point is, people forget that you can't ever really run away. Everywhere's the same place and you're always the same person. Just the way it is. Everything follows you, wherever you go. There's never any escape from it.'

He raised the bottle to his lips again and took a drink. I watched his movements, his outline in the darkness. He seemed to be a long way away from me; I was tempted to reach out and touch him, but he suddenly gave a laugh and looked at me and said, 'You know, I'm glad he ran away. One more off my client list, eh? Maybe I should encourage all my clients to do the same? The department's always looking for savings – getting rid of a few service users should do the trick.'

I thought about it for a moment. 'Nah,' I said. 'It'd never work. Other authorities would catch on and do the same. You'd only end up with a load of clients who had run away from someone else's area.'

Colin laughed, a strangely high-pitched laugh. 'A client exchange programme, eh?' Then he paused. 'But why would anyone run away to Nottingham?'

The humour had drained from his voice. I wanted to see his expression, to figure out what he was thinking, but it was too dark. I said, 'You said it yourself. Everywhere's the same place. Makes no difference where you end up.'

He didn't respond for a few moments, then said, 'Sometimes I wonder why we bother.'

'I think we all wonder that sometimes. I think you have to, to stay sane.'

'Yeah,' he said. 'I know. We're all just trying to do what's right. But what if we're having no effect at all? What if things just keep repeating themselves?'

'You don't really believe that, do you?' I asked. He didn't reply. 'You're just having a bad week, or a bad month, or something. It happens.'

'So, tell me I'm wrong.'

His voice sounded oddly strangled. I said, 'You're wrong.'

'You don't mean that.'

'Maybe not,' I said. 'But you have to carry on.' Again, he didn't respond. I said, 'But you have to just get on with it, don't you?'

'Yeah,' he said finally. 'It just seems like we're stuck on repeat, you know what I mean? The same stuff over and over. Get up, go to work, get stressed, come home, go to bed. I came into this job to try to change things, but it doesn't work. Nothing ever changes. You can't change the big stuff, and changing the small stuff is pretty fucking meaningless. Forget it.' He gave a laugh; a short, disappointed sound. 'But that's the thing, isn't it? Get on with it or get out, that's all there is.'

We sat in silence. I wanted to say something, to comfort him, to snap him out of these thoughts, but I didn't know what to say.

He sighed. 'Oh, just ignore me. I'm pissed. A hard week, you know how it is.'

'We all have those,' I said. I thought of Douglas

100

suddenly; sitting in his office, making things sound so easy. 'You can't take it to heart.'

'Sure, sure.' Colin drained the last of the beer from the bottle, then tapped me lightly on the knee. 'I need another beer,' he said. He sounded more cheerful. 'D'you want one?'

'Okay,' I said.

He stood up. 'Funny thing, though. All my clients seem to be running away right now. A proper little epidemic. Remember the Metcalfe kid? The one in Glen Parva? Turns out he isn't there after all. Absconded.'

'Absconded? How?'

'Dunno,' he said. 'Just legged it one day. They never told me how. Probably embarrassed, eh? Took 'em long enough to tell me that they'd lost him and I've got contact with the family, so I don't suppose they're going to broadcast how he did it.'

I said slowly, stupidly, 'So where is he now?'

Colin just laughed. 'Well, if they knew that—'

'But when did he run away?'

'A month or so ago. I don't know exactly. Where are you going?'

I had stumbled to my feet and was heading towards the house. 'I have to go,' I said. I felt a little sick, a little numb. I thought about Colin's words – the pointlessness of it all, and the week I'd spent so deep in work that I'd barely come up for air, and all the time he had been out there and I hadn't known. I wondered whether I should phone PC Short, tell him what I knew, but I was suddenly unsteady on my feet, and I wasn't sure if it was the drink or the skunk or the news that made me feel that way. I had a sudden image of Sean Metcalfe, the young Sean, the boy I'd known years ago, giggling as I tried to talk to him, not listening to the things I was trying to say.

I pushed open the kitchen door and was hit by the noise of the party: music, and people talking, and laughter. The air was warm. Colin made to follow me but I said, 'I'm okay, I'm fine. I'll see you later.'

He followed me into the house anyway. Everyone was dancing to The Specials in the front room, but Alex wasn't there. I found Simon by the stereo and yelled into his ear, 'I'm going. Where's Alex?'

He said, 'Leave it. Talk to him tomorrow.' I turned to go and look for Alex, but Simon grabbed my arm. 'Seriously. Don't argue with him twice.'

I was about to reply that I didn't plan to argue with Alex, but I saw how intent Simon's expression was, so I shrugged and said, 'I'll come round tomorrow.'

Simon nodded. 'But make it late,' he said, and grinned.

I was glad of the grin as I started to walk back to my house. I didn't like to think that Alex and I had argued – I always hated it when we argued, that bitter taste in the mouth and the resentment and waiting for the other person to back down just enough so that making up again wasn't a humiliation. I didn't want to think about Alex with Louise, unwrapping all that Lycra, peeling away the layers to get at the skin, the person under the fake tan.

I walked more quickly. My footsteps seemed louder in the darkness and I could hear the thump of my heart. The street was deserted and the street lights cast only a small amount of light; there were shadows everywhere, shadows that could all be the shape of men, shadows that could all conceal an attacker. I thought about Sean Metcalfe being free, wandering through the dark streets. I thought about the things that Colin had been saying; that desperate edge, that disappointment. I felt as though we were standing on the edge of something black, something miserable, and the tide was sucking at our feet, and I only had to slip and I would be washed away. I wanted to stop walking but I had the feeling that if I stopped I would never start again. There was so much that could happen – so many places a person could hide. I considered going back to the party, but when I turned the street behind looked darker and more sinister than the street ahead, and I was almost halfway home now, and would Alex even want me there if I did go back? I knew it was crazy to be scared – I hadn't been afraid when walking to the party earlier, and whoever had hit me had been just as likely to be waiting for me then. Hell, I didn't even know for sure that it was Sean Metcalfe who had attacked me – and even if it was, there was no reason to think he would be after me again.

I picked up more speed, felt the soles of my feet beating the pavement through my shoes. My breathing was too loud; I couldn't hear any other noises,

I couldn't hear the sound of someone approaching me. I kept looking around me, but I was alone.

But I hadn't seen him before. I hadn't realized he was approaching me. I remembered him arriving at my elbow, speaking to me, and turning to look into his face, and that feeling that I knew him. I tried to concentrate on that face, on the details of that face, and the more I thought, the more certain I became. Sean Metcalfe. Yes, a skinny lanky lad who played football in the street with his mates while I sat in his front room talking to his mother. She chain-smoked hand-rolled cigarettes so thin they were barely more than paper. She would squash the butt-end of one rollie flat in the ashtray and then start work on the next, her thumbs working the tobacco into a thread on the paper and tucking the end in, her tongue quickly licking the gummed edge. I had been telling her that Sean was in trouble, that he'd been skipping school, hanging around the city centre, shoplifting. She had listened with a frown, leaning forward, and I could tell that the moment I stopped talking she would be in with a defence of her son, so I kept talking, I kept going, trying to wear down her hostility.

And what had she said when I had finished talking? 'You don't know what it's like,' she'd said, with a little laugh. She wasn't going to take this from me, not when I knew nothing about it, she'd brought her kids up to be good kids and she wasn't going to let me interfere, not when I didn't have a clue what life was really like. Who did I think I was, coming round her house telling her how to bring up her kids? What the hell did I know about it, anyway; did I know what it was like to live round there, did I even have kids of my own? People get labelled, that's what she'd said. I'd tried to say that I hadn't come with any preconceptions, and she'd laughed a derisive sort of laugh and said, 'Yeah, but I know what your sort are like, looking down your noses, thinking you're so much better than us.' I'd gone away feeling very depressed, because how could I help?

But that was a long time ago. Things had changed – I'd changed. I didn't let it get to me, not now. Get on with it or get out, that was the thing. And the fact that it was so long ago didn't help with why Sean would hit me. Could it just have been a random thing – him passing as I came out of the office, recognizing me, remembering or imagining some slight, some reason why I was significant, acting on the impulse created in that moment? Had he been high on something? Did it make any difference? He had still hit me.

At last, I turned along my street and hurried towards my house. I was cold; my hands were getting numb. I clasped my keys tight in my hand, imagining striking out at someone, using a key as a small blade, jamming it into someone's flesh. My head was hurting and I felt slightly sick. I reached my house and walked up to the front door, body tensed for someone hiding nearby, someone waiting to rush me and bundle me into the house as I opened the front door. I turned the key in the lock, and then

I heard a sound behind me – a sort of rustling sound in the bushes that filled next-door's front garden. I looked over but I couldn't see anything in the shadows. It was probably nothing, I told myself; the wind, or a cat. But as soon as I was in the house, I bolted the front door and went to the front-room window without turning on the light. I don't know what I had expected to see – him, standing on the pavement looking at me, I suppose. But all I saw was the empty street.

I turned on the light and sat down. I had just got spooked, that was all. Then I heard another sound – a can being kicked in the street, or something like that: a metallic sound, and then silence. I went to the window again, but there was still nobody out there. I went into the kitchen to check that the back door was locked. Beyond the kitchen windows, the garden was a mass of dark shadows – I put on the kitchen light, quickly, to dispel the shadows, but the darkness outside became a wall that I couldn't see through. I went back into the front room. I wanted to go upstairs, but the rest of the house was very dark and empty, and I didn't want to face that darkness.

There were more sounds from the street: a stone skittering across the tarmac, someone whistling. I listened for footsteps but heard none. I wanted to go to the window again but I was afraid that the street would be empty still, and would that mean that someone was hiding? I didn't want to think about that, but the thought grew insistent.

Somebody hiding, and they had watched me come into the house alone, they knew I was on my own.

I went over to the phone. It seemed over-dramatic to dial 999, so I found the switchboard number for Radford Road police station in the phone book and rang that. Eventually, a man answered with a slightly sleepy voice. I asked for PC Short, more out of hope than any realistic chance he would be there at nearly one a.m. on a Saturday night.

'He's not on duty until tomorrow afternoon,' the man said.

'Oh, okay.' I hesitated, not sure what to say next.

The man took pity on me. 'Can anyone else help?'

'I don't know,' I said. 'I think there might be someone outside my house, hiding. Watching me.'

'You think there's a prowler?'

'Maybe,' I said. He didn't sound very concerned, and I found myself explaining that I had been assaulted two weeks ago, and PC Short knew all about it, and I thought it might be the same man outside my house.

My story didn't seem to impress him very much. I remembered what PC Short had said at the supermarket – that people often thought they saw their attackers, it was common. I was probably wrong – there was probably nobody out there anyway.

The man on the phone said, 'I could see if a car can come by, later on, if you want.' It sounded like a half-hearted offer that he was hoping I would reject.

'They are very busy this time of night. It might be a while.'

I sighed. 'No,' I said. 'Don't worry. I was probably imagining things. Spooked by the dark. Sorry to have bothered you.'

'I'll tell PC Short you phoned,' he said.

I wasn't sure that I wanted him to do that, but I let it go. After I had hung up, I stood where I was, listening for sounds from the street, but all I could hear was the occasional car on the main road. I switched on the landing light and went quickly upstairs. When I had got into bed, I lay there for a long time with my eyes open, listening, dreading anything that could be someone breaking into my house, but I didn't hear anything.

Eleven

P C Short came round to see me the next day. He had PC Andrews in tow and had obviously filled her in on the events at the supermarket, because as he talked to me about the previous night she had an almost dismissive expression on her face, as if she pitied me for being so weak.

PC Short sat on the sofa, forward in the seat so that his knees rose almost to his chin. He looked uncomfortably tall, sitting like that, but the expression on his face was attentive, as if he was trying to compensate for PC Andrews's attitude. I told him about getting my purse back, and about Sean Metcalfe being on the loose, and he listened politely and made a couple of notes in his notebook. Then he said, 'But you didn't actually see anyone around here last night?'

'No,' I said.

'And there's been nothing to suggest this man knows your address?'

'No.'

'I take it you're not in the phone book?'

'That's right.'

PC Andrews gave a sudden, derisive snort. We both looked across at her. She was standing by the front window, leaning against the wall as if prepared for a quick getaway. She seemed as surprised as us at how loud her reaction had been; she coloured slightly. 'Well, there's really nothing to go on, then, is there?'

She had directed the force of her comment at PC Short. I said, 'But I've told you who I think attacked me.'

'But there doesn't seem to be a reason for it,' she said, finally looking at me. 'Or do you expect your clients to be so dissatisfied that they come after you years later?'

PC Short was frowning at PC Andrews, but it didn't seem to have any impact on her. I wasn't sure where her hostility was coming from. I remembered Colin at the party; his comments about never making a difference, about patterns repeating themselves. I said, 'You really expect me to remember the details of every case eight years later?'

'Well, if you're right, then this Sean Metcalfe obviously does.'

PC Short looked at me then, as if he expected me to have an answer for that. I ran a hand up to the stitches on my head, where the skin was still sore. 'Okay, okay,' I said. 'I can remember some of it. Both the Metcalfe boys were taken into care. Fostering. But it was someone else in charge of their case by then, not me.' I could see that PC

Andrews wanted to ask why but I couldn't face a long discussion about departmental reorganization, not when I had a headache coming on. 'They were only fostered for three months,' I said. 'Just temporarily, while their mother sorted some things out. She'd recently been widowed. She was depressed, couldn't cope. You know the sort of story.' I had been going to add that they were on the At Risk for a while, when the father was around, but I suddenly couldn't see the point. 'It was a long time ago,' I finished.

'Yes,' PC Andrews said. 'But these things, they get emotions stirred up, don't they? Especially right now.'

She was talking about Chantelle Wade. I said, 'It wasn't like that. There wasn't any bad feeling. It was all very straightforward. That's why it doesn't make much sense. But I know – I'm sure I'm right about Sean Metcalfe.'

I thought PC Andrews was going to say something more, but PC Short closed his notebook and said, 'Well, there doesn't seem to have been anything disturbed outside.'

I nodded, not looking at either of them.

PC Short went on, 'But keep your eyes open. If you do see anything, give us a ring at the station.'

I wasn't sure if he was just saying that out of politeness. PC Andrews had already opened the living-room door. I said, 'Okay.'

PC Short followed PC Andrews out into the hall, and I went with them. At the front door, as PC

Andrews strode off down the path, PC Short turned to me and said, 'Look, don't worry. It was probably nothing, you know.'

I nodded, trying to look more confident than I felt.

'If I get a chance I'll pop back this evening, check you're okay.'

He had dropped his voice slightly, but there was no danger of PC Andrews overhearing as she was already at the car, unlocking the driver's door. 'Thanks,' I said, and he smiled, and followed PC Andrews to the car.

I waited until they had gone then looked up and down the empty street before shutting the door. My head was really starting to pound now – my heart was pumping hard, probably from the unpleasantness of PC Andrews. I didn't want to think any more about the reasons for her hostility; the unfairness pricked at me, but I knew it was pointless to react. The silence of the house weighed down on me – however cheerfully reassuring PC Short had been, I knew I was listening out for any noise that could be an intruder, or someone hiding outside, looking in through my windows. I wouldn't be able to settle to anything else, not while there was the chance that he would be back; but what would I do if he did come back? I could imagine the front door rattling as he tried to force it open, or the sound of glass breaking and cold air sweeping into the house. Even if I got to the phone the police would never get to me in time – PC Andrews would dawdle, not believing me; PC Short would think it was just the shock of the attack.

I gathered up my jacket and went out to the car. I didn't know where I was going; I just knew I had to get away from the house. So I drove, and smoked, and played cassettes, and the car filled with cigarette smoke but I wasn't going to open a window, not now, not yet. I drove out towards the suburbs and then back through the inner city, looping around the city centre, powering the car up hills and across junctions. He would have trouble watching me now, following me now. I could feel the weight lifting, and my mood improving. I rolled down the window, just a little, and felt fresh air on my face.

And then I thought about the argument with Alex. Another of those stupid disagreements. It had been a silly situation; there was alcohol involved, and things were said that weren't meant – I was sure he would be thinking the same thing. I cut down a side street and started to work my way towards Alex and Simon's house. They would be pleased to see me – they always were – and we would drink tea and listen to CDs and chat and laugh together, just like the old times.

Their front-room curtains were still drawn, but it was after three in the afternoon, so I knew they couldn't still be in bed. Simon opened the door, looking the worse for wear, dressed in a dirty white 'I stayed up for Portillo' T-shirt left over from the 1997 election and a pair of old tracksuit trousers that were a little too tight to be decent.

'You're still not dressed?' I said. 'Or do you dare go outside wearing those things?'

He looked down at himself but just shrugged. He led me into the front room, rubbing his hand over his face, and said, 'Give us a break. I only had a few hours' sleep.'

I started to open the curtains in the front room, but he winced and held his hand up against the sunlight, so I closed them again. He had flopped down onto the sofa and now offered me a cigarette from a packet that looked as if it had been slept on. I took one and nodded thanks.

'Alex is still in bed, I think,' he said. 'Haven't seen him since last night. Locked himself in his room early on, the lightweight. Rest of us stayed up playing games till four a.m.' He shook his head and laughed. I wasn't sure if he'd forgotten about my argument with Alex, or if he was just avoiding the topic. I decided not to mention it.

'It was a good party,' I said.

'Yeah. What time did you leave?'

'Just after midnight. I was knackered.' And then, without even meaning to, or realizing that I was doing it, I found myself telling him about Sean Metcalfe, and thinking he was outside the house, and getting freaked out, and phoning the police.

He listened carefully, his eyes on mine, and when I had finished he said, 'Christ, you should've said. You should've stayed here. Or got a taxi. Christ, I'd've walked you home if I'd known, or Alex would've.'

I waved that away. 'Don't be daft, it was just me

getting spooked. Besides, I don't think Alex would have been too happy.'

He was about to say something else, but we both heard feet coming down the stairs, and Alex came into the front room. He was wearing boxer shorts and a T-shirt, and looked as if he had just woken up.

I laughed at him and said, 'You look a picture.'

He scowled with hangover eyes and helped himself to one of Simon's cigarettes before slouching down on the sofa next to Simon. He didn't light the cigarette. 'What brings you round?'

'Can't I come and see my friends?'

He just shrugged. He wasn't looking at me properly. Simon opened his mouth and I could tell that he was about to repeat the things I had told him, so I shook my head. Simon closed his mouth again, frowning. Alex was too bleary-eyed to notice.

I said, 'I wanted to check you were okay, anyway.'

'Why?' Alex finally looked directly at me. 'Everything's fine,' he said, but I could hear the resentment in his tone.

I said, 'Oh, c'mon, don't be like that.'

'Like what?' Then he reached down, took a second cigarette from Simon's packet and stood up. 'I'm going back to bed,' he said. 'I'll see you soon, Jo.'

'Sure,' I said. I wanted him to say it was okay, to say we were okay, but the significance of the two cigarettes he held had not escaped me. I didn't say anything more, and Alex went back upstairs.

Simon and I looked at one another. Simon said, 'And there I was calling him a lightweight, the sly dog.'

'You had no idea she was here?'

'No,' Simon said. 'Not at all.'

It made me laugh, thinking about it, the way he had gone scampering back up the stairs with those unlit cigarettes. He must have had a shock, finding me sitting in the front room. I stood up and said, 'I'd better go.'

Simon nodded and followed me to the door. 'Are you going to be okay? You don't want anyone to come back with you?'

'No, I'm fine,' I said. I almost asked him not to tell Alex what I'd told him, but I couldn't think of a reason why Alex shouldn't know, so I just smiled and went out to the car. I glanced up at the bedroom windows, but the curtains were pulled tightly across and there was no way to be sure that Louise was up there with him.

Twelve

As dusk began to fall, I went round the house checking all the windows and closing the curtains. My bedroom at the front of the house gave a clear view of the street, the rows of red-brick houses stretching away up to the slight hill, curving towards the brow until they were hidden behind trees and hedges and parked cars. From the spare bedroom at the rear of the house, I could see the untidy backs of the houses on the next street – kitchen and bathroom extensions in mis-matched brick, jutting out into lawned gardens and concrete yards. Netted windows reflected the last of the sunlight back in flashes that burned my eyes, the surface of the glass silvery like mirrors a moment later. Behind one window, yellow electric light threw a shadow theatre onto the curtains as people moved around the unseen room.

I lay my forehead against the window pane and watched my breath fog the glass. I had looked at that view perhaps hundreds of times, but I wasn't sure I had ever really seen it before. All of those other people, all of those lives, and I didn't know anything about them. I wanted to feel reassured, to know somehow that their lives were straightforward, and ordinary, and safe. I put my palm flat against the glass, feeling its cool smoothness, and it made me shiver, suddenly. All those lives out there that I couldn't touch; being isolated, having that cushion of air, of space, of brick and glass around me had been a comfort, once. I would come home from work and close the door and the world and all its problems would be locked on the other side until morning.

The kitchens of the two houses directly behind mine were lit up, the blinds open. I watched a young couple drying dishes, dipping their heads towards each other as they laughed at an unheard joke. Next to them, just beyond the thin division of the adjoining wall, a teenaged girl made drinks, almost dancing, mouthing the words to a song as she stirred a teaspoon in a mug. I wondered whether each household was aware of the other; whether the couple washing up could hear the song as the girl sang along. I couldn't hear anything from my own neighbours; they could have been standing a few feet from me, beyond my wall, surveying the same scene.

I closed the curtains, quickly. I wanted to convince myself that I was alone; I wanted to feel a long way from strangers on the other side of the bricks, but when I closed the curtains my ears picked up the distant thrum of traffic snaking through the streets.

I went downstairs again, tried to distract myself with the TV, but there was nothing much to watch. I opened a bottle of wine and let the *Antiques Roadshow* play out in front of my eyes, but I was thinking about the previous night, and how scared I had felt. I thought about Alex, spending the night with Louise. I had spent the night alone and afraid, listening out for every little sound, and he had spent the night with her. It didn't really matter what he did – after all, we'd told each other often enough that we wanted the other person to find someone else and be happy. But I kept seeing the way Louise had leaned in towards Alex, and the jut of her body, her thin hips. All that black Lycra; those blood-red toenails. I could imagine them in bed, the way he would hold her, and the things he would say to her. I wanted him to be happy – but really, how happy could he be with that?

I flicked through the channels with the remote control, hoping for something to occupy my mind. Switching between a half-hearted sitcom and re-runs of *Fawlty Towers*, I heard a car pull up outside. I tensed, hearing the driver's door open and then crunch shut, and someone walking up the path outside my door; and then the doorbell rang. I went to the front window and peered out, hoping not to be seen by whoever was there. It was a man dressed in blue jeans and a beige anorak. The light spilling out from the front room attracted his attention and he turned towards me, and I realized it was PC Short. I hadn't recognized him out of uniform. He smiled at me, and I smiled back and went to the front door.

He was apologizing almost before I had the door fully open. 'I came round earlier but you weren't in,' he said, 'and it's on my way home so I thought I'd drop by. You don't mind, do you?'

'No, no,' I said, and led him back into the front room. I switched the TV off and turned to face him. He looked very different out of uniform – kinder, less severe. 'Please, sit down,' I said.

He chose the armchair, sitting forward on the edge of the seat. 'I just wanted to check you were okay. You seemed frightened earlier.'

I forced myself to smile. 'I was just a little freaked, I think. But thanks for coming round.'

'There's no sign of anyone hanging about, then?'

'No.'

He didn't seem to know what to say next. I didn't want him to go just yet – it was nice to see someone else, to feel that I wasn't so completely alone. I said, 'Have they found Sean Metcalfe?'

'Not yet,' he said. 'He's keeping his head down, I suppose.'

I nodded.

'These lads never stay on the run for long. Haven't got the nouse, most of them.'

I nodded again. He wasn't making any signs of leaving. The bottle of wine and my glass, half-full, were on the floor next to the sofa, and I realized he had been looking at them. I heard myself say, 'Would you like a drink? Some wine?'

If he was surprised at the offer he didn't say so. 'I shouldn't really,' he said, but I could tell that he was wavering.

'Why? You're not on duty now, are you?'

'True,' he said, and seemed to decide. 'Yes, okay, that would be nice.'

I went to the kitchen to fetch another glass. When I came back he had unzipped his anorak and was peeling it off. I poured out a glass of wine and handed it to him. 'Don't worry,' I said. 'I did pay for this bottle.'

He laughed politely at my weak joke, and I felt myself flush. I remembered Alex with Louise, and Colin teasing me that I had taken a shine to PC Short. To Dave Short. It wasn't that I was interested in him, I knew that – although he was much better looking than I had realized now he was dressed in civvies. But he seemed so kind, so thoughtful – he had come round after his shift had ended, after all. I thought about all the clients I knew who longed for someone to visit just to break up the tedium of their lives, and the excited way they offered tea and cakes and sometimes alcohol, and once, a long time ago and never repeated, a toke on a spliff sitting in the ashtray.

PC Short – Dave – said, 'This is a nice house. How long have you lived here?'

'Five years. Bought it with my partner at the time. He's gone, but I've kept the house.'

He didn't make any comment about that, but was looking around the room, eyeing up the proportions with a little smile on his face. 'I'm looking to buy,' he said. 'Haven't found anything yet.'

'Where are you looking?'

'Not really decided.' He took a sip of his wine. 'Don't want to live in the city, not when I work here, but a PC's salary doesn't go very far anywhere else.'

I had had two glasses of wine already, or I wouldn't have risked the question, but I said, 'You're looking on your own, then?'

He looked at me, and I noticed just how dark his eyes were – that reflective, liquid brown that looked almost black in certain lights. Like Alex's eyes. He was saying, 'I've been sharing with some colleagues, but I'm sick of their sweaty socks all over the front room.' He allowed himself a small laugh at that. 'Nice enough place, up in Beeston. I'd like to stay round there, but being so close to the university bumps up the house prices too much. Too many landlords cashing in. And spoilt middle-class students being bought houses by Mummy and Daddy.'

I hadn't expected a policeman to say something like that. It pleased me. I remembered Colin saying Dave Short was a nice guy, and caught myself wondering whether a social worker and a police officer were at all compatible. I put the thought out of my mind – he was just having a glass of wine, that was all. So I said, 'Did you always want to be a policeman?'

'When I was a kid?' He smiled, and creases

appeared at the corners of his mouth. 'No, I wanted to be a long-distance lorry driver. I always wanted to park my lorry outside the house, and the one next door, and the one next to that. Did you always want to be a social worker?'

'No way.' I couldn't imagine any child thinking of social work as a future career. I said, 'I wanted to be an air hostess, until I was eleven. Then I wanted to be a teacher, but the long hours put me off. Did some voluntary work at a children's home, organizing games and that sort of stuff. That swung it.'

'So you're in it for the good of the kiddies and the improvement of society as a whole, then? You're one of those woolly liberal, politically correct do-gooders the tabloids love to blame for all the ills of modern Britain?'

He had spoken in a light, mocking tone, and I laughed and matched my tone to his and said, 'Well, I didn't choose it for the paperwork, or the high status of the job.'

He laughed, too. 'Ditto with policing.'

'You're just out to catch the bad guys and make the world safe for law-abiding citizens,' I said. 'Or do you see yourself as an agent of the ruling classes defending the God-given Capitalist right to own property?'

He was about to respond, mouth open and twisted into a smile, when the sound of a car alarm pierced the air. His smile died. 'That's my car,' he said, and we both rushed to the front door.

The street seemed to be deserted. He switched off the car alarm with the remote control on his key ring and said, 'Stay here.'

I stayed. He went into the street. His car was parked nose to nose with mine, so close they were almost touching. He went round to the driver's door on his car; I saw him bend down to examine something. Then he stood upright and looked both ways along the street.

'Hey!' he shouted. 'Stop!'

He ran up the street and I saw a dark shape, a shadow, running ahead of him. In a moment they were both out of sight. I could still hear their footsteps, and then that sound also died. The air had a chill to it. The street was empty. I folded my arms and hugged them to my chest, waiting for Dave to return. A minute passed. I was standing with the door wide open, standing halfway between the house and the street, then I stepped back towards my house, away from the darkness. Anything could be happening – I didn't want to think what, I just wanted Dave to return.

Finally, he ambled back up the road, and examined his car and mine again before coming back into the house. I closed the door behind him and followed him into the front room.

'There was someone there,' he said. 'They ran off. Might've just been some kid, I couldn't tell. Little bastard scratched my paintwork with a key or something. Yours is fine.'

I nodded, unable to speak, and went and sat on the

sofa. I didn't want to show how much the incident had scared me, but I couldn't find my voice to say anything dismissive. I realized I still had my arms folded across my chest, but I was so cold, I didn't want to move at all. Dave was still standing, and he must have understood how I was feeling, because he came and sat on the sofa next to me, saying gently, 'Hey, it's all right, it's okay.'

He had put his arm across my shoulders to comfort me, and I felt myself turn in towards him and allow him to put his other arm around me too. I knew I shouldn't be doing this, I knew I should be strong and sit back and move away from him, but there was so much comfort in the warm, solid presence of his body. I felt myself getting close to tears, and it took an effort of will to break from his hug and reach for my cigarettes and light one with shaking hands.

He moved slightly away from me on the sofa, but didn't return to the armchair. I took a deep draw on the cigarette, wiped the back of my hand over my eyelids and swallowed down the tears. 'Sorry,' I said. 'Sorry.'

'That's okay,' he said, his voice still quiet and gentle. 'You've had a scare, that's all.'

The tears returned to my eyes. I wiped again, and sniffed them back, and took another draw on the cigarette. I wanted to ask him whether he thought it might have been my attacker out there, whether it had been Sean Metcalfe, but I didn't trust my voice. I wasn't sure how Dave would respond to the question anyway; I didn't want him to dismiss it. Scratching a car – that was the sort of thing Sean would do, he was always up to stuff like that, before. Hadn't he broken several windows at his school? I wasn't sure enough to mention it.

Dave sat back in the sofa. More distance between us. I twisted to face him. He said, 'Before you ask, I don't know if that was the person you think's been hanging around. Chances are it was just a kid being a prat. They're like that round here, eh?' He was looking for a smile from me so I gave him my bravest. 'Anyway,' he said, 'there's no reason to think they'll come back. And even if they do, they won't do anything.'

I just nodded.

'Have some more wine. You look like you need it.'

I picked up my glass and took a gulp and then looked at him, but he didn't seem to think I was being pathetic. I felt a little steadier, so I said, 'Should we report that to someone?'

'Like who?'

I felt a little silly saying, 'The police?'

'They couldn't do anything,' he said. 'Not worth my while getting the insurance involved, it'll only bugger my no-claims. Anyway, whoever it was'll be long gone by now.'

He wasn't looking at me as he spoke. He seemed to suddenly feel awkward, so close to me on the sofa, because he went back to the armchair, sat down and took a sip from his wine. Then he finally looked at me, and he was smiling again, a sympathetic, professional sort of smile. He said, 'Do you want me to check round the back of the house, just to put your mind at rest?'

'Okay.'

He stood up. 'Well, lead on.'

I took him through to the kitchen and unbolted and unlocked the back door. He stepped out into the darkness; the light threw my reflection back at me in the kitchen window, and through that, I saw the shape of him as he walked along the narrow path on the other side of the glass. I remembered seeing that face looking at me through the supermarket window, the surprise in the expression, but when Dave turned to look into the kitchen he just smiled.

He came back in, re-locked and re-bolted the door, then said, 'Nothing at all out there. Are you going to be okay on your own?'

'Oh yes,' I said, all bluster.

'Do you want me to check your windows, too?'

I thought about that, imagined me guiding him around my house, into the bathroom and the spare room and finally my bedroom. 'It's okay,' I said. 'I checked them all earlier.'

He nodded. I had the feeling that he didn't quite know what to do next. After a moment, he said, 'I suppose I'd better get off. Are you sure you'll be okay?'

'Yes, fine,' I said. I didn't want him to go, but I wasn't quite sure why.

He put his anorak back on and I followed him to the front door. At the door, he said, 'If you have any problems, give the station a ring, they'll send someone out.'

I nodded. He had adopted his professional tone again. I wondered suddenly how he saw me – he seemed so nice, but maybe that was all an act? Maybe he saw me the same way I saw my clients, and he was just being very polite? I shut the thought out.

'I'll drop by tomorrow evening,' he said, and added, off-hand, 'if you like.'

'Yes,' I said. 'That'd be good.'

Then he was gone. I closed and locked the front door and went back to the sofa. I wasn't sure why he had offered to come back – was it just that he wanted to reassure me? I wasn't sure why I had said yes, either, but I knew it was a bad idea to think too much about that.

I poured the remainder of the wine into my glass and turned the television on again, but I didn't really watch whatever programme was playing.

Thirteen

The slight edge of hangover curling the fringes of my brain wasn't the only thing that made it difficult to concentrate on my work. The office was noisy; the striplights were flickering; my eyes hurt as I read and re-read the file in front of me. I hadn't seen anybody hanging around outside my house when I left for work, and there had been nothing untoward around the office, but I couldn't escape the feeling that Sean Metcalfe was close by and was aware of my movements. It was silly really – I had no good reason to think he would be watching or that he was even interested in me, but I couldn't put him out of my mind.

There was a case conference to prepare for, but I knew even as I started to plan my report that I wasn't thinking clearly. It seemed so absurd, to think that I was supposed to predict outcomes, to foresee what was going to happen in someone else's life, and all the time I didn't even know what was happening in mine. I sat with my elbows on the desk, head resting on my hand, not looking at the others in the office.

They all knew what to do – I felt rising panic, that same fear I'd had when I first started in the job; that fear of acting in case I made a wrong choice, that fear of doing nothing in case that was even more disastrous. I tried taking deep breaths. I tried thinking slowly, step by step, but it didn't help. I thought about giving up, about asking someone else what they would do, but I could imagine how they would look at me, what they would think. I didn't want anyone to think I was losing it.

I knew I couldn't carry on like this. I needed to know what was going on, and why, and whether I was just paranoid. I packed away the case notes and signed myself out of the office. The cool air in the street helped; I realized I had barely been breathing and the sudden rush of oxygen made me dizzy for a moment. My heartbeat steadied.

I drove down to the street where the Metcalfes lived and parked up near the Adams' house. Katie Adams wasn't in; the front curtains were drawn and when I lifted the letterbox flap I saw that the baby buggy was gone from its usual place in the hall. There was a smear of something sticky across the front window. I stepped onto the patch of grass in front of the house and looked closer. Someone had been throwing eggs at the window; the yellowish gluey mess had dragged down the glass, encrusted with little bits of shell, and dried hard.

Smoking a cigarette, I stood by my car and tried to think. I had come all this way – I wasn't even sure why, because Katie Adams wouldn't be able to tell me much. I looked across at the Metcalfe house. Colin would hate me for talking to one of his clients, but I knew I couldn't leave the situation as it was. Mrs Metcalfe – Carla – must be able to do something, to tell me something. And I had a duty to help Katie Adams; it wasn't as if it was unreasonable for me to talk to Carla Metcalfe.

There was no visible sign of life at number five, and even as I rang the doorbell I was hoping there would be no reply. Curtains over the glass panels in the door prevented me from seeing if there was anyone on the other side, but eventually I heard the key turning in the lock and the front door opened.

Carla Metcalfe. She had aged considerably in the eight years since I had last seen her, and could have passed for ten years older than the mid-forties I knew her to be. She was thin, almost gaunt, her face creased and lined into a permanent frown, but her taut stance suggested that strength still ran through her limbs.

I said, 'Mrs Metcalfe, I'm Jo—'

'I know who you are,' she said. 'I'm hardly going to forget you, am I?' There was no move to open the door more fully. 'What do you want?'

'I wondered whether we could have a chat.'

She didn't change her expression or her stance.

'About Danny,' I said.

'What about him?'

Her tone wasn't exactly aggressive; there was the usual wariness, but no obvious hostility. I hadn't expected to be welcomed. I said, 'I'd rather not stand on the doorstep talking. Can I come in?'

She stood back from the door and signalled for me to go past, but it was a gesture of resignation rather than invitation.

'Thank you,' I said, and went through to the front room. The house was a mirror-image of the Adams' house, and it was a little disconcerting to see the reverse positioning of the identical fireplace, but all comparison stopped there. Katie Adams favoured wallpaper with small flowered patterns and brown velour furniture with tassled fringes, while Carla Metcalfe's front room was brightly decorated in citrus; orange paint on the lower half of the wall and yellow on the top half, with a green border dotted with yellow and orange cartoon daisies covering the switch between colours. The sofa and two armchairs were old-fashioned, high-backed seats covered with green throws. There was a recently applied look to the brightness of the paint.

'Nice room,' I said. 'Nice and cheerful.'

That elicited a nod of acknowledgement, but her lips didn't form anything I could interpret as the start of a smile. I sat down in an armchair and she sat on the edge of the sofa, legs apart, elbows on her knees, as if prepared to spring to her feet if provoked.

'So,' she said, 'did Katie Adams send you, then?'

'No, not at all. But she has told me what's been going on.'

She gave a short laugh. 'Yeah, I bet.'

I tried a neutral-friendly smile, but she wasn't going to be drawn that easily. I said, 'Why don't you tell me your side?'

There was something close to contempt in her expression. 'Why should I tell you anything?'

'I'm just trying to help,' I said.

Her expression didn't change. I had the feeling that she was angry, that there was a rage burning inside her. She hadn't been like that before, I was sure – I couldn't remember her being so fierce that it seemed to shine out from her. I was tempted to ask what was wrong, what had happened, what I could do to help, but I was scared to find out – I didn't want her to release all of that anger onto me.

I said, 'I'm trying to resolve the situation. There's obviously a problem with Danny and some of the other kids. I just want to stop things getting out of hand.'

I wanted to appeal to her – get her to see that she was strong, I was strong, but Katie Adams was not. I wanted her to realize that Katie Adams needed protecting, needed people to look out for her. But Carla's expression still didn't change. I could see her son in the line of her jaw, in the way she held herself. I could picture Sean next to me in the street; did she know what had happened, and what was going to happen? I wanted to ask if she knew where Sean was, if she knew what he'd been up to, but I knew I couldn't.

'I'm just trying to help,' I repeated.

'Help who?' she said. 'You lot are no help to anyone. I've seen it all before, remember?'

That was a challenge. I forced the neutral smile to remain on my lips. 'Look, whatever happened in the past, I'm sure we can agree that—'

'Agree?' she said. 'Agree? I don't have to agree with anything you say.'

I sighed. 'But surely you can see that this situation—'

'That woman's been making our lives hell,' she said. 'Ask anyone. But I don't suppose you care what we say, do you? You're all the same. Danny's a good kid if you lot would only give him a chance.'

'I'm not saying it's all down to Danny,' I said.

But she wasn't listening. 'That Katie Adams is the problem. She's not right in the head. It's her causing all the trouble.'

'I'm not saying it's Danny's fault,' I said.

'Good, 'cos it's not.'

I waited a moment before speaking, hoping that the silence would calm her. I wasn't sure how to handle the situation – Christ, she wasn't even my client. Colin would be furious if he found out about this conversation, but I knew I had to press on, had to get her to understand what I was trying to say. And she had always been hard work; before, I had put it down to the stress she had been under – the sudden death of her husband, the boys playing her up, Sean skipping school and being brought home in a police car. She had seemed on the edge back then, blaming me, blaming my lack of experience, and I had taken it all because it wasn't her fault, she was in a bad situation, she was grieving, and everyone has the right to lose it sometimes. I wondered whether she was always like this, whether the anger was always bubbling so close to the surface, or was it Sean's return that had caused this reaction? I was seized again by the desire to ask after Sean.

Instead, I said, 'I think we need to find a way to calm the situation down. If the lads didn't react to Katie Adams, or try to stir her up—'

'They don't—'

'I'm not blaming them,' I continued smoothly, and to my surprise she didn't try to interrupt me again. 'But if we could get one side to stop reacting, maybe it would all blow over?'

'Tell that to her. And that bloke of hers. But I don't suppose they mentioned what he's been up to.' I started to say that I wasn't interested, but she cut me off. 'He grabbed one of Danny's mates. Had him by the throat. Told him he'd sort him out properly.'

Her hand had run to her own throat, as if she could feel the pressure there. I remembered the bruises I'd seen on her face, the marks on her arms that she'd dismissed as accidents. I said, 'There's been unpleasantness on both sides.'

'Maybe,' she said, hand still at her throat. Then she leaned forward, looked at me and added, 'But it isn't right, is it? An adult, I mean, threatening a twelve-year-old kid. That isn't right.'

She seemed to expect a reply; she seemed to want to gauge my reaction. I said, 'No, of course not.'

'They're just kids,' she said. 'Nobody should treat 'em like that. I don't care what you say.'

I said, 'I'll be having a word with them, too.'

She sat back. She seemed slightly disappointed with my reply. I had expected her to seize the opportunity to end the conversation, but she made no move to do so. She seemed to be waiting – I wondered again whether she knew what Sean had been up to, whether she had been expecting me to ask about him.

I said, 'I'll let you get on.'

She followed me to the front door, that expectant frown still scoring her face. At the door, I said, 'Thanks for your time.' And then, as I was about to go, before I could stop myself, I heard myself ask, 'How's Sean these days?'

The frown disappeared. 'Why the fuck do you care?'

I was taken aback. 'Excuse me?'

'You've got some nerve,' she said. 'After all this time you want to know about him? Never cared before, did you?'

'I don't know what you mean,' I said, and I didn't. My pulse hammered. 'If you think I've done something wrong, at least tell me.'

But she had clammed up, as if she had said too much already.

'What's going on?' I asked, but she was closing the door on me. I put out my hand to stop her. 'Carla?'

She had put her weight behind the door and it slammed shut. I stood there, looking at the door, but I knew there was no point ringing the bell, she wouldn't open up to me again.

Fourteen

As soon as I got home from work, I shut the curtains, switched on the TV and camped out on the sofa with the small box that I kept my stash in. I built myself a medium-strength spliff and watched *The Bill* while the smoke knocked the edges off the day. I had moved onto re-runs of *Friends* and was considering rolling another spliff when I heard a car pulling up outside my house. I thought it might be Dave Short come to check up on me again, so I shoved the cling-filmed chunk of hash and my Rizlas into the lacquered box, put it back on the bookcase and was ineffectually fanning the air with my hands when the doorbell rang.

I opened the door. Alex. He came past me and into the front room; I followed him in, and before he had even peeled off his coat he said, 'Why didn't you tell me? Why'd I have to hear it from Simon?'

'What?' I asked.

'You know what. Someone hanging round here on Saturday night.'

'Oh, that.' It seemed like a century ago to me

now. I just laughed and said, 'Like you'd've wanted to know. Forgotten your little performance on Saturday night, have you?'

He said, 'Don't be ridiculous.' Then, 'Have you been smoking dope?' Before I could reply, he went on, 'I can smell it. And you're stoned. Look at you.'

I walked past him and slumped into the sofa. 'Sorry, Dad.'

He was about to respond to that, but then he changed his mind. He sat down in the armchair and rubbed the heels of his hands into his eyes. I waited for whatever argument he was going to start next. But he said, 'Can't we forget about Saturday? We were both – overwrought. Let's forget it happened, eh?'

I shrugged. 'Whatever.'

I knew that wasn't the response he wanted, but I wasn't in the mood to be magnanimous. He took a deep breath and made an effort to calm himself, then said, 'You should've called me. I'd have come round. I don't like the idea of you being frightened on your own.'

It would have been a lousy trick to tell him that he had frightened me on Saturday too, grabbing my arm and then storming off. The spliff had dulled my brain so I lit a cigarette and then offered him the packet, but he declined. I blew out a lungful of smoke, waiting for the nicotine to kick in. I said, 'You were busy. It was your party. I didn't think you'd appreciate being called away.'

He screwed up his face at that.

'Anyway, I'm not even sure there really was anyone there.'

'Yes, but all the same—'

'It's okay,' I said. 'The police've been pretty helpful.'

His expression suggested I'd missed the point entirely. 'It's not okay,' he said. 'You shouldn't be alone.'

'I'm a big girl. I can look after myself.'

'But the attack was only a couple of weeks ago. It'd be natural if you felt—'

'I'm fine,' I said, and there was more edge to my voice than I intended.

'But that's why you came round yesterday, isn't it? Because you were scared?'

'No,' I said. 'Not really. I wasn't scared. I just – I just needed company, that's all.' I could tell he didn't believe me, and although part of me was glad that he was so concerned, I didn't want to feel like a charity case. I said, 'Christ, I wish Simon hadn't told you now.'

'I'm glad he did.'

I didn't want to talk about it any more. I had been looking forward to a quiet night, just me and a few spliffs in front of the TV, and the warmth that would wrap me up and insulate me. My head was aching again. Alex was showing no signs of leaving. I reminded myself that his concern was sweet, really, however he chose to express it. He looked as though he didn't know what to do next, and I couldn't leave things like that, however big a part of me enjoyed seeing him suffer. I gave in to the hospitality urge and offered him a cup of coffee; he followed me into the kitchen to watch me wait for the kettle to boil.

While I was spooning coffee granules into a couple of mugs I said, 'So, tell me about this Louise, then.'

If he realized my casual tone was deliberate, he didn't comment. 'She's nice,' he said. 'She makes me laugh.'

'Are you seeing her again?'

'Maybe.' But it was defensive, so I took that to mean yes.

'I'm glad,' I said, and I did mean it, I did want him to be happy.

He gave an embarrassed smile, then said quickly, 'Simon said something about you knowing who mugged you.'

'Possibly.'

We took our coffees back into the front room and resumed our previous seats. 'It wasn't a mugging,' I said. He raised his eyebrows, and I added, 'At least, I don't think so.'

So I told him all about it, about my purse being returned to me and about Sean Metcalfe absconding and how I was certain – almost – that it was him. But I left out the stuff at the supermarket – I didn't want him to think I was losing the plot.

'And Dave Short's your knight in shining armour?'

'Oh, it's not like that,' I said, and laughed.

We drank our drinks in silence for a moment. I

had a horrible feeling that Alex was contemplating Dave Short, and part of me wanted to convince him that it really was nothing like that, but I couldn't help remembering Alex leaning in towards Louise at the party. There was some small justice in him thinking there was something – but I didn't want him to misunderstand, not really.

'What I don't understand,' Alex said, 'is why this Sean would want to attack you?'

'I was his case worker eight years ago.'

'Yes, but he's had others since. Why go for you? Why not Colin Fuller, for one?'

'He was taken into care eight years ago,' I said. 'Both the boys were. Foster care for three months.'

'But that's still not a reason.'

'No,' I said, and then I ran out of things to add to the speculation.

Alex said, 'Even if he blames you, which would be ridiculous, they were only in care for three months. And why wait this long?' I didn't reply, but he was still musing and didn't seem to notice. 'They didn't report any – any abuse while they were fostered?'

'Not as far as I know.'

'That wouldn't make sense anyway,' Alex said. 'He'd blame the foster carer, wouldn't he?'

I just shrugged. The pounding in my head was developing into a full headache. I wanted the second spliff I had promised myself; the effects of the first had been replaced by sore eyes and tiredness. 'Don't keep going over it,' I said. 'Best to just forget it.'

'Forget it? He attacked you, Jo. He could've really hurt you, or even killed—'

'Yes, yes,' I said. 'Be quiet, please.'

He was stopped more by my tone than by my words and said nothing else. After a minute of listening to him drinking his coffee, I relented. 'Sorry. I didn't mean that. I'm tired. It's been a long day.'

'S'okay,' he said. 'You've a right to be stressed. Christ, you're stressed at the best of times.'

'That's not fair—' I started to say.

'I don't mean any criticism. That's just the way you are.'

He was getting dangerously close to the subjects we'd had all those endless conversations – arguments – about before he moved out. I caught his eye, wanting him to understand that I had no intention of continuing those discussions.

He said, 'I just wish you'd called me on Saturday night.'

'I couldn't have,' I said.

'If you'd told me—'

'You'd really have told Louise you were coming round to mine?' I cut him off before he could respond to that. 'You didn't have to do that. I was fine. And anyway, what would she have thought?'

'She'd have been fine,' he said. His voice was low.

'That's not the point, anyway,' I said. 'We agreed to go our separate ways. I can handle this. It was nothing, really, I was just a little freaked. My own fault for walking home alone.'

He looked at me as though trying to work out

whether I really meant it. I steadied my gaze and looked back at him. After a moment, he looked away and gave a little laugh. 'Well, in future, don't hesitate.'

'Okay,' I said. 'Thanks.'

He took another sip of his coffee, the frown setting into a grim expression around his eyes. I waited for him to express whatever he was thinking, but I wasn't expecting it when he said, 'Do you want me to stay around tonight? I could go home and get some clean clothes and come back, if you want.'

I wasn't sure if I had imagined the slight reluctance in his tone. I wondered whether he had planned to see Louise again tonight, whether things really were progressing that fast between them, whether she really would have understood if he had said he was spending the night at his ex-partner's house. I said, 'No, it's fine, honestly.'

He was about to say something else, but there were footsteps coming up the path, and then the doorbell rang. It had to be Dave Short – I looked at Alex, not sure how he would take it, although there was nothing I could do but face it out.

So I said, 'Oh, that's probably PC Short. He said he might pop round. Check things are okay.'

Alex raised his eyebrows but didn't say anything. I went to the front door, leaving him in the armchair. It was Dave Short, out of uniform again, offering me a bottle of wine.

'To replace what we drank last night,' he said, with a smile.

'Oh,' I said, not sure how to react. Then I remembered my manners and took the bottle and said, 'Thank you. Come in, come in.'

He followed me through into the front room, where Alex had to twist in the armchair to see us both as we entered, and I said, 'Alex, this is PC Short. And this is Alex, a friend of mine. Dropped in to check how I was.'

I gave a nervous sort of laugh. Alex and Dave looked at each other. I retreated into the kitchen to put the bottle of wine out of sight. As I came back, Dave was saying, 'That's right, you know Kelly Andrews.'

'Yes, known her a long time,' Alex said. He smiled up at me. 'We've met before, Jo. I've worked with PC Andrews.'

'Oh,' I said. 'Good.'

Dave was still standing near the door.

I said, 'Come and sit down.'

Dave hesitated.

Alex said, with the kind of mischievous grin I'd been hoping to avoid, 'I've got to get off, anyway. I'll give you a ring, Jo.'

'Okay,' I said, probably a little too quickly for decorum. I saw him to the front door.

At the door, Alex gave a low laugh. 'I'm not the only one with romance in the air, eh?'

I hit him lightly on the arm and shoved him outside. I could still hear him laughing when I closed the door on him. I took a deep breath and went back into the front room.

Dave Short was over by the stereo, looking through my CD collection. 'You've got some good stuff here,' he said.

'Put something on, if you like.'

He turned and smiled at me, and I wondered whether that had seemed over-friendly. But then, he was the one who had turned up with a bottle of wine. That could hardly be considered a one hundred per cent professional act. He didn't pass any comment, though, selecting an old Chili Peppers album and kneeling down to figure out how to work the stereo.

When the music had started, he turned to me. 'I love this album,' he said. 'I take it you haven't had any strangers hanging around, then?'

'No, only Alex.'

He didn't pass comment, but didn't laugh either.

'He's my ex,' I said, and then wondered whether I should have said even that much about him.

'Fair enough.'

I felt awkward suddenly. 'Would you like some wine?' I asked. 'As it's yours anyway?'

'I wouldn't say no.'

I went into the kitchen and fetched the wine, a corkscrew and two glasses. When I came back, he was settled in the chair Alex had vacated, his coat folded over the arm, listening to the music with a smile of appreciation. I opened the wine and poured out two glasses, then gave him one and sat down on the sofa.

'There's been a sighting of Sean Metcalfe,' he said.

'Really? Where?'

'Not far from his mother's place. Down near the Arboretum. So he's definitely in the city.'

I nodded, wondering whether he meant that they were taking me more seriously than before. Was I no longer an unreliable and emotional victim imagining my attacker everywhere I went? And if so, did that mean there was more to Dave's visit than a quick check-up with social overtones? I wondered whether I should tell him that I had been to see Carla Metcalfe today, but I couldn't see the relevance.

I said, 'But he got away?'

'Yes. But don't worry, we'll catch up with him. These kids, they never stay on the run for long. Mostly we catch 'em having a cup of tea at their mother's or their girlfriend's – it's home they miss.'

I nodded. I didn't know what to say – I felt that I should be asking questions, pushing the investigation somehow, but I couldn't summon up the energy. Dave didn't seem concerned that Sean was on the loose still, and I knew it was unlikely anything would happen – he probably hadn't even planned the first attack, it had probably just been a chance encounter, hell, he probably regretted it as much as I did. He would be in even more trouble when he was finally caught, and I had no doubt that he would be caught. I could see why he was still running, and it had nothing to do with me. I even felt a little sorry for him, because they wouldn't be lenient when they did catch him, and, whatever he had done, I could picture clearly the boy I had known all those years before, a skinny little kid with a resentful frown, never meaning it but always, clumsily, in trouble for something, and looking as though he couldn't understand how any of it had happened.

Dave said, 'You seem very thoughtful.'

I shook the thoughts away, forced a smile and said, 'No, no, not at all. Just thinking about work, that's all.'

'Ah,' he said.

I was tempted to explain what I had been thinking about, but decided not to, in case he tried to persuade me that Sean deserved to be punished, that Sean wasn't the innocent little kid I remembered. I could imagine the sort of speech I might get from a policeman – reserve your sympathy for the victim, there're enough bad lads out on the streets without one more roaming free, you social workers are making our job harder, you don't know what it's like trying to stop your poor little misunderstood youths from bashing old ladies for their pension books, or peddling drugs to kiddies, or bottling each other in town on a Saturday night. I didn't want to hear anything like that, and particularly not from Dave Short. I didn't think he was the type to say those sorts of things, but I didn't want to risk finding out.

We sat in silence for a couple of minutes, both sipping our wine. I wondered whether he was starting to feel uncomfortable at having come round, at having created a situation that was more social than professional, but when I looked across at him he was listening to the music and seemed relaxed.

I had to break the silence, so I told him that the track playing was one of my favourites, even though it wasn't, and he smiled and said it was one of his favourites too, but I didn't believe him. We chatted about music for a while, and he told me that he had played electric guitar, badly, in a band when he was younger. I couldn't imagine him doing that – he seemed too clean-cut to ever have aspired to the rock 'n' roll lifestyle.

He just laughed. 'It's the job that forces me to shave.'

'You don't seem much like a policeman,' I said.

'Why? What did you expect, that I'd come into a room and bend at the knees and say "evening all"? We're not from another planet, you know.'

'I know, but usually policemen are so . . . I don't know. Conformist.'

'You mean stupid?'

I smiled. 'Well, I wouldn't have put it quite like that.'

'It's okay,' he said. 'I know all the things people say. Dull-witted plods. Corrupt thugs. Spend more time eating bacon cobs and telling dodgy jokes than catching criminals. Some of it's true. There're some real idiots on the force, but there are in every job, aren't there? That's just the way it goes.'

I wanted to say that policing was different – that it attracted people who liked having authority, that it brought out the intolerance in a person, that it represented so many negative things so how could anyone with a social conscience ever join? But I thought he would probably take offence at that, and besides, I had no evidence that he did have a social conscience, he might just have a polite visiting manner. Instead, I said, 'Yeah, there're a few idiots in Social Services, that's for sure. Usually the ones who get promoted.'

'Isn't that always the way?'

'Absolutely.' And I poured us both another glass of wine. The conversation had made me think of Douglas suddenly, and his instructions to leave Katie Adams alone, to stop her becoming dependent on me. It seemed unfair that someone who had never even met Katie Adams could decide something so important. She needed me. There was always time to squeeze in an extra visit.

I wondered whether Dave's bosses knew he was visiting me. It seemed unlikely, somehow – and what would they say if they found out? Would he be in trouble? I didn't see how; I was a victim, not a suspect, and all we had done was drink some wine and talk. There wasn't anything wrong with that, was there? And then I caught myself wondering whether he would be forbidden from anything more than a drink, whether he would be risking everything if he decided to take things further between us. But I dismissed the thought quickly – whatever jokes Alex made, I was not interested in Dave Short, I just liked his company, that was all.

And as we talked I realized that I really did enjoy his company. We talked about nothing and listened to more CDs and let the evening ebb away around us. Since Alex and I had split up, I had found myself alone more and more, and it was nice to be able to relax and chat and just enjoy someone's company. I thought about Alex with Louise and wondered what sort of conversation he got from her – was she really the way she seemed at the party, so self-assured and confident? I knew that was what Alex was looking for – Alex wanted to feel a little glamorous, like he was in with the right crowd, where all the action was, at the hub of the social circle, and that probably meant that she was better suited to him than I was. But would he be enough for her? I had the feeling that she wouldn't understand him, all his little hang-ups and neuroses, the ones that I understood so well. She would eventually reject him, and what would he do then? Find his way back to me, hide away with me to lick his wounds until he felt able to risk it all over again? It pleased me, in a way, that he would always return – but I didn't want to be forever linked to him, I didn't want an anchor holding me to my past.

Dave was telling me some half-funny anecdotes from his childhood, and I nodded and laughed in all the right places and tried to respond as well as I could. The wine on top of the spliff was having a bad effect on me. I had to focus hard to follow what Dave was saying, and to pick up the signals for when to laugh, but Dave didn't seem to notice. He was good-looking in a rather ordinary sort of way, but when he smiled it added a strange twist to his face, added character to the well-proportioned features, as though there was something more behind that kind façade, something that might even be worth finding. I wondered whether he was my opportunity for something new, something different; my Dave to Alex's Louise. I tried to imagine it, to build him into my picture, but my head was spinning slightly.

Dave finally said it was time for him to go, and turned down another glass of wine because he was driving, then started to put on his coat. All it would take was an invitation for him to stay the night, but as I walked him to the front door I knew I couldn't ask, I couldn't bring myself to utter those words, because once spoken they couldn't be taken back. I didn't think I could live with the embarrassment of his rejecting me. And he would reject me – as I opened the front door and the opportunity to ask drained away, I was certain that he would reject me.

'Well,' he said. 'You seem to be pretty safe now.'

I just nodded, hoping that he would offer to call round the following night.

He said, 'Give us a ring at the station if anything comes up.'

'I will,' I said, but it was all so formal, so impossible to ever follow up on. I added, quickly, before I could stop myself, 'I've enjoyed talking to you.'

His eyes met mine, but there was no moment of passion, no melting into an embrace, no sudden move to kiss. He said, 'I've enjoyed it, too.'

And did I imagine the moment's hesitation, the moment where it seemed that he was going to say something else, something more? I didn't know, didn't want to know. After he had gone, I went back to the sofa, poured the rest of the wine into my glass and sat with my legs pulled in tight and my arms wrapped around myself, and outside the street was very quiet, there didn't seem to be anyone else around.

Fifteen

I had hoped that work would be the usual grind through familiar routines, allowing me to recover from my hangover in peace, but as soon as people started to gather for the fortnightly staff meeting I knew it wasn't going to be like that. I was surprised to see a couple of workers from Referrals and Admissions sidle into our office, and it seemed that most of the long-term team were hanging around. There was a tension in the air, too; a palpable sense of expectation. I tried to think what this could mean, but my thoughts were muffled by the slight ache behind my eyes.

Colin came in, late as usual, and slumped down next to me. He looked tired, too. I said, 'What's with all the people?'

He seemed surprised. 'You haven't heard? They're saying Douglas wants to discuss Chantelle Wade.'

His expression brightened at the thought. I wanted to groan – didn't we already discuss the enquiry enough? I forced myself to smile, even though I knew it meant the office would be alive with rumour and analysis for the rest of the day – hell, the rest of the week, the way the others loved to tease out every nuance of meaning from the smallest detail.

Douglas got the meeting started, droning through the new referrals and the lists of unallocated cases. I kept my head down, and none of the cases came my way – I counted myself lucky for once. There was a time when I would have volunteered rather than see a case remain unallocated, but a sense of lethargy was creeping through me. I thought of the things Colin had said in Alex's garden at the party, and maybe he had been right? Maybe there wasn't any point to any of this? I glanced across at Colin; he was doodling patterns in the notebook resting on his knee, the thin line of black ink winding and wriggling across the page.

Douglas was talking now about the new objectives under the Quality Protects initiative, and how to tie policy in with the recommendations of the Laming Report, and the importance of multi-agency approaches, and making operational sense of new procedures. I stifled a yawn and tried to look interested. The room was getting warm with the heat of all the people sitting so close together. I shifted in my seat to try to wake myself up. My thoughts were drifting; I found myself wondering whether Dave Short would visit me again.

Colin made a sudden movement beside me and gave a grunt; I jerked my head up and realized that one of the women from the Referrals and Admissions team was saying, 'What about the Wade case? We want to know what's going on.'

There was a murmur of assent from around the room.

'I was coming to that,' Douglas said. He sounded a little irritated. 'There's not much to say, though. We need to focus on the job in hand, people, not on what might be being said at the enquiry.'

'But we know what's being said.' It was the same woman again. 'They've been trawling for anything they can throw at the workers. They're saying it's down to the individuals. How are we supposed to do our job with that hanging over us?'

The murmurs of assent grew louder. I sat more upright, looking around, and for the first time I noticed how strained everyone else looked, how tired and pale and grim-faced.

Douglas put down the papers he had been referring to and looked slowly around the room. He seemed to be thinking. 'Okay,' he said. 'Let's put paid to a few rumours, then. I know everyone thinks the enquiry's looking for scapegoats but that really isn't the way it's going. There were some mistakes made. Those have to be analysed, however painful it is, so that we learn from the experience.'

'That's not what's happening, though, is it?' The same woman again.

Colin said loudly, 'You know they're just trying to get someone to take the fall. We all know what went wrong, the department's too bloody disorganized and understaffed, that's the real problem.'

I had expected Douglas to respond angrily to that, but people were agreeing. The talk grew louder and he surveyed us all with a frown. For a moment, I couldn't make out what anyone was saying over the confusion of all the voices. I glanced at Colin and his expression was reddening, as though he was about to lose control. I put out a hand and touched him lightly on the arm; he flinched away from my touch, but looked across at me and forced a thin, terse smile onto his lips.

Douglas waited for the noise to die down. 'We don't know what the enquiry's going to say,' he said. 'The report will probably take weeks to come through. What we have to do is ensure that we stick to the Laming guidelines—'

'We do,' Colin said, and although he hadn't spoken loudly, the force he had put behind the words carried, stopping Douglas.

Douglas hesitated. 'Okay. Look, maybe we need to remind ourselves of the facts here. Chantelle Wade died, don't forget that. None of us ever wants that to happen again. Mistakes were made by the officers concerned.' He raised his voice above the protests that were bubbling up. 'Mistakes were made,' he repeated. 'A voluntary arrangement was made and it didn't protect the child. The Child Protection Plan failed. We have to ask why. We'd be neglecting our duty if we didn't ask why.'

'We know why,' someone said. 'It's because we're all stressed. We're all overworked. There aren't enough of us. Maybe if people weren't having to rush from crisis to crisis they'd make better decisions?'

'Maybe if we worked with the families more we wouldn't get to the stage where the kids are in danger,' I said. But I had spoken quietly, and only Colin heard me. The rest of the room was still protesting at Douglas's words.

I had a clear view of Douglas from my seat. He was looking uncomfortable now, pressing his fingertips into his forehead as if trying to push a headache away. I remembered the things I had heard him say on the phone, the day I came back from sick leave – he had been protecting the workers then. I wasn't sure what was going on now. I had the uncomfortable feeling that he had shifted his position, and if that was true, then maybe they were going to dump the blame for the things that went wrong on the individual caseworkers? I felt a little sick – I didn't want to think about it.

Douglas said, 'We have to just do the best we can. Now, I really don't see what we will gain from discussing this any further.'

His tone was firm. He waited for the grumbling to subside, then continued to talk about the importance of information-sharing for effective multi-agency practice. I felt the stupor of the warm room start to envelop me once more.

By the time the meeting dragged to its conclusion, I needed some fresh air to bring me back from the brink of sleep. Colin and I stumbled through the crowd and out into the yard for a smoke. I could see that Colin was still angry.

'Don't let it get to you,' I said.

He gave a little smile at that. I knew what Alex would have said: fine advice coming from me. But Colin was never that blunt when he spoke to me. He ground the heels of his hands into his eyes then looked up at the grey sky.

'It's just shit,' he said. 'Anyone could have made that mistake. How many times have you trusted what a client tells you? You have to sometimes. They were just unlucky that the mother was lying as much as the father.'

I didn't respond, concentrating on lighting a cigarette. I didn't think Colin would appreciate my thoughts – because I wouldn't have made that mistake. Don't trust anything they say, that was the rule I had always worked by. Evidence-based knowledge was how I phrased it to Douglas, but it came down to the same thing; don't just take their word for it. I had sympathy for the workers, of course I did – nobody likes to see a colleague under pressure – but it was their mistake, and it had cost Chantelle Wade her life.

Colin blew out a long puff of smoke. 'And now they're trawling, you know that? Going back through all their other cases to see if there's any other fuck-ups they can sling at them.'

I nodded.

'Can you imagine that?' he asked. 'People trawling through all your past cases, looking for every mistake you've ever made?'

I nodded again. I didn't really want to think about it. What would people have made of how I handled the Metcalfe case all those years ago? Carla Metcalfe obviously thought I'd done something wrong. I realized I should probably tell Colin that I had been round to see Carla, but I hesitated. I wasn't sure what there was to tell.

He said, 'I'd hate that. I hate anyone sticking their nose into one of my cases without me asking them to. It's just unprofessional. It's like saying I can't do the job myself. I really hate that.' He looked at me, and for a moment I thought he was going to say I had already done just that, and demand to know what I was playing at, but he just sucked angrily on his cigarette and said, 'You know what I mean?'

'Yes. It's an invasion. I'm the same.' I felt a little bad saying that, but he was so angry, so wound up. I'd never seen him like this. I thought again about our conversation at the party and I was about to ask him whether he was okay, whether there was anything I could do to help, when he flung his cigarette butt at the ground. He was about to go indoors again. I said, 'Have another smoke, Colin. You need the break, you look so stressed.'

He glanced at his watch. 'Can't,' he said. 'Got to get up to the Bulwell office. One of my cases has moved onto Alex's patch. Need to hand it over.'

'Alex won't mind five minutes.'

'No, but I'm already late, and it'll take twenty minutes to get there with all the roadworks.'

'Well, say hi to Alex for me,' I said, and watched him stomp back into the building. The door swung shut behind him. As the air calmed and settled around me, I felt the tension lift from me, releasing my shoulders from the awkward hunch I'd adopted without even noticing. The headache returned with a fury – I wasn't sure if it had ever gone, or if Colin's anger had merely drowned it out for a short period. I stood there, watching his cigarette butt burn itself out on the concrete.

I finished my cigarette and went slowly back to my desk. As I had predicted, people were still gathered in clusters discussing the morning's meeting and the latest rumours about the enquiry. Douglas was nowhere to be seen; hiding with a mound of paperwork in his office, I supposed. I slipped into my seat without being asked my opinion of the latest developments and tried to concentrate on the reports I had to write. I still felt uneasy that I hadn't mentioned visiting Carla Metcalfe to Colin, but I told myself that he was very unlikely to find out, and even if he did, I wasn't interfering in his case, I was working on one of my own.

However much I tried to focus on my work, I found my thoughts drifting. It wasn't just the Chantelle Wade enquiry – even the office appetite for gossip wasn't satisfied by the events of the staff meeting for very long. Every time I thought about my clients, about the difficulties they faced and how to support them, I was dogged by the echoes of the Metcalfe case. The children had been fine – like Katie Adams's children, they hadn't been in danger, not after the father's death. But I couldn't help feeling that safety wasn't the only issue. Chantelle

Wade had died, yes – the thought of that, the thought of a tiny little girl, a doll of a child, killed by her own parents, was enough to stop anyone's thoughts. But Sean Metcalfe – I had tried to support his family, I had done everything I could, and he had still ended up in Glen Parva, his life had still been ruined.

But I hardened my mind against that thought. Douglas was right, Alex was right – I couldn't allow myself to take on other people's responsibilities. However bitter, however angry Carla Metcalfe was, the way Sean had turned out was not down to my actions.

I gritted my teeth. I shut the thoughts out. I had a job to do, and worrying about all the kids I dealt with, dwelling on their futures and the problems that were yet to assail them, would only prevent me from taking the action that was required now.

I gathered all my faculties, all my mental energies, and started to write my reports. Get on with it or get out, Colin had said. He was right. And the work stretched on; the cases kept coming. There weren't enough hours in the day, in the week, to put things right, but I knew I had to do whatever I could to get through it.

Sixteen

When I dragged myself into work on Thursday morning, there was a message from Katie Adams on my voicemail, time-stamped nine p.m. She sounded distressed and was demanding to see me. I knew I should call her back and explain that she couldn't rely on me every time there was a little problem, and tell her that my line manager felt she was able to cope on her own, but it seemed likely that her call had something to do with the Metcalfes and I wasn't going to ignore that.

I stopped off at Colin's desk. He was struggling with some paperwork and seemed relieved to be distracted from it. I told him about the phone call from Katie Adams and invited him along to deal with the Metcalfes' end, as they were his case.

He said, 'I thought Douglas wanted you to back off from that situation?'

'He does,' I said. 'But I think it needs us. It's a developing situation. We can be pro-active.'

'It's just a neighbour dispute. Leave it to the Housing Association to deal with. Refer them to the Mediation Service, if you like, but don't involve us.'

'We're already involved,' I said. 'They're our cases.'

He was trying hard to ignore me now, making a show of looking through the pile of papers stacked in his in-tray.

'Oh, c'mon, Colin. If this gets out of hand they'll start pressing charges, and before you know it we'll have Anti-Social Behaviour Orders to deal with.'

'Might get 'em moved out of my area,' he said, and I knew he was weakening. I made eyes at him and tried to jolly him along. 'Aw, look, Jo, can't you see I'm snowed under?'

'Be even worse if they get ASBOs,' I said.

'Can't you do this without me?'

'If you like,' I said. 'But Carla Metcalfe doesn't like me.'

He sighed, and sat looking at his paperwork, then made a decision. 'Okay,' he said. 'Come on, then.'

After the things he had said at the party and his behaviour at the staff meeting on Tuesday, I had expected him to be quiet, a little down, even, as I drove us to the house. He looked tired, but he seemed almost jovial. I said, 'How are things, anyway? We haven't spoken properly since Alex's party.'

He laughed. I couldn't tell whether it was forced. 'Oh, that,' he said. 'I was just pissed. Stressed. Pissed and pissed off, you know? It was nothing.' I was going to push for more, but he said quickly, 'Anyway, where did you dash off to in such a hurry?'

Now, my laugh was forced; I wasn't sure it was as convincing as his. 'Same as you,' I said. 'Too much booze. I just needed to get away.'

'Away from Alex,' he said. It wasn't a question. But he must have realized that I didn't want to go into it, because he rattled off into an anecdote about getting his central heating fixed, and we had pulled up outside the Adams' house before either of us could raise the subject again.

Katie Adams had obviously been waiting for me, and didn't seem concerned or even surprised that I had brought someone else along. Colin and I sat beside each other on her sofa while she paced the room, the manic Katie I hadn't seen for a while, greasy hair and odd socks, not making eye contact, not stopping talking to catch her breath or allow us to speak. She rattled on about people shouting abuse and kids throwing things at her window, and all the time she was winding a strand of her hair around her finger, winding and winding. I knew Colin wouldn't have much patience with her, not while she was in this state, but he helped me try to calm her down and talk her out of the pitch she was working her way towards.

She rounded on me when I asked her to explain slowly. 'I've had enough of talking. I've been talking till I'm blue in the face and it hasn't done a blind bit of good. I've seen the politicians on TV, talking about getting rid of nuisance neighbours. Should be evicting the Metcalfes, that's what you should be doing.'

'That wouldn't be a solution, would it?' I said. 'That would just mean someone else would have to deal with them. It's best all round if we try to resolve the situation.'

'But it's getting worse,' she said, and her voice had taken on the whine I had hoped she would avoid. 'Since the older lad's back it's been loads worse. He winds them up, I'm telling you.'

'You've seen Sean?' I asked.

'Yeah. He stirs them all up.'

I looked at Colin but he frowned at me, so I said nothing more about Sean. We let Katie Adams talk until she had burned herself out, and I gave her my mobile phone number for if things got out of hand. Colin made a half-hearted attempt to suggest mediation, but Katie wasn't going for it and neither of us wanted to push too hard.

'You haven't seen what they've done,' she said. 'You've got to see.'

We followed her through the kitchen and out into the back garden, half of it a concrete yard with a rotary dryer full of baby clothes, the other half a square of untidy lawn. Katie stood by the kitchen window and pointed at the wall. There were words sprayed in red paint on the brickwork. It was hard to make out what the words read, partly because the writing was a foot-high scrawl, partly because there hadn't been much paint left in the spray can. I stood back and tried to make them out. *Psycho bitch*, I finally determined.

Colin said, 'When did this happen?'

'Last night. About nine o'clock. I heard a noise and came out the back but they were already over the fence by then.'

We talked to her some more, promising to have a word with Carla Metcalfe and asking her again to consider mediation. She didn't seem very impressed, but agreed to think about it. Colin and I left by the side gate and went back into the street.

'Well,' I said as we walked to the Metcalfe house. 'Sean Metcalfe, eh?'

'Better not mention that to Carla,' Colin said. 'Don't want to warn him off.'

I stood slightly behind Colin as he rang the doorbell. When Carla Metcalfe opened the door she stood with arms folded, looking from Colin to me and back again.

'So,' she said. 'What's that woman been saying this time?'

'Can we come in?' Colin asked.

'No. She can't, anyway, not after the way she talked to me on Monday.'

Colin looked at me, frowning. I realized I should have told him about our little chat. I said, 'I'm sorry if I upset you.'

'Whatever,' she said. 'You're not coming in.'

Colin said, 'How about just me, then?'

'That's okay, I suppose. Long as you don't talk to me the way she did.'

Colin looked at me again. I shrugged to show it didn't bother me. 'I'll wait for you,' I said.

Colin went into the house and I slouched back to

the car. I leaned against the bonnet and lit myself a cigarette. I looked up at the windows of the house but I didn't see anything; of course, I hadn't really expected to see Sean looking out of one of the windows at me. I was just grinding out my cigarette on the pavement when three boys on bikes cycled past. Danny was one of them; he pulled up short at the sight of me.

'What you doing outside my house?'

'Waiting for a friend,' I said. 'He's talking to your mum.'

Danny looked a little worried at that. His friends were calling to him from further along the street but he waved them away. 'What's he talking to my mum about?'

'What d'you think?'

He looked a little confused, then said, 'Don't care anyway.' But he made no attempt to cycle away.

I said, 'Shouldn't you be at school?'

'No.'

He still didn't move. I said, 'Seen much of your brother lately?'

His eyes widened a little. 'No,' he said, but this time the question was enough to make him decide to leave. I watched him pedal away after his friends.

I lit another cigarette, thinking. It was clear that Sean Metcalfe was hanging around, protected by his mother and brother. Danny I didn't blame – he was too young to know any better. But Carla Metcalfe – she should know better, she had to realize that hiding out was no solution for Sean.

How long did they think he would be able to hide for? I found it difficult to imagine someone hiding their son like that, actually breaking the law to help him when she must know that he would eventually be caught, and things would be much worse for everyone. I wondered again whether she knew that he had attacked me. And how did she really feel about it all, about all of the trouble Sean must have caused her before he was sent to Glen Parva, and the trouble he was in now? I could imagine the things Carla would be saying to Colin – the usual stuff, making the usual digs that we didn't know what we were doing. It wasn't only the Chantelle Wade enquiry being on the news every night – Carla had always been that way, had always tried to say that we were wrong. I tried to put the thoughts out of my mind – she wasn't my case, after all, and Colin could handle her. I had empathy, sympathy even, for Katie Adams, but I was glad that Carla wasn't my problem.

I smoked several more cigarettes before Colin finally came out of the house. He didn't say anything until we were back in the car and I was pulling out onto Forest Road.

Then he said, 'You should have told me you talked to her.'

'Yes,' I said. 'Sorry.'

'Made me look stupid,' he said.

'I know.' We had reached the traffic lights at the junction with Alfreton Road, and I drew to a stop in the queue of traffic. 'What did she say?'

'Oh, a great deal. About you sticking your oar in, and her rights, and harassment, and making a complaint. You've made it all worse.'

'Right,' I said, and eased us out across the junction.

'Is that all you can say?'

I glanced across at him. He was hunched in his seat, kneading his fingers in his lap. 'She's a very hostile woman,' I said.

'Is it any wonder?'

That surprised me. 'What do you mean?'

'She told me you used to be their caseworker. I should've known that from the files. Don't know why I forgot. I don't know the ins and outs of it, and I don't particularly want to, but it sounds like you two had quite a falling-out. She's still angry.'

'That was eight years ago,' I started to say.

'And then you go in all heavy-handed demanding to know about Sean. How was she supposed to react? Honestly, you worry me sometimes, charging at these cases like – like a bull in a china shop. She might've been willing to help if you hadn't been like that.' Then he threw open his hands and looked at me. 'Oh, what's the point, eh? You won't listen to me. You never do.'

'That's not fair,' I said. 'I'm just trying to do the best for Katie Adams, that's all.' He didn't respond. I pulled the car over into a side road and parked, then twisted to face him. 'So, tell me what she said, then.'

He seemed a little surprised that we had stopped,

but said, 'You're too hard on her. She's not in an easy situation.'

'Nor's Katie Adams.'

'Yeah, of course. But she's worried about Danny. You can understand that, can't you?' He sighed. 'Look, she's doing her best, but her relationship with Sean broke down when he was the same age that Danny is now. She's anxious. She doesn't want Danny going off the rails like Sean did, and all these accusations aren't helping.'

'They're not just accusations,' I said. 'You saw the state Katie Adams was in.'

'Yeah, I did, and you can't tell me Danny's responsible for that.' He hesitated, then said, 'You're concerned about your client and that's fair enough, but I've got to think about mine. Carla blames herself for the way Sean turned out. It's not so difficult to give her some support now, is it?'

'She said she blames herself?'

He looked irritated now. 'Well, no, she didn't say it. But it's obvious, surely? And you're making things ten times harder for her, steaming in making accusations—'

'I didn't,' I said. 'I was just trying to chat. A friendly chat, that's all.'

'So what's the obsession with Sean Metcalfe, then?'

'I'm not obsessed,' I said. 'All I did was ask after him. What's wrong with that?'

'When you know he absconded from Glen Parva? Do me a favour.' He drummed his fingers on his knee for a moment. 'Alex said something when I saw him on Tuesday. Told me you think you were attacked by an ex-client. He didn't tell me the name. It wasn't Sean Metcalfe, was it?'

'It might have been,' I said. 'I don't know for sure.'

'And what do the police say?'

'Just that he's been spotted in Nottingham, so it might have been him.'

He shook his head. 'Oh, Jo, Jo,' he said, as though he despaired, as though I was a child who wouldn't listen to him. 'You need to be so careful. You're getting caught up personally. It's a minefield. You know better than that, surely?' I didn't reply, so he added, 'What does Douglas say?'

'Nothing.'

'You mean you haven't told him? Christ, Jo, you should tell him, just to cover your own back.'

'Don't worry,' I said. 'It's all under control.' He didn't respond to that; I knew he wasn't convinced. I started the engine again and turned the car around. 'We've got to get back to work,' I said.

He didn't speak again until we were almost back at the office, when he suddenly said, 'I met him, you know.'

He wasn't looking at me. I said, 'Who? Sean?'

'Yeah. Had to write up a report for the court.'

'What's he like?'

He gave a little laugh. 'Oh, your usual dirty-minded, unhygienic teenaged lad. Snotty. Arrogant. Yeah, definitely arrogant.'

'What did he go down for?'

'Theft. And assault, I think. Jumped some kid in a park, something like that. Probably after their mobile phone, that's the usual, isn't it? Not his first offence.'

I nodded, trying to fit this into the picture I was starting to build up. We were approaching the office but I slowed down to give him time to say more.

He obliged. 'There was something I couldn't quite put my finger on with him. Something about his attitude. Like he was expecting something. It was nasty, whatever it was. Maybe it wasn't arrogance? No, it was more like he just didn't care about what anyone else thought. Or he didn't even recognize that other people thought at all. Very odd.'

'What, like he wasn't all there?'

'No, not exactly. He didn't seem slow on the uptake at all. The opposite, actually. He just – I don't know. Didn't care, I suppose.'

We had reached the office car park, and Colin fell silent as I pulled into a parking space. When we got out of the car, however, he looked at me across the car roof and said, 'You've got to talk to Douglas about all of this.'

'Don't worry,' I said, and then, to appease him, 'I will. Just leave it to me.'

He nodded, apparently satisfied, as if telling Douglas was going to resolve this whole situation. I felt far less confident about that, but I didn't think Colin would understand.

Seventeen

I dropped in to see Alex and Simon on my way home from work. Colin had unsettled me with his insistence that I was stepping into dangerous territory, and as I drove to their house I played back the events of the morning in my mind. I couldn't see why people would think I was doing anything wrong – all I was doing was offering the kind of support that it was my job to provide, and I had been in sensitive situations before. Douglas might think that I couldn't keep my professional distance, but I couldn't leave Katie Adams to face the situation on her own, and I'd taken Colin with me, so it wasn't like I was storming in without thinking.

Simon was out at a union meeting, but Alex was in. He looked tired. I had vaguely wanted to talk to him about my situation, ask him why he'd talked to Colin about me, but he looked too exhausted to deal with someone else's stress on top of his own. A problem shared is a problem two people have, and all of that. So we sat in his front room with music playing – Pogues, followed by the old favourites, Carter USM – and we chatted about this and that. He didn't mention Louise and I didn't ask. I didn't know how to ask without it sounding like I minded.

Alex had glanced at his watch a couple of times, and eventually I said, 'Have you got to be somewhere? Do you want me to go?'

'No,' he said. 'No, it's fine. Someone's coming round, but it's okay.'

'Who? Louise?'

He looked at me then, and I wondered whether he thought I was jealous, or whether he thought I would find the situation awkward. He said, 'Yes. But stay and meet her, if you like, she'll be here any time.'

I wasn't sure that I did want to meet her – my head was already aching from everything that had happened at work – but I thought he might read something into it if I didn't. So I smiled and agreed, secretly hoping that she would be far too late, or would phone and cancel, anything, because I couldn't imagine sitting in his front room and being polite to her.

But about ten minutes later she arrived. I saw her through the front window, getting out of a nice car, a newish Mondeo, dressed in a grey-blue trouser suit that showed off how sickeningly slim she was. Alex went to meet her at the front door and must have told her quickly that I was there, because she came into the front room with a smile already fixed on her face, extending her hand. I stood up and shook hands, and as our skin touched I found myself thinking how assured she was, how confident. I felt suddenly clumsy. Her hands were icy cold, the fingers thin, as if they were brittle, but I tried not to read anything into that.

'Alex has told me so much about you,' she said, and I wanted to laugh, because I had never heard anyone actually say that, it seemed such an unlikely thing to say. And had he really told her so much about me? What had he said? Had it been the usual lovers' conversation, about the break-up with the last partners, comparing notes, seeing who had been most hard-done-by, seeing who could get the biggest laugh? I didn't know what else Alex would be able to tell her about me – what else was there?

I said, 'Nice to finally meet you.'

She settled herself into the armchair, knees together, perfect posture, took out a packet of cigarettes and lit one with a slim gold lighter. Then she offered me a cigarette as an afterthought, but I declined.

'So,' I said, 'you're in the Chief Exec's department?'

'Yes.' She blew a small amount of smoke from the corner of her mouth, holding the cigarette as though it was an expensive accessory, as though she had a cigarette holder. 'Deal with the voluntary sector, mostly. SRB and European funding, all that, you know?'

'Oh right,' I said, with just the slightest veneer of interest, because I had only a vague idea what she was talking about. But that was enough to push her onwards, and before Alex had returned with her cup of coffee, she was explaining to me about the different phases of SRB and how the funding was allocated and all the monitoring and planning and consulting she did.

Alex sat down on the sofa next to me, but his attention was aimed at Louise. I sipped my coffee and watched him ask coy questions about her day, and listened to her answers, all the political intrigue between people I hadn't met in departments whose roles I didn't understand. If Alex didn't understand either he didn't say so, but listened with a slight smile of amazement or amusement on his face, as though he had never heard anything so interesting in all his life.

Then Louise must have decided that she needed to share out some of the conversation, because she leaned towards me and said, 'So, Jo, you're a social worker too, are you?'

'Yes,' I said. Alex had turned to look at me now, as though he was also interested in my reply. I decided I had to elaborate, to keep both of them happy. 'Dealing with families, mostly. Long-term cases, supporting them so they don't end up in crisis.'

'Like Alex does?'

'Yeah, but in a different part of the city.'

'It must be difficult,' she said. 'I couldn't do a job like that.'

'It's not that bad.' I was annoyed by her assumption – the usual assumption of the terminally arrogant – that a job had to be extreme if they couldn't imagine doing it themselves. I knew she wanted me to trot out the old cliché about it being rewarding, but I couldn't bring myself to do that. It always seemed like such a lie to me – what was the reward? Helping someone – yes, but what about all those others? Did helping one person really counterbalance all the others? Sometimes, the sheer numbers overwhelmed me – it was best not to think about it. I checked that the smile was still clenching my face and thought about Katie Adams and the graffiti on her wall. Had that been Danny? It was possible. I doubted if Colin had even mentioned it to Carla Metcalfe – he was too busy finding out why she didn't like me. But even if he had asked, she would have covered for him; after all, that was what she was doing for Sean.

Or – and the thought hit me only at that moment – maybe it hadn't been Danny at all? Maybe Sean had sprayed graffiti on Katie Adams's wall? I wasn't sure why he would do that, unless it was to help his brother, but I was seized with the certainty that it had been Sean. Hadn't the letters been sprayed quite high on the wall, and didn't that make it more likely that someone taller, someone older, had done it? After all, if Sean was willing to knock me unconscious in the street, he had to be willing to spray-paint abusive words on a wall.

Alex and Louise were discussing what they planned to do that night – go into town, see a film, maybe go for a drink – and I felt that my time in their company had run out. I wanted to be alone, anyway; I needed to think through this new revelation about Sean,

about the possibilities of the situation. So I drained
my mug and gathered my things.

They both looked up at me, and Alex said, 'Are
you going, then?' but there was no real disappointment in his tone.

'Yes,' I said. 'Got to get back. Have a nice
evening.'

They said goodbye, but Alex didn't get up off the
sofa so I left them where they were and went out of
the house. Once I was in my car and starting up the
engine, I thought about that, and it irritated me, that
he hadn't even shown that little courtesy, but I tried
to ignore it. We were close, after all – what were a few
formalities between close friends, between ex-lovers?
But I could feel a sour sort of mood rising through
me as I contemplated the fact that he was going out,
that he was going to have a good time that night, and
what did I have?

I drove. I didn't really want to go home just
yet, so I circled the streets for a while, trying to
calm down. I found myself driving up towards the
Adams' house, and although I didn't want to see
either Katie or Carla Metcalfe, I did start looking
for a group of boys on bikes, for Danny. I wasn't
sure what I would have done if I had found him
– asked him again about his brother? It seemed so
ludicrous to suppose that I would have found out any
information, but I felt that I had to do something, it
wasn't right to just go home and forget about the
things Sean had been up to.

When I did finally get home, it was dark, and the

house felt cold. I put the TV on and looked in the freezer for something to eat, but there was nothing that I fancied. I considered going out to get some food, but I couldn't face it, I was too tired. So I flopped down in front of the TV and tried to get interested, but there was nothing to watch.

After a while, I decided to phone Dave Short. I had the feeling that if I could only explain things to him, if I could only explain how Sean Metcalfe was involved in everything that was going on, then he would be able to do something, he would be able to resolve the situation.

The man on the police switchboard put me through to an extension that rang for a long time before anyone answered. It was a woman who eventually picked up, and when I asked for PC Short she said, 'He's not here right now. Can I tell him who called?'

'Jo Elliott,' I said.

'Oh.' The woman's voice seemed a little cooler. 'This is PC Andrews. Is there anything I can do?'

I thought about trying to explain it to her, but I couldn't imagine her understanding any of it. 'Not really. I just wanted to know how things were progressing.'

'We haven't got any news.' There was annoyance in her tone, and I wondered whether that was how she treated everyone, whether she viewed every victim as a nuisance, or whether I had been singled out for special treatment for something I had done or said.

'Okay,' I said, because I didn't want to prolong the conversation any further. 'Can you just tell him that I phoned?'

She said she would, and I hung up. I wasn't sure what I had expected, but I felt oddly deflated after that.

Eighteen

I woke in the middle of the night, jerked awake by the certainty that there was something wrong. I lay there for a while, tense, listening, but all I could hear was the clock ticking through its mechanism, and the occasional car on the main road, and the soft hum of the central heating. My heart was thumping. I wasn't sure what had woken me, but I knew I had been dreaming, about dark streets and people looming out of shadows and the certainty, the absolute conviction, that someone was reaching out to grab me.

After a while, when I knew I wasn't going to get back to sleep, I sat up. I could make out the bedroom in the dark now, but even so, I hesitated before I switched on the bedside lamp. I don't know what I had expected to see – someone standing over the bed, perhaps, a man with a knife or something to bludgeon me with, arms raised ready to strike. The more I strained my ears to hear the rest of the house, the more certain I became that I could hear something, someone, moving stealthily through the darkened rooms, coming slowly up the stairs, balancing his weight, creeping up.

I swung my feet over the side of the bed and put them flat on the carpet. For a moment, I had a flash of fear that something was going to grab my ankles from under the bed, that a man or a monster was lurking there, the old childhood fear. I forced myself to stand up, stepped away from the bed, wrapped my dressing gown around me.

There was a sudden noise from downstairs, a sort of scraping noise, as if someone was trying to force a window, or break the lock on a door. It lasted only a moment, and then there was silence again. I imagined whoever it was – I imagined Sean Metcalfe – crouching in the dark under a window or at the back door, screwdriver in hand, listening as tensely as I was, listening for signs that I had heard him. I tried not to think what would happen if he got into the house, if he came through the house with that screwdriver in his hand.

I got myself out of the bedroom and onto the landing, where I switched on the lights. The flare of light blinded me for a moment, but the shadows shrank back and there was nobody there. I edged my way down the stairs, listening for more sounds, but heard nothing. I wondered whether I had imagined that noise, that scraping noise, but the sound was so distinct in my mind – I didn't see how I could have imagined something in that detail.

In the hall, I switched on the next light and checked that the front door was still securely bolted.

It took me a few moments to gather enough courage to go into the through-lounge and flick on those lights, but nobody was there, and the windows were still tightly shut. Everything seemed to be the way I had left it.

That just left the kitchen. I tried not to think about the way the darkness of the garden became a wall when the lights were switched on. I tried not to think about how flimsy that back door was, and how none of the neighbours could see what was happening in my back garden, even supposing they had also heard the noise. The lights from the through-lounge cast reflections against the glass – a ghost of myself, almost translucent, looking back.

I switched on the kitchen light. I already knew there was nobody there – I knew there was nobody anywhere – but still it scared me, that final moment, that final moment when someone could have been hiding, waiting for me. The light flickered a little then brightened the room. Nothing.

But that noise – I was sure I had heard something. And what had woken me up?

As I went back into the through-lounge, my feet crunched against something sharp, and I jerked my foot back and looked down. There was a wineglass on the carpet, broken into fragments. I felt a sharp pain in my foot, and saw blood welling up between my toes. I pulled out a chair, sat down and turned my foot over to look at the sole. There was a small piece of glass caught between two of my toes. I pulled it out, carefully so it didn't splinter. The cut stung. It was only a small cut, a clean slice, but the blood was bright as it expanded across my skin – so much blood from such a small wound. I balanced my weight on my heel, toes pointing upwards, and fetched a roll of kitchen towel. I held a piece against the cut and watched my blood colour the paper. The woman in the shop, Davinder, had used kitchen towel against the cut on my head. That reminded me; I looked across at the window, but there was no face peering in.

And then I wondered how the glass had broken. I had put it on the table before going to bed, and it had been fine when I went upstairs, I was certain of it. So what had made it fall? Had someone been creeping through my house? Had I really heard someone getting inside? And what would have happened if I hadn't woken up?

It was suddenly very cold in the house. I tried not to think about the sorts of headlines that would have appeared in the paper the next day – the sorts of stories I had read; women tied up and robbed and raped and murdered, women beaten in their own homes, women attacked and left for dead. And who would come to find me? I was alone – the full extent of my isolation struck me.

I hobbled over to the phone, stood looking at the moulded plastic, the flimsy wire that represented my link to the rest of the world. I wondered who I should ring, what I should say. I realized that I wanted someone to rescue me; someone to take control, to push back the unknown, to puncture this isolation. Someone who could make the world safe and predictable again. I could phone the police – it was their job to keep me safe – but I didn't think they would understand, I didn't think they would know what it would take to make this feeling go away. And anyway, they would only tell me I had imagined it, nobody was breaking in, they would send a patrol car past when they had time but they were so busy, too busy. And what if they told Dave Short? They were bound to tell him, and PC Andrews would say I had phoned earlier, and what would he think, what would he read into that? Even if he came round, all he would say was that nobody had broken in, and the glass had probably just fallen from the table, and victims do get paranoid, they do start imagining things, and did I want help from Victim Support? But I wasn't a victim, not like that; I didn't want strangers telling me I needed to rebuild my confidence. I was strong, I should be able to cope; and yet, all it had taken was one minor incident to make me realize that I wasn't quite strong enough.

I lowered myself into the armchair with my cut foot raised off the floor and phoned Alex's house. I had to let it ring for a long time before anyone answered, and when they did, they sounded sleepy, and irritated.

'Alex?' I asked.

'Yeah,' he said, and then seemed to wake himself up. 'That Jo? What's the matter?'

I told him about the noises I had heard, and

the broken glass, and cutting my foot. He listened patiently, and then he said, 'But nobody's got into the house?'

'I don't know,' I said. 'Maybe they have – maybe they're hiding, waiting for me upstairs?'

He was silent for a moment, and I wondered whether he was thinking about that, about coming round and finding me murdered, and how he would deal with that, how he would feel. I could imagine him telling people, 'Yeah, she was my ex, my closest friend, she got killed by a burglar, she phoned me, she was terrified, but by the time I got there it was already too late.' I imagined the kind of sympathy he would get for that tragic story, the women who would want to comfort him, would want to help him deal with such a traumatic experience by talking, and cuddling, and maybe more.

Alex said, 'Have you been drinking?'

'No!'

'You're not stoned? Or speeding?'

'No,' I said. 'No, of course not.' Because how could he think such things, and how guilty would he feel later for having said those words, for having doubted me? I said, 'Alex, I'm scared,' and there was a crack in my voice that even he must have heard.

'Okay, okay, I'm sorry. There're no windows open, are there? Nothing like that?'

'Not that I can see,' I said, and then the cold overtook me in a sudden shudder, and I knew I was close to crying. I didn't want to cry right now.

'Have you called the police?'

'And say what? They won't come, I called them the other night, remember?'

There was another long silence. I imagined that now, right now, was when the thought process about my murder was kicking in, when he would feel its real effect. He said, 'What do you want me to do?' but there was reluctance in his tone.

'I don't know,' I said, because, after all, he was the one who had berated me for not calling after his party, when I had been so freaked out then, and what was different now?

'Christ, it's ten past three, Jo.'

'I know,' I said. 'I'm sorry. I'm scared.'

'Okay.' He sighed. 'Okay, I'll come round. I'll be there soon, hold on.'

I was still saying thank you as he hung up. The house felt cold and empty around me as soon as I had finished talking to him. I examined the cut on my foot, but it was more so I didn't have to look at the house, at the big empty spaces around me that could be filled with attackers, with people emerging from hiding places, with people who had only one aim, one motivation. On cue, the cut on my head started to ache, and when I flexed my foot the cut between my toes gave a sharp twinge and started to bleed again.

I tried to take a deep breath. I thought about Alex on his way to rescue me. I thought about him reaching the house, finding the door open, seeing me lying there. I tried to breathe, tried not to think about someone being in the house, hearing them approach me, turning, seeing them standing over me.

Alex would get here. Alex would be here soon. But what if he was too late?

Ten or fifteen minutes passed. I was wide awake, wired, alert to every sound, to every creak of the house or hiss of the central heating, to every distant car that could be Alex arriving, to every sound in the street that could be a prowler but was more likely a cat. I would begin to settle, begin to feel less frightened, begin to regret phoning Alex and dragging him out of his bed, and then another noise would come, something it took a moment to identify, and in that moment the fear flooded back through me, and I was glad that Alex was coming, I was glad he would arrive soon, soon enough to rescue me.

I was cold, but I didn't want to get up to put the fire on. I wanted a cigarette, but they were in my handbag on its hook in the hall. I wanted a drink, anything, to take my mind off whatever might happen, all the possibilities, the things that had happened to other women at other times; had they all felt like this?

Finally, I heard Alex's car draw up outside, and his door slam, and then he was coming up the garden path. I hobbled to the front door, putting my weight on the heel of the cut foot, and reached out to unbolt the door. But then it occurred to me that maybe someone would be waiting for this moment – maybe they would overpower Alex, attack us both, maybe kill us both, and what would happen then?

I forced those thoughts out of my mind, opened the door to allow Alex in and locked and bolted the door after him.

'Are you okay?' he said. 'You look freaked.'

'I am freaked,' I said. 'I'm sure someone's out there, I'm sure they're after me, they're trying to get in the house, and if you hadn't come maybe they would have got in and nobody would have been here and what would I have done then, I'm only short, I'm not strong enough to fight—'

'Stop,' he cried. 'Stop, stop.' And he caught my wrists in his hands and stopped me flailing about as I spoke. 'Nothing's going to happen, is it? I'm here now, it's okay. You've just got freaked, that's all.'

'I know,' I said, and I wanted to explain how I would have been found the next day, when I didn't show up for work. They would have phoned and got no reply; they would have said I was sleeping in, or had forgotten to tell them about a case visit, and later someone would say it was odd that I hadn't phoned, it was odd that I hadn't been in. And someone would try phoning again, and after a while someone would say they should come to my house to check everything was okay, because what if I was ill in bed, or had fallen down the stairs and broken my leg and couldn't get to the phone, someone ought to check. I could imagine them – Colin, perhaps – coming up to my front door, finding it slightly ajar, pushing it open, calling my name as they came into the hall. I could imagine him walking into the front room and finding me on the floor, my head bashed in, a bloody mess of skull and brains. Or upstairs, in bed, with signs of a struggle, the bedclothes kicked and wrapped around my feet, a ligature made from a bra or tights taken from the floor by the killer. Or in the bathroom, feet seen first as he came into the room, stab wounds, a gaping wound in my stomach, and pools of blood coagulating on the lino.

'Calm down,' Alex said. 'Everything's fine, okay?' He was guiding me into the front room, his hands against my elbows, a guiding figure behind me, and lowered me onto the sofa. He sat down next to me. 'Take deep breaths,' he said. 'You'll feel better.'

I took deep breaths, but they caught against the knot of fear rising in my throat.

'I'll get you some water,' he said. 'Stay there.'

I watched him go to the kitchen and heard the tap run. He came back offering the glass of water in front of him. I took it and drank a long sip.

He said, 'Do you want me to check round the house for you?'

I had a sudden flash of memory of Dave Short saying the same thing. I forced the memory back. 'Would you mind?'

'Course not.'

He went to the front window, pulled back the curtains and put his weight against the glass. It didn't budge. I followed him to the back window and he did the same. I leaned in the kitchen doorway, sipping my water as he checked the kitchen window and then unlocked the back door, opened it and examined the lock.

'Someone's had a go at this,' he said.

The nausea rose up through me again. I went over to him, looked at where he indicated. There were scrape marks along the paintwork, running under the metal handle, and the metal was twisted as if someone had inserted a screwdriver as a lever to prise the lock apart.

'Can't tell if it's recent,' he said. 'But anyway, the door was locked, so they didn't get in, did they?'

'No,' I said. He sounded pleased that nobody had got in, as if that proved that I was actually safe, but that seemed a little presumptuous to me – after all, if someone had tried to get in, that wasn't a lot better than someone succeeding. I remembered the broken glass on the carpet. If someone hadn't got in, how could that be explained?

Alex re-locked and re-bolted the back door and then went through to the hall. He opened the front door and examined the lock there, but shut the door and rammed the bolt home without saying anything. I followed him up the stairs. In the bathroom, he rattled the window and nodded approval. In the spare room, he did the same thing. He hesitated before going into my bedroom – I wasn't sure why. But then he went in, and the bedside light was still on, and he went to the window and opened the curtains and looked out quickly at the street before checking the window panes.

He turned and smiled at me. 'You see? It's all okay. There's nothing wrong.'

'There was the scrape on the back door,' I said.

'Yes, but that could have been done at any time.'

His expression didn't betray his thoughts. I was seized by the need to have him understand – to see some sort of concern, some sort of fear in his expression. I said, 'What about the broken wine-glass?'

'Chances are it just fell.'

I knew he was probably right, but it didn't help. A part of me wanted him to be wrong – wanted something more to happen, just so he would know how I felt. I wanted him to feel the same way, even as I was comforted by his certainty of my safety.

He must have seen that I was still rattled, because he said, 'Hey, hey,' and wrapped his arms around me. I lay my head against his chest, and felt the warmth of his body and the regularity of his breath. 'Don't worry about it, Jo. We all get spooked occasionally, and you're here on your own, and you're still shaken by the attack, it's no wonder you get scared sometimes. It's nothing to be ashamed of. It's perfectly natural.'

I could feel that I was close to tears, and tried to hold the tears back. It felt good, to be so close to him, to feel his warmth. I thought about Louise – had he left her in his bed to come and play the knight in shining armour for me? Would he have done the same, would he have rushed through the night to offer comfort if it had been Louise who had phoned him? But Louise wouldn't have phoned, I knew that – she would probably think even less of me if she knew that I had phoned Alex. She would have been strong enough to cope, she would have known what to do and what to say to the police to get them to take her seriously.

Alex gave me a squeeze and then released me. 'You should go back to bed. You need some sleep before work.'

I said, 'What are you going to do?'

For a moment, I thought he was going to say he would drive back home, and if he had said that I would have known that she was waiting for him, she was keeping the bed warm until he got back. Part of me wanted him to go – I wanted him to think that I was as strong as she was, that I could cope with this situation – but I didn't want to be alone, and I didn't want to find out that he thought I had nothing to be afraid of.

He said, 'I'll sleep in the spare room, if that's okay.'

'Yes,' I said. 'Yes, of course.'

'Okay. Get into bed, then.'

I felt like a little kid again, like a little kid being tucked in by my father. I took off my dressing gown and climbed under the bed covers, and he leaned over me and smoothed the covers down, and I looked up at him and smiled. He smiled back, but I couldn't tell if it was because he felt the analogy, too.

Then he said, 'Well, nighty-night.'

'Nighty-night,' I replied, still grinning.

He walked round the bed and switched off the bedside lamp, then went out onto the landing and pulled the bedroom door shut behind him. I lay there in the warm darkness, and I could still feel the weight of his hand against the covers; I didn't want to move in case I lost that sensation of weight, that sensation of being anchored down. I could hear him creeping around the house, but the sounds of movement didn't scare me any more.

Nineteen

I didn't sleep properly for the rest of the night, and at half past six I gave up the pretence and got up. I had intended to look through my filofax and plan the day at work, but I couldn't face thinking about anything that might remind me of Sean Metcalfe and the situation that seemed to be unravelling around me. Instead, I made some toast and a mug of tea and sat in front of the breakfast news.

Alex joined me shortly after seven. He looked tired and his clothes were crumpled as if he'd slept in them, but the first thing he said was, 'How are you?'

'Fine.' I forced a yawn. 'Didn't sleep well.' I felt awkward now, in broad daylight – my fears of the night before had shrunk back and I could see just how far out of proportion I had blown everything. I said, 'Listen, I'm sorry about last night. I shouldn't have called you.'

'It's okay, you did the right thing.' But there wasn't much enthusiasm in his tone.

'Were you with Louise?'

He flushed. 'Yes. I don't think she understood. I'll have to do some fast explaining.'

I nodded, digesting that. He had left Louise to come to my rescue. He had risked annoying Louise to help me out. I wasn't sure whether I should feel triumphant or guilty. I said, 'Well, tell her about the scrape on the back door, that might convince her.'

He shrugged. 'She thought you should've called the police.' Then he hesitated before asking, 'Why didn't you?'

'I told you,' I said. 'They wouldn't've come. They didn't come the other night.'

'But if you'd said—'

I wasn't in the mood for this. 'Believe me, they wouldn't come. Anyway, you said before that I should've phoned you.'

'I know, I know.'

I realized that he regretted saying that; he was thinking he had trapped himself into being on standby for any future emergency. I didn't want him to feel that way – the last thing I wanted was for anyone to feel obliged to help me. But I remembered how I felt the night before; how weak I had been, how much I had needed his – anyone's – strength. I hated myself for that weakness, but I didn't know what I could do about it.

He said, 'Why didn't you contact Dave Short?'

There was still the trace of bitterness in his voice. I wanted to say I couldn't have done at three o'clock in the morning, but I had after all disturbed Alex, so I said, 'I didn't think he'd be on duty.'

'He didn't look very on-duty last time I came round here. Or are bottles of wine part of victim support procedures these days?'

I tried not to be stung by that. 'There was nothing to it,' I said. 'We were just talking.'

He didn't dispute that, but I could tell that he didn't really believe me. I wondered what he was thinking – that I had been trying to make him jealous? That I had pulled a policeman and now felt embarrassed about asking the police for help? That I was playing some kind of convoluted game that would result in him losing Louise?

He got up suddenly. 'Right, well, I'd better get home.'

'What, now?' I said, surprised.

'Yup. Grab a shower before work.'

Grab Louise more like, I thought, but I kept that to myself. He didn't bother asking if I was going to be okay, but I was relieved that he didn't – I had already had enough of feeling weak.

After he had gone, I went into the kitchen and examined the back door. In daylight, the damage looked less pronounced and I couldn't tell how recent it was. There were burglaries all the time in my area – it could have happened at any time, it was hardly a sign that my fears of the night before had been well-founded. After all, I didn't often go into the back garden in the winter, and even when I did, I couldn't remember ever examining the lock.

I didn't really want to think about any of it, and staying in the house only made matters worse, so I gathered my things together and headed off to the office early. I was the first one there, apart from Douglas, who was sitting in his office with the door open, working through an intimidating pile of paperwork. I put my head round his door to say good morning and announce that I was there, and I was about to return to my desk when he called me into the office and came over and shut the door.

'We haven't had a chance to talk recently,' he said. 'Sit down for a few minutes, tell me how things are going.'

He sounded unusually friendly, and as I sat down I wondered what had been said to him, and whether Colin had decided to take the Adams matter into his own hands. But I gave a half-friendly, half-professional smile, and we chatted a little about workloads and backlogs and the continuing impact of the Chantelle Wade enquiry.

Finally, when I guessed he thought there had been enough casual chat, he said, 'And how's the head now?'

'Oh, fine. Hardly notice it any more. Should be completely healed soon.'

He nodded. 'And how are you finding it, going out on the streets? I know other people have found that difficult after violent incidents.'

I wondered whether I should tell him about the nightmares I'd been having, and the sickness I felt, but I wasn't sure that I wanted to discuss these things with him, not when he already thought I lacked professional distance. So I said, 'I was a bit shaky at first, and I haven't been sleeping particularly well, but it's getting better, and I'm sure it'll pass soon.'

'That's the spirit.' But he held my gaze for slightly longer than was necessary. 'Have the police found out who it was yet?'

If Colin had spoken to him, Douglas wasn't giving anything away. I said, 'No, nothing definite. They're still looking into it.'

'It's Dave Short who's dealing with it, isn't it?' I nodded, and he continued, 'A nice guy, Dave Short. Dealt with some of our more difficult cases. A little more understanding than some of his colleagues.' He allowed himself a small smile at that, but didn't elaborate. Then he said, 'I hear you've been getting on well with him.'

'What do you mean?'

He laughed, but it seemed like a calculated sort of laugh. 'You know what the department's like. Everyone knows everyone else's business. The police are just as bad. People can't help themselves, can they?'

I summoned coolness into my tone. 'Well, there's nothing for them to talk about. He's a nice guy, like you said, but there's nothing more to it.'

Douglas backed away, holding up his hands in mock surprise. 'I didn't say there was,' he said, but he still had a playful expression on his face. 'Just what I heard, that's all.'

My brain seemed to be working too slowly. 'Who did you hear this from?'

'Who? Oh, I don't know.' The smile was fading

from his lips now. 'I didn't think you'd be so touchy or I wouldn't have mentioned it.'

'It must have been from Alex,' I said. 'Or from someone in his office.' I was aware that Douglas was watching me now, with a little frown on his face, but I had to figure this out. If Alex had said something and it got back to Dave Short . . . I remembered PC Andrews's coolness on the phone. If Dave Short thought . . . but who would tell him, and who would believe anything Alex said about me? And yet, the rumour had got back to Douglas.

Douglas said, 'I didn't think you'd take it this way.'

'Yeah? What way did you think I'd take it?' I regretted the words as soon as I had said them, but there was no way to take them back. I rubbed my hand over my face and softened my tone and said, 'I'm sorry, I didn't mean that the way it sounded.'

'You're just stressed,' Douglas said, and his voice was kinder.

I didn't look at him. I wanted to tell him about the Metcalfes, and about Katie Adams, but I wasn't sure how he would take it.

Douglas went on, 'Maybe you're not coping as well as we thought, eh? Maybe you need help with your caseload, take off some of the pressure until you're back on form?'

Everyone would love that, I thought – me ducking out of my responsibilities, piling the work on them. 'I'm not the only one who's stressed,' I said.

'Yes, but if you're not coping—'

'I'm coping just fine,' I said.

'There's no shame in asking for help,' Douglas said. 'We're all a team here. People help out when they're needed, that's the way it works.' I tried to smile, but I was thinking that people would be far from happy to help me out when everyone was in the same situation. I didn't need help. I was about to say so when Douglas continued, 'There's no shame in needing a hand now and then.' He was leaning back in his chair, looking at me with an expression I guessed was meant to be sympathetic. 'Everyone needs a little support from time to time. It's only natural.'

I wasn't in the mood for platitudes. 'I can cope just as well as anyone else can. I just didn't sleep too well last night, that's all.'

'It's very easy to let things get on top of you,' Douglas said. 'It's happened to you before, after all.'

'Oh, great,' I said. 'Drag up ancient history, why don't you? That was years ago. I can cope perfectly well now, thank you very much.'

'I know, I know.' He was trying to be soothing with his voice, but it sounded forced. I was suddenly glad that I hadn't told him more about what was happening with the Metcalfes and the Adams.

I gathered my faculties. 'I wouldn't want to put any more pressure on the team, not at the moment. I didn't sleep too well last night, but once I've had some coffee and woken up it'll be fine. I came in early this morning to get my head around some cases, and once I've done that it'll all be okay. You just caught me off guard, talking about PC Short like that. I didn't realize anything so innocent could start a rumour, but now that you've told me, you can spread the word that it isn't true, can't you?'

I had spoken in a very calm, reasoning voice, and it must have had the right effect, because he sat back in his seat with a little smile and said, 'Good. I'm glad to hear it. It's good to know I can rely on you, Jo. I should really let you get on with your work.'

If he didn't really believe me, he gave no outward sign of it. I decided to take his words at face value. I got up and went to the door. When I had my hand on the handle, he said, 'I'm glad we had this little chat.'

Forcing a smile, I went out, pulling the door shut carefully behind me. I went back to my desk. The work was piled up in my in-tray, and there were more folders in my desk drawer, and there were all the files in my briefcase, and I had to finish reports and start on the next batch of visits, and there were a couple of case conferences coming up that I hadn't prepared for. I put my head in my hands and pretended to be looking at the file that was open on my desk. Gradually, the office started to fill up, and I could hear everyone talking and the jokes starting and the phones ringing, but I sat there for a long time, looking down at the paperwork, nodding and smiling at people as they said good morning, nodding and smiling as if everything was okay, but it wasn't, it wasn't. The paperwork was just going to multiply, and it didn't matter how long I sat here, how many times I reorganized and reprioritized, how many files I took home and how many weekends I spent on the stuff, I was never going to get through all the work. And out there, in the streets, the whole world was clammering for attention, waiting for us to solve their problems for them, and what could I do, how could I help, when I couldn't even sort my own life out?

I knew that I had to get out of the office. I was supposed to be in all morning, catching up on paperwork, but there were so many other people there, there was so much to be done and I didn't want to touch any of it. I wanted to get out into the wide open air, away from all the sour traffic fumes and the noise and all the cramped spaces. I wanted to see a clear blue sky and breathe air so clean it didn't taste of anything, so clean it felt icy cold in my lungs.

Shoving my filofax into my bag, I wrote on the whiteboard that I was off to see a client who I knew would not blow my cover by phoning the office while I was out. Nobody seemed to notice me leave. It was a dull, overcast sort of a day, and the vague plan I'd had to go driving out into the countryside didn't seem like such a good idea once I was in my car, negotiating the traffic. Besides, although I'd skived off work for a couple of hours on previous occasions, leaving the city boundaries felt a little too much like pushing my luck.

So I drove slowly through the city centre and

looped back round and out towards the northern outskirts. I was thinking as I drove, replaying the conversation with Douglas, trying to work out what exactly he had meant, how concerned he was about what was going on, how much was being said in the rumour about me and Dave Short. Alex was the only one who could possibly have said anything about Dave, and as I contemplated that, my anger grew. He had no right to even comment on my social life, let alone start rumours.

So I turned abruptly and headed towards his office, on the edge of the city. It was market day in Bulwell and the traffic was moving at a slow crawl over the railway bridge and round past the Market Square, but eventually I pulled into the car park at the side of his office.

Selima was just showing a client out as I entered the reception area. I hadn't seen her since Alex's party; I couldn't remember if she had still been there when Alex and I had argued. She seemed surprised to see me, and I wondered how much of my life Alex had discussed with her, what sort of impression she had of my situation. She said, 'If you're after Alex, he isn't in. Phoned in sick this morning.'

'Oh,' I said, and then covered up my surprise. I didn't want even more gossip to be spread about me. 'Oh, well, never mind, I'm sure I'll speak to him soon anyway.'

Selima didn't say anything to that, but adopted a sympathetic sort of expression as I escaped the office and went back to my car. Alex had obviously decided he needed a day off. I could imagine it – Louise had probably phoned in sick, too; they were probably spending the day in bed and sod all the things they should have been doing. I considered going round to his house, demanding to know what he had said about me and Dave Short, but I knew that would be a bad idea. Louise had probably already got her claws into him about my phoning in the early hours – the last thing I should do was make that situation worse.

I sat there in the driver's seat in the car park for a long time, trying to work out what I should do next. My eyes ached from lack of sleep; I would have loved to go home and sleep, or get horrendously drunk, or stoned – anything that would wipe out the way I was feeling. But I had to go back to work eventually, and I already felt too out of my head to deal with that.

I thought about my house, about Sean Metcalfe creeping around, peering through windows, testing locks and hinges. I wanted to know what was going on; I felt I was entitled to know. Was he tormenting me just for the fun of it? Did he have some master plan? Or was this just paranoia, just the aftershock of violent crime?

Putting the car in gear, I headed back towards the office. I was too strong to be beaten, I realized that. I thought about the Sean I had known years before; the skinny, foul-mouthed boy kicking out at the world while his mother whined and cried in the background. I was stronger than that.

And it wasn't right that he was being allowed to

affect my life. It wasn't right that he could do this to me and not have to face the consequences of his actions. Indignation – fury – surged through me at the thought that he was acting with impunity, and I was helpless to stop him.

I was driving down Radford Road, and as I reached the police station a sudden impulse made me pull off the road and stop in the car park. I sat steadying my breath for a moment, trying to think – but why shouldn't I demand to know what the police were doing to protect me? They had a duty, and I had every right to demand answers from them.

There were a few people waiting in the reception area of the police station, slumped in chairs with arms folded as if they had been there for a long time. I went to the policeman behind the counter and asked if I could speak to PC Short.

'I'll check if he's in,' he said as he picked up a phone and punched in a number. I looked around at the people already waiting, at their dull lack of interest, as if they had used up any curiosity they might once have had.

'What's your name?' the policeman asked. I gave it, and he repeated it down the phone with no trace of having recognized the name. Maybe the rumours hadn't reached here yet, I thought.

'Take a seat,' the policeman said. 'He'll be down in a minute.'

I took a seat between a teenaged lad in dirty jeans and an even dirtier denim jacket and an old man wrapped up in a ratty brown overcoat that smelled of cigarettes and urine and cheap white cider. Up on the wall, a clock ticked. I shifted in my seat. Behind the smell of the old man was that institutional smell of polish and cheap furniture that always made me think of waiting rooms, and interviews, and clients crying.

I wondered what I could say to Dave when he appeared. I wanted him to be pleased to see me, in a professional way – pleased that I was there but not reading anything into it. I wanted to find out that he had been thinking about me, with slight concern but not worry, with a certain fondness but nothing indicating interest. And he had spent time in my house – we had listened to music, and drunk wine, and we had laughed at each other's jokes – why shouldn't we enjoy each other's company, why did it have to be complicated by anything else?

The security door opened. Dave gave me a professional sort of smile and said, 'Jo, come through.'

I followed him through the security door and down a narrow corridor, then into an interview room. There was a table in the centre of the room, and four chairs. The window was a slit of frosted glass high up in the wall. The room smelled faintly of sweat.

Dave had pushed the door shut behind him and now he looked at me and said, 'What can I do for you, Jo?'

There was little sign of friendliness. I found myself stumbling over my words. 'I just wanted to know if you were any further forward,' I said.

'Not really.' He didn't seem concerned by the lack of progress. 'We'll pick Sean Metcalfe up eventually.'

I nodded, not sure what to say next. I wasn't sure what I had wanted him to say.

He said, 'Has something happened?'

'Yes. Well, I think so.' And I explained about hearing noises in the night, and the damage to the back door lock, but I didn't mention the broken glass, or that I had called Alex round.

He listened, but I wasn't convinced that he was giving my account the attention I felt it warranted. I wanted to shout at him, demand to know why they weren't scouring the streets for Sean Metcalfe, how it was that a nineteen-year-old lad could evade them for so long, how they expected me to feel when they weren't offering me the protection I felt I deserved. I was a taxpayer, after all – they should be taking this more seriously.

Dave said, 'You probably scared off whoever it was when you came downstairs. There's not much we can do about it. I mean, you didn't see anyone, and nothing actually happened.'

'But it could've been Sean. He might still be after me.'

'Is there anything that leads you to believe that might be the case?'

He wasn't making proper eye contact with me, I noticed. I wondered whether the rumours had got back to him, whether he thought I was playing games. I wanted to tell him that I wasn't, that there

209

was nothing for him to feel awkward about, but I didn't know how I could phrase that.

I said, 'He hit me – isn't that enough?' I could see that he was about to say something about unplanned attacks, and how it was unlikely to be anything more than that, so I added quickly, 'There's just too much stuff. I mean, the damage to your car, and now someone trying to break into my house. How can you say it isn't connected?'

'But it probably isn't,' he said. Then, more kindly, 'I think you're getting overwrought, Jo. You need to find a way to relax. Have you talked to the Victim Support people?'

I was tired of him mentioning them. 'I don't need that sort of help. I need you to find Sean Metcalfe. How difficult can it be?'

'We don't even know if he's still in Nottingham,' he said. 'We've had intelligence that he's left the city.'

'One of my clients has seen him.'

'In the last couple of days?' It didn't sound like a real question. 'I'm sorry, Jo, but we can't spare all our resources to chase a teenage boy who probably isn't even in the city.'

I stared at him. 'But he attacked me.'

'You're not certain it's him, though, are you?' He gave a little sigh, as if he was tired of explaining this to me. 'We do have other priorities.'

I could feel the energy seeping out of me. I couldn't believe I had ever enjoyed this man's company – he wasn't concerned about me, and probably never had been. He didn't have a clue what I was going through – I had been a fool to think otherwise. I said, 'Look, fine, if that's all you've got to say, I might as well go.'

I started towards the door. He said, 'Jo, don't be like that.'

'How do you expect me to be? I'm telling you this is happening, and you're telling me it's not a big enough priority. How am I supposed to react?'

I pulled open the door and headed back towards the entrance area. He followed behind me – I heard him call my name, but I didn't want to stop, I could feel tears swelling in my throat and filling my eyes and I didn't want him to see that, I didn't want anyone to see that I was scared. At the security door, I tried to work out how to open it but couldn't see the release catch.

He arrived at my elbow and put his hand over the release button on the wall. 'Calm down,' he said. 'I never said it wasn't a big enough priority.'

I knew the moment I turned he would see the tears in my eyes, and that would only confirm his opinion that I wasn't coping, and needed help. I wanted to shout at him that I didn't need help, it wasn't my problem, it wasn't down to how I felt, it was down to Sean Metcalfe still being out there, terrifying me, and their not doing anything about it. I glanced across at his hand, cupped over the release catch.

I steadied my voice and said, 'Let me go, will you? I've got to get back to work.'

He said, 'Jo—' but didn't continue the sentence. Then he let out a long sigh and pressed the release button. I heard the lock click open, and pushed my way out into the reception area. At the street I glanced back, but he had already retreated behind the door.

Twenty

Even after I had bolted my front door I didn't feel that warm, safe, homecoming feeling. The house enclosed me, solid brick walls on either side, but there were windows front and back, and doors, and the locks were so flimsy, and glass could be broken, and whatever Dave said I was certain that Sean Metcalfe was out there somewhere, watching, waiting for his opportunity.

I stood at the front window. The street appeared to be empty, but how could I be sure? It was still light outside but the colours were fading to a blue tint as evening drew in. When it was dark I wouldn't be able to see the street; I wouldn't be able to tell who was in the shadows.

I pulled the curtains shut; at least he wouldn't be able to watch me move around the house. Then I went round closing all the other curtains, pulling down the blinds in the bathroom and the kitchen, double-checking that the latches were secure. The house was very quiet, holding its breath, but I didn't want to play music in case I covered up the sound of someone breaking in.

Clare Littleford

It was going to be a long weekend. There was no way I would sleep, not while I was waiting for whatever was going to happen.

So I uncorked a bottle of wine and sat with the TV on, volume turned down low, and I smoked and drank and waited. The wine was heavy and sour in my mouth, but I drank on towards oblivion, because what else was there, what other comfort was there?

I was three-quarters of the way down the first bottle and halfway through my first packet of cigarettes when I heard a car pull up outside, and the car door opening and then clumping shut, and footsteps coming up the path towards my door. I waited. The doorbell rang. I considered hiding, pretending I was out until they went away, but they rang the bell again, and then the letterbox flap was lifted and I heard Dave's voice calling my name, calling, 'Jo? Are you in there?'

I got up and went to the front door. Before I could change my mind, I drew back the bolts, turned the latch and opened the door.

He was out of uniform again. I stood looking at him. He said, 'Are you going to let me in?'

I just shrugged, but stepped back from the door. I was slightly drunk already. He followed me into the front room, took in the wineglass on the floor, and the full ashtray, and the amount of wine left in the bottle. He said, 'I take it you're feeling stressed?'

'I'm trying to get out of my skull,' I said. 'I want to forget about everything.'

He allowed himself a short laugh. 'And me coming round isn't going to help that, is it?'

I just shrugged again, slumped down onto the sofa and lit another cigarette.

He sat down in the armchair. 'Why did you storm off like that?'

'I didn't storm off,' I said. 'I was just frustrated.'

'Well, what did you expect from us?'

Us. That bit into me. I wanted to say that I didn't expect anything from them in the plural, I had just wanted some reassurance and that wasn't a group activity. Instead, I said, 'I don't want to talk about it.'

He considered that. 'Moping around the house isn't going to help, is it?'

'What's it to you?'

I had expected him to take offence at that – I think I had wanted him to take offence. But he didn't. He said, 'I could do with a pint. Come to the pub with me.'

'Which pub?'

'I don't know. Any pub. The closest pub. Get yourself out of this house.'

I wanted to refuse. I wanted to still be angry, but I couldn't find the energy. So I agreed, and we headed off onto Sherwood Rise, the Star Inn, which was a bad choice really but better than the other options around. The place was half full; a few students had crept in among the old men who made up most of the regulars. Dave sent me to sit down at a table by the window and came back from the bar with two pints of lager.

'Right,' he said, when he was settled. 'Are you going to tell me why you think Sean Metcalfe has it in for you?'

I was surprised. 'I don't know why.'

'But you're pretty convinced he's after you. You must have some idea.'

'No,' I said. 'Not really.'

'Not really?'

'Not at all, then,' I said. I took a long sip of my pint. Trying to think had made me very – and coldly – sober.

He leaned back in his seat, seeming to consider something. Then he said, 'I asked Carla Metcalfe about it.'

'You did what?' I took another gulp of beer. 'When?'

'This afternoon. I went round to see her, after you stormed out. She had no idea Sean was being accused of attacking you.'

'So she says,' I said. 'He must've told her what he'd done.'

He just shrugged. 'Well, she wasn't going to admit to me that she'd seen him, was she? But she did say she'd seen you. Told me all about your little visit, you and Colin Fuller. I don't get it, Jo,' he said, and now he was looking at me, puzzled, as if he really couldn't figure it out. 'If you think her son's after you, why go round to her house?'

'I had to,' I said. 'For my client.'

'You could've got Colin Fuller to go alone. You didn't have to go yourself.' He was watching me closely now, and I wondered what he thought he was going to find out. But then he changed tack, abruptly. 'Carla told me about what happened eight years ago.'

I was feeling slightly dizzy, and I remembered that I hadn't had anything to eat. I took another sip of beer and tried to concentrate on what Dave was saying. 'What about eight years ago?'

'She said you were cracking up. She said you looked like you were on the edge, about to have a breakdown the way she tells it, and when she asked for someone else to take over the case, you flipped out and told her she was causing trouble.' He hesitated. 'The way she tells it, you got nasty with her.'

'No, no,' I said. 'It wasn't like that. I was stressed, yeah, that's true, but I never said anything to her. She wanted someone else to take over because she thought I was too young. Inexperienced. She was always saying I didn't know what I was doing, but she was just being difficult. Didn't want to admit that her husband was abusive. Kept telling me everything was fine. I believed her at first. She can be very persuasive.' I stopped, took another mouthful of beer. Dave was waiting for me to say more. 'Eventually I realized she was covering up for him, and that's when she kicked up a storm. If I'd known he was going to drop dead a couple of weeks later I'd never have said anything. You know how people get – the second someone's dead they go from being a selfish bastard to one miracle short of sainthood. That's why my line manager assigned someone else to the case; the department didn't want to be accused of insensitivity to a bereaved woman's wishes.'

'That's not how she tells it.'

'Well, it wouldn't be, would it? She's bound to twist it all so she comes out looking wonderful.'

'She told me you grabbed Sean and pushed him against the wall.'

That did make me laugh. 'An eleven-year-old kid? I don't think so.'

Dave didn't say anything.

'Oh, c'mon. You know what these cases are like. She had to blame someone for the situation. Much easier to blame me than face the real problem.'

'That's true,' he said. I let him consider for a moment, then he added, 'She's a bitter woman. Wants to blame someone for how Sean's turned out. It's understandable. Sad, but understandable.'

'Sean going off the rails is not my fault,' I said.

'No, I know. But she thinks Sean changed when he went into care. Thinks that's what stopped her being able to control him. I can understand why she wants to blame you.'

I wanted to point out that Sean had been a problem before then, that was why we had got involved in the first place, but I suddenly couldn't see the point. These things never came down to being any one person's fault – life would be a lot easier if they did.

Dave leaned in across the table, as if afraid that

someone was going to overhear us, and said, 'She might try to cause trouble for you, if you keep pushing this.'

I met his gaze, trying to work out what he was saying. It seemed so ridiculous, it was just too stupid to be true, and he seemed to think – I had no idea what he thought. I said, 'How's she going to cause trouble for me? There's no truth to what she says. I'd've lost my job if that was true. She's the one with the son who attacked me. The son who's absconded from Glen Parva – Christ, what sort of trouble could she cause for me?'

He looked down at his pint glass as if he was thinking seriously about it, but there was a little smile on his face.

'You don't believe her, do you?'

He looked up at me then, ran his hand over his face, took a long sip of his drink. Then he said, 'Not really, no. But it would explain why he attacked you. How else would you explain it?'

'Random,' I said. 'Just a random thing. He was walking past and saw me and acted on impulse.'

'But if that's the case, why would he still be after you?'

That did throw me. The truth was, I didn't know why any of this was happening, I just knew that it was. I remembered suddenly that Davinder had told me that someone had been outside her shop that day, saying 'apologize'; someone had been demanding an apology. Had that been Sean? And if so, what could he possibly want me to apologize for?

I said, 'I don't know why he's after me, just that he is.' Dave was going to keep talking about this all night, I could see that, and I was fed up with it already. 'Can we change the subject?'

He shrugged and took another sip from his pint.

I said, 'It's the weekend. I want to forget about work. I want to forget about everything.'

'Well, you're going the right way about it.'

I couldn't tell whether he was disapproving or joking, but I decided to take that as a joke. I had finished my pint, so I said, 'Do you want another?'

He nodded, and drained his glass quickly. He looked tired, too, I realized – he was probably as relieved it was the weekend as I was. I went to the bar and ordered the drinks and some crisps, because I knew I had to try to soak up some of this alcohol somehow or I'd end up making a fool of myself. I was surprised to find that I cared what Dave thought of me. That reminded me of the rumour Douglas had mentioned that morning, and when I took the drinks back over and sat down and opened the crisps, I said, 'My line manager told me there's a rumour flying around about us.'

'About us?' He seemed surprised.

'Yeah. My ex must have said something, and then the Chinese Whispers – you know how these things are.'

He was frowning. 'What does this rumour say?'

'I don't know. That we're friendly, I suppose.'

He gave a short laugh, and I wondered what he found so funny. Then he said, 'Kelly Andrews said something, too. It's daft, though; I mean, there's nothing for people to talk about.'

'No,' I said. I had a sudden, reckless urge to suggest we give them something to talk about, but I swallowed that down.

Dave went on, 'I really hate that. People just assume that any time a man and woman talk to each other it means there's something going on. Why can't people just keep their dirty little thoughts to themselves?'

I was surprised at the strength of feeling in his voice. I took another sip of my pint and tried to work out if it meant anything, but my head was too light.

Dave said, 'They make everything sound so bloody sordid, don't they?'

He had looked up at me suddenly, and his eyes caught the light; a reflective, liquid brown. I felt cold. 'I know what you mean,' I said, but I couldn't summon much feeling into my voice.

He gave another short laugh, then seemed to have made a decision. 'Come on,' he said. 'Drink up. Let's go somewhere else. Somewhere more lively than this.'

He indicated the whole room with a contemptuous jerk of his head. I looked around. Most of the students had gone and now the pub was occupied by a few old men, huddled over their pints, and friends of the staff leaning against the bar with listless boredom. I drank my drink as quickly as I could, but the beer didn't go down easily, not on top of all the wine I'd had, and he had to wait for me, adjusting his coat collar, looking at me with a frown.

Outside, I said, 'Where are we going?'

'I don't know. Anywhere.' He was looking around him, as if the answer would present itself to him. 'This is your area. You suggest somewhere.'

I thought about it. There was the Frog, but Colin Fuller drank in there, and besides, I didn't like it much. Or the Lion, but Simon and Alex liked that pub. 'Horse and Groom?' I suggested.

'Near the police station? I don't think so. How about the Lion, that's all right?'

I hesitated, but he was looking impatient. Friday night – Simon would be off in town with his union mates, and Alex was probably tucked up in bed with Louise. I tried to calculate the odds of Alex and Louise fancying a pint after all their exercise, but my head was spinning so much that I couldn't think straight, and besides, I couldn't think of anywhere else. So I agreed, and he set off at such a fast pace down Northgate that I had to almost run to keep up with him. He had forced his hands into his jacket pockets and was walking with a purpose, almost an anger, it seemed.

'Slow down,' I said. 'I've only got little legs.'

He stopped and waited for me, and seemed to realize how unreasonable he was being, because he forced a smile onto his face and said in a tone that was intended to be light, 'It's all that wine, girl, not the length of your legs.'

I allowed myself to laugh at that. He linked his arm through mine, in a totally casual kind of a way, as if he was just helping me to walk although I wasn't anywhere near that drunk. At the pub, he held the door open for me, and I led him inside.

The place was crowded – the noise and heat of so many people thickened the air. There was a band playing a feeble cover version of 'Don't Look Back in Anger' at the far end of the room. We found a table in the furthest, darkest corner, tucked away near the fireplace with a coal fire burning in the grate, and I sat there while he went to the bar. The walk in the cold air seemed to have cleared my head a little, and as I warmed with the heat of the fire, I watched Dave and wondered how on earth I'd ended up coming in here with him. I was seized with a sudden panic – was this a date? Was he seeing this as a date? Was he going to walk me home at the end of the night and then try to kiss me on the doorstep – or worse, would he expect me to walk home alone? He had his car outside my house – but he wouldn't be able to drive, not by then, even now he probably wouldn't want to risk it. What was he planning? I wanted to ask him, but I didn't know how to phrase it, and I wasn't entirely sure what I wanted the answer to be.

And then I realized that he was talking to someone at the bar, and I recognized Alex. Louise was beside him. I watched Dave and Alex talk, their heads bowing towards each other, and then Dave indicated where I was sitting, and Alex and Louise were nodding, and the place was so crowded, of course they were going to join us, where else would they sit?

Dave brought our drinks over and settled himself next to me. 'I just bumped into Alex and his girl-friend. They're coming to join us.'

His tone didn't betray whether he was pleased or annoyed. I said, 'I didn't realize they'd be here.'

He shrugged and took a sip of his pint. 'How could you know what they were planning?' Then he glanced at me. 'Oh, you're not still thinking about that stupid rumour, are you? Honestly, people can think what they like, we know there's nothing to it.' He hesitated slightly, then said with a laugh, 'Even if there was, so what?'

Before I could react to that, Louise arrived at our table. She was wearing a heavy fake-fleece jacket, and as she shook that off I saw that she was clad in her usual Lycra trousers, but with a strappy little maroon silk camisole top that underlined the fact that she wasn't wearing a bra, she didn't need to, she was perfectly pert without one. I fixed a pleasant smile on my face. She reflected the same smile back and sat down on a stool across the table from Dave.

'So,' she said. 'How are you, Jo? Recovered from your scare last night, I hope?'

'Thanks to Alex. It was very good of you to let him leave like that.'

She held my gaze for a moment. 'Well, it's under-standable that you'd get worried, being on your own.'

Before I could reply, or Dave could intervene with the comment I could see he was preparing, Alex came to the table, set down his and Louise's drinks and sat on a stool opposite me. He looked around the table at all of us and said, 'Well, cheers, then.'

We all said cheers, and I took a long sip from my pint and tried not to look at Louise, or Dave. Which left me with Alex to look at. He looked well – something to do with the kind of day he'd had, I assumed. I said, 'I went to see you at your office this morning, but they said you were sick.'

He just grinned. 'Took the day off. I needed to go back to bed, after last night.'

Dave was frowning at me, and I remembered that I hadn't told him that Alex had come round when I had heard the attempted break-in. But he seemed to have worked it out for himself and didn't look too pleased. I reminded myself that it really wasn't anything to do with him.

The same thought seemed to occur to Dave, because he swallowed his expression, turned to Louise and started to talk to her. I heard him asking about her job, and she launched into some sort of convoluted explanation of what her department did. Dave was pretending to be interested, and Louise was so bloody self-obsessed she actually believed him.

Alex said to me, 'Why'd you come to see me, then?'

I gave a little laugh. 'Because Douglas told me

there was a rumour about me and a certain police-man getting too friendly, and I wanted to ask you about it. I wanted to convince you there was nothing to make a rumour out of.'

He looked surprised. 'I didn't think there was,' he said, but then he was glancing over towards Dave, who had leaned his head in slightly to hear what Louise was saying over the noise of the band. 'I didn't start any rumours,' he said.

'Well, someone in your office did.'

He frowned, then said, 'Oh, I know what it must've been. I was talking to Jill – you know Jill – she was asking after you, about the attack, and I said you were fine and had a friendly policeman paying house calls to check you were okay. That was all. I was just messing around, I didn't think she'd take that seriously.'

I didn't quite believe him, but I couldn't be bothered to challenge him. The band had just started a rendition of 'Run to You' that made Bryan Adams sound soulful, so I shrugged and smiled as if it didn't matter and waited for the music to stop bruising my eardrums. The band seemed to have a policy of playing so loud that the audience had no choice but to listen. The conversation died – drowned out – as I sipped my pint slowly, trying to work out what the hell we had to say to each other anyway. But that was churlish, I knew – I had to make an effort to get on with Louise, just for Alex's sake.

The evening wore on. The band calmed down a little but seemed determined to play until the last moment of drinking-up time, and my head had started a dull thumping that echoed the drummer's efforts. Louise had been regaling us with anecdotes – the kind of anecdotes that sounded so polished I wondered whether she rehearsed them in the mirror for maximum effect. Alex had an admiring expression on his face, his mouth open ready to laugh as he listened to her stories. Dave was looking interested, but at one point I caught him yawning. When he saw that I had seen, he grinned at me and squeezed my hand under the table. It was an innocent sort of squeeze, but when he released my hand I could still feel the pressure he had put against it, and the warmth of his skin.

The drink was having a serious effect on me, and I got to my feet and staggered off towards the toilets. It was brightly lit in there, and the music was muffled, but the thump in my head had grown heavier. I sat in the cubicle, trying to rub the effects out of my eyes, but I was drunk and there was nothing I could do about that. I thought that splashing some water on my face might help, but when I left the cubicle I found Louise in front of the mirror, applying more lipstick as if that really had been her aim in following me.

She turned to face me. 'All right?' she said, but she didn't sound particularly friendly.

'Fine.' I stood next to her to wash my hands.

She said, 'What is your problem, Jo?'

There was such aggression in her tone that I turned, surprised. 'I haven't got a problem,' I said.

'Yes, you have. You've been giving me filthy looks all night.' Before I could deny it, she added, 'Alex is with me now, so don't think you can weasel your way around him. He's not going to come running every time you claim to need him.'

I had to laugh at that. 'He was happy enough last night,' I said.

'Yeah,' she sneered, 'but who'd he come back to, eh?'

There was an unpleasant tilt to the way she held her head. I said, 'You can have him, anyway. I'm not interested.'

'Now you've got your little policeman friend, you mean?'

'That is none of your business,' I said.

I felt the anger rising up through me, and I knew I wouldn't be able to control it, so I pushed past her to get out into the pub again. I must have pushed more roughly than I intended, though, because she fell back against the sink with a thump. I heard her say, 'Bitch,' as the door swung shut behind me.

I took deep breaths as I headed back to my seat. Alex and Dave were laughing about something, and when I sat down Alex said, 'Why do women do that, Jo?'

'Do what?' I asked.

'Go to the loo in pairs.'

They were giggling about that, but I wasn't in the mood to humour them. I wondered if Alex had any idea what Louise was really like. I wanted to tell him, but he was smitten and I knew he wouldn't believe me.

I said to Dave, 'I want to go home.'

Dave looked at me with surprise. 'Okay, we'll go after this one.'

We all had most of a pint left. I took a sip from mine, trying to steady my thoughts, but the room was starting to spin a little and I needed air. Louise returned to the table and sat down, glancing at me but making no comment. I gritted my teeth and waited for Dave to be ready to leave. He was talking about football with Alex; they were both Forest fans, and were deep into nostalgia about standing on the terraces in the days before all-seater stadiums, and the classiness of the team under Cloughie, and the never-forgotten spell as European champions. I avoided eye contact with any of them.

Finally, Dave was ready to go, and I put on my coat and stood waiting while they talked about the prospects for next season and whether the club's finances made a return to the glory days impossible. Louise was sipping her drink, not looking at anyone. I wondered whether she was going to tell Alex about me pushing her, but I decided she probably wouldn't – she couldn't be sure that Alex would side with her yet.

Outside, the air had become damp and I huddled myself into my jacket as we walked. The cold air helped – I felt more sober, more in control.

Dave said, 'How come you wanted to go in such a hurry?'

'I'd just had enough,' I said.

'Of Louise?'

I looked at him in surprise, wondering whether he had seen through her when Alex couldn't, wondering whether he really was that observant.

He said, 'I could see the way you were looking at her. Christ, if looks could kill.'

'It wasn't like that,' I protested, but I was worried, because if it had been that obvious then Alex probably would have noticed as well, and that would have fitted right in with her game plan. I said, 'Oh, I can't help it. She's just such a bitch.'

'She seemed okay to me,' Dave said.

'Well, she's a bitch,' I said. 'Take it from me.'

We walked in silence for a while. It started to rain, a light sort of drizzle that soaked through my jacket, but I couldn't be bothered to hurry.

Dave tried again. 'Alex is a nice guy.'

'Yeah,' I said.

'Why did you break up? You're obviously still friends.'

'It just didn't work,' I said. 'Happens, doesn't it?'

He shrugged. His tone had been very casual, but I could tell that he was thinking hard, and I wondered whether he had come to the same conclusion as Louise, that I wanted Alex back. I wasn't sure how I could explain what was really going on. I wasn't even sure that I wanted to – after all, it wasn't really any of Dave's business.

I said, 'We wanted different things, you know? He's still my best friend, but nothing more.'

'But how long will that last?'

'What do you mean?'

He sighed. 'If you can't handle him being with someone else, how are you ever going to stay friends with him? And how are you going to move on, find someone else yourself?'

I thought about that. I wasn't sure what he was implying, whether he was implying anything at all. Finally, I said, 'I didn't think there was a problem. I don't like Louise, I wouldn't like her even if she wasn't with Alex, it's got nothing to do with Alex.'

He didn't respond to that.

We had reached my front door and I unlocked it and went inside. He followed me into the living room.

'I should go,' he said.

I wanted to tell him not to. I wanted to ask him to stay, but I didn't know how. Instead, I turned to face him and said, 'Surely you've drunk too much to drive?'

'Probably. I could get the bus. Pick up my car tomorrow.'

I waited for him to make his decision.

'Will you be all right on your own?' he asked. 'I wouldn't want you to go phoning Alex in the middle of the night.'

He was trying to make light of it. I gave a little laugh and said, 'I wouldn't dare. I don't think Louise would be impressed.'

He smiled at that. I met his gaze; those dark eyes, liquid eyes. I felt I should say something, do something, but I didn't know what. I was suddenly aware of how close we were; I could feel the heat of his body, hear each of his careful breaths. My own breathing hammered like a pulse. He leaned forward, and his lips touched mine. I closed my eyes. I felt his hand, light against my arm, and the pressure of his lips against mine. I couldn't breathe, didn't want to breathe. Then I thought suddenly of Alex, and how his lips had felt against mine, and his mouth touching Louise's mouth, and his arms holding her the way Dave now held me. Before I even realized I had done it, I broke free of Dave, stepped back a little.

He said, 'What's wrong?'

His voice had an urgency to it. I didn't want to look at him, because I didn't want to see the flushed expression I imagined from his tone. I put my hands over my face, over my eyes.

'What is it?' he asked, more gently.

He was a nice man, a good man, a kind man. I was being unfair. I was being unreasonable. I took my hands away from my face and looked up into his concern. 'I'm sorry,' I said. 'I didn't mean that.'

'Didn't mean what? The kiss? Or breaking it off?'

I wasn't sure I could answer. I felt a little breathless. I sat down on the sofa, hunched up, and lit myself a cigarette. I offered the packet to Dave but he just shook his head. He was waiting for a reply. I said, 'I do like you, Dave.'

'I like you, too,' he replied. 'But there's a "but", isn't there?'

'No,' I said, too quickly, unconvincingly. 'Not at all, you caught me off guard, that's all.'

He let out a long breath. 'I'd better go.'

'No,' I said. 'Don't. I didn't mean—'

'It doesn't matter,' he said. Then, 'It's late.'

'You don't have to go just yet. Stay for a little while.'

He looked defeated. 'What would the point be?' Then he relented a little. 'I like you, Jo, but I don't want to get used.'

'Used?' I said. 'I wouldn't use you. I'd never use anyone.'

He didn't refute that, just gave a little shrug as if it was irrelevant anyway. He was about to leave – I had the chilling feeling that if I let him walk out now he would never come back. I tried to find the right words, tried to think what I could say that would persuade him to stay, but my mind seemed frozen, I couldn't think.

He said, 'I'll see you around.'

I followed him to the front door. 'You don't have to go.'

He had his hand on the lock, ready to turn the mechanism. He said, 'Take care, eh?'

I didn't know what to say to that. I didn't know what to say to any of this. I wanted to blurt out that I was sorry, that I wanted him to stay, that this was all a silly misunderstanding, anything that might stop him from leaving me. But I just said, 'Yeah, you too.'

He stepped out into the front garden and walked

slowly down the path. I wanted to call after him, tell him that I was scared of being on my own, but I knew that would be the wrong thing to say. So I watched him walk away up the road, and he didn't look back, he just walked with shoulders hunched and his hands in his pockets, as though he had a lot on his mind.

Twenty-one

I woke with a bad head just before lunchtime and sat in front of re-runs of *The A-Team* with a pile of Marmite on toast and a large glass of Diet Coke. Hangover food. My stomach was uneasy with the alcohol of the night before, and when I moved too quickly I felt sharp pains in my head. I sat still.

I had checked on Dave Short's car when I got up, but he had already been back to collect it. I wondered whether he had knocked on my door to say hello, or whether he had deliberately come early in the hope that I would still be asleep. I had been very drunk – I was only now becoming aware of just how drunk I had been. He must have had such a bad impression of me. And I could remember Louise in the pub toilets – I remembered knocking against her, so hard, I realised now, and the hissed 'Bitch!' she had called after me. Had she deserved the way I had treated her? I couldn't remember, but no doubt she would already have started convincing Alex that I was unbalanced, or still in love with him, or a nasty piece of work.

By mid-afternoon, I was starting to feel better. I had a long bath and felt more normal after that. I decided to go for a walk, to get some more cigarettes and to clear my head with some fresh air.

There was a boy on a bicycle circling in the road. He stopped circling when he saw me, and I realised that it was Danny Metcalfe. I crossed the road to where he was and said, 'Hello, there.'

'Hi,' he said, but he didn't look directly at me.

'What're you doing round here?' I asked.

'Just out for a ride.' He leaned forward against his handlebars and looked over at my house. 'Is that where you live?'

There wasn't much point denying it, so I said, 'Yes.' I waited, hoping that he would offer an explanation for being in my street, a mile and a half, maybe further, from his house, but he just leaned there and said nothing.

I said, 'Have you seen your brother lately?'

His eyes widened for an instant, and then he shook his head. 'Not for months.' I didn't believe him.

The street was quiet, empty. There was no sign of anyone hanging around; I doubted that Danny would still be here if Sean was nearby. I said, 'Well, see you, then,' and started to walk away.

He scooted himself along beside me with his feet on the pavement. 'Where are you going?'

'Just to the shop.' I was confident that he would follow me and he did. He was chewing gum or something similar, smacking his lips as he chewed. I said, 'So, what's the story with Mrs Adams?'

He screwed up his face. 'She's a witch. She tells lies about us. She just don't like kids.'

'She gets scared easily,' I said. 'Think about it, she's stuck in that house with those two small kids, and she gets things thrown at her windows and people shouting rude things at her and stuff spray-painted on her walls.'

'That wasn't me,' Danny said quickly.

'Who was it, then? Was it Sean?'

His eyes widened again, but he just said, 'Why would Sean do that? Anyway, I don't know where Sean is.'

We crossed over Northgate and went past the garage to the corner shop. He took up position outside the door, and I realised he would still be waiting when I came out. I had the feeling that there was a purpose to his visit, but I couldn't understand what it could be. I was aware of him watching me as I pushed open the shop door; I stepped into the gloomy interior, and remembered the feel of the blow on the back of my head, and falling, and everything going black. I stopped, stood there, aware of Danny's presence in the bright sunlight behind me, and the sudden disorientating gloom in front of me. For a moment, I couldn't remember what I had come for, and the shop seemed to be laid out wrong, and it should have been Davinder watching me from behind the counter. I forced myself to smile at the shopkeeper. I was shaking a little. I took a deep breath and stepped forward and let the door clatter shut behind me, between me and Danny. I picked up a bottle of Diet Coke and ordered my cigarettes, and when I went back out with the bottle under my arm Danny was still waiting for me.

He rolled himself along beside me, sitting on the bike's saddle but scuffing his shoes on the tarmac. He said, 'Do you like it round here?'

I looked at him in surprise. He was chewing away, and his expression didn't tell me anything. 'It's okay. Yeah, I suppose I do. What d'you think?'

He looked around him, as if he hadn't bothered to properly see the place before, and then he shrugged and said, 'It's okay.'

'You prefer where you live?'

He gave no sign that he recognised that my area was nicer than his, but said instead, 'I've got my mates there.'

'Fair enough.'

We crossed over Northgate and headed back up the hill. Past the Star Inn, and I thought of Dave Short again with a crushing flash of embarrassment – what must he think of me now? And Alex – I would have to do something to try to limit any damage that Louise might have caused.

Danny didn't say anything until we were almost back at my front door. Then he said, 'Mum says you're causing trouble for us.'

I had been putting my key in the lock, but I stopped and turned. A dark frown cast shadows over his face. I said, 'That isn't what's happening. Nobody's in any trouble. We're trying to stop things getting to that point.'

He was still frowning. I had the feeling that he was struggling to understand something.

I said, 'Do you want to come in? Have a glass of Coke or something?'

I knew I shouldn't have said it – Douglas would have had a fit – but there was always the chance, however slim, that Danny would listen to me when his mother and his brother and his friends weren't around to influence him. I felt a surge of confidence that I could sort out Katie Adams's situation, if I could only get Danny to understand. And Sean, too. If I found out something about Sean's whereabouts at the same time, that would be a bonus. Danny hesitated for a moment but then shrugged and agreed, and I helped him lift his bike over the doorstep and lean it against the banisters at the bottom of the stairs.

We went through the living room and into the kitchen, where I poured out two glasses of Coke and handed him one. 'Let's go and sit down,' I said, and he followed me back to the front room and sat down. He was looking around him, a critical sort of expression on his face, but didn't say anything. I said, 'I'm not trying to cause trouble for your family, Danny.' I wondered suddenly whether he knew that Sean had attacked me, whether Sean had told him – would Sean have been laughing about it? Was that why Danny was here? But I cleared that thought from my mind and said, 'Your mum doesn't seem to like me much.'

He shrugged, but I couldn't tell whether he disagreed or just didn't care.

I said, 'All I want to do is help.'

He didn't believe that, I realised, but I didn't know what I could say to convince him. Then he said, 'She reckons it's your fault Sean turned out like he did.'

'She said that? How does she work that out?'

'I dunno. Says he was okay till we got put in care.'

'Do you remember being in care?'

'Course I do. Sean goes on like it was terrible but it wasn't that bad. They had satellite telly and took us bowling. It was okay.' Then he looked embarrassed, as if he'd admitted something he hadn't planned to tell me. He hardened his voice. 'Mum says you're why we ended up in care. Mum says you were really nasty about it.'

'That isn't true. Your mum wasn't coping, that's all. She needed a bit of time to herself to get everything sorted. And she's been fine ever since, hasn't she?' He didn't answer, still brooding. I said, 'Is that what Sean says, too?'

He got up out of his seat and went over to the mantelpiece to look at the ornaments. He picked up a vase Alex and I had brought back from Greece one year, turned it over and then put it back. 'Sean don't know what he's talking about,' Danny said. He was looking up at the print in a clip-frame above the fire. 'Who painted that?' he asked.

'Kandinsky,' I said.

'Yeah? Who's he? Some other kid?'

I stopped myself from laughing. 'No,' I said. 'Famous artist.'

'Never heard of him.'

There wasn't much I could say to that. I watched him do another circuit of the room, thinking about getting him to tell me what was going on. 'What does Sean say, then?' I asked.

'Sean says Social Services fucked us over. He's started saying he remembers being hit and stuff, when we were in care, but I don't remember nothing like that, and he's only saying stuff like that since he – since recently.'

I allowed myself a little smile at what he had nearly given away. 'He never mentioned it before?'

'No.'

I was relieved about that – if all the allegations Carla Metcalfe was making were based on recent conversations with Sean, there was nothing for me to worry about. Not that there was anyway, I reminded myself.

Danny sat back down again. I said, 'Why are you here, Danny?'

'What d'you mean? You asked me in.'

'No, I mean why did you come to my street?'

He rolled his eyes. 'I toldja. I was just cycling around.'

'You didn't come with Sean?' He laughed at that, but he looked slightly worried. 'Did you follow Sean?' I asked. It was getting clearer to me. 'Sean doesn't know you're here, does he? He doesn't know you followed him? When was it, Thursday night?'

'No,' he said, but he couldn't look at me. Then he got up. 'I got to go now.'

I followed him out to the hall and watched him struggle to wheel his bike back out through the front door. I leaned against the door jamb with my arms folded, and he wheeled his bike down to the pavement then threw one leg over and heaved himself onto the seat. The bike was a little too big for him – probably a hand-me-down from Sean, I thought, and the irony of that made me smile.

I said, 'Danny, if you ever want to talk to someone you can always come back here.' He frowned at that, but I added quickly, 'I don't mean about anything or – or anyone in particular. I mean about anything at all.'

He considered that for a moment, then said, 'See ya,' and launched himself off the pavement and onto the road. I watched him picking up speed, standing on his pedals to gain momentum. Then I looked the other way up the street, but I couldn't see anyone watching the house.

I returned to my sofa and the gradual recovery from the excesses of the previous night, but as my hangover wore off, the sense that Danny's visit could not have been a coincidence increased. I found it difficult to see what Sean could have achieved by sending Danny to see me; but Danny himself had seemed unsure why he was in my street. I wanted to believe that Danny had no idea what Sean was up to – maybe he had simply followed Sean to my house on a previous occasion. Maybe he was just the innocent little brother – but it was possible that he was in with Sean, that he was acting out a role just to help his brother, and I had let him into my house, and what if that had told him something? What if Danny had spotted a way for Sean to get in, and was telling Sean about it even now as I sat on the sofa? I had to do something – I couldn't just wait for nightfall to see what happened.

I wanted to talk to Dave Short, explain this new development, get him to act, but there was no way I felt I could ring him after being so drunk the night before. And that kiss – I couldn't phone him, no matter what. So I considered calling on Alex; he was usually good for logical, rational thinking, but the thought of seeing Louise again and the things she might have said to him in the meantime was too much. I wanted to face the Metcalfes; engineer a big showdown that would force them to explain what was going on, but I knew that I couldn't do that.

And that left Katie Adams. The idea seized me – she knew Danny, would happily tell me everything she knew or thought she knew about him. I could sift the information, locate the truth within the things she said – I knew her well enough for that. I could imagine myself in her front room, listening as she gave away more than she would ever realise, listening as she told me that one fact that would unlock whatever was going on. I didn't allow myself to think too long about it. I had to act, I had to do something to bring the situation to a head, whatever Douglas would have said about it. After all, it was my life that Sean Metcalfe was disrupting.

So I drove over to the Adams' house. There was

no sign of Danny or any of his friends when I reached their street, which was a relief. I parked and locked my car, and Katie Adams had opened her front door to me before I had even started up her path.

She said, 'How did you know to come? Did they phone you?'

'Who?' I asked.

She was leading the way into the front room, and I could see that she was agitated. She turned towards me, then away again, as if she couldn't decide. 'The police,' she said.

'Why have you called the police?' She wasn't listening to me, so I took her gently by the shoulders and guided her into a chair. I crouched down beside her. 'Tell me slowly.'

'He smashed my kitchen window,' she said, signalling towards the back of the house with a wave of her hand. 'Put the whole thing in. I was in here with the babies, I mean, what if Jack'd been in there? Glass everywhere. My kids could've got hurt.'

She was going red in the face; I was worried that she would hyperventilate. I took her hand in mine, rubbed it slowly with my other hand. Her eyes were wide, but her breathing calmed a little. 'Now,' I said, 'who smashed the window?'

'The Metcalfe kid, who else?'

'You mean Danny?' She nodded, but I wasn't sure if she was really listening. She pulled free of my grip and scrabbled over the crowded surface of the coffee table, strewn with children's toys and a colouring book and crayons, to pull a tissue out of a box. I repeated, 'You're sure it was Danny?'

'Yes,' she said, her words muffled by the tissue clamped over her face. She blew her nose, then added, 'Course it was, I mean, who else would it be?'

The quiver had returned to her voice; I had to head off her tears. I said, 'Listen to me, eh? It's okay, it's okay.' Then, 'What time was this?'

'A coupla hours ago. I called the police but nobody's been yet. Typical, isn't it? Never here when you need 'em. What they gonna do about it, eh? I'll tell you – they'll do sod all, because they never do.'

I looked at my watch. I had seen Danny three hours ago – did that mean he'd come straight back from talking to me and smashed her window? It didn't seem very likely to me, but then, I hardly knew the kid, for all I knew he was as uncontrollable as his brother. I said, 'Did you see Danny?'

She wasn't listening to me, sniffing into her tissue.

I repeated, 'Did you actually see him?'

She shook her head. 'Not really. Not clearly, but I know it's him.'

I sighed and sat back on my heels. I wasn't convinced that she actually had seen Danny – I wasn't at all convinced that Danny had broken her window. I said, 'Sit there. I'll make you some tea, eh?'

She nodded, and I went into the kitchen. The

window pane was completely smashed, with only a few jagged pieces of glass still held in the frame. There were shards all over the sink and the work surface, spilling onto the floor. I stepped across carefully, filled the kettle from the tap and switched it on. On the floor, there was half a brick, slightly muddy. I left it where it was. I unlocked the back door and went out into the garden, but there was nothing to see. The graffiti that had been there the other day had been washed off.

I went back into the kitchen and carefully re-locked the door. I made a mug of tea and carried it back through to her. She took it without a word, and I sat down in the opposite armchair.

'Where are the kids?' I asked.

'Gary's taken them over the park. Should be back soon.'

It seemed to me that he shouldn't have left her alone after something like this, but it wasn't my place to comment. Instead, I said, 'Do you want me to help you clean up?'

'The police said to leave it till they've been,' she said, and there was fear in her voice, as if I had been suggesting something illegal.

'Okay.' I sat there for a moment while she tried to dry her eyes and gather herself together. I wasn't sure what to say, now that I was here. My plan to have some sort of logical discussion with her had been knocked off course by the latest developments.

Finally, she screwed up the tissue in her hand,

threw it onto the table, then looked at me. 'If the police didn't call you, why are you here?'

'I just wanted to see how things were.'

She looked doubtful. 'On a Saturday? Why?'

'I just wanted to make sure things were okay.'

If she didn't believe me, she didn't say so, but we were interrupted then by a key in the front door lock as Gary brought Jack and the baby back from the park. Katie got to her feet and rushed into the hallway to help him bring the pushchair over the step. Jack came tearing into the front room, still in his coat and mittens, and stopped when he saw me sitting there.

'Hello, Jack,' I said.

He hesitated for a moment, then went to the table and shook off his gloves, threaded on elastic through his sleeves. He picked up a crayon and started colouring. I heard Katie Adams say something quietly in the hall, and then a man's voice saying, 'About time and all.'

They came into the front room. Gary led the way with Katie just behind, holding the baby to her chest. Gary was small and lean with a mess of brown hair over a weathered face. His jeans were splashed with paint and streaks of dirt; work clothes. Blue tattoos of indistinguishable design were scattered on his tanned forearms, folded across his chest.

I stood up and held out my hand. 'Nice to finally meet you.'

He regarded me with suspicion for a moment, then shook my hand. The skin on his palm was rough and hardened. He stretched himself out over the nearest armchair and said, 'What brings you here?'

Katie Adams had retreated to the kitchen. I heard the kettle being filled from the tap. I said, 'I wanted to check how things were. Seems there's been more problems. I can come back another time if you'd prefer.'

He shrugged. 'No skin off my nose what you do.' He glanced towards the kitchen, leaned forward and said, 'But you've been stirring it, haven't you, talking to that Metcalfe woman?'

'I wasn't stirring it. I was trying to stop the problems. Make life easier for everyone round here.'

He looked at me as if I was stupid. 'You can't stop people like them,' he said. 'Nowt but scum, that's them. They need a proper sorting out.'

I said, 'Now, that's not —'

'Oh, don't fret, I wouldn't do nowt.'

He had taken a tin from his pocket and started to roll himself a cigarette. I watched him for a moment, trying to work out what I was going to do or say next. Katie Adams came in and gave Gary a mug of tea, then perched herself on the arm of his chair and looked at me.

Gary said, 'So, what're you going to do about it?'

This wasn't the right time, I could see that. Gary was not as receptive as I had hoped he would be. I wanted him to go away again – take the kids back out, go to the pub, anything – because I knew how to handle Katie Adams, I knew how to get her to agree with me. I said, 'We need to get people communicating. Sort out whatever the problem is and start again, with none of the bad feeling that's been going around recently.'

Gary just laughed. 'That won't do no good. Ask anyone round here, they'll tell you. Everyone knows what's been going on.'

'That's right,' Katie put in, then flushed and fell silent.

Gary put the rollie between his lips and lit it, watching me as he did so. He seemed to be waiting for me to respond. I had hoped we could keep the situation quiet, but that clearly wasn't going to be the case. I wondered whether all the neighbours were getting involved, whether this feud was escalating to involve the whole street, or the whole neighbourhood. It didn't bode well for Danny, especially as Katie Adams was sure it was Danny who had smashed her window.

'Need to give that kid a good scare,' Gary said. 'Make him think he'll end up like his brother, that's what'll stop him.'

'That's a little over the top,' I murmured.

'Over the top? You're joking. That little bastard's put our window in, but you don't seem to care about that.'

'I do care —' I started to say, but he cut me off.

'You don't get it. I know what you bloody social workers are like. Fucking do-gooders. You haven't got a clue. You let that kid run wild and never mind what it means for the rest of us. You're supposed to protect people, aren't you?' Katie Adams looked like she wanted to say something, but didn't. I wanted to tell her it was okay, I understood how she felt, but Gary was still talking. 'You just let people get away with it. You're all too soft.' He picked up his lighter to re-light the rollie between his fingers, and then signalled towards me with it, as if he'd thought of something else. 'You let the police deal with it, they know how to handle a kid like that. Or just leave it to us. Wouldn't've got away with that sort of stuff when I was a kid, I can tell you.'

I thought he was going to drift off into some rant about beat bobbies giving cuffs on the ear, or that getting a good beating had never done him any harm. I couldn't bear to hear such things, not from a face like his, lit up with anger. I wondered where Danny was now, whether I should try to get his side of the story, but I knew I had to back off.

I said, 'I'm not here to take sides or say what should be done. I'm here to offer support. If the police find evidence that Danny Metcalfe broke your window, I'm sure they'll act.'

'If?' Gary said, outraged. 'What d'you mean, "if"? Nobody else would've done it, would they?'

I held up my hands to indicate that I didn't want to get pulled any further into this dispute. I had already got more involved than I should have done. My hangover had returned with a fury. I said, 'Look, I've got to go now. Tell the police exactly what you saw, and I'm sure they'll do what they can for you. But please, don't do anything about this yourself, you'll only make the situation worse.' Katie Adams nodded, but I wasn't convinced that Gary was listening to me. 'This is up to the police now.'

Gary let out a sigh, of frustration or anger I couldn't tell, but Katie Adams got up and said in a low voice, 'Don't worry, we won't do anything, we'll talk to the police when they get here.'

I nodded and allowed her to take me to the front door. I heard Gary turn on the TV. At the door, I said to her, 'Please, tell the police exactly what you saw. It might not have been Danny you saw. It'll only make things worse if they accuse him and it wasn't him.'

She frowned. 'I'm pretty sure,' she said, but she did sound a little doubtful.

I could imagine the way Gary was going to work on her before the police arrived. 'Just picture what you saw and describe that. Let the police work out who it actually was.'

'Okay,' she said, but I wasn't sure that she grasped the significance of what I was saying.

I left her there and went back to my car. There was no sign of Danny or any of his friends in the street, to my relief, although I did want to see Danny. I wanted to ask him if he had been involved, to see his reaction for myself, and to judge whether he was telling the truth. But I knew it would just make the situation worse, so I got into my car.

I couldn't face going home just yet. I felt a little depressed – I wasn't sure if it was an effect of the drink from the night before, or whether the situation at the Adams' house had dampened my spirits. I drove round to Simon and Alex's house. I was nervous about going there, in case Louise was hanging around, but I had to go somewhere, I didn't want to be alone. I wanted to tell them all the details of the case, but I knew I couldn't really do that, it wasn't right to break confidentiality.

Alex answered the door. He didn't seem very pleased to see me, but opened the door wider and allowed me to go through to the front room. I said, 'Is Louise here?'

'No.' He looked tired. 'She had to go and meet some mates. What d'you want, Jo?'

'That's a fine way to greet a friend,' I said, trying to be jocular about it.

He sighed. 'I'm not really in the mood. Why'd you have to be so nasty to Louise last night?'

'Why? What's she said?'

'She didn't have to say anything. I know you, Jo. You can be a bitch when you want to.'

'That's not fair.' It hurt me that he thought that, that he had used the word Louise had used. 'I was a little drunk last night. If I came across as though I didn't like her, I didn't mean it. I'm just stressed at the moment.'

'Yeah, yeah.' He fetched his cigarettes from the side table and lit himself one, but didn't offer me one. Then he sat down slowly, wearily. 'You're always stressed,' he said. 'It's no excuse.'

'I was attacked a couple of weeks ago. Don't you think I've got the right to be freaked out by that?'

He waved that away. 'That was ages ago. Get over it.'

'Get over it?' I couldn't believe what he was saying. 'Get over it? I've had fucking Sean Metcalfe trying to break into my house, and you tell me to get over it?'

'You don't know if anyone tried to break in,' he said. 'Christ, people get burgled all the time. Doesn't mean there's someone out to get you.'

'It's not just that,' I said. 'There's been other stuff.'

I wanted him to ask what stuff, to push for more details. If he pushed, I knew I would tell him everything, and then he would have to help, he would have to say something.

But he just shook his head. 'Don't be so fucking paranoid, Jo. Get a grip.'

'I'm not paranoid,' I said.

'You are,' he said, with a kind of authority, a firmness that reminded me of all the times we had nearly had the final, explosive, friendship-ending argument when we lived together. 'The whole world doesn't revolve around you, Jo. You're not the centre of everyone's thoughts. And there isn't some great conspiracy against you.'

'I never said there was,' I said.

'So what's all this crap about some client being out to get you, then?' Before I could answer, he shook his head again and said, 'You're not right in the head. You need professional help. The way you behave is unacceptable.'

'No. I was drunk, that's all.'

'That's no excuse,' he said. 'You drink too much. You need to sort yourself out.'

'This isn't about me having a few drinks, it's about someone being out to get me.'

'No,' he said. 'It's about you refusing to see what your problem is.'

'No—' I started, but then I stopped, because what could I say to that? That I could handle it? There was no way to counter him – he had me trapped by all those denials we'd been trained to discount. So I said, 'You're not listening to me.' And, louder, 'Why won't you listen?'

'I don't have to listen to this.' He stood up, looked down at me. 'Who do you think you are, coming round here, shouting at me like this? I don't owe you anything, and I don't appreciate the way you're behaving.'

I stood up, too, nearly a foot shorter than him but ready to bridge that gap if I had to. 'I'm telling you,' I said. 'Sean Metcalfe's been hanging round my house, and I don't know what he's planning to do, and his brother's causing trouble for one of my clients, and everything's getting out of hand, and I don't know what to do about it.'

He looked at me for a long moment, but there was a coldness in those dark eyes, there was a harshness I'd never seen before. He said, 'I don't give a shit. Go and tell someone who cares. Go and tell your policeman friend, if he hasn't blown you out already. Go and tell Douglas, unless you've done your usual trick of ignoring what he says until it's too late.'

'That's not fair.' I heard the wail in my voice, but he just turned away from me. He strode over to the door, threw it open, went into the hall. I followed; he was opening the front door now. I said, 'Don't do this, Alex. I need you.'

He turned to look at me then, and for a moment I thought that had done it, that had won him back, but he just let out a tutting noise and opened the door a little wider. 'I don't need you,' he said. 'Get some professional help. Get yourself sorted out. But don't come round here unless you're willing to be civil, and you're ready to apologize to Louise.'

I wanted to laugh in his face. I wanted to tell him that that would never happen, but the hardness growing inside me seemed fit to choke me, and I couldn't say anything. As I left the house, he slammed the door behind me, loud enough to attract his neighbours' attention. I stood in his front garden and stuck my finger up at the door, but I knew he wasn't watching, I knew he wasn't paying me any attention.

I stormed down to my car and sat in the driver's seat. I felt the tears welling up in my eyes – frustration, anger, I didn't know what. I had to get out of there, I had to get away, back to my house. Lock the door, shut myself in, do something – anything – to get completely out of my skull and forget that today had ever happened.

Twenty-two

I didn't want to go to work on Monday. I had slept badly, jerked awake by every noise from the street, and when the alarm went off I didn't want to get out of bed, or get dressed, or collect my stuff together, or drive out into the rush-hour traffic. But I had to, and I did it on auto-pilot, eyes still bleary, head pounding. I hadn't dared look at my face in the mirror, I'd just brushed my hair and rubbed my face with the flannel and scrubbed the taste out of my mouth with toothpaste. I felt like shit, but I probably deserved it. I had spent Sunday in a stupor, hoping that Alex would phone or call round, or that Dave Short would, or wondering whether I should phone them. I wanted to hear Alex's voice – I wanted to hear him laugh, and tease me about something, and be friendly, the way he used to be. Or Dave – he could have found a pretence to phone or call round; he could at least have shown some concern for me. But nobody called.

At the office, I tried to bury myself in paperwork at my desk, hoping to sleepwalk through the day, but Douglas came to me almost before the day had begun to tell me that he wanted to see me and Colin Fuller at eleven o'clock. It had to be about the Metcalfes; I could imagine the sorts of stories Carla Metcalfe would have been spreading after her little chat with Dave Short on Friday.

I knew I should do something to prepare for the meeting – go over my casenotes, or talk to Colin, anything. I did find the energy to go and look for Colin; I saw him across the other side of the office and called his name, but he couldn't have heard me, because by the time I got to the corridor there was no sign of him. I even went and checked in the yard, to see if he was having an early cigarette, but there was nobody out there. And my head was pounding so much, and my vision swam when I moved, so I retreated back to my desk. All I was capable of doing was drinking fizzy pop and stuffing my face with chocolate, in the hope that the caffeine and sugar rush would carry me through.

I took a couple of paracetamol with a large swig of orange Tango before heading into Douglas's office at eleven o'clock. Colin was already there, hanging his jacket over the back of the chair as if he'd just come in from the street. I sat down in the other chair set out in front of Douglas's desk and forced myself to smile at both of them. Douglas gave me a sympathetic sort of smile in return, but Colin seemed embarrassed and avoided meeting my gaze.

Without preamble, Douglas said, 'Jo, I've received

complaints about how you're dealing with the Metcalfe and Adams situation.'

I nodded my head slowly. 'Who from? Carla Metcalfe?'

'Yes. And from Gary Adams.'

Both sides. I suppressed a giggle. They were finally agreeing on something.

Douglas went on, 'Perhaps you'd like to tell us what your recent involvement has been?'

I took a deep breath and told them, in a low tone, about what had happened when I visited the Adams on Saturday. But I left out having seen Danny earlier that day – it didn't seem wise to admit that I had allowed him into my house.

I waited for Douglas to ask why Gary Adams had felt it necessary to complain after my visit, but he didn't. Instead, he said, 'Colin tells me there was an incident on Sunday night. Last night. Do you know anything about that?'

'No.' I glanced at Colin. He had crossed one leg over his knee and was doodling on a pad he was resting against his thigh, deliberately not looking at me. I wondered what else he had let slip during the secret meeting they had obviously already had.

Douglas said, 'The police were involved. We don't know the details, but Gary Adams was arrested. Cautioned for Breach of the Peace.'

This seemed to be a cue for Colin, because he did finally look at me, quickly, his cheeks flushing up. 'Carla Metcalfe's distraught,' he said. 'She told me she thinks you wound him up. Put him up to it.'

'Oh, that's just great.' I slumped back into my chair. 'Just what I need.'

'Carla doesn't like you,' Colin said, as though that wasn't already obvious. 'I told Douglas about her refusing to speak to you when we went there last week.' He kept his tone flat, as if that would stop my noticing that he had spoken to Douglas behind my back. I wanted to ask why he had felt the need to say so much to Douglas when I wasn't even there to put my side, but he continued, 'She phoned me on Friday, said she wasn't happy about you being involved.' He glanced across at me, all apology now. 'I was going to talk to you about it but I didn't get a chance on Friday.'

They were both looking at me. 'Did she say why?' My voice came out slightly strangled, and I coughed to clear my throat, and then added, 'I mean, was there a reason?'

'She said she didn't think you were impartial.'

He had spoken with that same flat tone, and I realized that he was holding something back, she had said more than that. I remembered Dave Short saying she had accused me of threatening her and Sean eight years ago. Dave Short had spoken to her on Friday – had that been before or after she had decided to phone Colin? I rubbed my hand over my face, feeling the headache returning. It was difficult to breathe in the stifling heat of the office, but they were waiting for me to speak, so I cleared my throat again and said, 'These disputes are like that, aren't they?'

'That's why we shouldn't get so involved,' Douglas said. 'Leave it to the Housing Association, or get the Mediation Service in.'

I didn't look at Colin. I didn't want to know whether he had expressed this opinion to Douglas already or whether Douglas considered this a basic principle.

Douglas let out a long sigh. 'Look, Jo, we have two complaints against you now. We have to investigate them. It's probably best if you don't have any contact with the Metcalfe or Adams families until we've dealt with these. You understand, I'm sure. Colin can handle anything that comes up.'

I had to laugh at that. 'You're joking,' I said. 'You can't just bounce me off a case I've spent so much time on. I've built up a relationship with Katie Adams. She trusts me. It'll take weeks, maybe months, for anyone else to get in that position. You don't understand what she's like.'

I was looking from one to the other as I spoke. Colin was looking down with concentration at the notes he'd made in among the doodles on his pad. Douglas did look at me, but with a slightly con-descending smile, as though he needed to explain something simple to me. 'Jo, I know we say we shouldn't pander to this sort of thing, but we don't want to make the situation any worse now, do we?' I opened my mouth to object, but the expression on Douglas's face stopped the words. He went on, 'Colin, you may as well go. I'm sure you've got plenty to be getting on with.'

Colin gathered his things and stood up quickly. I avoided eye contact with either of them. Colin was in such a rush to get out of the office that I realized he knew Douglas wanted to berate me in private. He brushed against me as he passed me, but there was no supportive squeeze from his hand. I felt cold inside.

Once Colin had gone, Douglas moved his chair slightly towards me, as if that would make this easier, and said, 'I don't understand why you went round there on Saturday.'

I wanted to defend myself – there had to be something I could say to defend myself. I wanted to say that Colin was selling me out, that Douglas and Colin were playing right into the Metcalfes' hands, that Sean Metcalfe was behind all of this. But I bit those words back – a sour taste – and said, 'I haven't done anything wrong. They're just using me to score points.'

Douglas nodded, as if he agreed that this was probably the case, but then said, 'It would have been better if you hadn't gone. You certainly shouldn't have gone there when you weren't even supposed to be working, and you should have come to see me first, anyway. I warned you about this.' He hesitated, then continued, 'We talked about you getting too involved, didn't we? We seem to have this same conversation over and over.'

'I'm just trying to do my job,' I said.

He ignored that. 'Carla Metcalfe has complained to her Councillor,' he said. 'He's fuming about it.

You know what it's like when the department gets complaints from Councillors. I've had the Director's office on the phone to me half the morning.'

The headache started a fresh attack on the inside of my skull. I lowered my head into my hand and tried surreptitiously to massage the pain away. I wanted to be back in bed, curled up with the duvet over my head, and all of this a million miles away. But Douglas was waiting for me to say something, so I let out a long breath and said, 'Carla Metcalfe just wants to cause trouble. She's just a troublemaker. You know what it's like – they think if they cause a fuss they'll get what they want.'

He said, 'What I don't understand is why she feels the need to stir? I mean, you're not even dealing with her case. Why's she so angry with you?'

'It's because of her son,' I said. I was about to explain about Sean Metcalfe being the one who attacked me, but Douglas held up his hand to stop me saying more.

'There's going to have to be an investigation,' he said. 'Whatever Danny Metcalfe's been up to, we'll get to the bottom of it.'

I wanted to explain that it wasn't Danny I had been thinking about, it was Sean, but I suddenly didn't have the energy. I forced myself to give the smile he was looking for, and pretended to be reassured by his words. I felt slightly sick. Colin wasn't going to stand by me, he'd made that much clear already, and if he didn't then why would Douglas? I'd slogged my guts out for the department but they wouldn't do anything to jeopardize their precious reputation, not after Chantelle Wade and all the stuff in the papers.

Douglas said, 'You've allowed yourself to get too drawn into this, haven't you?'

'No. Not really. I've just been doing my job.'

'But you've allowed yourself to become embroiled. You've lost your professional distance. Come on, Jo, you can't pretend you've got everything right, can you?'

I wanted to laugh. I wanted to ask him just how many people he'd been out to see recently. I wanted to ask what he would do if someone phoned him up and asked for help – tell them to wait for their next appointment? Tell them it would damage his professional distance if he got embroiled? But I didn't say any of that.

Douglas went on, 'Colin's worried about you.'

I bit back a derisive, 'Oh yeah?' and said instead, 'There's no need.'

Douglas said, 'He's not the only one. You don't seem to be coping very well at the moment. You seem to be under pressure.'

'We're all under pressure,' I said. 'Goes with the territory.'

'Yes, but—' and then he hesitated, as if trying to work out how best to phrase this. He softened his tone. 'If there's anything we can do to help – I mean, I'm sure other people in the office would be willing to help you out. If you need a few days off, I'm sure you've got some in-lieu owing to you.'

'I'm fine,' I said, but he took no notice.

'We don't like to see one of the team under the weather.'

I didn't say anything. I was remembering the brush of Colin's hand as he left the office – how much concern had there been there? He was like everyone else – so scared of a scandal he'd rather cover his own back than help me out when I most needed it.

'There's no shame in admitting you need help, Jo. You must realize that from last time. We don't want this to make you ill. Much better to ask for help now than end up unable to cope at all, wouldn't you say?'

'Last time was a one-off,' I said. 'I was new to the job back then. You remember what things were like. This has nothing to do with then.'

He was looking at me with a soft smile that suggested he didn't believe me. I knew I shouldn't blame him for that – after all, the Metcalfes had caused problems for me back then, too. But it made me angry – I wanted to remind him that back then he had told me not to worry, it wouldn't affect my career, nobody would remember that I hadn't been coping, not once I found my feet, not once I knew what I was doing and had some experience under my belt. I wanted to remind him about that, but I knew I couldn't. I said, 'Everyone feels stress now and then. But I'm fine. There's no need to be concerned.'

'Well,' Douglas said, 'I do have to look at the things Carla Metcalfe's been saying, you know. She's made some accusations about when you looked after their case eight years ago. I know she's only trying to stir things up, you've told me that already, but it's quite a coincidence, isn't it? The same family?'

'She's just looking for things she can manipulate,' I said. 'Oh, come on, you can't possibly think there's any truth in the things she's saying?'

'Of course not,' he said, but it wasn't convincing.

'It's ridiculous,' I tried again. 'The whole thing.'

'Of course,' Douglas said.

'Colin must have told you that.'

'Of course,' Douglas said again. The same flat tone. Then he said, 'You're in the union, aren't you?'

'Yes,' I said, surprised.

'Talk to your union rep. You need to talk to him before this goes any further. Now, I suggest you go back to your desk and write some reports or something. You look dreadful. You're in no state to be talking to clients.'

I nodded and stood up.

When I got to the door, he said, 'Jo,' and I turned and looked at him. 'Make sure you get plenty of sleep tonight. And don't go drinking. You don't function well with a hangover.'

Normally, I would have laughed at that, but he wasn't smiling and it didn't feel funny. So I just nodded and pulled his office door shut behind me. I went to my desk, found my cigarettes and headed out into the little yard at the back of the office.

Colin was already there. He looked embarrassed

when he saw me. 'Are you okay?' he asked, but I had the feeling it was because he felt he had to ask.

'Oh, just great,' I replied, and he grimaced at my tone. I lit my cigarette and smoked it hard, but there didn't seem to be enough nicotine, or tar, or whatever, in the cigarette to give me any kind of lift.

'Was Douglas okay about things?'

What 'things', I wanted to ask, but I knew I shouldn't be angry with Colin, it wasn't his fault. I'd put myself in this situation, after all; Douglas was right about that much. And Colin – Colin was just trying to protect himself, and who could blame him, really? I was the one in a mess, and it didn't matter that all of this came back to Sean Metcalfe; I was the one who should have been following the book, and keeping a professional distance, and realizing what the game was. But Sean Metcalfe – Sean fucking Metcalfe – he was the one who had attacked me, he was the one who had done something wrong, and I was the one in trouble for it. I remembered him coming up to me in the street, that twisted face, the sudden violence. I imagined myself striking out first; my fist making contact with his jaw, the snap back of his head, the jarring impact to my knuckles and hand and wrist as I drove him backwards. I could imagine the blood, a burst of blood as his lip punctured, and the cry he would have made as he fell, his hands coming up to protect himself as I watched him fall back. I was in trouble anyway now, so what difference would it have made?

Colin was waiting for an answer. I said, 'He told me to talk to my union rep.'

'Oh.'

I rounded on him. 'Is that all you can say? I'm in the shit and that's all you've got to say about it?'

'What do you want me to say?'

'I don't know, do I?' I turned away from him, hunching myself up, because I was so angry; I felt so much anger, and my head was pounding, and why had I got so drunk this weekend, why did things have to work out this way, now, when I wasn't in any fit state to cope with it? I threw my cigarette down and ground it against the concrete with my heel.

Colin said, 'This isn't my fault.'

'I didn't say it was,' I said, through gritted teeth, with my back still to him. No, if it was anyone's fault it was Sean Metcalfe's. I balled my hands into fists.

Colin said, 'I wish I'd found you on Friday, told you what Carla Metcalfe was saying.'

That made me laugh, because I'd already known what she was saying, Dave Short had told me, and had it made the blindest bit of difference to me? No, I'd blundered in there, thinking I could sort things out, and I'd just landed myself even further in the mire. I said, 'It wouldn't have mattered.'

'It might've.'

I turned to face him, hoping for sympathy, but the expression on his face stopped me. He had told Douglas all these things but he hadn't even bothered to find me. He could have phoned me –

he had always claimed to be my friend, but what kind of friend wouldn't have warned me? He didn't care that I was in trouble. He was protecting himself and now he wanted me to say that it was okay. And it wasn't okay – I wasn't going to absolve him of his guilt. Why should I? If he had spoken to me – warned me – it might have changed things. I might have listened more to Dave, I might have realized what was happening. I felt a sudden, reckless certainty that Colin could have saved me if he had wanted to, so why should I forgive him?

I said, 'Why didn't you talk to me on Friday, then, if it seems so vital now?'

He looked stung. 'I did try,' he said. 'I couldn't find you.'

'I was here. Most of the afternoon I was at my desk. You can't've tried very hard, can you?'

'I tried. Don't put this on me.'

'Why not? You should've said something to me instead of going running to Douglas.'

He shook his head and threw his cigarette to the ground as he moved towards the door. 'I don't have to listen to this,' he said. 'I warned you about getting too involved, I said you were getting sucked into their dispute, but you didn't listen to me, did you? You think you know so much more than me. You think you're the only one who knows how to do the job. Go on, admit it, that's right, isn't it?'

'No,' I said. 'No, it wasn't like that.'

I saw him stepping back towards the door; his fingers closed around the door handle, and he was half turning as he spoke. I couldn't hear his words any more. He was turning away from me and in a moment he would be gone. It was all his fault but he was walking away, like Sean Metcalfe, like everyone else. I wanted him to stop, to face me, but he wasn't listening to me. I saw his face in profile and all I could feel was a rush of something, anger, hatred, I didn't know. I couldn't breathe. I saw my hands fly out towards him, felt the rough cloth of his jacket, felt myself pull against him. I saw his stagger of surprise as he twisted towards me, as he fell, his shoulder against the doorframe. His hand gripped mine on his arm; I felt the pressure of my hand on his jacket sleeve, and his hand pushing against my grip. I remembered Sean Metcalfe at my elbow; his presence against my arm, and the contact of his fist against my head. My hearing seemed to have faded out; for a moment I heard nothing, then, as my grip broke and I fell back against the fence, there was the roar of sound again. Traffic on the main road, Colin yelling, me yelling. I struck the fence with a jerk, and I closed my eyes, and I remembered the feel of that first blow against the back of my head. I felt my fists making contact with something solid; I felt the impact all through my hand and along my arm. I could feel the energy packed up into my arm as I struck out again; energy running out along the muscles and through my wrist and out through my fist and knuckles and into Colin's face.

Colin. I opened my eyes, dropped my hands. He was standing in front of me, clutching one hand over his mouth. My knuckles hurt. 'Oh, oh God, Colin, I'm sorry.' I put out my hands to comfort him, to rub out the fact that I had punched him, to somehow take it back, but he backed away from me, still clutching his face.

I said, 'Colin, I didn't mean that, I'm sorry.'

He finally took his hand away. His lip was swelling up fast. He opened his mouth to speak but didn't seem to know what to say. There was blood gathering around his top teeth; dark red blood bubbling onto his lips. He looked at me, tried to speak again, changed his mind. Then he turned and went into the building, quickly, and I had to run to follow him.

'Colin,' I cried as I followed him along the corridor. 'Colin, I'm sorry, I didn't mean that.'

He didn't turn to look at me, but hurried on towards the toilets. I considered grabbing his arm, forcing him to stop and talk to me, but I didn't really know what else to say. I said again, 'Colin, I'm so sorry.'

As we were approaching Douglas's door, it opened, and Douglas stepped into the corridor. He blocked Colin's path and I stopped behind them.

'What's all the racket?' Douglas demanded.

Colin had his hand cupped over his mouth. When he glanced back at me, I saw blood spilling onto his chin. But he said, 'Nothing.'

'What happened to your lip?' Then Douglas looked from Colin to me. He seemed to be working it out for himself. He said, 'Jo, wait in my office.'

I squeezed past Colin and Douglas and went into

Douglas's office. Douglas pulled the door shut and I heard the low murmur of his voice, then Colin's voice, but I couldn't make out the words. I went over to Douglas's desk. There was a pad of paper on it, and I saw my name written along the top. I glanced at the door, then turned the pad towards me. He must have been making notes during a phone call, because there were random words written at odd angles across the paper, some of the words decorated with doodles and underlinings, as though he'd been colouring while talking. I saw 'unprofessional' and 'threatening' and 'PC Dave Short' and 'Danny' crossed out and replaced with 'Sean'. I turned the pad back to how it had been before and sank down into a chair. I felt weak. My head pounded.

Finally, Douglas came back into the office and shut the door carefully behind him. He sat down in the chair next to me and said, 'Did you just hit Colin?'

'I didn't mean to,' I said. 'I don't know what happened.'

He looked at me for a long moment, then looked away and said, 'Go home, Jo. Pack up your stuff and go home.'

'Home?' I said stupidly.

'Yes.' He rubbed his hand over his face, and went over to sit behind his desk. 'We can't have members of staff hitting other staff. It's just not done. It's not professional. Go home and cool off.'

I stood up slowly.

Then he said, 'No, actually, Jo. Go home and stay there. You're suspended.'

'Suspended?' I said, as though I was incapable of anything apart from repeating the last words he had said. 'You can't just suspend me.'

'I can,' he said. 'Go home. I'll make sure your union rep contacts you there.'

I felt that I should say something, anything, to avoid this happening, but even as I tried to think of something to say, I realized that it didn't really matter anyway. The Metcalfes might have had it in for me, but I had managed to wreck my career all by myself. I wanted to laugh, but I didn't think Douglas would get the joke.

As I went to the door, Douglas said, 'You know this means you can't go near the Adams family?'

'Yes,' I said.

'Or the Metcalfes?'

'I understand,' I said.

He nodded, and that was that. I went to my desk and collected my handbag. I emptied the files out of my briefcase and dumped them in my in-tray. I opened my drawers and took out everything I might need while I was at home. I was aware that everyone was watching me. All business had come to a standstill. I could see Colin at the far end of the office, sitting on a desk with the First Aid kit open next to him as someone dabbed his lip with a lint pad. I deliberately didn't look in his direction. Nobody spoke the entire time I was there – the only noise I could hear was the banging of the items in my drawer as I collected the things I wanted. Then I hoisted my handbag onto my shoulder, picked up my briefcase and swept out of the office and into the car park.

I didn't look back or even hesitate until I had pulled out of the car park and was heading up Alfreton Road. Only when I was out of sight of the office did I pull into a side road and sit there for a moment. I put my head down against the steering wheel and felt the cold plastic against my forehead, and I wanted to scream out loud but my throat was already tight with tears.

Twenty-three

I bought a large bottle of rum on the way home, but by the time I got back I realized that I didn't want to drink it. I put it on the side in the kitchen, went upstairs and ran myself a hot bath. I lay in the water for a long time, trying to wash away the day, but I knew it was a futile effort. By the time I was dressed again, in jeans and a sweater, the familiar feeling of nausea had returned to my stomach. I wandered around the house, trying to decide what to do. Cool off, Douglas had said. I felt very cool, very calm, but when I went into the kitchen the bottle of rum beckoned me again. I ignored it, went through to the front room, switched on the TV.

Then I rolled myself a large spliff and smoked it while I rolled the next one. Take the edge off the day. I was considering sparking up the second spliff when the doorbell rang.

I wasn't sure who I hoped would be on the other side of the door, but I certainly wasn't expecting Danny Metcalfe. He didn't have his bike with him this time, and stood hunched up, half leaning against the door frame.

'What are you doing here?' I must have sounded less friendly than I intended, because he jerked away from the door and looked at me with surprise. His face was red; it took me a moment to register that he had a bruise developing under his left eye.

I said, more gently, 'What happened to you?'

He gave a miserable kind of shrug and simply stood there, waiting for a reaction from me. I couldn't leave him standing there on the doorstep. I knew Douglas would go mad, but there was nothing I could do but stand aside and let Danny into the house. He came in, hesitantly at first, but then carried on through into the front room. He slumped down onto the sofa and huddled his arms around himself, not looking at me.

I sat down in the armchair, leaned forward, said, 'Danny, what's happened?' He didn't reply. I wanted to ask him who had hit him, but I knew he wouldn't tell me, not yet, so instead I said, 'Would you like a drink? Some Coke?'

'Yeah,' he said.

I went into the kitchen and poured out two glasses of Coke. When I returned to the living room, he was still sitting in the same position. I held out a glass but he made no move to take it, so I put it on the floor by his feet.

I sat down and waited.

Eventually, he said, 'You've been smoking.'

He glanced at me then, and there was a little

smile on his face. I said, 'Well, you know how it is.'

'Can I have a cigarette?'

I was about to say no, he was too young, but that playful smile was still there, so I offered him my packet and said, 'I won't tell if you don't.'

He took a cigarette, lit it and smoked it. He seemed to be thinking about something. He wasn't as huddled any more.

I said, 'How's your brother these days?'

He shrugged. He leaned back and blew cigarette smoke up towards the ceiling.

I waited.

He stubbed out the cigarette and drank some of his Coke. Then he looked at me, as if he was expecting questions and was ready now. I said, 'Who gave you the black eye?'

His hand ran up to it, fingers touching the edges where the swelling yellowed into a bruise. 'Who d'you think?' There was something in his tone – anger, bitterness perhaps. I didn't supply an answer, so then he said, 'They think they can do what they like. They think they can get away with anything 'cos nobody believes me. Fucking think they own the street.'

'Who?' I asked.

His expression told me I was stupid for not knowing. 'Gary fucking Adams,' he said.

'Gary Adams hit you?'

I had been careful not to sound as though I didn't believe him, but he still gave me the same resentful look. 'He said I'd get worse if I caused any more trouble, but I haven't done nothing. I can't stop other people doing stuff, can I?' I didn't say anything, but it didn't seem to matter. A whine had come into his voice and he put a hand up to cover his eyes, but I didn't think he was crying. He said, 'Everyone always blames me. It's not fair.'

I wanted to retort that life wasn't fair, that he had done things in the past so what did he expect? But he had drawn his knees up towards his chest, and if he wasn't crying yet he wasn't far off. He looked so small; a boy, a child sitting there. I thought of Gary Adams, a grown man; I imagined him grabbing hold of Danny, towering over him, having to reach down to hit him. My knuckle still ached slightly from its contact with Colin. I couldn't imagine ever being angry enough to hit a child.

I said, 'You should tell the police.'

He didn't reply, rubbing his fists into his eyes.

I said, 'The police would sort Gary Adams out. More than just a caution this time.' Then I thought of Katie Adams, alone with those kids, and how it would be for her, and what Danny's friends would shout at her. 'It's not right, him hitting you,' I said.

He pulled his hands away from his face. 'But you're not gonna tell them, are you?'

'Why? Don't you want me to?'

'It'd make it worse.' He looked uncomfortable. 'Don't want them involved.'

There was no more explanation coming. I considered explaining that I had a duty to report these things, it was part of my job; but then, I wasn't even working at the moment. And how could I explain Danny being at my house?

I said, 'But you can't just let him get away with it.'

'He won't,' Danny said. 'He'll get his.'

There was nothing nasty in his tone; it was a statement of fact. I said, 'You don't want to make things worse, do you?'

'But he deserves it,' he said. 'They all do.'

But there was a slight waver, a slight hesitation in his voice. He wasn't looking at me again. I said, 'What do they deserve?' He just shrugged, so I said, 'Danny?'

'I don't know. Jesus Christ, stop asking so many questions, will you?'

'But you sounded like you knew.'

'No,' he said. 'No, I don't.'

'So what did you mean?'

He got to his feet, faced me. 'How the fuck am I supposed to know?' I stood up, too, and he looked at me, then drew in breath and forced himself to smile. 'It's just natural justice, isn't it?' he said. 'What goes around comes around.'

It was a strange thing to hear him say, and he didn't seem entirely comfortable with the words himself. I had the feeling he was imitating someone else, putting on a performance for me. I sat down again, looked at him standing there, his fists clenched as though it was an effort to appear relaxed.

'Danny, sit down, won't you?'

He was almost glowing with resentment.

I said, 'I don't know why you told me this stuff if you don't want me to do anything about it.'

He still stood there, but I could see he was relaxing.

I said, 'Why did you come here?'

He blinked twice, as if snapping out of the act. Then he sat down again, said, 'But you're not going to say anything, are you?'

I wanted to laugh, because what could I say? That Danny Metcalfe believed in natural justice? That Gary Adams had hit Danny when Danny would only deny it? That I had invited Danny into my house? I said, 'Tell me why you came here.'

He just shrugged.

I considered pressing on, asking about Sean, but I didn't think he would tell me anything.

He was preparing to leave. I said, 'You're not going, are you?'

He nodded. I was about to ask him if he was sure he would be okay, if he was sure he didn't want me to phone anyone, when he said, 'You're not going to say anything to anyone.'

It wasn't a question. I said, 'Why not?'

'Because there's nothing to tell.' Then he smiled. I had the strange sensation that he was imitating someone else again, a threat implicit in each of his words, each of his movements. I thought of Sean;

my throat tightened. Then he said, 'Besides, about the dope smoking, I won't tell if you don't.'

Before I could react to that, he had started towards the front door. I followed him, caught his arm as he went to open the door. 'You can't threaten me,' I said.

He twisted to release his arm but I gripped it tighter. He was looking up at me and for a brief moment I thought he was afraid. He pulled his arm free and said, 'It wasn't a threat,' and the whine was back in his voice.

I said, 'You should watch what you say, then.'

I hadn't intended that as a threat, but he seemed to take it that way. He opened the door and ran outside.

'Danny!' I called, but he only stopped to undo the latch on my gate. 'Danny, come back here.'

He ran out into the street and across to the opposite pavement, where he stopped to look back at me. I stepped out onto the path, but I didn't have my shoes on and the concrete was rough under my feet.

I called out, 'Danny, I didn't mean that. Come back, please.'

He hesitated for a moment, but then started to run again. I stood and watched him until he was out of sight at the junction with the main road. I stood there a while longer, but he didn't reappear.

Back in the front room, I sat for a long time trying to decide what to do. I should tell somebody what Danny had said, and what Gary Adams had done.

But who could I tell? Colin certainly wouldn't want to hear from me, and Douglas would be angry, and who else was there? Besides, I could imagine what they would say – if Danny refused to press charges then nothing could be done, and a vague notion of 'natural justice' didn't amount to any kind of useful information. All I would end up doing was making my own situation worse.

So I smoked the second spliff that had been waiting for me, and rolled a third. I sat there and let the haze engulf me, until I was barely awake. The TV played out before my eyes but I had no idea what I was watching.

Later, the phone started to ring. The rumour-mill grinding on, spreading the news through the department – my situation must have reached Alex's ears by now. I let the phone ring on and allowed myself to sink further towards sleep.

Twenty-four

Morning came too quickly, another dreary day. I woke with aching knuckles. I could remember the impact of my fist against Colin's face, but it felt a lifetime ago. I lay on my back, massaging the hard bone of my knuckle and the soft flesh around it, feeling the ache, thinking about Colin falling and Gary Adams hitting Danny. Gary Adams with knuckles bruised against a child's face. And Sean – did his hands ache after he attacked me? Did he wake the next morning to pain that reminded him of what he'd done?

It took me a long time to get up. My throat was sore with the sticky aftertaste of all the spliff I'd smoked. I sat on the sofa drinking tea in front of daytime TV – an American chat show discussing kids who were out of control, in which the kids slouched and grinned and played up to the camera while the audience shouted abuse. I imagined Gary Adams watching the show, smacking his knee with his hand and giving approval while his kids watched and his wife said nothing. I imagined Carla Metcalfe as one of the tattooed mothers on the show, at the end of her tether. I imagined Douglas and Colin in the office, and all the other people at their desks, making their phone calls, writing their reports, and all the time it was having no impact, it was making no difference. The TV audience's bleeped-out insults chiselled further into my skull. The whole department would be talking about me by now, examining and re-evaluating everything I'd ever said and done. The Chantelle Wade enquiry would be old news, positively pedestrian in comparison to this scandal.

I switched off the TV and rattled around the house, waiting for someone to phone me up, waiting for someone to come knocking at my door, but nobody did. They had already decided – they knew what they thought.

But I had to talk to someone, I had to find out what was going on. By six o'clock I was going stir-crazy, coming down with cabin fever. Alex and Simon would be back from work soon; they would know what was being said, and what I could say or do to save my skin. Alex knew me so well, Simon was a union rep – they would listen to my side, understand why this had happened, surely they would? I had the feeling that if I didn't get to them soon, if I wasn't there to put my side of the story, I wouldn't ever be able to correct it, I wouldn't ever be able to convince anyone of what had really happened. I could imagine Alex listening with his usual frown of concentration, and Simon maybe cracking the odd joke, and everyone realizing that I had been in a difficult position, I had acted the way anyone would have acted, I had nothing to worry about.

I made sure my mobile phone was charged and put it in my handbag, then collected my jacket and headed out to the car. All the way over to Alex's house, I ran through what I would say in my head. They would understand – they were my friends, Alex knew me better than anyone, Simon was always representing people who'd got themselves into trouble at work, it went with the territory. I felt almost calm as I headed up the path to their front door.

Louise answered the door. I pushed in past her. She said, 'Uh, Jo, he's not here.'

'Yes, he is. I know he is. You wouldn't be here on your own, would you?'

She recoiled slightly at my tone but followed me into the front room, and then into the kitchen-diner. I headed back into the hall, but she tried to block my path to the stairs. I couldn't believe that she was being so blatant, that she thought she had this much control.

'I told you, he doesn't want to see you,' she said. She had her hand on the banister, blocking my way.

'He will.'

She wasn't going to move. I looked up the stairs, willing him to appear at the top, willing him to see what she was doing, what she was really like.

'Just leave it,' she said. 'I'll get him to call you.'

But I knew she wouldn't pass on any message. I tried to push past her, but she stood firm. 'I want

to speak to him now,' I said. She couldn't stop me –
he was my friend, he was still my closest friend, and
I knew he would want to see me. 'It's important,' I
said, but I knew she wasn't going to move.

Louise sighed, then leaned in towards me. 'When
are you going to get it into your thick skull that he
doesn't want to talk to you? When are you going to
learn? He's not interested, he's with me now. He
doesn't want to talk to you.'

'No,' I said. 'You've got it all wrong. I don't want
Alex, you're welcome to him, but he's my friend,
and I want to talk to him. You can't stop him from
talking to me, you can't stop us being friends.'

And then there he was, at the top of the stairs,
wearing jeans and buttoning up a shirt, his feet still
bare, his hair damp as if he'd just got out of the
shower. I wanted to run to him, get him between
me and Louise, so that he could see what she was
like, that she was twisting everything, so he could
see that I was his friend, not her. But I just stood
there, and I could feel the tears on my cheeks.

As he came down the stairs, he laid a hand on
Louise's shoulder. She looked up at him. He said,
'It's okay.' She let out a loud huff of frustration,
pushed past me and went into the kitchen-diner.
Alex watched her go, then signalled that we should
go into the front room.

I led the way, and as soon as he had come into
the room behind me and shut the door I turned and
said, 'You see what she's like, Alex?'

He looked a little taken aback, but he just went

and settled himself in one of the armchairs and said, 'I hear you're in trouble?'

The calmness of his tone knocked me off course for a moment, but then I remembered what I had come to say. 'It wasn't my fault. Everything kind of got out of hand. It's all gone crazy.' I could feel the tears starting up again, and I tried to fight them back, because I had to be able to explain this, I had to convince him that I had behaved the way anyone would have, and that none of this was my fault.

He looked at me for a moment, then turned to a packet of cigarettes on the table. He removed two, lit both and handed me one. I was still standing, still full of the energy of the moment, but I took a deep drag of the cigarette and said, 'Douglas suspended me.'

'Why?' But he didn't seem very surprised, and I realized that he already knew, he was just being nice, giving me time to put my side of the story. That irritated me. He had already made up his mind, he had already held some sort of kangaroo court in my absence and declared me guilty – Christ, he'd probably talked to Louise about it, got her opinion.

I said, 'I lost it for a moment. I'm stressed, Alex. I'm not coping very well. It's not my fault, it's this – it's since the attack. I can't seem to think straight.'

He looked at me, as if waiting for more of a reason, as if he'd already heard and rejected this explanation.

I said, 'I didn't mean for things to go this far. I don't know what I'm supposed to do.'

A moment of silence, a moment I'd hoped he would fill with reassurance, or sympathy, or advice. His expression didn't change.

'It's not my fault, honestly. It's – things have just got out of hand.'

'What things?' he asked.

He didn't sound sympathetic. I wanted to convince him but I didn't know how, I didn't know what explanation would satisfy him. I said, 'The Metcalfes. This case. I know how it looks, but,' and I took a deep breath, 'Sean Metcalfe's the one who attacked me. His mother's got it in for me. They're spreading lies about me, Alex, they're trying to cause trouble for me, but I don't know why.'

'The Metcalfes didn't hit Colin, though, did they?'

'No,' I said. 'But it's all part of the same thing, don't you see?'

He frowned. 'I doubt Colin sees it that way.'

'No, but it's all linked,' I said. 'Carla Metcalfe's hiding Sean. That's where the trouble's coming from.'

He said, 'So, tell the police, then.'

'I can't. I mean, I have, but they won't listen to me.'

'Is it any wonder?' He was looking up at me as I strode around the room, but his face was partly in shadow as the cigarette smoke rose in front of him and I couldn't make out his expression. He said, 'Look at yourself, Jo. You're a mess, you're fried. You need to calm down. Sober up.'

That stung me. 'I am sober. And calm.' I wanted to add that it was only Louise's presence that had stopped me being calm beforehand. 'I'm very calm, I'm ultra calm. I'm trying to tell you what's going on.'

'I know what's going on,' he said. 'You're getting obsessed with this thing. You're blowing it up out of all proportion. You're taking it out on the wrong people, too. And now you've got yourself suspended from work, and I can't say I'm surprised, the way you've been lately.'

'No, that's part of all of this,' I started to say.

He cut me off. 'You need to worry about yourself before you start fighting other people's battles for them, Jo.'

'But that isn't what this is all about.'

He didn't seem to be listening to me. 'You're alienating everyone,' he said. 'People at work, everyone. Even Colin's saying you've lost the plot, and he usually leads the Jo Elliott fan club.' He sounded bitter, and I wondered where that was coming from, but I didn't have time to think too much about it. 'Even Colin says you went too far this time.'

'It's not like that,' I said. 'I haven't done anything wrong.'

He just laughed, but there was no kindness in the laugh, none of the affection I'd been hoping for. He said, 'Done nothing wrong? You're lucky Colin isn't pressing charges.'

I opened my mouth to respond to that, but I didn't know what to say. I'd been so sure Alex would understand – I'd been so sure he would take my side, or at the very least listen to me, but he was no better than anyone else. I wanted to shout at him, shout that he was being led astray, that Louise was poisoning his mind against me, that the gossipers in the department were warping his thinking, that he shouldn't listen to what everyone else was saying. But I found I didn't have the energy to speak.

I sat down in the armchair, and Alex leaned across to me, took my hands in his and squeezed them. When he spoke, his voice was very gentle. 'Look, Jo, you've got issues you need to sort out. You need to get some distance, deal with this rationally. You're not making sense at the moment.'

I wanted to tell him that he had to listen, he had to really hear what I was saying to him. But my mouth was dry.

He said, 'We've known each other for a long time. I used to think I knew you really well, but just recently I can't figure you out at all.' Then he stopped, and withdrew his hands from mine. 'I don't think I want to figure you out, not at the moment, not the way you're behaving. I hoped we'd always be friends, but it doesn't seem to be working out that way.' He hesitated again. I wanted to meet his gaze, but he wouldn't even look at me. He said, 'I'm with Lou now. I'm happy. I haven't got the emotional energy to deal with all your shit. I don't want to deal with it, not any more.'

'But you're my friend—' I started to say.

'I can't cope with it,' he went on. 'It's too much.'

I suddenly saw. 'This is Louise, isn't it? She's got it in for me, Alex. I don't know why. I've never done anything to her—'

He cut me off. 'This isn't about Louise. Stop blaming other people. Face up to yourself.'

His voice sounded slightly strangled. I said, 'Help me to do that. Please, Alex, I need—'

'No.' He let out a long breath. 'I can't. I haven't got the emotional energy.'

That phrase again. I tried to think what I could say, how I could win him round, but there was a distance in the way he looked at me; a coldness. I didn't know what to do. I didn't know where to turn to next. I got up, in a kind of daze, and walked out of the room and back to the front door. Alex followed me – I heard him ask me where I was going, and what I was going to do, but I didn't answer him. I went back to my car and got in and drove. I didn't know where I was going – I didn't even really care that much – I just drove.

I was up towards the edge of the city, almost at the motorway, heading out towards Derbyshire, when my mobile phone rang. I would have ignored it but I thought it might be Alex – I wanted it to be Alex – apologizing, telling me he had thought again, telling me he knew I needed him and would I come back and it could just be the two of us, he'd tell Louise to go, and we could really talk, like we used to.

But it wasn't Alex on the phone. It was Katie Adams, and as soon as I heard her voice, the tremble in her voice, I wanted to break the connection and switch the phone off. Then I heard her crying, and I knew I couldn't hang up on her, not just like that, so I pulled over to the side of the road, cut my engine and said, 'What's wrong?'

She was crying so much it was hard to make out what she was saying. I could hear noise in the background: a heavy engine idling, people shouting, as though she was standing in a busy street. She was into a torrent of a tale; I had to listen hard to make anything out.

Finally, I said, 'Slow down, slow down. Did you say your house is on fire?' I couldn't understand what she was saying; she wasn't giving herself time to breathe. So I said, 'Okay, don't worry, I'll be there in a few minutes.'

Driving over there, I started to decipher her words. Someone had set her house alight – I couldn't work out what she had been saying about her kids. And was that heavy vehicle behind her a fire engine? I wasn't sure. I didn't know if she was in the right frame of mind to have dialled 999. I pulled over to the side of the road again and rang the emergency services, but when I gave the address, the woman on the other end of the line told me that the fire brigade were already there.

It was too much to think this was a coincidence. I remembered Danny's comments about natural justice, about Gary Adams 'getting his'. And did that mean I could have prevented this? Did that mean that this was something else that was my fault?

As I pulled off Alfreton Road and headed towards

their street, there were crowds of people out on the dark pavements; kids drawn in from all the neighbouring streets, attracted by the fire engines, clusters of women with their arms folded, a group of young men clutching cans of Special Brew. I parked my car at the top of the street and walked down towards the fire engine outside the Adams' house. There was still some smoke drifting out through the front window, through a blackened hole in the glass. I could taste the sour edge and my eyes began to smart. And then Katie Adams was there, throwing herself into my arms, her face streaked with grime and tears, coughing and sobbing into my chest. I gave her the briefest of hugs and then eased her away from me, eased her snotty face away from my clothes.

I said, 'How are the kids?' and she dissolved into another fit of sobs. Before I could read anything into that, I saw Gary Adams standing on the pavement nearby, holding the baby, Jack at his side. I guided Katie back over to him. He just nodded in acknowledgement.

'What happened?' I asked him.

'What d'you think happened? He chucked a fucking petrol bomb through the window, didn't he?'

'Who?' I asked.

'Who d'you think?' Before I could reply to that, he continued, 'Hope they catch the bleeding bogger an' all. Needs locking up, he does. Could've killed them all.'

Katie Adams let out a wail at that, and Gary put

out one arm to comfort her, still hugging the baby to his chest. Jack clung to his father's legs and started to cry too.

I looked back at the house. One of the firefighters was inside, examining the buckled window frame, while a couple of others talked to him through the hole in the glass. A tapering black scorchmark ran up the brickwork and licked the glass in the window above.

'Have you got somewhere to stay tonight?' I asked.

'Yeah,' Gary said. 'Cousin up at Strelley.'

I nodded, relieved – I wouldn't have wanted to sort their accommodation out when I shouldn't even have been there at all. I left them to it and went over to the fire engine. I showed the nearest firefighter my Social Services ID card, asked who was in charge and was directed to a firefighter rolling up one of the hoses. He was still wearing his heavy fire suit and boots, but he had taken his helmet off. I introduced myself and asked him if he knew what had happened.

'Looks like a petrol bomb. We'll know once the investigators have been.'

I wanted to ask more, but I wasn't sure that a Social Services ID was going to get me very far, and besides, I had just seen the police, over at the far side of the house talking to neighbours. I watched them for a moment, but PC Short and PC Andrews weren't among them, so I felt safe enough to go over and speak to them.

There was a CID man there, standing looking

at the mess as if he could find some answer in the ruins. I showed my ID card and said, with a kind of professional disinterest, 'I'm the Adams' caseworker. So, do we know what happened?'

He shrugged. 'Firebomb, by the sounds of it.'

'But you don't know who?'

He was annoyed by that, I could see. 'Give us a chance. We only just got here.' Then, as if aware that he sounded rude, or remembering some policy to cooperate with other agencies, he said, 'Have you got any ideas? The family got any enemies?'

I was about to give a brief run down on the history of the case when another police car arrived on the scene, and the detective turned to greet the officers getting out of the vehicle. I turned, too, and came face to face with Dave Short and PC Andrews.

Dave said, 'Jo. What are you doing here?'

'Katie Adams called me.' I waited for him to point out that I was suspended and shouldn't be having any contact. I was sure someone would have told him by now.

But he didn't say that, he just frowned. 'She tell you anything about what happened?'

'Nothing definite,' I said. I was oddly reluctant to point out that we probably all knew who was behind this.

He brought the subject up anyway. 'You think it was the Metcalfe kid, I suppose?'

I wasn't sure which kid he meant, but I didn't want to get pulled into a discussion so I just shrugged. 'Could be. How would I know?'

The detective looked from Dave to me and said, 'If you know anything, you should tell us.'

Dave wasn't going to help me out, I could see that, so I said, 'Ask PC Short, he knows as much as I do.' And I turned and walked away, back to where Katie and Gary Adams were watching. As I glanced back, I saw that Dave was talking to the detective. I could imagine the sorts of things he would be saying.

When I reached Katie Adams, she said, 'Did you tell them who did it? Did you tell them it was Danny?'

I said, 'But do you know it was him?'

'Of course it was him,' Gary started to say. 'All the stuff that's been going on.'

I was tempted to ask whether he meant it was revenge for the black eye he'd given Danny, but I stopped myself. My head was aching. 'But did you actually see him?'

'I don't need to have seen,' Katie Adams replied. 'Just look at my house, that's proof enough, isn't it? Who else would do it?'

I said carefully, 'I'm just saying that you have to be sure. This is so serious, you have to be absolutely sure.'

'We are,' Gary said, and it was more a snarl than a statement. 'We know it was him. He'll get what he deserves, you watch.'

I started to say that retaliation wouldn't solve anything, it would only make matters worse, but Katie was crying again. Gary put his arm around her, hugged her head to his chest and the bundle of baby, and glared at me.

I got the hint. I stepped away from them. My head was spinning a little, from the smoke or the strain, I couldn't tell. I wanted to tell someone that this wasn't Danny, Danny wouldn't do this; but then, Danny had that edge too, that nasty streak, and how could I be sure? Danny was the one who disliked Katie Adams so much; Danny was the one with the black eye. There was no reason for Sean to be behind this, not when he was already in so much trouble, not when he was already supposed to be in hiding.

I was still trying to work it all out when Dave Short and the detective came over to me. The detective said, 'I think we need a chat, Miss Elliott.'

There wasn't much I could say to get out of it, so I agreed. We went over to the low wall at the far end of the street, away from listening neighbours, and I sat down on the wall while the detective stood facing me and Dave Short hung around somewhere behind him. I took out a cigarette, lit it and then forced a smile onto my face. 'So,' I said, 'fire away. What d'you want to ask?'

The detective was in his forties, I guessed, but had the creased face of an older man. He was wearing a brown polyester suit that was slightly too tight for him, and his hand kept running to his waistline as if he could smooth away a slight beer gut if he tried often enough. 'So,' he said, 'PC Short has filled me in on the background. Neighbour dispute, eh?'

'Yes,' I said. He waited, but I didn't know what else he wanted me to say.

Finally, he continued. 'You're – er, close with the Adams family, that's right, isn't it?'

'I'm their caseworker,' I said.

He ignored that. 'You take a lot of interest in them?'

'I have to,' I said. 'It's my job.'

'Quite,' he said, and smoothed his hand over his stomach once again. 'But you're, er – involved?'

I wasn't sure where this was going, but I didn't like it. 'How d'you mean?'

'There was an incident over the weekend,' he said. 'The Metcalfes were threatened. Carla and Danny. By Gary Adams. Carla Metcalfe seemed to think you'd put him up to it.'

'Oh, that's ridiculous,' I said.

'Quite,' he agreed, but he wasn't making eye contact with me. 'Now Gary Adams claims the firebomb was the work of Danny Metcalfe.'

I just nodded.

'What do you think?' he asked.

'I don't know,' I said carefully. 'I mean, Danny's a little wild but he's only twelve. A petrol bomb – I mean, it seems unlikely.'

'Petrol bombs are very easy to make,' the detective said. Then he smiled brightly, but not with his eyes. 'It's just a bottle and a rag, isn't it? Find instructions on the Internet easily enough. Could find out how to build an atom bomb if you knew where to look. And kids these days, they know how to, don't they?'

'I suppose,' I said. 'But still—'

'Unless,' he continued, 'you have any better ideas?'

I opened my mouth to mention Sean Metcalfe, but there was something in his expression that didn't seem right, that got me worried. So I said, 'I really don't know. You're the detective.'

He didn't show any offence at that. 'You know the Metcalfes, though?'

'Yes,' I said.

'And it's fair to say you're not on good terms with Carla Metcalfe?'

'I don't see what that's got to do with anything,' I said. He was frowning, so I added, 'I'm a social worker. We're not always popular people.'

'But you've taken a lot of interest in the Adams family, haven't you? And their dispute with the Metcalfes?'

'So?'

'That dispute in particular, isn't that right?'

I threw down the butt of my cigarette and ground it under my heel. 'I'm a social worker,' I said. 'It's my job to take an interest.'

He gave a thin sort of a smile. 'But you've been suspended,' he said. 'After Gary Adams and Carla Metcalfe both complained about you.'

'And?'

'Well, I know I'd be pissed off if people got me suspended.'

That made me laugh. 'Don't be ridiculous,' I said. 'I'm a professional. I don't take these things personally.'

He gave an apologetic laugh, as if he, too, thought his comment had been ridiculous. 'So why the interest? Why are you here now?'

'Katie Adams phoned me. She was distressed.'

'There must be other workers available?'

'Not any who know her like I do,' I said. 'Look, is there a point to all these questions? I don't see how this could possibly be relevant.'

The thin-lipped smile again, showing slightly yellow teeth. 'Just background,' he said. 'Helps to build up a picture.' Then he glanced over to where Dave Short was talking to Gary and Katie Adams. 'That'll be all for now,' he said. 'Why don't you go home?'

It wasn't a suggestion. I wanted to refuse, but I couldn't see what that would achieve. I got up and walked back towards my car while the detective crossed over to Dave Short. I walked quickly along the opposite pavement before anyone else could collar me. When I reached my car, a couple of Danny's friends were circling on their bikes, but they didn't say anything to me. I called them over and they circled a little closer, eyeing me with suspicion.

I said, 'Do either of you know where Danny is?'

'No,' they replied, and then they cycled off. I wasn't sure that I believed them, but it didn't make any difference. I hadn't expected them to tell me anyway. So, deciding there was no point wasting my time looking for him, I headed home.

Twenty-five

I knew something was up as soon as I opened the front door. The house felt wrong, almost indefinably; the familiarity disturbed. I could hear the TV playing, so quietly I could have mistaken it for next-door's. I pushed open the living-room door. Nobody was there, but I could smell recent cigarettes. I switched off the TV and stood listening, but I couldn't hear any sounds.

I advanced further into the room. There was a glass of Coke half-drunk on the dining table, and a denim jacket hung on the back of the chair. I stepped towards the table. A pair of trainers, old and grubby, on the carpet. They were a child's size, a boy's size.

I called out, 'Danny? Are you here?'

No reply. I went through to the kitchen. Someone had smashed the pane of glass in the back door; there were shards of glass all over the lino, broken as if someone had stepped on them to get into the house. I felt strangely calm.

I went back through the living room and into the

300

hall. At the bottom of the stairs I called, 'Danny?' again, but there was still no reply. I wondered whether I should phone someone – the police, or the office, or Carla Metcalfe – but I didn't know what I would say, or how I would explain that he was here. The silence chilled me. I went slowly up the stairs, because what if he wasn't alone, what if he'd brought Sean with him, into my house? I gripped the banister hard as I went up, listening for the sound of someone else's presence, someone waiting for me, crouching at the top of the stairs.

I went into my bedroom first, but it didn't look as if anything had been disturbed in there. In the second bedroom, he had closed the curtains and it took a moment for my eyes to adjust to the darkness. The duvet was heaped up, moulded around his shape, and I thought suddenly of Alex in this room. I switched on the light, prepared to remonstrate, prepared to demand that he leave, but he only gave a slight moan and barely moved at all. I pulled the duvet away from his face – peaceful, sleeping, a small boy sleeping – but there was a smell rising from him, unpleasantly sweet. I pulled the duvet off him completely – he shifted and curled in protest but didn't wake. He was fully dressed; his sweatshirt had risen up his back, exposing pale skin and the trace of his spine underneath. He was hugging my bottle of rum, the lid off, the contents soaking out across the mattress. I pulled back as I recognized the sour smell mixed with the sweetness, and saw his wet clothes, the wet jeans bunched up around his groin.

I couldn't tell how much of the rum had spilled out onto the bed, but he had obviously managed to drink a fair amount of it.

I picked up the bottle and stood it on the floor next to the bed. I didn't really want to wake him; I didn't want to have to deal with this but I didn't know what else I could do. So I shook him, gently, and he tried to shrug me off. I hooked my arms under his and tried to lift him; he was heavier than I expected and struggled against me, eyes closed. Then he threw his hands over his face, but whether it was to protect himself or to block out the light I wasn't sure. I manoeuvred him into the bathroom and managed to turn on the shower. He struggled slightly as I undressed him, protesting as I reached his underpants. I left those on; I didn't know what else to do. I put his clothes in a pile on the floor and helped him to get into the bath, and while he leaned against the tiles I used the shower attachment to rinse him off. Hose him down. He was starting to wake up, starting to cry. When I got him out of the bath and began to towel him dry he struggled against me a little, but I could see that he was almost asleep again. I rubbed him more roughly, wanting him to wake up, wanting him to understand what he had made me do; he tried to push away but I persisted, and I saw his skin turning pink under the effort. I didn't want to stop; I kept rubbing, wanting him to feel this, wanting him to remember this.

He started to cry again, but still didn't open his eyes fully or look at me. And I felt bad and stopped what I was doing; I wrapped the towel around him more gently, and tried not to look at the raw patches on his skin where I'd rubbed. He leaned against me, snivelling; a snivelling little boy with my arms around him. So I guided him through to my bedroom, half-walking, half-stumbling, and I helped him into my bed and wrapped the duvet around him. I stood looking at him, so small curled up in my bed, his face pale except where the bruise under his eye was slightly green with a yellow edge. He seemed to be asleep again before I had even left the room.

I collected up his clothes and the bedcovers from the other room and went downstairs. I emptied out the pockets of his jeans – there was nothing much in there, just a few sweet wrappers, a couple of pounds in small change and a scrap of paper with what looked like a mobile phone number written on it. I put these things on the kitchen work surface and loaded everything else into the washing machine. With luck, I would be able to get his things dry enough to wear by morning.

Once that was done, I sat down on the sofa. Danny had left his cigarettes there, so I took one out of the packet and lit it. I wasn't sure what I should do. I couldn't imagine who I could phone, or what I could say; how could I explain his being here, passed out in my bed after drinking my rum? Whatever I said, Douglas would say it was an issue, would take it as yet another sign of my unprofessionalism. Alex was right about one thing; I had to worry about myself first, get some distance from this whole situation. Besides, Danny had come to me, and that was because he trusted me. How could I betray that trust?

So I left him where he was and didn't phone anyone. I fetched a sleeping bag from the cupboard under the stairs and made up a bed on the sofa for myself. I wasn't tired, though; I uncorked a bottle of red wine and sat drinking in front of the television until gone midnight, listening out for sounds from upstairs, although I heard nothing. I put his clothes out on the radiator to dry and lay down, not convinced I would be able to sleep.

I did sleep, though. I slept and dreamed about a dark house, and a broken window, and the smell of smoke, and flames engulfing me. I dreamed about faces looming out at me from the darkness, through the smoke, and hands against my face, and someone standing over me.

I woke with a jolt. A shadow across my face. I sat up quickly, gave a little cry, saw him standing there, saw Sean in his features.

He laughed.

I rubbed my eyes open. Danny was standing there. He had wrapped a towel under his armpits and around his chest to cover his whole body, and was holding it up with his fist.

'Christ,' I said. 'You gave me a fright.'

He laughed again. 'Who'd you think I was, eh? Jack the Ripper?'

I sat up awkwardly. The sleeping bag had twisted

around my legs during the night and I had to kick myself free of it. 'Never mind that,' I said. 'What are you doing here? Nearly had the fright of my life when I got in last night.'

He ignored that. The usual resentful scowl had returned to his face. 'What've you done with my clothes?'

'On the radiator,' I said, signalling with my hand. I unzipped the sleeping bag, stiff from having slept awkwardly, and lit myself an early morning cigarette. The clock on the video said just after seven. Danny stomped past me with his clothes in his hand and went upstairs again without another word.

But when he came back downstairs a few minutes later, dressed in his clean clothes, he had obviously decided that he needed to behave himself. He sat in the armchair and looked at me and then said, 'How come you didn't phone the police?'

'Doesn't mean I'm not going to. You seemed to need some sleep before any of that.'

He considered that, frowning, but didn't say anything. If he remembered anything about the shower I'd given him, he showed no signs of it.

I said, 'Why did you come here, anyway?'

He just shrugged and looked at me as though I had asked the least intelligent question I could have thought of. I wanted to ask him about the fire at the Adams' house, but I suspected that he would have been even less tolerant of that question. He got up out of the armchair and collected his packet of cigarettes from the mantelpiece where I'd put them, took one out and lit it, looking at me with a challenge in his eye as if he was testing my reaction. But I had only just put my own cigarette out, so I didn't really see what I could say.

He was walking around the room while he smoked, looking at all my things, the way he had the first time he had come to my house. I forced a yawn. 'What do you want, Danny?'

He was thinking, I could see it in his eyes. He went back to the armchair and sat down, drawing his socked feet under him. 'Why didn't you call the police?' he asked.

'I told you,' I said. 'I thought you needed sleep.'

'Well, I've slept now. You gonna call them?'

'Do you want me to?'

'You're the one who doesn't want to,' he said.

I couldn't read his tone. 'What do you mean by that?' I asked.

He gave a little smile. 'Did they tell you about the fire?'

'At Mrs Adams's house? Yes. It was lucky nobody got hurt, it could have been really dangerous.' I hesitated, but I had to ask. 'Did you start that?'

'No,' he said, but quickly. 'Course not. Is that what they think?'

'I don't know.' I didn't want to tell him that they had asked me what I knew, that they'd been so strange towards me. I thought he would probably laugh. I said, 'Do you know who started it?'

'That'd be telling, eh?'

I was starting to get impatient. 'This isn't a joke,

Danny. It's very serious. Was it you?' Watching his expression. 'Or was it Sean?' His eyes widened for a moment but he hid his expression quickly. 'It was, wasn't it? Do you know where Sean is?'

'No,' he said, with relief.

'But you've seen him?'

He was calculating as he looked at me and I thought he was going to find a way not to tell me, but then he said, 'Yeah, I saw him, but he's gone now. They'll never catch him.'

'Where's he gone?' He just shrugged, but there was something – I thought I was starting to be able to read his expressions, and there was something. 'But you can find out?' I asked. Then I realized. 'You've got his mobile phone number, haven't you?'

He looked at me with alarm and his hands ran to his empty pockets.

'It's in the kitchen,' I said.

He went into the kitchen, and I heard him scooping up the coins. Then he was back, a little more shyly. 'About the window,' he said. 'In the door.'

'Yes?'

'I didn't know where else to go. And you did say I could come back. I'll pay for it, I swear.' He anticipated my derisive, 'How?' and said, 'I can get the money, no problem.'

'What, from Sean? He's on the run, he won't have money to replace my glass.'

'It'll be okay,' he said. 'We're gonna be together, he told me. Everything'll be great, he's got it all worked out, a place and everything.'

'He told you that?' I had been about to laugh, but I saw Danny's expression and he suddenly seemed so young, such a kid. I said, 'Danny, you can't go on the run with Sean. They'd catch up with you eventually, and then what'd happen?'

He shrugged.

I changed tack. 'Tell me about the fire. Was that what you meant when you said about natural justice?'

His hand ran to the bruise on his face, but he just shook his head and said, 'Think what you like. I never started the fire.'

'I don't think you did,' I said. 'I think it was Sean.'

He didn't respond to that.

I said, 'People think it was you.'

'So?'

'Don't you want to tell them it wasn't?'

He turned and looked at me then, and I realized that he didn't want to because suspicion would fall on his brother. I said, 'You can't protect Sean from the things he does, you know. He's old enough to make his own decisions, and old enough to take the consequences.'

He didn't say anything to that.

'What goes around comes around,' I went on. 'That's got to apply to Sean too, hasn't it? All the things he's done?'

His whole body seemed to sag at that. He sat down in the armchair, bit on his fingernail. Then he said, 'He's not so bad, not really.'

I wondered whether I should tell Danny that Sean had attacked me, knocked me unconscious. I wondered whether Danny would even care – I realized that I didn't want to know. Instead, I said, 'Sean's in trouble and there's not much you can do about that.'

He sighed. He was twisting the hem of his sweat-shirt round in his fingers, twisting and twisting the material, a frown on his face. Then he said, 'I'm not like Sean. I know people think I am. I know what people say about me, but I don't want to end up like him.'

'Why do you keep getting into trouble, then?' I asked. 'All this stuff with Mrs Adams – you've been involved with that, haven't you?'

'I don't mean to,' he said. I thought he was going to start making excuses, and maybe he would have, but his hand had run to the bruise around his eye again and that seemed to have an effect on his mood. 'Sometimes stuff happens,' he said. 'Everything gets out of hand, you know what I mean?'

I felt I should say something about taking respon-sibility for your own actions, or thinking before acting, but I couldn't bring myself to say those words. I didn't know what else to say, so I just nodded.

He said, 'Sometimes one little thing happens and everything goes crazy. Seems like you should be able to undo stuff, but it doesn't work that way, does it?'

'No,' I said.

'Like Sean. He doesn't think, he just does stuff, and then he ends up in a huge mess, and he just leaves it for other people to sort out. I don't want to be like that.'

'That's a very mature attitude,' I said.

He looked at me quickly, as if I'd disappointed him somehow. After a moment, he said, 'I'm not stupid, you know.'

'I know that,' I said. 'I can tell.'

That seemed to please him. 'Don't get me wrong, I mean, he's my big brother, you know? He looks after me, protects me. But I don't want to be like him, I wouldn't ever do what he's done, I mean, I'd never—' He stopped himself suddenly.

I ignored whatever he had almost said. 'So what do you want to do?' I asked.

'Dunno. Get away. Live somewhere nice. Have lots of money.'

'Go to college?'

He looked at me as though I was stupid. 'No way. Boring. Leave school as soon as I can.'

'And do what?'

He just shrugged. I knew I should ask him what he was planning to do now, but I thought I would get the same response. I knew I should try to persuade him to go home again, maybe even tell someone what had happened and where Sean was, but I was reluctant to broach the subject.

He said suddenly, 'Haven't you got to go to work?'

'No,' I said. 'Not for a few days. Do you want something to eat?'

He followed me through into the kitchen. I put some toast in the toaster and he fetched the margarine from the fridge while I put the kettle on. I was just forming my next question when someone rang the doorbell. I glanced at Danny, then went through the living room and out into the hall. I opened the door. PC Short and PC Andrews.

'Sorry to call so early,' Dave said.

'That's okay,' I said. I wasn't sure what to do next. They wanted to come in, I could see by the way they had angled themselves at the door, and I knew it would seem odd if I didn't let them in. But if they found Danny here – what would people think?

'Can we come in?' Dave asked.

'It's not very convenient,' I said.

'We won't be long.' He was trying to look past me. I realized I had no choice, so I opened the door wider and led the way through into the front room.

Danny had closed the kitchen door and was out of sight. The sleeping bag was still on the sofa, and the two of them looked at it then at me. I smiled and said, 'I was watching telly till late.' I moved the sleeping bag onto the floor, looking around surreptitiously to see if there was anything else that would give away Danny's presence, but I couldn't see anything. I sat down quickly. 'What can I do for you?'

Dave Short said, 'We're looking for Danny Metcalfe. He didn't go home last night.'

'Oh,' I said, and then I couldn't resist adding, 'So you've lost both Metcalfe boys, have you? Their mother must be so pleased.'

Dave scowled at me and looked around the room, and I wondered whether he could spot any differences since the last time he was here, whether he suspected that Danny was hiding behind the kitchen door.

PC Andrews said, 'Come on, Jo. Don't be hostile.'

'That's not hostile,' I said. 'I can do hostile if you want, but that wasn't hostile. Anyway, what am I supposed to do? According to everyone it seems like all this is my fault.'

'Nobody thinks that.' But Dave's tone was cool and he didn't look directly at me. 'We know you've been suspended from work. We've been told all about it. I'm sure that'll get sorted out. We're not interested in that, we're just looking for Danny.'

'Why, so you can accuse him of starting that fire? I don't believe it was him.'

Dave shrugged. 'Maybe it wasn't. We won't know until we speak to him.'

PC Andrews said, 'Do you know where he is?'

'No.' I wondered whether they could tell that I was lying. I wasn't even sure why I was lying.

'Have you seen him since yesterday?'

'No,' I said.

Dave was wandering around the room. He walked through to the back area and I stood up, unable to stay seated as he got closer to the kitchen. I could imagine Danny, crouched in there, trying to make himself small and invisible.

Dave's hand had run to the handle on the kitchen

door. He was looking closely at me, and so was PC Andrews, and I wondered what they were thinking, what they thought they could see in my face.

PC Andrews said, 'Do you know anything about the fire yesterday?'

'No,' I said, still looking at Dave. 'I was asked about it yesterday. I don't know.'

'What about Danny or Sean?'

'I've told you,' I said. 'I don't know where they are.'

PC Andrews looked at Dave Short, and Dave stepped towards me, gave a pleasant sort of a smile and said softly, 'We're only here to help, Jo. I'd hate for you to get even more mixed up in all of this.'

He seemed to actually think that talking to me that way might have some sort of an effect. He hadn't grasped that I had moved beyond all of that. I smiled a sweet smile and said, 'That's very kind of you, Dave, but there's really nothing for you to worry about.'

He held my gaze for a moment. 'Why do I feel as if you're hiding something?'

'Hiding something?' I forced myself to laugh. 'Like what? I mean, d'you think I've got the Metcalfe boys tucked away upstairs?'

Dave frowned. 'No,' he said. 'Of course not.'

They headed back towards the front of the house. I allowed myself to breathe again. When we got to the front door, Dave turned and smiled at me and said, 'I'm not fooled, you know.'

'Fooled?' I said, as innocently as I could.

'I know he's around here somewhere. I just don't understand why you'd be protecting a kid when you think his brother attacked you. It doesn't make any sense.'

'I'm not protecting anyone,' I said. 'I'm hardly in a position to do that these days, am I?'

They looked at each other, but seemed to have nothing further to say. I opened the front door. Then PC Andrews said, 'Listen, Jo, if you do see them, please call us. It'll only make things worse for everyone the longer this goes on.'

I didn't think they believed I would contact them, but I played along anyway. 'Sure, sure,' I said, and gave them an encouraging smile as they headed down the path.

When they had gone, I lit myself another cigarette. I was surprised to find that I was shaking. I'd never lied to the police before; I wasn't sure why I had now, but there was no way back. I couldn't see how I could extricate myself from this situation.

I went to the kitchen, but Danny wasn't there; he must have slipped out of the back door. I had lied to the police, and now I really didn't know where Danny was. I wanted to laugh but I thought I might end up crying instead. Douglas had told me I needed distance; Alex had said the same thing. At that moment, it did feel that I needed distance – as much distance as I could put between myself and Nottingham. I smoked the cigarette right down to the filter while I waited for Danny to return, trying to figure out what I should do next.

Twenty-six

I was on the phone to my union rep when Danny returned. I was standing cradling the receiver against my shoulder while I folded clothes and put them in my holdall. My union rep had phoned up to explain the definition of Gross Misconduct to me. Every so often I said, 'Uh-huh,' or 'Right,' just so she wouldn't feel that she was wasting her breath.

Danny came strolling into the house through the back door and sat down on the sofa. He was crunching his way through the contents of a tube of Smarties. When I finally extracted myself from the conversation with the union rep and hung up, he said, 'What you doing?'

He was indicating the holdall. 'Packing,' I said. 'Thought a few days away would do me good.'

He frowned, but gave no other response to that news. Then he said, 'You're suspended from work?'

'Yes,' I said, wondering how much more of the conversation with Dave Short he'd overheard before clearing out of the kitchen. 'Where have you been?'

'Around.' He pushed some more Smarties into

315

his mouth, then said, 'Police'll be back soon. With a search warrant.'

I was surprised. 'You think so?'

'Yeah.' But he didn't expand on that. I wondered whether he really did know, or whether he was just trying to show off.

But I picked up the lacquered box with my stash inside it and put that in the holdall, just in case. I put the clothes on top of the box, then zipped the bag up. In my handbag, I had an envelope containing my bank books and cheque books and the credit card I reserved for household emergencies. I had about four grand in savings, the cheque books were pretty new, and if I hammered the credit card creatively I could get hold of a fair amount of cash. Surely that was enough to keep me going, for a while at least?

I made myself a strong mug of coffee and sat in the armchair drinking it. Danny had turned on the TV and was channel hopping with the remote control, crunching his sweets noisily and glancing over at me, as if waiting for me to comment. I knew I should phone someone and tell them that he was here, but I couldn't bring myself to do that. He would be okay – he would go back to his mum's house once I had left.

I had expected to feel some sort of emotion at the prospect of just clearing off, even if I was saying it was only for a few days. But I felt nothing, except a sort of numb sickness in the lower regions of my stomach; a sensation I didn't want to find spreading through the rest of my body. I remembered Colin's story about the client who ran away, and I thought of all my clients who had done the same – the women who escaped their husbands, with or without their kids; the teenagers showing off that they didn't want to be like their parents; the depressives who escaped into drink, or drugs, or some grand-gestured attempt at suicide. I didn't think I could do that. But escape – I could imagine escaping, just turning my back on everyone and everything, getting into the car and driving away into the horizon.

I drained the last of my coffee and stood up. 'Right,' I said. 'I'm getting out of here. Time for you to go home, Danny.'

He feigned reluctance. 'Can't I come with you?'

'No,' I said. 'You've got to go home.'

'But if I go back they'll start asking about the fire, and I know they won't believe me, and I'll get in trouble for something I never did.'

'You just have to explain,' I said. 'Tell the truth. The police'll listen to you if you tell them about Sean.'

He ignored that. 'Gary Adams'll be after me again,' he said, touching the bruise on his face and adopting a pitiful expression. 'He'll kill me if he catches me.'

I was pulling on my denim jacket. I rolled my eyes at him and said, 'Don't be so melodramatic, Danny. You just have to face this. It'll be fine.'

His expression changed; irritation, anger, I wasn't sure. I hoped he wasn't going to have a tantrum, or start crying. He said, 'Well, I'm not going back home. If I can't come with you, I'll phone Sean. He said I can go with him.'

I looked at him, trying to judge whether he was serious, but I couldn't tell. He had his jaw clenched shut, a frown darkening his face. And how did I know whether he would really do it? He was just a kid, after all, a kid who wanted to get away from his normal life for a while, a kid who was too stupid to realize what he was saying. If he did find Sean, if they did head off together, they wouldn't last five minutes, I was certain of that. They'd be picked up in a shopping centre for loitering with intent, or on a city street for aggressive begging, or for breaking into a car or a shop or a house.

So I sat down and thought for a moment and said, 'Danny, running away isn't an answer, you know. You have to sort these things out otherwise it'll all get worse for you. As for Sean—' I had been about to say that going off with Sean would make them both fugitives, but I realised that that was a bad choice of words. Instead, I said, 'Being with Sean wouldn't be much fun, you know. It might seem like a big adventure to you now, but running away with Sean would just make everything worse.'

He was silent for a moment, and I thought maybe I'd got through to him. Then he said, 'But you're running away, aren't you? What's the difference?'

I rubbed my hand over my eyes and took a deep breath. 'I'm not running away,' I said. 'I'm just going away for a few days. A break. A holiday.'

'Yeah, right,' he said. 'That's what you call it when you've got money for a hotel. Still the same thing, isn't it?'

'No,' I said. 'Not at all.' I knew there was no point arguing about it, though, so I continued, 'You need to go home, Danny. Your mum must be worried sick.'

He shrugged; I wasn't sure if he meant that she wouldn't be worried or that he didn't care if she was.

I said, 'If you go with Sean you'll be in danger. The streets aren't very nice, you know.'

'So let me come with you.'

'No.' I picked up my holdall and went to the front door.

He followed me. 'Don't you want to know why Sean's got it in for you?'

I turned and looked at him. He had a smile on his face. I wondered again whether he knew that Sean had hit me – whether he knew how little it had taken for Sean to hurt me. But I kept my expression blank and said, 'Grow up, Danny.'

He followed me out onto the front path and watched me deadlock the front door. I was surprised that it didn't seem to concern him, being locked out of my house, until I remembered the broken glass in the back door.

He said, 'How d'you think I knew where you lived?'

I ignored him and went down to the car. He followed me. I put my holdall in the boot. I wanted him to stop talking to me, to leave me alone; I didn't want him to say any more about his brother.

He said, 'Sean said he was going to sort you out.'

I stopped with my key in the driver's door. I wanted to ask when Sean had said that; before or after he attacked me? Instead, I said, 'This won't work. You're not coming with me.'

Danny shrugged, fake-casual. 'But if I was you I'd be curious about why he's been watching the house. I mean, what if he wanted to firebomb another place? Doesn't that scare you?'

'No,' I said, and made myself laugh. 'Don't be ridiculous, Danny. Just go home. Back to your mum and be grateful that I'm not going to report you for breaking into my house.'

'Report me? Hah! After all the things I could say about you?'

He was cocky now, confident. I gritted my teeth. 'What makes you think I'd be worried about anything you could say?'

He smiled, showing yellowish teeth. 'I know you smoke ganja,' he said. 'I know where your stash is.'

I unlocked the driver's door and got in. But the central locking had released the other doors, and before I realized what he was doing he had opened up the passenger door and was sitting next to me. 'Get out,' I said, with as much authority, as much coldness as I could gather.

'If I went back, I'd get to talk to that PC Short,

wouldn't I? Wonder what he'd do if I told him you'd lied to him?'

I softened my tone. 'This isn't going to work, Danny. You can't make me take you with me.'

He leaned back in the seat, crossed his arms over his chest, looked at me. But he didn't seem comfortable; he was playing out a role again, imitating his brother. Then he said, 'What would they all say if they knew you took my clothes off and put me in the shower?'

I felt a chill run through me, but tried not to show it. 'For Christ's sake, Danny. Don't be ridiculous. Now get out of my car immediately.'

'But what would they say?' he insisted. 'They wouldn't like it, would they? You're not supposed to do stuff like that. Anything could have happened.'

'Nobody would believe you.'

'Yes, they would,' he said. 'They told us at school. Anything like that, they take it dead seriously.'

'Don't be stupid.'

He just laughed. 'My mate at school got a teacher sacked by saying he touched him, you know, down there.'

I didn't believe him – but how would people react? I could imagine Douglas saying they had to be seen to investigate, there was nothing he could do. I said, 'They'd know you were lying. Now get out of the car.'

He pretended to be surprised at my anger. 'But I wouldn't be with you for long,' he said. 'All you'd have to do is take me to Sean. You could even drop me off nearby, if you wanted. I wouldn't tell anyone, honest I wouldn't.'

It was a ridiculous suggestion – as if I could do anything of the sort. I could imagine Douglas's reaction if he found out. And Alex's. And Colin's. And Dave's. I leaned forward and rested my arms and head on the steering wheel. I just wanted Danny to leave me alone – I wanted everyone to leave me alone – was that really so much to ask?

I said, 'I can't take you to Sean.'

'Why not? Nobody would know.'

I thought about Colin betraying me, and Alex and Dave refusing to listen, and Douglas telling me I needed to sort things out. I spent my whole life worrying about people like them, worrying about what they thought, and they had all betrayed me. What difference did it make? Danny was asking me for help. I'd lost everything by trying to stick to the rules – maybe I should take control? I could imagine it – me and Danny finding Sean, talking him round, setting things straight.

I heard myself say, 'Where is Sean?'

'Skegness.'

'That's a long way,' I said. 'I hadn't planned on going to the east coast.'

'Well, that's where he is.' Danny waited a moment, then said, 'Oh, come on. Please.'

And if I brought Sean back, got him to admit what had been going on, would people believe me then? They would have to understand the position I'd been in, the trouble that Sean had stirred up. Would it still be Gross Misconduct if I brought Sean back? I could imagine Douglas saying that he understood, and Colin laughing and telling me to forget about the punch, and Alex telling me he'd been upset, he hadn't meant any of it. I raised my head from the steering wheel and said, before I could change my mind, 'Okay, okay, I'll take you there.'

Danny did his seatbelt up quickly, as if afraid I would change my mind part way there and push him out. I started the engine without another word.

We headed out along Gregory Boulevard and up the Mansfield Road, out through the northern edge of the city. Danny was very quiet as we drove, looking out of the window; I wasn't sure whether he was deep in thought or was trying to avoid reminding me of his presence.

We passed the estates that ring the city, and then we were out between brown fields. I saw how dark the sky was, how cold the air was growing. It was not the time to be heading towards the coast – the weather forecast had predicted high winds, rain, a drop in temperature.

Danny glanced across at me a couple of times as the city receded into the distance. I ignored him. Then he said, 'I wouldn't have said any of that stuff, you know. I wouldn't have dropped you in it.'

He sounded boyish again. There was pleading in his tone; he was waiting for me to tell him it was okay. I gripped the steering wheel hard. I wasn't sure if I had actually believed he would say those things – but I knew it was possible, and those things would have finished me. I forced myself to look across at him and smile and say, 'I know. It's okay.'

He watched me for a few more minutes, as if afraid that my expression would change to anger. But I wasn't angry, not now that we had left the city. The black sky rolled in before us, weighed down by impending rain, but I could see a hazy sort of horizon across the flat fields, and that was something. Back in the city we were hemmed in by red brick, by a skyline of factories and warehouses and high-rise blocks until there was no sky to see. It all seemed so very far away. I could imagine just keeping going, never coming back; nobody would miss me. I could keep on driving until I merged with the grey blur of the horizon, until I was just another part of the smudged and hazy distance. They would miss Danny, that was true; people would look for him, would put out reports and print posters with his picture to paste up at railway stations. But what was he really leaving behind? I was rescuing him, that was all; saving him from the bleak future that his brother had mapped out for him. And if by saving him I could save myself – well, Sean owed me that much after everything that had happened. I felt strangely confident – for the first time in a long time, I felt in control.

Danny said, 'Can I put the radio on?'

'Sure,' I said, and he leaned down and tuned it in to Radio One. We drove on with a soundtrack of something I didn't recognize, garage or techno or something. He hummed along and beat out the bass rhythm on his knees and looked out of the window, and I just kept driving.

The rain started as we reached Newark, and we negotiated our way through the town with the windscreen wipers battling against the deluge. We got onto the A46 towards Lincoln and drove through the spray of lorries, and I remembered all those holidays I'd had as a kid, all those wet August days sitting in traffic jams waiting for a glimpse of the rusty North Sea below an iron sky.

'Do you go to Skeggie a lot?' I asked Danny.

He nodded. 'Mum's sister's got a caravan at Ingoldmells.'

'And that's where we're going?'

'Yeah.' Then he hesitated, and said, 'But you won't tell anyone, will you?'

'No, not if you don't want me to.' We drove in silence for a bit, and then I said, 'Does Sean know we're coming?'

He hesitated again. 'I told him I would.'

I nodded. I had half expected Danny to repeat that I didn't need to take him all the way, but he didn't say that. I tried to imagine just dropping Danny off, and I knew that Danny was right; I did want to know what had been going on, and why. I wasn't sure how Sean would take my arrival, but now that it was going to happen, I realized it didn't really matter. He had wanted me to apologize for something he believed I had done – I might not be offering an apology, but bringing his brother to him had to be worth something. And even if he was angry, he wouldn't hit me again, not with Danny there, not as long as Danny didn't want that.

But how close were they? Did Danny know everything Sean had done? Did Danny know that Sean had hit me? I didn't want to ask. I kept quiet, and kept driving.

When we came into Lincoln, it stopped raining. The growing distance from Nottingham was helping me to think more clearly, and I parked the car near the railway station.

Danny said, 'Why have we stopped?'

'I need to get some money. Anyway, I'm hungry. Aren't you?'

He scrambled out of the car after me and walked with me into the shopping area. It was not very busy, and the sun shone weakly on pools of water from the recent rain. Danny waited outside while I went into the Building Society and withdrew some cash. I had already decided that I wouldn't withdraw all of it, not just yet – I didn't want to alert the Building Society to anything odd. But while I was standing in the queue waiting, it occurred to me that there was nothing wrong with me withdrawing all my savings, there was nothing to stop me closing all my accounts if I wanted to. It was my money, my life. The further I got from Nottingham, the less important everything seemed. So what if the department had suspended me? I didn't want to go back to work anyway, and it wasn't a crime to walk out on a job, there was nothing that said I had to stay.

So I told the cashier that I wanted to withdraw everything except just enough to leave the account open. I had expected her to be surprised, or to pass comment on what I was going to do with four thousand pounds in cash, but she didn't say a word, just handed over the form for me to sign and then counted the money out onto the counter. She bundled it up into five-hundred-pound wads, held together with elastic bands, and gave me an envelope to put the money in. I stood at the counter holding that envelope, looking at the boredom on the cashier's face, and it struck me that all my life I had been working, and saving, and worrying about money, and in the end it came down to an envelope of cash and a scale of economy that didn't even raise the interest of the person handing me the money. I tucked the envelope into my handbag and walked out of there feeling almost deflated.

Danny wanted to go to McDonalds for lunch, so I took him. We sat in the window of the restaurant looking out at the people milling through the streets. I ate my burger and fries, but they tasted like cardboard to me. I watched Danny eating and wondered yet again what I thought I was doing. There was no magical fix, I knew that. I was running away, and it wouldn't solve anything. I just had to hope that facing Sean would have an effect, because I couldn't imagine going back to the situation I had left behind.

Twenty-seven

We reached Skegness in mid-afternoon and I drove through the town centre to the junction where the clock tower surveyed the promenade. The fish restaurants and shops selling rock and tourist souvenirs were open but there weren't many customers. Across the road, beyond the shuttered seafront kiosks, the sky was a dirty grey mass of rolling clouds, imitating the swell and froth of the sea.

'Looks cold for swimming,' I said, but Danny didn't laugh. He had burrowed down into the seat and drawn his knees up to almost touch his chin, and he looked around him with a gaze that showed no surprise or excitement or disappointment.

I turned north. The road followed the line of the coast for about half a mile; the amusement arcades were open, soaking up the small number of visitors, but the Pleasure Beach and the crazy-golf courses were closed. A few half-hearted raindrops fell from that heavy sky then gave up again.

Danny gave me directions in a flattened tone. He

was looking directly ahead the whole time. I had no idea what he was thinking. I wanted to ask him; I wanted him to tell me without my asking. I wanted to reassure him that everything would work out fine, but I didn't know what he was expecting to happen.

The road turned away from the coast. The amusement arcades were replaced by guest houses and blocks of holiday flats, then, gradually, large mock-Tudor houses that hadn't become hotels, followed by ordinary housing estates and streets of bungalows with tiny gardens. I had expected some nod towards open countryside, but instead the straggles of housing on the edge of town were interspersed with caravan parks and sales yards. We passed Butlin's and Fantasy Island and turned along Sea Lane towards Ingoldmells village. The road was fringed with corrugated buildings hiding behind neon signs: more amusement arcades, takeaways, pubs, discount clothing stores. Further up, there were more bungalows, and the driveways between the bungalows gave access to the caravan parks behind.

Danny directed me down to the end of the road. I caught a glimpse of brown water before the view was blocked. A moment later, he said, 'Turn off just ahead.'

I obeyed. Sunny Bay Holiday Park. We drove past the bungalow that functioned as an office, now closed up, and followed a waterlogged gravel road along a winding route past rows of static caravans planted on the grass.

'There,' Danny said, and pointed to a caravan parked on a scrap of hardstanding towards the back of the site. Someone had built a narrow wooden decking along the side of the caravan but the wood didn't look as if it had been treated recently, and there was green mould lapping around the edges of the caravan's roof.

I guided the car across and parked next to the wooden decking. The caravan's curtains were drawn; there was no sign of anyone watching our approach.

'You're sure he's here?' I asked.

Danny just nodded and got out of the car. I followed him across to the steps and up onto the decking. He seemed a little nervous. He knocked lightly on the caravan door, looking round at me as if to check that I was still there. I listened but couldn't hear any movement inside. Danny turned the door handle and pulled the door open. I followed him in.

It was gloomy inside the caravan, but the curtains were only thin and allowed enough light in to see the interior. It was larger than it seemed from the outside. We were standing in a lounge area that occupied the caravan's nose. Cushioned benches faced each other across a melamine table that was attached to the wall below the large front window. There was a small portable TV on the table, switched off. A kitchen area took up space in the centre of the caravan, and a narrow corridor led from there into the shadows of the other rooms.

'Sean?' Danny called, but he kept his voice low. 'Sean, are you here?'

A noise from down the corridor. I turned – someone coming straight at me, fast. I threw myself out of the way, banged heavily into the table, let out a cry that I stifled immediately. And there was Sean, standing in front of the door, as if afraid we would try to escape, looking at me and Danny, looking at us with an expression that I couldn't – didn't want to – interpret. That face – the face I had pictured for so long, but slightly different, unaltered by my memory. A thin sharp face with sickly pale skin, pinkened around the corners of his mouth by acne, and eyes so dark they reflected.

Sean said, 'What's she doing here?'

Danny was behind me, wedged in against the seat as if it could protect him. He said, 'She gave me a lift.'

'You told her where I was?'

'It wasn't like that,' Danny said. There was a little pleading in his tone. 'How else was I supposed to get here?'

'You could've blagged the train, like I did.'

Sean was as tense as Danny, watching me, body primed as if I was going to attack, or run. I said, 'I won't tell anyone where you are.'

He laughed, a sharp burst of laughter. 'Too fucking right you won't.'

There was a feverishness to his movements, to the way he spoke. Danny hadn't moved from his position; I realized I'd been relying on him knowing

what to say. I remembered my plan to persuade
Sean to come back with us and explain what had
been happening. I felt slightly sick at the thought,
but there had to be a way – I would find a way, I
just needed time. I tried to steady my breath, steady
my thoughts.

But Sean was thinking, too. He said, 'Sit down,
both of you.' It was a command, not an invitation.

Danny and I sat down, facing each other across
the table. I didn't look at Sean directly, but angled
myself so that I could see him clearly from the corner
of my eye. Danny sat stiffly upright, looking at Sean
with wide eyes. Sean was still standing. He opened
his mouth slightly, as if about to speak, but ran
the tip of his tongue quickly over his lips and then
turned away from us for a moment. Danny lowered
his gaze to the table top. I waited. The way Sean was
huddled, I had the impression that he was struggling
with how to react, and what to do next.

Suddenly, Sean laughed to himself, then turned
back to face us. He was making an effort to seem
relaxed. 'Sorry, you threw me there. Didn't mean
to seem rude. I wasn't expecting visitors.' Then he
added quickly, 'I mean, I was expecting you, Danny,
just not so soon, you know? I thought you'd take
your time getting here, eh, kiddo?'

Danny didn't react; I couldn't tell if he believed
Sean.

'Now then,' Sean said, all smiles. 'Cuppa tea,
anyone? Jo?'

He was playing the role of the host; I expected

his next question to be about the journey – a polite discussion of A-roads and roadworks and traffic. But it was a better reaction than we could have got; it was probably a better reaction than we deserved, arriving unannounced. I needed time; he was giving us time, so I forced myself into the role of guest and said, 'That would be lovely, thanks.'

'Danny? I've got some orange.'

Danny shook his head. Unlike his brother, he didn't look relaxed. I wondered what sort of welcome he had really been expecting.

Sean went over to the little galley kitchen and filled an aluminium kettle from the tap. He turned on the gas and lit it with a match; I heard the whoomph of flame and the kettle spat for a moment, then all I could hear was the hiss of burning gas. I realized that I couldn't hear any traffic outside, or any sounds at all apart from the occasional seagull crying in the air.

'It's very quiet here,' I said.

Sean glanced at me, a grimace of a smile. 'Yeah,' he said. 'Hardly anyone comes here this time of year. We shouldn't be disturbed.'

I wanted to be appalled at that thought. I felt I should be. After all, I was here with an absconder, a fugitive; he was the man who had attacked me and firebombed the Adams' house. I looked at his back as he stood waiting for the kettle to boil. He was skinny, lanky; he didn't look as if he had any strength at all, but I had felt the power in his arms, in his body, I had felt that strength.

And what was I doing here, sitting in a caravan with the man who had attacked me, waiting for a cup of tea when we were so far from help? And if anything did happen what could I do to prevent it?

I was suddenly aware of how gloomy it was in the caravan. The blue flame on the hob seemed to deepen the shadows elsewhere. I said, 'Can we open the curtains? It's very dark in here.'

I thought Sean would probably say no, he didn't want people to see that the caravan was occupied, but when he turned again, Danny was already opening the nearest curtains. Sean forced a smile and said, 'Yeah, why not, eh? Open the windows, too, let some fresh air in.'

Danny grinned at me, suddenly, as if we had passed some sort of watershed and he was now free to relax. I grinned back. I didn't understand whatever Danny had recognized, and I didn't know how to feel about my uncertainty. I concentrated on opening the curtains and winding the mechanisms that released the windows from their catches. Danny had opened the curtains on the big window that ran the width of the caravan's nose. I saw a couple of rows of caravans beyond and then a concrete wall; I had the impression that the sea was on the other side of the wall.

Danny said, 'Can I go down to the beach?'

He was looking out of the window and I wasn't sure which of us he was addressing. I glanced at Sean and caught him looking at me, as if he wasn't sure either. Something in his expression held my attention and I felt a slight chill as our eyes locked.

I said, 'It looks like it's about to chuck it down.'

'No, go on.' Sean still held my gaze. 'Just don't be too long.' Danny scrambled out from his seat. Sean said, 'And don't go near the water, eh?'

Danny went out, slamming the door shut behind him. I broke Sean's gaze to watch him running towards the concrete wall. He disappeared from view behind a caravan, and then his head bobbed past on the other side of the wall.

'He's a crap swimmer,' Sean said. 'Always has been.'

I looked back at Sean, but he had turned away to place teabags in two mugs on the draining board. He wrapped a tea towel around the kettle's handle and poured out the water, turning off the gas with his other hand.

'Do you take sugar?' he asked.

'No thanks.'

'That's good, 'cos I haven't got any.' And he laughed too hard at his own joke.

I looked back towards the sea wall but Danny was out of sight. I forced myself to take a slow deep breath, concentrating on that grey sky and the contours of the clouds rolling in from the sea. Sean was placing a mug of tea in front of me, and as I turned my movement brought me close to him; too close. I was aware of his solid presence; I could smell the sudden scent of his sweat, and feel the heat rising from his body. I jerked back, away from him, but he was so big above me, I had to fight to hide the jolt of fear.

He didn't seem to notice, just slouched down into the seat opposite me. I had no choice but to look at him. His expression was wary but not hostile, not as far as I could tell. I tried to remind myself that he was the one on the run, he was the one who didn't want to be found. I was in a strong position – he didn't know all the things that had happened to me, and that nobody would be looking for me. I could persuade him to come back with me – I just had to work at it. I just needed time to think. It had seemed so easy, coming here with Danny at my side. I had thought . . . what had I thought? That Danny's presence would be enough to make Sean realize? It seemed so ridiculous now. I looked into Sean's face, hoping I would see whatever I was looking for, but I couldn't read his expression. He was a good-looking sort of kid, I realized; he seemed younger than I remembered, looked younger than the nineteen years his file listed. If he found himself some clean clothes he was the sort that girls would find attractive, in that listless teenaged way, and older women would like the expression in his dark eyes. I had always been a sucker for boys with dark eyes.

I thought he was going to ask me what I was doing here, and I wasn't sure how I could answer that. It had seemed logical, driving over here; as if everything had been leading to me confronting Sean. But now that I was here, sitting drinking tea with the seagulls in the background, I wasn't sure what I had expected to achieve, what questions I had expected to find answers to.

Sean sat back in his seat and looked out of the window towards the sea wall. I wondered whether he was thinking the same as me; wondering what would happen next. But all he said was, 'Danny's always loved it here. I did, too, when I was a kid. So much space, you know?'

I nodded.

He went on, 'I can understand why he wanted to come. Bet he thinks this is a holiday, eh?'

He glanced at me this time, as if he really did want to know the answer. As if he thought I could explain. I thought about Danny slumped in my car as we drove through Skegness. 'I don't know,' I said.

He said, 'I don't think he gets it.'

I had to say, 'But you invited him.'

'Yeah, but—' and he stopped himself. A more guarded expression was creeping onto his face. 'Why are you here, anyway?'

He sounded almost angry. I said, 'Danny asked me to drive him here.'

'But you didn't have to say yes. Most people wouldn't have.'

'It was better than leaving him to hitch-hike,' I said. I wanted to add that Sean should have thought about this, he should have realized what Danny was like, but I didn't say any more.

'You could've just given him the train fare,' Sean said.

There was a sulk in his voice now, as if he was blaming me for this, as if he was blaming me for spoiling his fun. I wanted to remind him that he was the one who had told Danny to come, it was hardly my fault if Danny took him seriously. I was tempted to explain that I was trying to help Danny – give him the chance to break free, to turn out differently – but I realized that Sean wouldn't understand.

He seemed to be waiting for me to speak. I wondered what he was expecting me to say; that I had really come to see him? That I wanted him to explain why he had attacked me? Now I was here, the question seemed absurd. All that time in Nottingham, I had allowed myself to believe that there was some reason, some logic, to his attack on me, but what if there hadn't been? What if he didn't have any good reason for it? There was a little knot of nausea expanding in my stomach; I had been through so much, and come all this way, and what if there really wasn't anything behind it all? He didn't seem to have thought through what he would do if Danny came and joined him – was it so hard to believe that he hadn't thought about anything very much when he attacked me? I had wanted there to be a reason – of course I had; nobody would want to feel that something so momentous, something with such a big impact, had been random, meaningless, motiveless. But I looked at Sean, looked at him as he struggled to think, and the whole incident suddenly seemed so small, so squalid, almost nothing at all.

He said, 'I know why you're here.'

'I've told you why. I brought Danny.'

He shook his head. 'No, I know why you're really here.'

I made myself laugh. 'Oh yes?'

'Yeah,' he said. His eyes had narrowed slightly, and there was a slight shift, an increased tension in the way he held himself. I waited, feeling my heartbeat. I think I had expected him to mention the attack; to offer an explanation or to threaten me with more – I wasn't sure which. But after a moment he simply gave a little smile and said, 'Bet you've told the police where I am, haven't you? Bet they're on their way right now, eh?'

There was menace in his tone. I wished I had told someone where I was going – I wished I had been able to speak to Alex, or Colin, or even Dave Short, but I knew that none of them would have listened to me. I was on my own. The thought chilled me. Nobody would come looking for me. I didn't want to think about what would happen if Sean ever realised that.

So I said, carefully, 'I haven't told them where you are, but they know where I am. They'll come and look for me here, in the end.'

He hesitated, then said, 'Liar.' Before I could work out whether he meant I was lying about telling them where he was or about them coming to find me, he said, 'Anyway, it don't matter. They'll never catch me.'

'Everyone gets caught in the end.'

'Not everyone,' he said. 'Not me. I'm too clever, aren't I?'

I didn't respond to that. I didn't trust myself to say anything he would accept. He had put one foot on the cushion next to him and was playing with a small hole in the knee of his tracksuit trousers. There was a smile lurking around his lips. 'Me and Danny,' he said, 'we're gonna be all right. Gonna be smart, the two of us together. Invincible team. Never gonna get caught. You'll see.'

That didn't seem worthy of a response. I looked out of the window, allowed him to see that I was bored, that he wasn't impressing me with all his talk. I wondered whether he was scared of being caught, of being taken back to Glen Parva. I wondered whether Danny had thought about that; whether Danny had considered the reality, and the situations they would end up in, and how it would be when they finally were caught. Sean might be capable of blocking it all out, but I didn't think it would take Danny long to realize the truth.

Sean was looking at me. When he was sure he had my attention he said, 'What do you think about me?'

I was surprised. 'Think about you?' I said. I wasn't sure how I could respond to that. That he was a child, an arrogant little boy in a young man's body, thinking only about himself, putting his brother in danger for no good reason? That he acted without thinking about the people he affected, or the likely results of his actions? I remembered Danny telling me that he didn't want to end up like Sean. I realized that I had to take Danny back to Nottingham, no matter what happened. I couldn't leave him here with Sean. I realized I should never have brought him. I let out a sigh and said, 'Sean, why on earth would I think about you at all?'

I thought he might take offence at that, but he just giggled and said, 'You know why,' and pushed his fingers further into the hole in the knee of his trousers. 'You think about me, I think about you. It's all the same.'

'No,' I said, and then stopped, because what was the point? He wouldn't believe me anyway. I needed air. I needed to get out of that caravan, away from him. I realized I had been wrong about him. I already knew all I needed to know – there was nothing he could tell me, nothing that would be worth listening to. I would fetch Danny and we would go back to Nottingham together, and maybe people wouldn't even question where Danny had been or how he had got there. Sean could stay in hiding if he wanted to – I didn't have the energy to care.

I got up and said, 'I'm going for a walk. I need some air.'

He didn't change his expression, and didn't move until I had already opened the caravan door and was stepping onto the decking. Then he was there, right behind me; he clutched my arm and pushed himself up close to me and said, 'Not without me.'

I pulled free of his grip. 'Suit yourself.' I shifted my handbag onto my shoulder and strode towards the concrete wall where Danny had disappeared, then climbed some metal steps that led over the wall and onto the path at the top of the sea defences. Sean kept a couple of paces behind me. I followed the path round to a slipway giving access to the beach. The wind was picking up and had a wet, icy edge to it; I wasn't sure if it was rain or seawater. Sean followed me. I walked round the edge of the beach in the shelter of the sea defences. The concrete had been cast into a crescent shape so that when I sat down I had a solid crest of concrete wave breaking at my back and over my head. I opened my handbag and took out my cigarettes. Sean sat down next to me; I offered him a cigarette, more out of politeness than any desire to please him. Sean took it and turned his head away to light it.

I watched Danny while I smoked. He was at the water's edge, a long way off, but I could make out that he was digging a stick into the sand and then jumping back as the sea surged in around it. After a moment in which Sean and I sat in silence, both smoking, Danny saw us and waved. We waved back. He stood where he was, looking at the stick and the sea, as if trying to decide, then he started to walk towards us, swinging the stick in his hand.

Sean said, 'What're you going to do?'

'Go back to Nottingham,' I said. 'Take Danny home.'

'But what about me?'

'You do what you like,' I said. 'I don't care.'

'But the police'll find out where I am. You'll tell them.'

He sounded worried, scared even. I said, 'I won't tell them, but they'll find you soon enough anyway. You can't hide for ever.'

Sean gave no sign that he had heard me. Danny was approaching and stopped a few paces away. He was flushed red by the wind. Sean raised his voice. 'I was asking little miss social worker here what she's going to do next. She says she's taking you back to Nottingham.'

Danny said, 'But she can't. She said she was bringing me to you. That's what she said.'

'Can't trust social workers.' There was mocking in Sean's tone. 'Haven't you figured that out yet, eh, kiddo?'

Danny said nothing, digging the stick into the sand.

Sean continued, 'She says she won't tell the police where I am, but I don't believe her. I bet she's told them already. I bet they're already on their way. The police'll take me and the social workers'll get you.'

Danny said, 'They wouldn't believe her. They're trying to sack her. And she lied to the police already, this morning. I heard her.'

'That's not true,' I said quickly, and stood up, but Danny backed away from me. 'Danny, you know we've got to go back, don't you?'

Danny was looking around, as if contemplating running away from me. 'I'm not going back,' he said. Then, accusing, 'You said you weren't going back. That's why you took all that money out, isn't it?'

'I was wrong,' I said, and stepped towards him.

Danny turned and ran towards the slipway off the beach. I called out, 'Danny, wait,' but he didn't. Before I could run after him, Sean blocked my path. I tried to get past him but he pushed me, hard; I felt a tangle of his feet around mine. I staggered and fell; Sean was above me, kicking out at me to keep me down. I was about to get up, but then I saw him standing over me and I knew he would hit me properly, he had no problem with hitting me properly. I flung my hands over my head to protect myself. I thought he was going to kick me again, but he didn't, and then I heard him laugh, softly. I stayed where I was for a moment longer, then I sat up. The sand was wet and coated my jeans and one sleeve of my jacket. I felt bruised around my elbow and hip. Sean was approaching Danny, who had stopped at the edge of the slipway and was looking back at me with surprise.

I thought, he doesn't want to be like Sean. That gave me some satisfaction. I got to my feet and started to brush sand off my jeans and jacket, but the sand was wet and scraped the skin on my palms. I gave up and walked towards Danny and Sean. Sean was standing over Danny; I wondered what he had been saying, how nasty he had been to Danny. Danny was talking but I couldn't hear his words.

When I reached them, Sean turned to me, smiling. 'Let's go back to the caravan, shall we?' he said, and took hold of my arm, loosely. 'We need to talk.'

Danny stayed where he was. He started to dig the stick into the sand. I thought about breaking free of Sean's grip – it wasn't tight – but I could still feel the impact of his body against mine, and the grit and damp on my clothes, and my hands stung where I had fallen against the sand. I wanted to get away – I could get away, I realized; I could get to my car and drive away and call the police and they would come and pick Sean up. The whole situation could be over within minutes.

When we had crossed the sea defences and descended the steps back into the caravan park, Sean's grip around my arm tightened and he turned, quickly, and pushed me back against the concrete wall. His weight pressed against me; I felt the solid wall behind me. It took me a moment to understand what he wanted, and in that moment the nausea rose up through me again. Then he jerked away from me and I realized he had my bag gripped in his fist.

'Give that back,' I said, stupidly, but he wasn't listening. He turned to walk away. I felt a rage of helplessness, and I remembered hitting Colin, I remembered that I had hurt Colin. I reached out, took hold of Sean's arm, the top of his arm. The muscles hardened under his jacket. He swung round, swung his other hand towards my head. I let go of him.

'Don't you fucking touch me,' he said.

He still had my bag. His fists were tight. His whole

body was tight. I wanted to reach out again, challenge him again, but I couldn't stop myself thinking about his fist against the back of my head, and a shiver took hold of me, and all that bravery washed right out of me. He was watching me; something close to contempt came into his expression and he strode away, back towards the caravan.

I stood there, trying to breathe slowly, trying to calm my thoughts and my pulse. I looked around, hoping to see someone, anyone, who could help me, but all I saw were rows and rows of caravans, as far as the horizon, all of them empty. I considered walking to Sea Lane and finding a phone, but he had my handbag, he had all my money and my car keys and my mobile phone. I could imagine him watching me through the caravan window; if he saw me heading off the site he would leave. He would take my money and my car. He would collect Danny and they would disappear.

So I took a deep breath and started to walk back to the caravan. I was making a show of looking relaxed, but every step shook right through me, a violent trembling that betrayed me. I climbed the steps onto the decking and went into the caravan. He was sitting at the table looking inside the envelope of money, fingering the stack of banknotes. He had placed a large kitchen knife on the table beside him, blade pointing towards me as I came through the door. I stood there, looking at the knife, at the sharp blade, the clean metal surface and the teeth of the serrated edge.

He said, 'Sit down. Take your jacket off.'

I did, opposite him, trying to seem confident. He shoved my handbag across at me. I looked inside but my car keys, mobile phone and purse were gone.

He said, 'So, been lying to the police, have we? Been suspended from work, eh? Cashed in all your savings? You've kept this very quiet.'

'It's nothing,' I said. 'It makes no difference.'

'Not what Danny says. Not what Danny says at all.'

'He's a kid,' I said. 'He doesn't understand.'

Sean just laughed. The knife wobbled on the table top, tap-tapping in agreement. 'Here's the situation. You're going to be a good little social worker and keep your trap shut. We're going to stay here, all three of us, until I figure out a plan. And you're going to keep Danny happy. As far as he's concerned, this is just a weird little holiday for everyone, right?'

I should have laughed at that, refused, shown him how ridiculous this was, but there was that knife on the table top, and he seemed so sure of himself, and I couldn't find the right words. I cleared my throat, said, 'You're joking.'

'No, I'm not.' He sat back, smiled. 'You should be scared of me,' he said. 'You know what I'm capable of.'

I forced myself to laugh. 'I'm not scared of you,' I said, but I knew there was a wobble in my voice. 'You're just a kid. Why should I do anything you say?'

'I was a kid,' he said. 'I'm a grown man now.

A big man.' His hand had run out to touch the handle on the knife. 'You might've been able to ignore me when I was a kid, but you can't now. I'm in control. You have to listen to me. You have to do what I say.'

'I don't.' I stood up. 'I'm leaving right now. Give me my car keys.'

'No.'

I realized that he was still afraid of me – however confident he seemed, however strong, he was still afraid that I would finish him. I felt myself smile and fought the smile back. If he was afraid then there was still a chance that I could talk him round.

I said, 'Sean, you know this is never going to work. You can't hide for ever. Come back with me. Help Danny out.'

He said, 'You have to listen to me now. Nothing you say counts any more. I'm in control of this situation.'

'No, you're not,' I said. 'This situation's controlling you.' But I could see that he didn't understand. 'This won't work,' I said.

The keys were on the seat next to him. I reached across, tried to take them from him; he swung his arm towards me and I felt a hot slash of pain. I looked down and saw blood, a deep line of blood across my forearm. I expected him to be as surprised as I was, but he had the knife in his hand and was pointing it at me.

'I told you. I warned you. That was your fault.'

I looked back at my arm. The blade had cut

through my shirtsleeve, a quick tear in the fabric. I rolled my sleeve back and saw the red streak underneath. It wasn't a deep cut, but it started to hurt as I examined it, filling with blood.

I said, 'I can't believe you just did that.'

'I warned you,' he said again. 'You made me do that.' Then he stood up, blade still pointing at me. 'Sit down.'

I did as I was told, seeing that blade so close to me. I closed my eyes for a moment, feeling a little sick.

'You asked for that,' he said, but he sounded less certain. He was looking at my arm, at the blood spreading out from the cut, deep-red globules of blood. The knife wavered in his hand.

I said, 'There's no need to use that knife. I'm not going to do anything.'

'I didn't mean to do that.' He sounded a little frightened. A boy pretending to be a man.

I felt a knot of anger inside me and fought it back. I took a deep breath. 'It's okay,' I said.

I didn't think he was going to use the knife again. He was gripping it hard, fingers going white from the pressure he was exerting. I watched him; the concentration in his expression, his lips pressed too tight over his clenched jaw, the slight hunch to his shoulders. The blood on my arm started to run, dark ribbons of blood spreading out across my pale flesh. He said, 'Sit still.' He went over to one of the kitchen cupboards and returned with a plastic box, which he put on the table and opened. A First Aid kit.

'Keep your sleeve out of the way,' he said.

I did. I felt a little numb. The blood was thickening on my skin. I found it hard to believe that it was my blood I could see, that he had actually cut me. He took hold of my arm with one hand; I jerked away at the harshness of his grip.

'Hold still,' he said.

I did. He was standing over me, frowning as he looked at the cut. He wiped the blood away with a disinfectant pad. The wound shrank back to little more than a scratch, then started to fill with blood again. He had my blood on his fingers, orange smears across his fingertips; he left smudges on my arm where he touched me.

'Hold this,' he said, and put the fingers of my other hand over a lint pad he had placed on top of the cut. I obeyed, feeling the wound stinging under the slight pressure. He unwrapped a bandage and started to wind it around my arm, moving my fingers to hold the bandage in place on each loop. He tucked the end of the bandage under and said, 'There. That'll hold.'

He sat down, opposite me, placing the knife carefully on the table top. It was still close enough for him to grab, but I felt oddly confident that he wouldn't pick it up again. I looked at the bandage on my arm. 'Thanks,' I said, and then realized how ridiculous that was. I hardened my tone. 'You have to give me my car keys.'

'No,' he said. Then, 'Christ, don't you get it? Leave if you want to, I won't stop you, but don't expect me or Danny or your car to still be here by the time the police arrive.'

I should have been tempted by that. I wanted to leave – every part of me ached to walk away – but I had come here to help Danny. I remembered my plan to persuade Sean to return with us and it seemed ludicrous now. I could imagine what would happen if I left Danny and Sean alone with my car and my money – a great adventure for them, and what kid wouldn't love it? I thought about Danny telling me that he didn't want to end up like Sean, and I realized that if I left him here he wouldn't have a chance of turning out any other way.

So I said, 'You can't really think it's a good idea to take Danny with you?'

'It's his choice.' There was a slight sulk in his voice. 'I'm not gonna tell him he can't come with me.'

'Even when it'll get him in trouble? You can't want him to end up like you, can you?'

His head jerked up at that. 'Not my fault if he does,' he said. 'Anyway, I'm not that bad.'

'You're wanted for arson. I'd say that was pretty bad, wouldn't you?'

'It wasn't like that,' he said.

'It was a petrol bomb,' I said. 'What did you expect it to be like?'

'It wasn't like that,' he repeated. The sulk in his voice had grown. 'I made sure they were okay. Nobody got hurt. They were asking for it.'

'There were kids in that house,' I said. 'How did

you know it would be okay? Anything could have happened.'

'But it didn't, did it? I made sure. Anyway, you've seen what that Gary Adams did to Danny. A grown man hitting a kid. I couldn't just let that go, could I?'

I wanted to push him further, make him understand what he had done, what could have happened, but I didn't think he would listen. And the knife was still close to his hand, and the cut on my arm was throbbing. I wanted to shake him, make him see the effect he had on other people, but I knew I couldn't. He didn't seem to care – he didn't seem to even realize what he had been doing. I wanted to despise him for the way he treated other people, the way he had treated me, but I discovered that I couldn't hate him. He wasn't even worth that much thought. The only person I should be thinking about was Danny, and getting him to come back to Nottingham with me.

I looked out towards the sea and saw that Danny was coming back to the caravan. Sean looked out of the window, too, then said, 'Remember, you're keeping your mouth shut.'

I realized that he wasn't sure what I was going to do. He was frightened. It gave me hope – he wasn't sure how Danny would react, whether Danny would stand by him. I said, 'I'm going to take Danny back to Nottingham.'

'No. Danny can stay with me as long as he likes.'

'But what if he wants to come back with me?'

'He won't.' Sean gave a little laugh. 'Why would he go back? Nothing there for him.'

I was about to say that there was nothing for him if he stayed with Sean either, but it didn't seem wise. I watched Danny approaching the van. He had his hands in his pockets, his shoulders hunched; I had the impression that it was only the rain now coming down that had brought him back.

Sean said, 'So you're going to do like I said?'

I looked at him. He had picked up the knife again, was playing with it, as if he had forgotten the threat it had posed. 'For now,' I said. He just nodded.

Twenty-eight

We went out for supper, Sean's largesse coming from the envelope containing my savings. Fish, chips and mushy peas at a plastic table in the window of a takeaway on Sea Lane. I ate slowly; all I could taste was grease, coating the inside of my mouth. Danny stabbed his food with his plastic fork, not speaking, not looking at either of us. Sean was the only one who ate with any appetite, picking up chunks of fish and stuffing them into his mouth, feeding in soggy chips, his lips not quite closed as he chewed, eating as if it was a race to finish first. His fingers were shiny with grease, coated in the stuff. As I watched him rub his hands on a paper napkin, I remembered the feel of his hands against the cut on my arm, and seeing my blood on his fingers. Danny hadn't asked what had happened but I knew he had spotted the bandage. I wanted to explain – tell him that this was what his brother was really like, this was why I wanted him to come back with me. But I didn't say any of that.

I had been thinking about what I could do once

we left the caravan. Whispering to someone to please call the police, or scribbling a note on the paper napkin tucked under my polystyrene tray of chips. I knew I could just leave – walk up Sea Lane, use one of the phone boxes or walk into an arcade or a café, or catch the bus into Skegness and present myself at the police station. But actually doing that— even if I didn't know that Sean and Danny would be gone before the police arrived, I couldn't imagine explaining the situation to anyone. There was no explanation that could justify bringing Danny to Ingoldmells. I wanted to leave, walk away from it all, but when I looked at Danny and the frown that was like a scar across his face, I knew I couldn't leave without him.

It was dark as we walked back to the caravan and the air had thinned out. I was cold. Danny was huddled into his jacket, walking slightly ahead of me and Sean, kicking the pavement as he went. Sean gave no sign of feeling the drop in temperature. He walked close to me; I could hear him breathing.

When we got back to the caravan, Danny switched on the portable TV and fiddled around with the aerial until he got a decent picture. Sean filled the kettle to make tea. I sat down opposite Danny, who had angled himself to see the TV screen more clearly.

The local news was just finishing, leading into the weather forecast. Storms, rain, wind. I shivered at the thought. 'Not the right weather for the beach, eh?'

Danny glanced across at me but didn't comment or even smile. I didn't turn to see Sean's reaction.

I said, 'Funny to think of everyone in Nottingham, going about their daily business.' Danny gave a grunt that I took to be agreement. Sean was preparing the tea; I heard the fridge door open. I said, 'What do you think your friends'll be doing right now, then, Danny?'

He shrugged. 'They'll just be hanging around, I guess.'

'Cycling around, eh?' I said. 'They seem like good mates. You known them a long time?'

He was half-watching the programme that had just started – vets doing unpleasant things to small animals – but broke his gaze away and said, 'Since always, I suppose.'

I gave him a moment to think about that. Sean was fishing out the teabags with a spoon. I said, 'Don't you miss them? Don't you want to see them again?'

Sean slammed a mug of tea down in front of me, slopping tea onto the table. 'We agreed we weren't going to talk about this.'

'I was only asking him about his mates. What's wrong with that? I was only wondering whether he was going to miss them. And what about your mum, Danny? Aren't you going to miss her?'

Danny was looking at the screen again, trying to pretend he was engrossed, but I could tell from the slight frown he was trying to control that I was having an effect.

'I said shut it,' Sean said.

'But I was only asking—'

He grabbed my arm, half-pulled me up to standing. 'Get off,' I said, but he didn't let go.

'I need to talk to you,' he said.

'So talk,' I said, breaking free of his grip and sitting down again.

'Not here. In the bedroom.'

Danny frowned and reached over to turn the TV volume up. I realized I wouldn't gain anything by arguing with Sean in front of him, so I stood up. I felt oddly confident that I could face Sean alone. He followed me down the narrow hallway to the room at the end. It was a small bedroom, almost filled by a double bed with a violently flowered bedspread. The curtains were drawn.

Sean turned on a lamp. 'Sit down.'

He sounded angry. I sat on the bed, trying to keep my expression relaxed. The mattress had lost its shape and gave way beneath me to an unnerving depth. At the other end of the caravan, Danny must have changed TV channels; I heard the sounds of an American cop show – screeching tyres and sirens and snatches of dialogue. Sean was still standing. The dim lighting left most of his upper body in shadow; I couldn't make out his expression, but I could see that he had the knife in his hand again.

I said, 'You're not going to use that knife.'

He gave a little laugh. 'I might.' Then he sat on the bed next to me; I felt the mattress subside under his weight. He was very close to me. 'You don't know what I'm going to do.'

I forced myself to look at him but I still couldn't read his expression. My breath felt very tight in my chest. 'But Danny's only in the next room,' I said.

He didn't reply for a moment, then said, 'I know what you're trying to do. Danny isn't going to suddenly change his mind about being here just because you mention his friends.'

'I only want to show him what this means,' I said. 'He's a kid. He doesn't understand.'

'He understands more than you think.' He gave another little laugh. 'But that's typical, intit? You thinking you know best?'

My mouth was very dry. 'Oh, c'mon, you know this is no good for him.'

'Like you care.' But before I could protest that I did care, that I was concerned, he continued, 'I want to know what you're up to. Why you're here.'

'You know why,' I said. 'I brought Danny. He asked me—'

'No,' he said. 'That's not the real reason. You're up to something. You bring him here and now you want to take him away again? It don't make sense. You're after something.'

'I just want what's best for Danny.'

He jumped to his feet, a sudden thrust of movement. I could see his expression now; the glint of anger, of passion. 'You don't care about Danny,' he said. 'You don't care about anyone except your-self.'

My heart had started to pound. I tried to steady myself, but he had that knife. I wanted to tell him that he was the one being selfish, but I could feel the cut on my arm throbbing under the bandage, and how did I know what he was capable of? I said softly, 'I do care about Danny. That's why I want to take him back with me.'

'Oh, change the record,' he said. 'Danny's not going anywhere with you.' He strode over to the window, stood there for a moment with his back to me. I could see the back of his neck as he looked down at the knife in his hand. I could strike him there, a sharp blow on the pale patch of skin below his hairline, where the nape of his neck dipped. My breath caught in my throat. I couldn't move. Then he turned and came back to me, stood in front of me, the knife between us. 'Danny doesn't want you here. Why don't you just go? Why do you always hang around where you're not wanted?'

I was about to respond that I didn't, but he had turned his back on me again. He kicked out at the caravan wall; I heard the dull thump of his shoe against the fibreglass. He kicked it again, harder, as if he wanted to cause some damage. I remembered the things Colin had said about him, when we were sitting in the car together, and I felt an ache of nostalgia for that moment; two friends sharing things, two friends who were so close, and Sean had cost me all of that. Colin had said he thought

Sean didn't care about anything, but that couldn't be it. He was reckless, yes, but he seemed to know what he wanted to happen next.

Sean turned back to face me. He was a little calmer after that outburst of energy. He said, 'There's so much I wanted to say to you.' He gave a nervous giggle. 'I've been thinking about it a lot. What I was going to say, I mean.' He hesitated, as if expecting me to comment. 'Oh, c'mon,' he urged. 'You must have some reaction to that. Don't you want to know what I've been planning to say?'

I gave a slow, exaggerated shrug. 'You'll tell me if you want to.'

He let out a loud breath of frustration. 'You've got no idea,' he said. 'I've been looking after you and you act like there's nothing—' He stopped himself, grinned. 'All the time I was in Glen Parva, I was thinking about you. About all the stuff you've done to me.'

His voice had a dangerous edge to it, a wild edge. I remembered Colin trying to describe Sean's attitude, trying to pin down with words something that was so – so animalistic. I was very aware of Sean's movements, of the energy running through his body, of heat and strength. I said, 'I've done nothing to you—'

He cut me off. 'You don't realize what I've done for you,' he said. 'You don't seem to realize just how vulnerable a woman on her own is.'

I wanted to tell him not to be so ridiculous, but I couldn't speak.

He said, 'Remember that night you woke up hearing noises? When you got your wimpy bloke to come running round? Remember that?'

'That was you,' I said, and a chill went through me.

'No. You should be thanking me. It's a dangerous neighbourhood round your way. I was protecting you.'

'Protecting me?' I said, and then stopped, because I had been about to demand what kind of protection had led him to attack me, and I didn't want to hear his excuses.

'I sorted him out. Stupid little tosser would've been there all night, messing around with that lock. A crowbar in the doorframe, that would've got him in quicker. That's what I'd've done. He didn't have a clue.' He laughed and jerked the knife into the air. 'I sorted him out.'

I tried to take a breath but the air seemed so thin. I didn't know what to say.

He said, 'You really thought that wimp of a bloke was going to protect you? Pathetic. You need someone like me. Someone who'll sort out thieving little bastards. Someone who'll look after you.'

I heard myself say, 'Why?'

He was standing a little too close to me. Then he leaned over me, and I wanted to back away but there was nowhere to go, and his legs pressed against my knees, and I would have to fight to get free of him. I stayed still, held my breath.

He said, 'All the time I was locked up, I was

thinking about you. Had a lot of time to think, I did. You know what I was thinking?'

I shook my head, but he wasn't expecting an answer.

'I was thinking about when my dad died and my mum went to pieces, and how you was there. You was always there. Never left us alone.' He giggled. 'You know, I even convinced myself that it was your fault my dad died.'

I forced myself to laugh, too. 'That's ridiculous.'

'Yeah,' he said. 'That's what I thought. But then, he was on his way to meet you when he died.'

I felt a cold chill. 'That's right,' I said. 'But he never arrived.'

'That café on Denman Street, wasn't it?'

'Yes,' I said. I didn't like the expression on his face, the knowing smile. 'I waited for three-quarters of an hour, but he never came. I saw the ambulance up the road, but I didn't know it was for him.'

'No,' Sean said. 'Why would you?'

I waited for him to make his point – I had no idea what he was trying to say – but he snapped the smile off his face and said, 'Yeah, so I'm sat behind my door, thinking about you and my dad, and then I get out, and I find you're already a mess. You're nothing special. I've seen you, out of your face half the time, stumbling around, fawning all over blokes that aren't interested. Fucking pathetic. I've seen you, so fucking scared of being alone, hiding away in your house like a few locks are going to protect you.'

He held out the knife so that the tip of the blade touched the collar of my shirt. I forced myself to sit completely still. I held his gaze; those dark eyes that showed none of the emotion coming through in his voice. After a moment he looked away, then lowered the knife. 'Relax,' he said. 'I only want to talk.'

'So talk,' I said, although it was the last thing I wanted. 'You don't need a knife to get me to listen.'

Sean didn't speak for a moment. I could still hear the TV in the other room. I wondered whether Danny had turned the volume up to drown us out; whether he could hear what was being said.

'You don't listen,' Sean said. 'Maybe things would be different if you did?'

I frowned but said nothing, waiting for him to explain.

'I mean, look at the Adams family. Fucking appropriate name, that, eh? They just try to cause trouble for us, and there's you, not even bothering to listen to our side, just going along with everything they say. Never believe us, do you?'

'I don't take sides,' I said, but he wasn't listening.

'You've always had it in for me,' he said. 'Right from back then. But I was only a kid, you know? It wasn't right, what you did.'

I let out a breath. 'What did I do?'

'You know,' he said. 'You know what you did.'

He turned away from me abruptly. I had the feeling he'd been building up to this for a long time – I could picture him in Glen Parva, looking out through a barred window, planning his revenge. Because that was what this was – the culmination of a plan he'd been thinking about for so long that now the moment had arrived he didn't know how to finish it off.

I said, 'Look, Sean, this isn't getting us anywhere.'

He didn't seem to have heard me. 'Everything's your fault.'

'My fault?' I said. 'I didn't send you to Glen Parva, did I? Christ, I haven't had anything to do with you for eight years, how can it be my fault?'

'You don't get it,' he said. 'You haven't been listening. You told us everything was going to be fine, and then my dad got killed and nothing was fine ever again.'

I said, 'Oh, please. Your dad dying had nothing to do with me. His death was an accident, a hit-and-run – if you're going to blame anyone, blame the driver. I'm sorry he died, but—'

'You're not sorry,' he said. 'Suited you just fine. You wanted Mum to kick him out anyway.'

'That's not true.' But I didn't sound convincing to my own ears. And it had solved the problem – but I hadn't wanted the man dead, of course I hadn't.

'He was coming to meet you when it happened,' Sean said. 'He'd never even have been there if it wasn't for you.'

'It was just a terrible accident, Sean.'

He still had his back to me. 'That's what it's

always like with you, eh? It's never your fault. Always going on about how you know best, and when it all fucked up you just said it wasn't your fault.'

I didn't respond.

'And you never even admit it, do you? Never even fucking apologize, do you?'

He had swung round to face me. He was winding himself up to act, I could see that; winding himself up, and the knife was in his hand. I said, 'I don't know what you're talking about, really I don't—'

But he cut me off. 'You just can't stand to see other people happy, can you? You've got to come in and stuff it up for them just to make yourself feel better. Just because your own life is so fucking pathetic. They'd have been fine if you hadn't come along.'

'That's not true.' I had a sudden memory of Carla Metcalfe, sitting forward on her sofa with her elbows on her knees, hands over her face, telling me that she couldn't cope, telling me that she wanted to be away from the boys' father, and how could I help and what could she do and was it ever going to be okay? Her whole body had shaken as she talked; she looked wretched. I said, 'Your mum was scared.'

'No, that's not true. You made all that stuff up. Our dad was the best. He was always good to us, but you just wanted to stuff everything up for us.'

'It wasn't like that,' I said. 'Your mum asked for my help. That's why I was meeting him, to talk about things and work out what to do to make things better.'

'That's not true. You're lying.'

'No.' I kept my voice calm, tried to seek out eye contact. 'Don't you remember, Sean? Your mum was so unhappy. Can't you remember that?'

He did make eye contact then. I held his gaze, but I knew I was only stalling him, delaying his next accusation. I could see myself reflected in his eyes – a distorted self in the curve of his iris – and I jerked my gaze away from him.

'Yeah, that's right,' he said. 'Twist it all. It wasn't like that. Scared now though, aren't you? Used to think you were so fucking clever, but you're scared of me now. You can't get away with those lies any more. I'm not a little kid any more. I'm a grown man. I'm a strong man. I can do you over. I will if I want to, you can't stop me.'

I tried to seek out eye contact again, but he wouldn't look directly at me. His jaw was tense; his whole body was tense. I realized with a chill that this was hatred; that he hated me with a passion I couldn't imagine feeling. I felt almost dead next to the extremity of his emotion.

He said, 'You get off on all this stuff, don't you? You just love stirring it up. Gives you a kick to interfere with people's lives, doesn't it?'

'No, of course not.'

'You do.' He sounded almost amused. 'This is how you get your kicks, isn't it? Getting wrapped up in other people's lives? Your own life's so miserable you have to use other people's.'

He sat down next to me, grabbed my arm with his left hand, pushed his body up close to mine. I felt a sharp pain along the cut on my arm but said nothing. He had the knife in his other hand. 'I know why you're here,' he said, and he had dropped his voice slightly, as if he didn't want Danny to hear this bit. The knife came closer to my body; I found myself watching it, watching its slightest movements, as he gripped my arm harder and said, 'You want me, don't you? That's why you're here. Don't try to deny it, I've seen the way you look at me. You want me to do things to you. That's right, isn't it?'

I had to struggle to find any voice. The knife was almost touching my shirt, almost touching my breast. 'No, that's not it. Of course not. I just want to help. Really, Sean, I'm just here to help.'

'Don't deny it,' he said. I looked into his eyes. He had cruel eyes – I couldn't believe I hadn't noticed it before. He moved the knife up; I felt its blade touch the skin on my neck, under my chin. I jerked without meaning to; I thought I could feel how sharp the blade was even with that gentle contact. He laughed, a quiet, low laugh. 'Don't deny it,' he repeated.

I knew I had to speak. I spoke very carefully, calmly. 'Sean, I'm not interested in you. Nothing would make me interested in you. I'm only here because I'm worried about Danny.'

'Danny?' He let out a long breath, and then he pushed me away and was up on his feet, standing over me, holding the knife out. 'You're fucking obsessed with Danny. What are you, some sort of pervert? You like little boys, is that it? Maybe

I should go and talk to Danny, eh? See what you've been getting up to with my kid brother, eh?'

'That's not it,' I said. 'Honestly.'

I didn't know whether he believed me. I thought about him, outside my house, watching the things I had been doing, watching the people come and go from my house. Then he said, 'I'd fucking kill you if anything happened to Danny.'

I held his gaze. The anger seemed to be subsiding a little. I said, 'I only want to help. Like I've said all along. I just want to see Danny safe, that's all.'

'You don't care about safe,' he said. 'You shove kids off to live with strangers. What's safe about that?'

I didn't speak. I felt raw, drained. I wanted his words to run out; I wanted him to shut up. He lowered the knife to his side and went over to the window again. This time he parted the curtains and looked out. I was aware of the sound of the TV once again, and then the bedroom door opened and Danny stood on the threshold of the room, looking from me to Sean and back again.

He said, 'Sean, there's a film starting.'

'Okay.' He seemed a little deflated. 'I'll be along in a minute.'

Danny nodded and left the room, leaving the door ajar. I looked at Sean. He said, 'Danny never heard none of that. He knows better than to listen.' I thought he was going to say more, return to the things he had been saying before, but his shoulders had dropped a little. I wasn't sure whether he was trying to convince me or himself about what Danny had overheard. Either way, his anger seemed to have dissipated.

I said, 'I'd appreciate it if you'd put that knife away.'

He looked at me, then down at the knife. 'Whatever,' he said. Then he added, 'You sleep in here tonight. Me and Danny'll take the fold-down in the living room.'

'Fine,' I said.

He went back up the hallway to the other room. I went to the bedroom door. I heard the sound of a muffled conversation but I couldn't make out the words. I closed the door but there was no lock. I looked around for something to move in front of it but every item of furniture was screwed to the walls so I jammed a couple of towels under the door in the hope that that would at least slow down anyone coming in.

Then I sat down on the bed again. My head was thumping; my chest hurt. A sickening trembling took hold of my body. I lowered my face into my hands and tried to think, but all I could feel was the nausea rising up through me. I could see him standing over me still, as if his presence hadn't yet left the room. I didn't know if he would have used the knife – I didn't know how far he would have gone, and that thought stayed with me.

I sat without moving for a long time – perhaps an hour, perhaps longer. Occasionally, I heard voices from further down the caravan; once, I thought I heard a car coming across the caravan park and I looked out of the window into the darkness, hoping to see people, but there was nothing but that black void of night. I couldn't even see any stars. I was overwhelmed by the thought that nobody knew where I was, and nobody would be looking for me.

I went to the bedroom door and opened it a crack. I could see a little way into the living room at the other end of the caravan. The table and benches had been converted into a bed; I heard murmured conversation, and then Sean came into view, dressed only in boxer shorts, smoking a cigarette. I shut the door again. I wasn't sure if he had seen me.

My holdall with clean clothes was still in the boot of my car. I took off my shoes and socks but got into bed wearing everything else; I didn't want to strip down any further. I lay under the duvet, sinking into the middle of the mattress, but although I was tired I knew sleep would be a long time coming. I thought again about my holdall; there was the little box of gear inside it, and a spliff would have knocked me right out, but there was nothing I could do about that. I turned off the lamp and lay there in the darkness, willing myself to sleep, but my mind would not rest. I couldn't fix my thoughts clearly; I couldn't see how this situation was going to be resolved.

At some point, I heard movement at the other end of the caravan. I lay completely still, trying to listen for more, trying to work out if the sounds were drawing closer to the bedroom, but I couldn't tell.

Death Duty

I heard the flare of a match and smelled cigarette smoke. Then I heard slight creaks as Sean – it had to be Sean – moved around in the hallway. I wondered whether he was having the same problems as me finding sleep. I expected him to push open the bedroom door, to at least check whether I was awake, but he didn't. When I finally drifted into sleep, it was with the impression of him on the other side of that door, waiting for sleep to overtake him.

Twenty-nine

When I woke, Sean was standing in the doorway, watching me. I wasn't sure if his arrival had woken me, or if he had been standing there for a while, watching me sleep – I didn't want to know. I drew the bedcovers up to my chin and frowned at him, but he made no move to leave.

'Where's Danny?' I asked.

'Out. Sent him to buy a paper.' He approached the bed and I gripped the covers tighter. He said, 'I wanted to check you remembered what we agreed yesterday.'

'Which bit?'

'The bit about keeping your mouth shut.'

There was a decisive edge to his voice; he must have come up with a plan during the night, but I didn't bother asking what it was. My own plan seemed so inadequate – he was never going to agree to come back with me. Part of me had been expecting to wake to find both of them gone, along with my car and all of my money. I knew I should be relieved that they were still here, that I still had a chance; I couldn't imagine what I would have done if they had left me.

Sean said, 'Let's give Danny a really nice day, eh?'

'Why?' I asked. 'Do you think it's going to be the last one?'

His face screwed up. 'Oh, don't start that again. You never fucking shut up, do you? You're going to keep your trap shut all day today, that's all you need to know.'

'I just don't want Danny to end up in trouble,' I said. 'You can understand that, can't you?'

'You brought him here,' Sean said. 'If he wants to stay with me that's his choice.'

'You can't stop him coming back with me.' But the words struck me as absurd even as I said them, because he obviously could.

He didn't point that out, just said, 'I don't have to stop him. He don't want to go with you. Now get up. We're going in a bit.'

He left me alone. I sat up and straightened my clothes as best as I could, but they had that warm, stale feeling from having been slept in. When I went through to the other room, Danny had returned and Sean was sitting at the table reading the front page story in the *Mirror*. He put the paper down and said, 'Let's go, then. I'll drive.'

Danny didn't comment on the fact that Sean had my keys and was driving my car. Danny didn't comment about anything, just got into the back of the car and sat there leaning forward between the two front seats, elbows wedged, resting his chin on his hands.

In Skegness, we played the arcade games for a couple of hours; me with a plastic cup of two-pence pieces, working the Penny Falls, while Sean and Danny blasted aliens and drove fast cars round pixellated racing circuits. I got bored quickly. I leaned against a fruit machine to watch them; two dark figures in a gloomy room, huddled side by side in front of a bright screen that cast bluish light across their faces and hands. Sean and Danny were laughing as they played, elbowing each other, hammering the buttons. They wouldn't have noticed if I had left them to it.

I remembered the brief plan I'd thought about in the night – whisper to someone, get them to call the police, stand by while they took Sean away. I could imagine it happening: darkly-clad figures swarming through the arcade, surrounding the boys as they giggled and jostled at the game controls, and Danny's distress as they took hold of Sean, and Sean turning to stare at me as they handcuffed him. I could imagine the look on Sean's face; that absolute hatred. He had said I would betray him – but Danny didn't think I would. I could imagine the police taking Sean outside to a waiting car, and Danny standing there on the pavement, trying to stop them, pleading with them, maybe even crying. They would ignore him, and what could I do about that? Danny trusted me. I didn't want him to turn against me; he was a good kid, a nice kid. He would see sense, if I kept talking to him.

They abandoned the video games and moved over to play Air Hockey, sliding the plastic puck backwards and forwards across the air-cushioned table, laughing at each near-goal, cheering when they scored. I went over to watch; Danny didn't react to my presence, but the scowl returned to Sean's face.

'Let's have a go,' I said.

The air supply to the table cut out. Sean flung the puck at me and said, 'Go on then.' He seemed angry at my intervention, but I didn't let that worry me. Danny was crouching down at the side of the table, feeding in coins to start the game again, and didn't seem to notice Sean's change of mood. When the game started up, I knocked the puck down towards Danny and he slammed it back, sending it bouncing off the sides of the table. The game was fast. Danny played with a frown of concentration that soon changed into a smile at how feeble my returns were. When he scored his first goal he gave a whoop and laughed and looked at me. I laughed, too. I knocked the puck back to him and he hit it back and scored again. Sean was hanging back, watching us; I was aware of him standing there, a rigid expression on his face. I tried to ignore him, tried to concentrate on the game, but I could sense the hostility coming off him.

When the air cut out and Danny was celebrating his victory, Sean came closer and said, 'Right, let's really thrash her, eh?'

Danny stood back as Sean put some more coins

into the machine. He took off his jacket and stood there in his T-shirt. He meant business. We faced each other across the length of the table. He had a nasty smile on his face as he held my gaze for a moment before launching the puck with a vicious hit. I knocked the puck back and it skidded past his hand and into his goal.

'One nil.' I couldn't keep the glee from my voice. Danny laughed. 'Go, Jo.'

Sean glared at Danny but Danny didn't notice. He sent the puck down the table again and I knocked it back; it went backwards and forwards for a while, a click-click as we knocked it along the table. Sean's face screwed up in concentration; I realized that he was determined to beat me, that he wanted to humiliate me. I fixed a relaxed smile onto my face and made a show of how easy it was to play. Danny stood beside the table, laughing and commenting at each near-goal. I scored again. Sean roared and whacked the puck with all the strength he could find. It flew down the table but rebounded harmlessly off the end wall.

I made myself laugh and said, 'You'll have to do better than that, Sean.'

Danny was hopping from foot to foot, clapping his hands together, laughing as he watched the puck. Sean's expression darkened; he punched out at the puck as it reached him and it flew up from the surface of the table and bounced off onto the carpet.

'Oh, good one,' I said.

His hands curled into fists; I could see the tension

in his upper arms. I fetched the puck and knocked it down to him; he knocked it back with such ferocity that I had to lift my hands off the table and step back. The puck hit the end of the table and bounced into the slot of goal, then bounced out again.

'Hah!' Sean said. 'Take that!'

Danny stopped laughing.

I knocked the puck to Sean and he sent it back with the same force, and again I pulled my hands out of the way, and again he scored. Sean said, 'Oh, and see the master play! He's unstoppable. He's thrashing the opposition.'

'In your dreams,' I said, and hit the puck at him but didn't score.

The puck came at me again, bouncing up against the end of the table. I had to jump away to avoid being hit. Sean laughed, an angry laugh. He didn't seem to notice that Danny wasn't cheering any more but was standing watching, a frown growing across his face as he looked at Sean.

Sean scored again. My hand hurt from contact with the puck. Sean said, 'And there's no stopping him now. What a game from the young Nottingham player. He's tearing the opposition apart. He's pulverizing her. He's smashing her completely. And what a humiliation, how will she ever live this down?'

I looked over to see Danny's reaction. He was huddling into himself, watching Sean but saying nothing. I forced myself to relax, to keep a smile on my face as if I was enjoying the game. Sean didn't seem to be aware of Danny's reaction. When the time ran out and the jets of air on the table cut off, he went straight to Danny, hand up for a high-five. Danny just gave a weak smile, still huddled.

'What's up with you?' Sean demanded. 'Didn't you see that? That was class, that was. I pulverized her.'

'Yeah, I saw,' Danny said, and looked at me.

I seized the opportunity. 'Let's get something to eat,' I said, and linked my arm with Danny's. 'What d'you want?'

He wanted burger and chips. We crossed the coastal road towards the Pleasure Beach and went to a café at the back of one of the arcades. The woman behind the counter took our order then slouched over to the fryers to refry some chips. We found a table near the back of the café, away from the arcade where a handful of old people were feeding their pensions into the fruit machines.

Sean was sulking a little, one foot up on the bench beside him, playing with his shoelaces with one hand. He wouldn't look at either me or Danny. I ignored him, listening to Danny tell me about a trip to Skeggie in the past, and how going on the rides after a cheeseburger had nearly made him throw up.

'Well, no rides after this, then,' I said.

Sean said, 'They're all closed, anyway.'

Danny frowned. I said, 'What would you like to do next, then, Danny?'

'Buy a gun,' Danny said. 'Kyle's got one. It shoots pellets. It's cool.'

'Who's Kyle?' I asked.

'I met him on the beach.'

Sean said, 'What did you tell him about us?'

Danny seemed surprised by the ferocity of Sean's tone, and hesitated before saying, 'Nothing.'

'You did, didn't you? You were fucking stupid enough to tell him who we are.'

'I didn't,' Danny said. 'Honest, Sean, I never.'

I thought Sean was going to say more, but the woman was bringing our tray of burgers and chips to the table and he just shut his mouth and looked away, arms folded across his chest. I thanked the woman and she gave me the sort of conspiratorial look that said she had teenaged boys herself and could see what was going on. I smiled back at her, wondering what she thought – that I was their mother? Did I really look that old? I shared out the food. The burgers were burned around the edges and the bread rolls were a little stale, but nobody commented on that. Nobody said anything at all as we ate.

When Danny had finished, he looked at Sean. 'Can I have some money for the machines?'

Sean sighed, but reached into his pocket and pulled out a handful of coins. Danny cupped his hands and Sean dropped the money in. 'Don't spend it all at once,' he said.

Danny smiled, back to his old self again, and headed off to explore the games.

I said, 'You were a bit harsh on him before.'

'You can shut up,' he replied. 'Playing up to him. I know what you're doing. Makes me sick.'

'You said to make sure he enjoys himself. I'm only doing like you asked.'

He dismissed that with a wave of his hand. He lit himself a cigarette but didn't offer me one. 'Pretending like you care about his holidays in Skeggie,' he said. 'You don't give a shit.'

'Of course I do,' I said.

He didn't seem to have heard me. 'We used to come here with Mum and Dad, but he don't remember that. He hasn't got a clue.' He sounded resentful.

I said, 'It's hardly Danny's fault if he can't remember, is it?'

'No,' he said. 'It's yours.'

'Oh, not this again.' I let out a long sigh. 'I don't know why you keep saying this. What happened then has nothing to do with me.' Before he could launch into another diatribe about how everything was my fault, I added, 'Frankly, I'm not interested in your paranoid little fantasies. I'm just worried about Danny, that's all.'

'Yeah, yeah,' he said. I thought he was going to say more than that – get back into the discussion we'd started in the caravan – but he just spat out a derisive sort of laugh and looked away, across the arcade to where Danny bashed the controls on a machine. We sat in silence for a while, then Sean said, 'You lot are never going to give him a chance.'

I wanted to tell him that it wasn't true, but I knew he wouldn't listen.

He said, 'You're all the same. Coppers, magistrates, everyone. You think it's all so easy, like stuff'll just work out if you keep your head down, but it ent true, is it? You keep your head down, you just get walked all over.'

'That's a very negative view,' I said.

'Yeah, but it's true, though.'

I wasn't sure if he wanted me to disagree, or even to agree, but I didn't want to get into any meaningless discussions. I wanted to shake him, tell him things were never that bad, there were always choices, but I couldn't summon the energy. I was tired; my head was pounding, a hangover without the booze. I kept watching Danny, not wanting to meet Sean's gaze.

Sean said, 'Dad used to bring us to this arcade. I'd forgotten. Used to give us a couple of quid's worth of two pees each and money for ice-cream and leave us here half the afternoon. Dunno where he went – the pub or the bookie's, I suppose. Danny was only about four. Mum used to go mad about it.'

I nodded, but didn't comment.

'But Dad was a laugh,' he said defiantly, as if I'd criticized him. 'He always had a joke and he always had time for us. All that other stuff, it's just exaggeration.'

Again, I didn't speak. He didn't seem to notice, though, just kept watching Danny. 'He was always buying us stuff, too. One time he bought me a glider, just one of them little polystyrene things where you have to slot the wings through the body. I loved that glider but it broke, one of the wing tips snapped off. Dad fixed it with Sellotape, but then one wing was heavier than the other so he had to put Sellotape on the other wing to balance it out, and then on the tail fin to stop it nose-diving, and then on the nose to keep it level.' He laughed softly to himself. 'In the end, there was more Sellotape than polystyrene. He should've just bought me another one, they were dead cheap things really.'

He glanced across at me then, an anxious glance, as if he wanted me to be as amused by this memory as he was. I smiled, nodded my head to show I appreciated the story.

His expression darkened. 'Oh, what's the point?' he said. 'Mum never mentions him and Danny don't even remember him.'

He wanted me to respond, I could see that. I was surprised by how desperate he seemed. I said, 'People cope with bereavement in different ways. Just because your mum doesn't mention him doesn't mean she's forgotten all about him.'

He spat out a laugh. 'Like you even care. Bet you were relieved when he died. One less thing for you to worry about.'

'That's not true—' I started, but then I couldn't be bothered to continue. I had been about to trot out a few platitudes, but I realized there was no point. He wanted me to make everything right; he wanted me to fix something that nobody could mend. He wanted me to take the blame for something that was none of my doing, and I would never do that. I thought about the number of cases I'd dealt with over the years. There was no reason why I should have any answers, any explanations – there was no reason for me to fill up my memory with the details and intricacies of other people's lives. Christ, I had enough trouble just dealing with my own; I had no intention of taking on responsibility for whatever had happened to Sean. He was the one who insisted that this was my responsibility, but he was just a kid, so why was I paying him any attention? He was just a selfish little boy who liked to hit out at the big wide world for the wrongs he thought had been done to him, and why should I play along? As I watched Danny on the machines, so involved in what he was doing, I could feel Sean's gaze on my face but I didn't look at him. I just hoped he couldn't read my thoughts in my expression.

Danny had finished his game and stood for a moment considering whether to put another coin in and have another go. Then he slumped his shoulders and came back to us and sat down.

I said, 'What d'you want to do now?'

He shrugged.

Sean said, 'Let's go for a walk along the sea-front.'

Danny seemed about as enthusiastic as me at the prospect of spending time outside. But we all dutifully went out onto the promenade and stood by the low sea wall, feeling the chill of rain in the wind. Danny stood close to me, hands deep in his pockets, jaw set firm, gazing out to the cold mass of the sea. The beach was deserted; an exposed strip of sand that had taken on the consistency of mud where the water lay in pools. I wondered what Danny was thinking; whether he regretted being here yet.

Sean said, 'I guess it's too cold for the donkeys to be out, eh?' Neither Danny nor I answered him. He walked away, further along the promenade towards the huddle of closed-up kiosks near the entrance to the beach. Danny and I trailed along behind him. Sean forced cheerfulness into his voice and said, 'Remember when Mum and Dad used to bring us to see the donkeys, Danny? You used to love it. You always had a favourite. Lightning, I think it was called. You always wanted to ride on Lightning, even if we had to wait 'cos someone else was on that animal. Remember that? Dad used to pretend you were a cowboy.'

'I don't remember,' Danny said. He sounded sullen, shivering into the collar of his jacket.

Sean stopped and looked at him, but didn't say any more. I could see that he was disappointed. Danny just looked miserable.

I said, 'How about we go and see about that pellet gun, then, Danny?'

Danny smiled, but Sean glared at me. I counted that as a success.

Thirty

The gun was a cheap plastic toy on sale in one of the tourist shops near the clock tower. Beyond the racks of T-shirts and baskets of flip-flops and sunglasses, there were shelves of novelties decorated with badly drawn cartoons and explicit jokes, and, on the floor, shallow boxes of toys in blister packs with most of the information in Japanese or Korean – I couldn't tell which. We were the only customers; the salesperson loitered near us, as if afraid we would leave without buying anything.

Back at the caravan, Sean and Danny sat with heads close together, examining the pellets that had been included in the blister pack. I held the toy gun in my hands. It was light and fairly crudely made from moulded plastic pieces shaded various tones of grey and black. Close up, it looked plastic, but I held it away from me and squinted at it, and in the gloom of the caravan and with my eyes slightly out of focus, it could almost pass for real.

I said, 'This'd look real from a distance.'

'Don't be daft.' But Danny was grinning.

Sean laughed, 'Anyone can see it's a toy.'

Danny's expression dropped. He looked up at Sean, so close to him, but Sean didn't notice. I said, 'Not from a distance, though.'

'Only from so far away that you couldn't even see it, you mean.'

Danny let out a little cry of protest and pulled away from Sean. He came over to me and stood there, looking at the toy gun in my hands. Sean glared at me, as if this was my fault; I met his look and felt our gazes lock. I could imagine the gun having a different weight, a different feel – cold, heavy, metallic. I could imagine raising the gun, holding it steady with both hands, feeling the resistance of the trigger against my fingers as I squeezed it. I could imagine the kick the gun would give as it fired, and Sean flung backwards by the force of the shot. I could imagine him falling. I felt slightly sick. I broke eye contact with Sean; with those black eyes. He was the one who fantasized about violence, who spent his days thinking about hurting someone. I could never hurt anyone. As I turned away, half closing my eyes, I felt Danny take the gun out of my hands. I took a deep breath, forcing the air into my lungs – it was just a toy, after all.

When I turned back, Danny was examining the gun at the table, trying to fit the pellets into the clip. Sean was watching Danny; when he saw that I had turned, he grinned, reached over and grabbed the gun from Danny.

'Give that back!' Danny cried.

Sean laughed and stood up, holding the gun out of reach. He looked across at me, as if he expected me to join in.

'Oh, let him have it,' I said.

Sean laughed again, but didn't give Danny the toy. Danny wasn't laughing – he reached up, trying to get to the gun, but Sean twisted and held it higher. Danny pulled at Sean's arm, then, as Sean laughed and pushed him away, he drew back his foot and kicked Sean, hard, just below the knee. Sean let out a yell and dropped his hands to his leg; Danny scooped the gun out of Sean's grip and headed out of the caravan.

'Little bastard,' Sean snarled, clutching his leg.

I looked out of the front window. Danny had hesitated halfway to the sea wall, looking back at the caravan, but then he must have seen Sean straightening again, because he ran, head down, for the beach.

I said, 'You deserved that. You were upsetting him.'

'Didn't give him the right to kick me, though, did it?' Sean sat down on the seat and pulled his trouser leg up to reveal a red mark on his shin. 'Stupid kid shouldn't take things so seriously. I was only messing with him.'

I just shrugged.

He rolled down his trouser leg again and looked out of the window, but there was no sign of Danny. 'Shit,' he said. 'Better go after him.' Then he looked at me. 'You're coming, too.'

There didn't seem much point arguing, so I went with him to the sea wall and then climbed onto the path at the top of the sea defences. Danny was further along the path, a small shape at that distance, running towards three figures almost at the far end of the bay. One of the figures was smaller than the other two; Danny's new friend Kyle, I assumed.

'Christ,' Sean said. 'What's he gonna say to them?'

We walked along the path towards the other people. It wasn't even four o'clock yet, but the sky was darkening with more rain and the temperature had dropped. The wind had picked up and I huddled down into my jacket but I still felt cold. I wanted to be back in the caravan, but as I watched Danny approaching the other group of people it occurred to me that I might be close, very close, to being able to persuade him to come back to Nottingham with me. Sean must have been thinking something similar, because he took hold of my arm and said, 'Just remember, we're on holiday, nothing more.'

'Okay,' I replied, but it was so cold, and there had to be a storm coming, and who in their right mind came on holiday to the Lincolnshire coast in March?

The other people came into focus as we drew a little closer. A black couple in dark clothes, wrapped up against the wind. Danny looked back at us as we approached and said something to the boy, and they both headed down a set of steel steps leading from the sea defences to the beach below.

The couple leaned against the steel rail that topped the sea defences, watching Danny and Kyle. We approached them.

Sean said, 'Seems you've met my brother.'

He wore an odd sort of smile; an attempt at friendliness that looked slightly overdone, a little too much. The couple turned in unison to face us. The woman was a little taller and older than me; the man, a lot of both.

Sean held out his hand to them. 'I'm Sean,' he said. 'This is Jo.'

They responded politely, holding out their hands to each of us in turn. Sonia and Derek, up from Nottingham for a few days out of the city.

'Same here,' Sean said, and they gave no indication that Danny might have told them otherwise.

'Nice weather for it,' I said, and everyone smiled a politely amused smile.

We stood watching the boys on the beach. They were play-fighting, kicking the sand at each other. The wind was picking up and the sand caught in the air, twists of dust spraying back over the boys. I could hear their laughter.

'Getting cold,' Sean said. 'Looks like rain coming.'

'They're forecasting a storm,' Sonia said. 'Just our luck, eh? A few days away and it blows a storm. Still, that's what you get this time of year.'

'Yeah.' Sean gave a false, forced laugh. 'We're a right load of mugs, standing around like this.'

I wasn't sure how it had happened – certainly, Sean didn't seem that charming to me – but Sonia was warming to him. She had half-turned herself towards him and was reflecting his smile back at him. I didn't want to watch the unfolding spectacle, so I leaned my arms against the railing and looked out across the sand to the boys playing. They were near the water's edge now; Danny had tried to kick water at Kyle, as he had done with the sand, but he just soaked his leg and got a faceful of spray. Kyle's wild laugh carried on the wind.

Derek had come to lean next to me while Sean kept chatting to Sonia. He said, 'So, what brings you here, then?'

I looked at him with a little surprise. 'How do you mean?'

'A nice lady like you, here with two teenage boys.'

I met his eyes. Dark-brown eyes, a slight yellow hue to the whites. I wasn't sure what he was asking me – I wasn't sure how I could respond. But before I could say anything, Sean was by my side, flinging one arm over my shoulder and laughing as though he did this all the time, as though I often let him touch me. I flinched away from him. I covered my reaction quickly, but I could feel that Derek's gaze was still upon me, and I wondered what Danny had said, what he had revealed to them without even realizing it. I forced myself to smile, feeling the tension in the arm that was looped around my neck.

Sonia said, 'It's too cold to be hanging around here. Why don't you come back to our van for a drink? Warm ourselves up a little, eh?'

'Oh, I don't know,' Sean started to say.

'No, please do,' Derek said. I avoided his gaze. 'Please, we'd like it.'

Sean had unlooped his arm from around my shoulder and now looked to me. I realized he didn't know how to say no without rudeness. I said, 'We wouldn't want to put you to any trouble.'

'No trouble.' Sonia beamed at me.

I looked at Sean and shrugged, and he looked at Derek and then said, 'Yeah, why not, eh? Can't do any harm.'

But he gripped my arm hard as we walked up the path. Derek and Sonia were busy attracting the boys' attention and didn't seem to notice, but I knew what Sean was saying in that twisting grip on my flesh. I didn't – wouldn't – look at him. I didn't want to give him any extra confidence, or let him believe that I had any interest in keeping the truth from Derek and Sonia. In reality, I was hoping that Derek and Sonia would realize that something was wrong and would call the police. I was tired. Nottingham seemed so far away now; all the problems there seemed so far away that I found it difficult to see what I was gaining by protecting Sean. Danny was my only concern. I was hoping that Derek and Sonia might turn out to be our saviours.

They were in the next holiday park along from Sunny Bay. The caravans on this site were larger and newer; some had gardens planted next to them, trimmed with small white fences. There were more people about, too; cars parked next to the vans and lights burning behind curtained windows. The inside of their caravan was more like a flat, with proper furniture that wasn't screwed to the walls and a kitchen with full-sized appliances. We drank hot chocolate and listened to Sonia telling us how long they had owned the caravan (three years) and how often they came (most weekends in the summer) and how Kyle loved the freedom of the site and the beach and how safe everything seemed. While she talked, Derek watched us, and I couldn't work out what he was thinking.

'It's so difficult these days,' Sonia was saying. 'There's so much traffic, and you never know who's around, drug dealers and paedophiles everywhere, and there's so much crime. All those kids who get robbed of their phones. It's terrible.'

'Yeah, I know.' Sean took another biscuit, his expression so concerned. 'I worry for Danny, really I do.'

I looked at Sean, expecting to see some small sign that he felt awkward saying these things, that he felt some sense of responsibility, or guilt, or something, but his expression appeared to be genuine. And he did care about Danny, I knew that; but Christ, Sean was one of the people Sonia was worried about, and how could he sit there coolly and pretend it was nothing to do with him?

'You do hear such terrible things,' Sonia said, and rattled on into a story about a neighbour's son being pushed off his bike by a gang who cycled away on the bike, laughing.

'Kids these days,' Derek said. 'No respect for anything.'

I could sense Sean stiffen at that; I wondered whether Derek had intended to create that effect, and whether I was the only one who had noticed. I expected Derek to go on, to say something about how things used to be different, how kids these days didn't know how lucky they were, that they needed sorting out, needed discipline. But he only said, 'Kyle's a good kid. Danny seems like a good kid. But what are they going to do when they get older? You see it all the time.'

Sean had a frown on his face; I thought he was going to say something, but Sonia said sharply, 'Those boys won't be trouble.'

'No,' Derek said. 'No, of course they won't.'

'That's right,' Sonia said. 'They'll do well, eh, Jo?'

She leaned in towards me; the conspiracy of women. I wondered again what Danny had said, who they thought I was, but I just forced a smile onto my lips and sipped my drink.

'Danny'll be fine,' Sean said. There was an edge to his voice, as if he expected one of us to disagree. 'He's got his head screwed on right.'

'Yes,' Sonia said, and lapsed into silence.

I looked at Derek, sitting so upright on the sofa, his expression neutral. I couldn't tell what he was thinking. I felt suddenly that I didn't know what anyone was thinking. Then Derek stood up and said, 'It's going to rain. I'll fetch the boys.'

Sonia looked a little surprised but said nothing. Outside, the skies had darkened further, the same brown clouds that had greeted our arrival the previous day. I watched Derek through the window, striding away from the van, head bent, protecting himself from the weather. Sean was watching him, too. We saw Danny and Kyle returning, meeting Derek, and then they started to walk back to the caravan. Derek was talking to Danny and Danny was listening with a frown; it was impossible to tell anything from his expression.

Sonia said, 'Why don't you let Danny stay for his tea? Kyle doesn't get to see many kids his own age when we're here. Do them both good, I bet.'

Sean said, 'Oh, no, that's okay.'

I ignored Sean's glare. 'That's very kind of you.'

'But we were going out tonight,' Sean said. 'Remember?'

The last word was said with force. I just smiled as the caravan door opened and the boys were followed in by Derek.

'I just invited Danny to stay for dinner,' Sonia said.

Derek gave a brisk nod of his head. 'Good idea.'

'But we're going out, aren't we, Danny?' Sean said.

Danny just shrugged. 'Can't I stay?'

Sonia said, 'We could have him back at yours by seven.'

Sean was outmanoeuvred. He looked at me, but I wasn't going to help. My heart was thumping. So

Sean gave in. 'Okay, okay, but don't be late back, eh, Danny?'

Danny nodded. Sean looked at Derek; I saw their eyes lock, and that chilled me. For a moment, I considered blurting out what was going on, throwing myself on Derek's mercy, hoping he would wrestle Sean to the ground, something. But I looked at Danny and Kyle, an excited pair giggling away, and I knew that I couldn't do it, not just then, not with them watching.

Sean and I got up and headed to the caravan door. As Derek stepped aside to let us pass, he suddenly said, 'Oh, have you read a paper today, Sean?'

'No,' Sean said. 'Didn't have a chance this morning. Why?'

Something changed in Derek's expression – I wasn't sure what, something in the eyes perhaps. He said, 'I just wanted to know the football scores, that's all.'

Sean hesitated for a moment, looking directly at Derek. I wondered whether he had seen the same thing as me. Then he made himself smile and said, 'No, sorry mate, can't help you there.'

And then we were out into the cold air, with the wind blowing hard against us and rain spattering down. We walked quickly, sheltering our heads, and didn't speak until we reached the caravan. My thoughts were in turmoil. I wasn't sure what had just happened, but I had the feeling it carried great significance.

When we were back in the caravan, Sean said, 'He's onto us.'

My pulse hammered. 'What makes you think that?'

'It's obvious, intit?' He glanced at me with contempt. 'All that effort to get Danny away from us. They're calling the police right now, I bet.'

'You're paranoid,' I said, as lightly as I could. 'You're just seeing stuff that isn't there.' But even as I said those words, I could imagine police cars driving slowly through the caravan park, and officers getting into position outside, and Derek and Sonia comforting Danny, telling him his ordeal was over, telling him he could go home.

Sean had found the paper Danny had bought that morning. He laid it out on the table and started to turn the pages, his finger marking a trail down the page as he scanned the headlines. On page five, he stopped. 'There,' he said. 'Paranoid, am I?'

The headline read 'Police Fear Kidnap of Boy and Social Worker'. I read the article over Sean's shoulder, feeling cold.

Police in Nottingham are growing increasingly concerned about the whereabouts of a twelve-year-old boy and a social worker. The boy, who has not been named, and 33-year-old social worker Joanne Elliott disappeared some time yesterday, it has been revealed. Police say there were signs of a break-in at Elliott's home in the New Basford area of the city, raising fears that the disappearance of the

*two may be linked and that they may have been
taken against their will. A police spokesman said,
'It's too early to speculate at this stage, but we
are concerned that something untoward may have
occurred. We urge anyone who thinks they may
have information relating to the whereabouts of
these two persons to come forward.' Ms Elliott's
car, a blue Renault Megane, is also believed to be
missing. Police refused to comment on speculation
linking the missing pair to Sean Metcalfe, 19,
who absconded from Glen Parva Young Offenders'
Institution last month.*

I didn't say anything for a moment. I felt a little sick.
But I wanted to laugh, too – they thought Sean had
kidnapped us. All this time I had thought I was in
so much trouble; I had thought people would be
thinking I had lost the plot completely, and here
they were, convinced that Sean had kidnapped me.
There might still be a way out of this mess – I just
had to think of it, that was all. My head thumped –
I couldn't seem to think straight, but I knew I had
to start quickly or Sean would do the thinking and
take my car.

I said, 'You really think Derek's read this?'

'Yeah,' he said. 'He'll be calling the police right
now.'

'What are you going to do?'

He closed the paper. 'Don't know. Get out of here,
I suppose.'

I realized his dilemma – should he wait for Danny

or go without him? Should he leave me here to reveal everything I knew? I had to stall him. 'Maybe Derek doesn't know,' I said. 'Maybe we convinced him? There's no reason why he would guess. He might not even have read the article. They call me Joanne in the paper but he knows me as Jo. Danny isn't even named in the article. Why would he suspect?'

Sean didn't say anything.

I said, 'Derek wouldn't really think Danny was kidnapped, would he? I mean, surely it's obvious? After all, he's been running around the beach on his own.'

I realized I was talking too much while Sean wasn't talking at all. I stopped, waiting for him to speak. I was hoping that he would decide to leave Danny here; that he would just take my car and go and leave us behind. I didn't know how I could explain to the police that I had stayed here with him, but I knew that I just wanted it to be over.

He said, 'I can't believe this.' He flung the newspaper away, onto the floor. 'This is all your fault. Never would've happened if you hadn't shown up.'

'That's not fair,' I started to say.

'You're always interfering,' he said. 'Christ, you make everything worse.' He turned to face me then, and I saw how angry he was. 'I should've kicked you out yesterday. Christ, I should've sent you and Danny packing. See what you've done? Fucking idiots.'

I said, 'We haven't done anything.'

He stepped towards me – without meaning to, I moved away from him and found my back against the wall. 'You brought Danny here,' he said. 'The police are after you, not me.'

'You invited Danny.' But he wasn't listening to me.

'I'd've been okay if it wasn't for you showing up,' he said. 'Why couldn't you leave us alone? Why are you so obsessed with Danny? It's not normal. You've wrecked everything.'

'I just want to help,' I said.

'You never do help. You just fuck everything up. You're not interested in helping me, you just want Danny. What is your problem? You can't get a man so you got to make do with a little boy, is that it? Fucking freak. Fucking pathetic.'

He swung his fist towards me as he spoke; I flinched away, but he didn't hit me, just struck the fibreglass wall next to my head. Then he turned away from me, strode across the caravan and back again. He raised his finger, pointed it at me. 'I told you,' he said. 'Danny don't want to go with you. What d'you think, that he don't know what I know about you? That he don't know that everything's your fault? That he don't know about me giving you a battering before? He knows everything. Thinks it's fucking hilarious.'

'That's not true,' I said.

'Yeah? How d'you think he knew where your house was? 'Cos I told him, that's how.'

'You're lying,' I said. 'He followed you one day,

that's all. He doesn't know anything about the day you attacked me. He'd have told me.'

'You reckon?' Sean laughed. 'You think he's so fucking wonderful. You haven't got a clue. Got you wrapped round his little finger, eh?'

He was close to me again, crowding in on me. I needed air; I needed to get some space. I pushed past him and went over to the table, then sat down. He stayed where he was, looking at me, smiling. I looked away. I didn't believe him – I thought he was just trying to cause trouble, to stir things up. But then, what if he was right? I thought about Danny in my street, breaking into my house, persuading me to bring him to Skegness. He hadn't persuaded me, I realized; he'd blackmailed me. He'd threatened me. Maybe he hadn't been as physical as Sean – but then, he didn't have the physical strength that Sean had.

I said, 'So what? So he got me to bring him here. Are you trying to tell me this was all some plan to get me here?'

He screwed up his face. 'Christ, you don't half like yourself, do you? I never wanted you here. I dunno why Danny brought you, but I never wanted him to. Stupid kid. He'll get me caught if I hang around here.'

His expression brightened slightly. I realized he had made his decision. I wondered whether Derek and Sonia had called the police yet. Sean moved around the caravan, putting things into a small rucksack – my mobile phone, my wallet, my money, my car keys. I tried to think, tried to work out how I could delay him until the police arrived.

Behind Sean was the caravan door. It was slightly ajar; I could see the dark night beyond. Every so often, Sean glanced back at it, looking out, as if he expected to see the police. The forecast storm was approaching; the wind was rattling across the caravan park and rain started to drum on the caravan roof. I wasn't sure Sean would be able to hear a car approaching.

I said, 'So, if this isn't about me, why were you watching my house?'

'What does it matter? I got you back, anyway. Your life's screwed up just like mine is. No more than you deserve.'

He opened the kitchen drawer and took out the knife. For a moment I thought he was going to threaten me with it again; he saw my expression and laughed softly, then wrapped the knife in a tea towel and pushed it into the rucksack. 'Like I said,' he said, 'you're so far up yourself you're completely paranoid.'

He looked around at the open door again, then started searching more drawers but I didn't know what for. I was watching the darkness outside, waiting for the arrival of headlights or maybe even the flashing blue lights that would signal the end of this situation. I saw a sudden movement out there – a dark shape appearing on the decking.

I said, 'You're leaving without Danny, aren't you?'

Sean laughed. 'Gotta go,' he said. 'I can't hang around here chatting, can I?'

The shape on the decking hesitated. I said, 'But you told Danny he could go with you.'

'I never meant it, though, did I? Stupid kid. He'd be a fucking liability.'

'You mean you lied to him?'

'I didn't know he'd be stupid enough to take me seriously, did I?'

The door flew open. Danny. He was soaked with rain, his hair plastered down against his head. Sean turned to face him – I saw him step back, surprised, and then Danny threw himself at him. Sean fell back, off balance, but quickly recovered; he grabbed out at Danny's hands, gripping them in his fists as he struggled to stop Danny hitting him.

I heard Danny shout, 'Bastard!'

Sean threw his arms around Danny, pinning him, holding him tight. Danny struggled. 'Calm down, calm down,' Sean was saying.

Danny broke free of Sean's grip and faced him, faced both of us. 'You lied to me.' He was crying, but it was anger I saw. 'I came to tell you,' he said. 'They've called the police. I came to protect you. You said I could come with you.'

'Jesus, you didn't really think you could, did you?'

'But you said—'

'That was before.'

Danny stopped, open-mouthed. I thought I could see his brain working – I thought I could see realization in his expression. He screwed his face up into a snarl. 'You're just the same as everyone else. I thought you was different. You said we could be together.'

'I didn't know things would turn out like this.' Sean's voice was surprisingly calm – I had expected him to be as angry as Danny. 'Danny, you've got to be realistic. There's no point getting mad about this.'

'I'm sick of being realistic,' Danny said. 'I done like you told me and now you're bailing on me. I don't want to go back.'

I thought he was going to start crying again. His posture had slumped; he looked crumpled. I remembered the kid who had come to my house, the boy who had asked for my help – I could help him, I knew that, even if his brother had abandoned him. I said, 'Danny, you have to come back home with me. We can sort all of this out, but you've got to come home.'

He rounded on me. 'I'm not going nowhere with you,' he said. 'Fucking freak, you are. You really think I'd want to go with you? I'm going with Sean.'

He was so angry. I looked at him, looked at the expression on his face. I wanted to see the boy I had tried to help but all I could see was that expression, and it reminded me so much of Sean. I looked from one brother to the other, and really, what was the difference between them? I had risked everything for Danny, I had thrown everything away to help him, and he was no different to Sean. He was just as selfish, just as unpleasant. He said he didn't want to end up like Sean, but he already was like Sean. I felt so stupid – I had believed him. He had fooled me, and I had thrown everything away to help someone who didn't deserve it. I thought of Katie Adams, and her children crying outside their damaged house, and all the things these boys had put her through. Katie Adams was the one I should have been helping – she was the one who needed me, and appreciated me, and deserved my help. So I said, 'Go on, then. Go with Sean. You deserve each other. You're as bad as each other, anyway.'

If I had expected that to have any kind of impact on Danny, I was mistaken. He just laughed, a high, hysterical laugh.

Sean said, 'Danny, you've got to go with her.'

'No—' Danny started.

'Mum'll be missing you,' Sean said. 'And all your mates, eh? Don't you want to see them?'

'No. You promised. They don't give a stuff, nobody does. That's what you said, intit, Sean? Nobody gives a stuff except us. Just us two together, that's what you said.'

Sean looked away from him, then over at me, as if he was appealing for me to say something more. I hardened my expression, folded my arms, tried to show him that I didn't see what this had to do with me. Danny watched Sean, narrowing his eyes. Then he said, 'I don't need either of you.' And he flung something at Sean; Sean threw up his hands to ward off the object as Danny headed for the door again.

Sean looked round at me – I registered that he had the toy gun in his hands, then he dumped it onto the table, called out, 'Danny!' and followed him out.

I only hesitated for a moment before I followed the two of them out into the storm.

Thirty-one

Outside, it was dark. Rain carried on the wind soaked me. I heard them running, their feet pounding across towards the sea wall. I followed. There was a small amount of sulphurous light from the street lights strung along the seafront path, and I saw Danny climbing the metal steps over the sea wall. Sean was ahead of me. I followed both of them over the steps and out onto the path. I ran towards the slipway onto the beach; Sonia and Derek were there, standing still, as if they didn't know what to do. Sonia called out to me as I passed, asking what was happening, but I didn't stop to explain. When I reached the bottom of the slipway, both Sean and Danny had disappeared into the darkness.

I stepped out onto the sand and walked straight ahead. I could hear the suck and crash of the waves somewhere to my left, and the wind battering against the sea defences and rattling down into the caravan parks. The rain was soaking through my clothes and I was cold, a deep cold that penetrated right into me, but I didn't turn back. I couldn't see anything at first, but gradually, I started to make out the lines of white breakers as the waves crashed onto the sand. Then I saw two dark shapes, contours of people rather than full figures, standing further along the beach. I walked towards them but they didn't show any signs of having heard or seen my approach. Their voices were raised, loud enough to be heard over the sound of the sea.

Sean was saying, 'You can't come with me, you've got to understand that.'

Danny didn't reply.

'I'll come back. I'll see you again. I won't forget about you, I promise.'

'You promised before,' Danny said. 'You lied to me.'

'I know. I was stupid. I'm sorry. But it'll all be fine now.'

'No,' Danny said. 'It won't be. You'll get arrested and they'll send you away again and everything'll be worse than before.'

I drew closer, but they still hadn't heard or seen me.

'It'll be okay,' Sean said. 'Jo'll make sure it's okay.'

'No, she won't,' Danny said. 'She don't care. She's just like everyone else.'

I reached them and came alongside Sean. He jerked as he realized I was there; both of them seemed surprised. I said, 'Danny, I just want what's best.'

'No, you don't,' Danny said. Shouted. He backed

away from us, towards the black mass of the sea. 'You're just out for yourself, like everyone else.'

'That's not true,' I said. 'I brought you here, didn't I? And now it's time to go back.'

'No,' he shouted. 'I don't want to.'

Both Sean and I moved towards him. He moved further away, into the surf. He looked down at the water surging around his feet, then laughed and kicked water towards us. It was swelling over his shoes, over the bottoms of his jeans.

'Come on,' I said. 'This is stupid. You're getting soaked.'

He looked down at the water again, then over his shoulder at the white glow of the breakers. He stepped further into the sea as Sean and I approached. My feet were at the edge of the surf now; I felt the sand shifting as each wave sucked around the shape of my shoes. The wind was picking up and the rain came down more heavily. The night had darkened – the string of street lights on the coastal path flickered through the rain, suddenly so far away. Danny started to laugh as the rain came down; he held out his arms, lifted his face up to the sky to feel the rain pelting down onto his skin, then backed further into the water, backing out of sight and into the darkness.

Sean waded into the water, towards Danny's laughter. I stepped further into the sea, feeling the surf foam and crash around my calves and thighs. It was a struggle to stay upright against the suck of the tide and the growing storm.

'Danny,' I called. 'Danny, come back, this is getting dangerous.'

The water came up around my legs, and the next wave crashed around my waist, so cold it sucked the breath out of me. I stumbled as I was caught by the swell of the breaker. I tried to keep my balance, the water breaking around me, my clothes filling with water and chilling me. I could only just see them ahead of me, but I heard Danny shriek and laugh at the thrill of the night sea, an uncontrolled sound, and I was scared, so scared, with the icy cold of the water gripping me and the suck of the tide so strong and the wind and the rain in my face, my hair, my clothes. I heard splashing, and Danny wasn't laughing any more, and I couldn't see or hear either of them in the darkness. I waded out further, the water breaking around my chest and lifting my feet from the sand. Sean was reaching out, trying to grab at Danny, but Danny backed further away. I wanted to call them back – I wanted to call Sean back, tell him that we were only forcing Danny into deeper water, we had to go back to the shore and let him come in, back to where it was safe. But I couldn't find my voice – I couldn't form the words, and even though I knew what we needed to do, I was still wading out towards them. I could hardly hear anything over the shrill wind and the roar of the breakers. My hands were icy and stiff as I reached out to grab Sean's arm – he tried to push me away, but I hung on, and my weight on his arm pulled him down, and he stumbled in the water.

'Get away,' he said. 'Leave us.'

'No.'

I wanted to say that we needed to get back to shore, that we had to get Danny into shallower water, but he broke free of my grip. I felt the contact of his fist in my face; a cold, hard fist driving into my eye, and I fell back towards the dark water. I grabbed out at anything I could find, grabbed out to stop myself falling, and I felt Sean fall with me. I was under the water suddenly, churned in the breakers, thrown head forwards towards the sea floor. I felt my face scrape the bottom, the gritty sand ripping at my cheek. My throat filled with salty water, and I struggled to get back upright, but I couldn't get my head above the water. More waves crashed over me – I was turned and twisted – I felt my head crack once, and then my arm twist heavily under me, and then finally I broke the surface, retching out seawater, gasping and coughing for air. My heart hammered; my head felt as if it had split open. I was disorientated – everything was so black, so dark, I couldn't see – and then I found my feet on the sea bottom and managed to stand and look around.

I couldn't see Sean but I saw Danny, a few metres away; I saw a flash of his white face, the sudden fright in his expression as the shock of the cold started to numb his body. I struck out towards him, half-swimming. I grabbed him in my arms, but even as I did so a breaker hit us, and I lost my footing, and I felt him going down under me, under the water, caught in the suck. I felt him struggling against me, struggling to get his head above the water again. He kicked out, and I remembered the feel of Sean's fist, and being spun around in the water, and falling as he hit me in the street, and the feel of the knife cutting my arm. I felt Danny writhing between my arms as I clutched him, and I held him tighter, and I remembered all the things he had said, all the things he had done. I had risked everything for him and he didn't even trust me – I had risked so much to save him and he was just like Sean, there was no difference between them. I felt my hands against his body, I felt his movements, and then my fingers closed around his neck, and even as I gripped him harder he kept struggling. I was trying to help him and all he ever did was fight against me – I had tried so hard for him and for Sean, and all they ever did was hurt me in return. I could feel him under the water, the kick of his body, his struggle for breath, but I kept holding him there, I kept hold of him.

I heard my voice, over and over, the same thing. 'I can help you. Don't worry. Trust me. I can help you.'

I felt my grip, so tight.

I felt the water heaving around me, the swell of each wave lifting me as the tide surged on.

And then I felt Sean, grabbing my arms, pulling my arms away. He was shouting something at me but I couldn't hear him – all I could hear was the wind and the sea and the storm. He struck out at me, knocked me away; I wanted to reach him, strike him back, show him what it felt like, show him what he had done to me and what I could do to him. I got myself upright again and waded towards him, but he wasn't looking at me. He was struggling to pull Danny in towards the shore. I went to him, started to help him, and he didn't push me away. Danny was heavy, his clothes heavy with water. I couldn't see his face – Sean was cradling him, lifting him into his arms as we reached the sand.

On the beach, I saw torchlight. People ran towards us. Sonia and Derek. They pulled Danny from Sean's arms, pulled him down onto the sand. He didn't seem to be breathing. Derek was on his knees, ripping open Danny's clothes, starting mouth-to-mouth resuscitation. I saw Sonia's shocked face, and the frantic activity around Danny as he lay there. I was struggling for breath myself. I waited for Danny to cough, splutter, retch out seawater and come back to life, the way they always did, the way it was on TV, the way it had to be. Sonia was on her mobile phone, calling for an ambulance, shouting the instructions, and the wind and the sea were so noisy, and then Sean was there, in front of me, and he looked more angry than I had ever seen him, than I had ever seen anyone. He was shouting at me, I knew that, but I couldn't hear him, I couldn't understand what he was saying.

And then Sean pulled back his fist and hit me, a blow to the chin, and I fell back, I fell onto the sand, and for a moment I gagged for breath, gagged against the salt in my throat. But I had to get up – I forced myself to get up, to face him. I could feel the impact of the punch, I could feel the sting of the long scrape down my face where the gritty sand had torn my flesh, I could feel the salt in the cut on my arm, the itching of the remnants of the wound on the back of my head, the salt eating into the flesh where the stitches had been. I remembered the feeling of falling into darkness, hitting my face on the shop floor, the other blows that had followed. I got back onto my feet and launched myself at Sean, and felt my fists, hard-clenched, driving against his face. I felt the contact of flesh with flesh, bone with bone, and pain ran through my knuckles but I hit him again, and he fought back, he hit me back, and there was nothing real apart from the feel of each blow, my fists against him, his fists against me.

Then I hit the ground. My knees hit the gritty sand, and I felt the sting of the sand and I opened my eyes and there was Danny, I could see him. I was down on my knees and I could see Danny, so pale, his body jerking as they tried to force the life back into him. I knew I should be helping, I knew there had to be something I could do to help, but I couldn't see what.

I got to my feet again. Somewhere far off I could hear sirens, and I looked at Sean, and he had heard the sirens, too. Before I could call out to him, before I could do anything to stop him, before I could tell him that his brother was more important, he was running away across the beach, back towards the caravan site.

'Sean!' I shouted. 'Sean, come back!' But he didn't turn, just kept on running, working his legs hard to get up the beach, across the sand and through the wind and the rain. 'Sean!' I shouted. 'Sean, wait!' But he didn't wait.

I looked at Danny, lying there on the ground, and all the activity around him; I heard the sirens drawing closer, and I knew I couldn't stay around, I didn't want to know what I already suspected. So I started running, too, up the beach, after Sean, my feet pounding against the loose sand, dragged down by the weight of my wet clothes.

I could hardly breathe as I reached the sea defences. I could see Sean running across the caravan park, and as I climbed the steps over the wall and onto the site, I saw him go into the caravan. I stopped to gather breath, to get some air into my lungs, and then he was out again, with his rucksack, running towards my car.

I ran again, towards the car, towards Sean. He started the engine; the car's headlights lit up the area suddenly, and I had to shield my eyes, but I kept on running. He was backing away from the caravan, preparing for a three-point turn to face the gravel track. He was really leaving – I hadn't expected him to actually go, not without Danny, not without me. I ran onto the gravel track, in front of the car. I could see him through the windscreen, gripping the steering wheel. I saw the concentration in his expression, and then he revved the engine, and he drove straight at me.

I stood there, stood up straight. The car acceler-
ated towards me. I realized that he thought I was
going to get out of the way, but I knew that the time
had come to finally make a stand. I wasn't going
to move, not for him, not for anybody. I spread
out my arms to block his path, waiting for him to
slow down, to stop, to yell at me, anything. I saw
again the image of Danny lying there on the sand,
and I closed my eyes. I thought about their father,
knocked down and killed on his way to meet me.
I thought about Alex telling me that he couldn't be
my friend any more, and Dave Short walking out of
my house that night, and the feel of my fist against
Colin's face. I thought about Katie Adams crying
into my blouse as the fire brigade dampened down
her house, and Danny telling me that he didn't want
to be like Sean, and Sean's face, his expression as he
told me that he would kill me if anything happened
to Danny. I kept my eyes closed. I didn't want to
feel any of this any more.

The car hit me. I felt the sharp crunch of metal
against flesh and bone, my knees crumpled, and I
was flung into the air. I felt myself tumbling through
the air. I felt as if I was floating, as if this was never
going to end. Everything was silent. There was cold
air all around me. Then I hit the bonnet of the
car with my shoulder, and my head smacked hard
against the windscreen. I could feel metal crumpling
under the impact. I could feel the heat of the engine.
I could feel everything.

Thirty-two

The first thing I became aware of was the pain in my knees. It started as an ache that cracked open the darkness; as I identified the sensation as pain, it expanded into a deep throb burning on the peak of each pulse beat. Then my head started to hurt; the sharp, stinging pain of cuts to the scalp alongside a tightness inside the skull. I took a long breath, felt the movement of my chest through every part of my body. I know I let out a moan; I heard the sound but it seemed disconnected from me. I opened my eyes, slowly. I tried to focus my eyesight but everything was blurred – colours smudged together, spots of light so bright that I had to squeeze my eyes shut and moan again.

'You're awake.'

The voice seemed to come from a long way away. I wasn't sure if it was a question or a statement. I wasn't sure whose voice it was. I opened my eyes again and the blurring began to clear. I recognized the caravan ceiling above me – the brownish hue, the slightly curved edges. I realized I was lying on my back on the bed, on the impossibly soft mattress, on top of the covers, still fully dressed. My clothes were stiff with salt and slightly damp under my body; my skin felt chilled where it rested on damp cloth.

I turned my head. Sean was sitting on the floor next to the bed, his back against the caravan wall, head just below the level of the window. The curtains were drawn but I could see light through them. Daytime. Sean watched me. He was holding the knife in his hands, playing with it, as if its shape gave him some comfort.

I tried my voice, cleared my throat, tried again. 'What's going on?' I asked.

He gave a feverish sort of laugh. 'What's going on?' he repeated, as though the question was absurd. His voice was very soft. 'The police are here. They're outside. They've been out there all night. They want me to release you.' That laugh again. 'They think I've got you hostage.'

'Why do they think that?'

'They think I kidnapped you from your house. Like the papers said.'

I could see that he was finding it difficult to take that seriously. I said, 'Did you tell them what really happened?'

'What's the point? They wouldn't believe me. Anyway, this way I get time to think.'

I tried to think about that, but my head hurt too much. I experimented with moving my legs; they hurt, but not as much as I had expected. My left arm wouldn't move; I thought of the car hitting me, that jolt of impact, and being flung into the air, and the slam against the bonnet and windscreen.

He said, 'They've got an ambulance outside. Different to the one that came for Danny.'

I wanted to ask how Danny was, but I didn't want to hear the answer I feared. I could imagine Sean sitting here all night, seeing the activity outside, all alone and nothing to do but think about things. I said, 'Sean, you've got to go out there. Give yourself up.'

'Give myself up?' He gave a little laugh. 'You actually think—' He stopped himself, hesitated, then said, 'Not until I'm ready. I told you, I need time.'

Before I could say any more – before I had thought what more I could say – I heard a mobile phone ringing somewhere in the other room. Sean looked at me, then went down to the other end of the caravan. I lay there, feeling the throb of my wounds, looking up at that brown ceiling. I didn't know what to do – I knew I had to do something, but I didn't know what. My brain felt a little numb, a little frozen – I wasn't sure I was capable of planning, of thinking straight.

I heard Sean answer the phone, then listen. He came back into the bedroom and handed me the phone. He was still carrying the knife.

'The police,' he said. 'Dave Short. He wants to talk to you.'

I felt my heart give a jolt, felt the rush of my pulse. I took the phone from Sean and held it to my ear. I was thinking about Dave driving all the way out from Nottingham; about the Lincolnshire police phoning him and asking, and Dave thinking about it, Dave deciding he needed to be here, Dave being so concerned. I put the phone to my ear and said, 'Dave?'

'Jo?'

That familiar voice, deep and calm. I wanted to smile. I could imagine him out there, huddled over a phone – or would it be more hi-tech than that, would there be a group of them listening in on headphones? I wondered whether they had planted microphones around the caravan to listen to me and Sean talk, or if they had a trained negotiator and armed officers on standby, just in case. I couldn't help shivering.

'How are you?' Dave asked.

'Okay,' I said. 'I'm hurt, though.'

'Did Sean hurt you?'

'He didn't mean to,' I said, eyes fixed on Sean.

I felt that I had to find words that would unravel the situation – there had to be something I could say. I almost blurted out that this wasn't what it seemed, that I wasn't a hostage, not really, but I didn't say that – after all, I didn't know what Sean was thinking. I didn't know how I could explain my being here, not without time to think. I didn't know how sympathetic Dave would be if he knew the truth, but before I could think of another way to explain, Sean had taken the phone away from me again. 'That's enough,' he said to me, and then, down the phone, 'See? She's fine, I told you.'

I heard a mumble of voices but couldn't make out

what was being said. Sean turned his back on me and paced the room again, the phone to his ear. Then he said, 'No, you listen to me.' There was force in his voice, determination; I realized that he did have a plan, he did know what he was going to do. 'I want a car,' he said. 'You bring me a car, I drive off, you get Jo. That's the deal.'

He cut the call off, put the phone in his pocket and rubbed his face in his hands. He was sweating, I could see that now – a sheen of sweat across his face. He seemed to be playing out a role; a role that he'd seen in too many movies, too many action thrillers with desperate men holed up in a bank with ski-masks and semi-automatics.

I said, 'They'd pull you over the second you left here.'

'Shut up.' Then he rubbed his hands over his face again, paced around a little more and said, 'Not if I take you with me.'

'You can't do that.'

'Why not? I'd let you out as soon as we were clear. You'd be fine.'

'It wouldn't work,' I said. 'They'd find you.'

'What do you care, anyway?'

'You need to give yourself up,' I said. 'Tell them now. Tell them you're going to go outside. That's all you've got to do.'

He came over to me, leaned in over me. I felt his weight against the bed, the mattress giving under his hands. He was gripping the knife, the blade flat against the bed covers, so close to my body

– I wanted to turn away from him, turn my head away from his face, but I didn't dare move. He was so close that I could see the dried salt on his face, crusted around the spots near his mouth, and the yellow of his teeth.

'You never shut up, do you?' he said. His teeth were almost clenched even as he spoke. 'You're always the fucking same. Just shut the fuck up while I think.'

Then he was away from me again, pacing the room. He had squeezed his hands into fists, elbows bent, his fingers gripping the knife.

'I told you,' he said, 'I told you I'd fucking kill you if anything happened to Danny.'

He seemed to be deliberately winding himself up, building up the energy to act. I wanted to demand what his intentions were, but I didn't know whether I could trust my voice. My mouth was dry. I tried to move, tried to roll myself onto my front – if I could get to the window, if I could only get there – but the pain swam up from my stomach to the back of my throat and I had to squeeze my eyes shut to stop the dizziness from making me vomit. I thought of all those people I read about in the papers, people who crawled from car wrecks with broken legs, people who chose to jump from tall buildings when flames licked up behind them, people who cut off their own hands when they got trapped in machinery. I didn't feel that brave. I couldn't move, however much I told myself I needed to.

'What happened to Danny was not my fault,' I said.

He stopped, mid-stride. 'How can you say that? How the fuck can you say that? I saw! I was right there!'

'I was trying to save him,' I said. I remembered the coldness of the water, the texture of his wet clothes between my fingers, the water expanding the fibres, the weight of his clothes. I had touched his jeans – the stiffness of the heavy cloth, and the lighter material of his T-shirt, material that floated out as I held him. He had been heavy in the water – I had thought he would float, I had thought he would be weightless but he was so heavy, struggling against me. I could remember the sound of the waves crashing around us, and seeing the white foam bursting over us, and the tug of the backsurge that had pulled me off my feet. I said, 'You said yourself he's a weak swimmer. You said that yourself.'

'I know what you did,' he said. 'Don't deny it. You weren't dragging him up, you were holding him under. You think I'm blind? You think I'm stupid?'

He had his back to me, but I could see that he was tense, almost hunched over. I said, 'Why would I hurt him? I was trying to save him.' I remembered how cold the water had been, so cold I could hardly breathe. I had felt Danny against me; I had felt the solidity of his weight, and his skin against my skin. I said, 'He was scared. It was dark. He was struggling. I tried, you have to believe that.' My words didn't seem to have any effect. 'Sean, why would I ever hurt Danny? You know I'd never hurt him, don't you? You know I was trying to help him, don't you? I wouldn't ever hurt Danny – I couldn't. You know that, don't you?'

He didn't reply right away. I wasn't sure if he believed me, but his shoulders had slumped slightly. He went over to the window, pulled back the curtains a little. I caught a glimpse of cloudy sky, then he dropped the curtain and turned to face me again. 'That's what I want to know.' There was a small crack in his voice. 'What's Danny ever done to you? What've any of us ever done to you?' He gave a low laugh, but it had a desperate edge to it. 'I'm the one you should want to hurt,' he said. 'This is between you and me. Danny should never have got dragged into this.'

'But he did get dragged in,' I said. Sean looked defeated. 'Come on, Sean, you need to end this. Stop things getting completely out of hand.'

'They're already out of hand,' he said. 'Danny's dead.' And then I saw the fury coming back – a flicker that came alight in his eyes and rushed across his expression. 'But you don't care, do you? Look at you. The only person you care about is yourself.'

'That's not true—' I started to say.

'It's your fault Danny's dead. You killed him.'

He was holding himself very still, very taut. I said, 'Why does there have to be someone to blame? It was an accident. A tragic accident. It wasn't anyone's fault.'

'You always say that,' he said. 'Danny was a tragic accident, but you killed him. My dad was a tragic accident, but it wasn't, was it? Someone knocked him down and left him to die. That wasn't an accident, was it?'

'Come on,' I said, gently. 'This isn't helping.'

He had turned his back on me. For a moment, I thought he might have been crying; his hand had gone up to shield his eyes. But then he turned again and I could see his anger. 'Tell me the truth,' he said. 'Did you have something to do with my dad's death?'

I was surprised. 'No,' I said. 'No, of course not. I was waiting for him in the café.'

He came closer and I saw that, despite the anger, there were tears in his eyes. 'Tell me about it,' he said.

'Why? I told you, I wasn't there.'

'Tell me anyway,' he said. 'I want to know.'

I didn't know what to say, but I could see that he was serious. I tried to think back – but it was so long ago, and what was there to remember? I said, 'I don't know. It was dark. Late on a winter afternoon. Raining. I got to the café – I can't remember what time. I had a drink and waited. I waited forty-five minutes. When he didn't show I drove home.'

'You said you saw the ambulance?'

'Yes, I did. Pulling out of the side road by the café. I was turning left. I looked to the right to check it was clear and saw an ambulance and a police car. I saw them loading a stretcher. That's all.'

He frowned, as if disappointed.

Before he could say anything more, I said, 'Did they ever charge anyone?'

'No. Fucking animals. They just left him there to die. Didn't even stop to see if he was okay.' Then he gave a short, bitter laugh. 'When I was in Glen Parva, doing all that thinking, I did wonder if you were the driver.'

His eyes had flicked up to look at mine, as if searching for a reaction. 'Me?' I said, and made myself laugh. 'Don't be daft.'

'Yeah,' he said, narrowing his eyes slightly. 'It was daft, wasn't it? But then again, everything does come back to you. It's your fault that all of this started.'

'You started all of this by attacking me in the street.'

He dismissed that with a flick of the hand. 'That was nothing. Christ, I hardly touched you.'

'You knocked me out,' I said. 'I needed stitches. Anyway, I don't just mean the head wound.'

He had an ugly sneer on his face. I thought he was going to laugh, maybe tell me I'd been feeble, I'd asked for it, I'd been too easy to scare, but he didn't. I remembered how scared I had been; tormented by the feeling that someone was out there, someone was after me, and the conviction that something nasty was going to happen. But I was the one who had come out here – I had brought Danny and now Danny was— But I hadn't intended any of this to happen. All I had wanted was to face Sean, to get him to explain, to justify, make him understand the enormity of what he had done to me. It occurred to me that we were both after the same thing; we were locked together by the same question. And I had no answer for him – I had no idea why he blamed me for everything that had happened to him.

He said, 'You still don't get it, do you? After all this, you still don't see what I mean. I'm not just talking about Danny, I'm talking about everything. Everything that's gone wrong comes right back to you.' He gave a little laugh. 'You're supposed to help, you know? That's meant to be your job. But no, you just cruise in and wreck everything. Wrecked my whole family. My dad died, my mum thought she wasn't worth shit, and then you took me and Danny away. Some help that was.'

'It wasn't like that. It's a hard job sometimes.'

'It's not about the job,' he said. 'It's about you. You fuck things up for people. You just can't help yourself. You think you're the only fucking social worker I've ever met? They're not all like you. Some of them even act like human beings, but not you. You say you'd never hurt Danny, but you hurt me, didn't you, when I was only his age? Remember that, eh? Remember punching me? I had a black eye for weeks.'

'That's not true,' I started to say, but he wasn't listening. He was prowling the room again, banging the handle of the knife against the palm of his other hand. I felt cold – I didn't know what he was building up to.

I said, 'We have to end this, Sean. This is getting

us nowhere. You need to tell the police you're coming out. We can talk all of this through after that, when we've got plenty of time, when we can think properly.'

He laughed, that same feverish laugh I'd heard when I first woke up. 'That's all you lot ever want to do, isn't it? Talk doesn't change nothing, though, does it? You know it – that's why you hit me when I was a kid. Couldn't get me to listen so you fucking punched me. And I was such a stupid kid I thought I'd be the one in trouble for making you do it.'

'It wasn't like that,' I said. I had been about to explain – explain that I had been trying to do the right thing, that things would have worked out fine if his mother hadn't made such a fuss, if he had only listened to me instead of fighting me – but why should I explain to him? He didn't deserve explanations, not when he would only use them as excuses for his own behaviour. Maybe I had lost control, but that was a long time ago – and why should I suffer for that now, all these years later? I was young then, I hadn't known as much as I knew now. So I said, 'That isn't true, Sean. Social workers don't go round hitting people, you know that. It just – it just doesn't happen.'

He let out a loud, derisive laugh – 'Hah!'

I said, 'I'd never do that. I'm not a violent person. I've never hurt anyone.'

He was approaching the bed again; my voice died away until it was barely audible. He sat down on the edge; I felt the mattress give under his weight.

He held out the knife, as if admiring its sheen, and then he leaned in and touched me, gently, on the throat with the flat of the blade. I felt the pointed end pressing into my skin. I held very still, not even breathing. I moved just my eyes to look at him as he pushed his face closer to mine and said, 'Scared?'

I found enough voice to whisper, 'No.'

'You should be,' he said, and pulled away from me slightly. He held the knife up for me to see; that sharp blade between our faces. 'You don't know what I'm capable of.'

I wanted to say something; I wanted to find the words that would break the tension, but I didn't know what to say. He actually believed that I had damaged his life – he didn't seem to realize that I had been helping him. I had only ever wanted to help. I had never expected him to thank me – even back then, when he was just an arrogant little boy, even then I had known that he wasn't the type to ever thank me. But still, it angered me that he wouldn't listen; even now, when he was most in need of my help, he still wouldn't listen. It was so – so self-destructive. It didn't matter what I said to him; he was never going to acknowledge that I had tried to help. And he seemed so certain of the things he said that I wondered whether he was delusional, if he had ever been tested for a mental illness.

I said, 'What are you hoping to achieve with this, Sean?'

'Achieve?' He seemed a little thrown. 'I don't know. A fucking apology would be a start.'

'Fine,' I said. 'I apologize. I'm sorry. Now tell the police you're giving yourself up.'

He brought the knife closer to my face. I saw the slight nicks in the serrated edge, a small blemish on the metal. His hand was shaking slightly. 'You don't mean that,' he said.

'I do,' I said. 'Honestly.'

He was looking into my eyes; his eyes moving over mine as if he was searching for something there. 'You're lying,' he said. 'I know you are.'

It didn't matter what I said; I realized that now. He was never going to accept that I knew what was best for him, he was never going to accept the simplest truth of this situation. I tried again. 'I'm very sorry that you think I've harmed you.'

'I don't think—' he said. I saw confusion, frustration, I don't know, in his eyes. He grabbed me: a fistful of shirt collar. The knife dropped from his hand. I cried out, but it was more out of surprise – fear – than pain. He said, 'You're never going to admit to nothing, are you?'

I tried to tear his hands away from my clothing. My left shoulder burned; my fingers wouldn't grip. He twisted my shirt collar, twisted it against my skin. I could feel the cloth tightening around my neck, pressing into my throat. I was struggling; he climbed onto the bed, climbed on top of me, and I felt his weight pushing me down into the mattress. I tried to kick him away but the sudden movement sent pain through my legs, and I sucked in all the air I could, but I couldn't breathe, he was stopping me breathe. I could feel the pressure in the flesh of my face, and the press of his fingers in my neck, and I needed air – I couldn't see – my vision was black with panic. I could feel myself going under – I could feel that I was losing, and he was holding so tight, squeezing, and I writhed under his weight.

He released me, suddenly. I fell back into the depths of the mattress. My throat was still constricted; I tried to cough, tried to suck air down, and my lungs burned. Then, finally, I could breathe, and the water cleared from my eyes, and I saw Sean standing over me, his hands stretched towards me as if he didn't know what to do.

'I didn't mean that,' he said, and he sounded scared.

I coughed again, put one hand to the sore skin around my neck. I didn't think I could have spoken even if I had wanted to.

'I wouldn't hurt you,' he said. 'I'd never hurt you.'

I would have laughed at that if I hadn't felt so sick. But there was something pleading in his tone, as if he desperately wanted me to agree. I closed my eyes. My fingers felt cool against my neck; I could feel my pulse against my fingertips.

The phone in his pocket started to ring. I heard him answer it, and a muffled voice, then he said, 'No, she's fine. Nothing's happened.'

He was approaching me. I opened my eyes and saw that he was holding the phone towards me, close to my mouth. He said, 'Tell them you're okay.'

'I'm okay,' I said, and I was surprised by the strength of my voice. I wanted to say more – tell them that he had nearly strangled me, anything – but I didn't even have a chance to hear a voice in response, Dave's voice, before Sean took the phone back.

Sean put the phone to his ear and said, 'Are you listening? I've got something important to say.' His voice was calm, but he didn't sound reasonable. 'I've told you what I want,' he said. 'I tell you, I'll fucking kill her if I don't get what I want. I mean it. I've got a gun.'

'No,' I cried. 'Sean, no, don't tell them that, don't say that,' but he ignored me. He cut the call off and put the phone back in his pocket. I said, 'Sean, why did you tell them that?'

'Shut up.' He reached down and picked something up off the floor, but I couldn't see what.

'But if they think you've got a gun—'

He was coming at me. I didn't know why – I threw my arm out to push him away but it didn't stop him. He climbed onto the bed, knees sinking into the mattress, and then he was astride me, his weight against my belly. He had something dark – dark material in his hand, and he laid the other hand against my forehead; a cold, sweaty hand. He pushed my head backwards; even as I protested he stuffed something into my mouth. I didn't know what it was – a cloth, a sock, something that tasted musty and dry. I tried to gag against it, spit it out, but he was forcing it in, his hand flat against my lips.

Then the cloth was near the back of my throat, and I thought he was going to suffocate me, and I couldn't breathe, I was going to pass out, but I couldn't get free of him.

He kept his hand pressed against my mouth; I felt the pressure against my teeth, felt the flesh of my lips crushed against my teeth. His other hand pushed underneath my shoulder blades, and he turned me over, quickly, so that I was lying face down. His weight in the small of my back pushed me down into the mattress. He wrapped something around my mouth and tied it behind my head. He forced my arms behind my back – my left shoulder crunched and I tried to cry out but my tongue was trapped, my mouth was full, I could feel the tightness in my throat. I felt him tying my wrists together behind my back, and then he got off the bed and stood up. Before I could do anything – kick out, or struggle, or something – he had grabbed my ankles, and I felt him wrapping the bedding around my feet until I couldn't move them. Finally he stepped away from the bed, into my line of view, and he was smiling.

He said, 'I told you to shut up. Now you'll have to, won't you? And I'll have a chance to think. They won't come bursting in now they think I've got a gun, will they?'

I didn't want to look at him any more, so I closed my eyes. I didn't want to open them again until this was all over. I heard him walk away, down towards the other end of the caravan. I tried to concentrate on the sounds I could hear from outside. There was a car engine, idling somewhere, and the distant murmur of voices, too far away to distinguish. I thought about Dave Short, crouched out there, talking to his colleagues. I wondered whether he was worrying about me – whether he was wishing he had done more to help me.

I felt the pressure on my wrists where Sean had tied me up. I flexed my hands, felt them move against the material he had used to bind me. I twisted my hands, tried to squeeze my thumb into my palm, tried to make my hand thin enough to slide out under the knots. The material scraped my skin, burning a little, but it had stretched – I had felt it stretch.

Sean came back into the bedroom and I felt the mattress dip as he sat down on the edge of the bed, somewhere near my knees. I opened my eyes. He was holding the knife in one hand and, in the other, Danny's toy gun, the stupid plastic pellet gun he had made such a joke of.

'You know,' he said. 'You're probably right about this gun. It probably does look real from a distance. What d'you reckon?'

I wanted to tell him not to do it. I could imagine them outside, discussing whether he really did have a gun. Did they have an Armed Response Unit there? I didn't want to think what they were predicting would happen next. I made a half-hearted attempt to speak through the gag but it was no good. Sean smiled. 'Yeah, I agree,' he said as he got up and went to the window. He stood there for a moment, looking at the gun, then pulled back the curtain and waved the gun quickly across their line of view. He dropped the curtain back into place and came back to me.

The phone started to ring. He took it from his pocket and answered it. He raised his voice. 'Of course it's fucking real,' he said. 'You want me to shoot her just to prove it?'

I tried to moan, wriggle, struggle, anything that might be heard by them and interpreted. The material around my wrists loosened a little more, but I couldn't pull myself free, not with him so close to me. I wanted to send thought-vibes down the phone – get Dave to think about this, because where would Sean get a real gun from? Dave couldn't possibly think he was that well connected – Dave couldn't possibly think he would go that far.

'And get us some food,' Sean said. 'Fish and chips or something. We're starved in here.'

He didn't look at me when he said that. I remembered the role I had thought he was playing earlier; the lone movie hero, outnumbered, outgunned. I wanted to tell him not to be so stupid – I wanted to tell him that this wasn't a game, but there was nothing I could do.

He cancelled the connection and put the phone back in his pocket. 'That should do it,' he said. 'Reckon they'll fall for that? Yeah, I think so, too. The food was a nice touch. People always ask for food, don't they?' He laughed again, sat down next to me, clapped his hand against his knee. 'So, here we are, eh? Alone at last. Who'd've thought I'd end up with you tied up in my bed, eh?'

He obviously found that funny. I didn't react. The bindings on my wrists felt looser, but I didn't move.

He said, 'Well, this is good. I can say anything I like and you won't answer me back. That makes a change, 'cos you've got a big mouth. Anyone ever tell you that, Joanne Elliott? You should shut your mouth and listen sometimes. Put a sock in it.' He giggled at his own joke. 'Well, got no choice now, have you? Got no fucking choice.'

He was silent for a moment. I tried to seek out eye contact, hoping I could get some sympathy, some sort of connection from him, but he didn't look at my face. Instead, he put the knife down on the mattress, near my head, and reached one hand out, touching the gag around my mouth. I thought he was just checking it was still secure, but then he said, 'Did I hurt you before? I never meant to.' His voice was surprisingly gentle. 'All this,' he said, very quietly, 'all this, it's just a show, intit? I mean, if I really wanted to hurt you I'd have done it already, wouldn't I? You were unconscious on that bed for most of the night. I could've done it then if I was going to.'

I wondered again whether the police could hear him, whether microphones were picking up his words. Surely they would know by now what was really going on here – know that the gun wasn't real? Sean had said as much himself – but I couldn't remember what he had actually said, I couldn't work out how the police would have interpreted it, and they did seem to be taking Sean's threats seriously. But whatever was going to happen to Sean wasn't my problem – I had to force myself to remember that.

Sean went on, 'I don't know why I'm so worried about you, anyway.' There was a little anger in his voice now; he pulled away from me, hardened his tone. 'I'm the one in the shit. Don't matter what I say to them, you'll still come out okay.'

But that wasn't true, I realized. I thought of Danny with a jolt of nausea. If they ever knew what had really happened – if they found out I'd chosen to bring him here myself – what would happen to me?

Sean said, 'Christ, I'd've been long gone if you hadn't got in the way. If I hadn't stopped to check you were okay. I must be mad. I should've cleared off when I had the chance.'

And if he had – if he had disappeared and never been found, I would have been in the clear. If they never heard his version of events, they would think I was the victim. Which I was anyway, of course, but they wouldn't understand that, not the way things stood.

He said, 'But I know why I stayed.'

His hand was still resting lightly against my cheek. He had a slight smile on his lips but it couldn't disguise the frown around his eyes. He said, 'Everything comes back to you, don't it? Everything just fell apart because of you.'

He hesitated, then ran his finger along the shape of my chin. I held still, feeling the tingle of his light touch. I wasn't sure whether to feel sick or scared. He went on, 'I reckon there's some people whose lives just get all tangled in with each other. Know what I mean? You're right in there, all tangled up with why things are the way they are. We're linked, you and me. Karma, intit?'

He seemed to expect an answer. There was nothing I could do, so I showed no reaction.

He said, 'You know about karma, right? What goes around comes around? I used to think it was a load of crap, but you know, maybe it isn't? Maybe everything gets balanced out in the end. What d'you say to that?'

Again, I couldn't answer. I wasn't sure what I could have said if I had been able to speak. He edged a little further up the bed, towards my head, and moved his hand across my face to stroke my hair, smoothing it where it fell across my forehead. I felt the soft warmth of his touch. I could see the knife lying on the mattress close by, but he didn't pick it up.

He let out a long breath, then took his hand away. 'Shame this has to come to an end, eh? I could get used to this. But you know what they say, all good things and all that.' He laughed, a high, unnatural sound, and looked down at me, right into my eyes. 'All these years,' he said, 'and it comes to this. A flea-blown caravan in Skeggie with the police waiting outside. Who'd've thought it?'

I looked up at him. I wanted to know why he thought that this was the end, but the possible answer scared me. I was surprised to see tears collecting in his eyes; the lids of his eyes reddening and liquid swimming over his dark irises until I could see myself reflected there, distorted but reflected. I remembered the boy he had been; the boy who had needed my help so badly that he hadn't known how to handle it when I offered it to him.

He said, 'I don't want things to end like this.' He gave a little laugh, a bitter, angry sound, rubbed his sleeve over his eyes, and laughed again. 'You can make this right,' he said. 'I know you can. You can explain it all to them. Explain why you came here. Why you brought Danny.'

I lay very still, barely even breathing. I wanted to tell him that things couldn't be undone, that he had already made his choice. I wanted to tell him that there was nothing to be gained in sacrificing myself for him.

'You can tell them about when I was a kid,' he said. 'Tell them what really happened.'

He didn't seem to realize that it wouldn't make any difference, not for him. I had acted in his best interests; the way things had worked out was his fault, not mine. I wanted to tell him that the world wasn't as unforgiving as he seemed to think, but I knew he wouldn't believe that. I wasn't even sure that I believed it. And did he really think that I could undo all the years? There was nothing I could say – and I didn't want to, anyway. I had tried to help him, but I couldn't take responsibility for his actions. If I let him go out there – if I let him tell people his version of the truth, they would never understand. He would twist it, distort it, and it wouldn't help him but then they would never believe me, and where would that leave me? He couldn't end up much worse off than he was already, but me – I could lose everything, and what would happen to me then?

He said, 'Tell me what to do. Tell me how to get out of this. I don't know how to get out.'

There was no way out, not for him or for me. If he told them about Danny, I would be out of a job at the very least – career over, and what else did I have?

He was reaching over me. I had a moment of panic, not knowing what he was doing, and then I felt him untie the gag and remove it. He pulled the cloth out of my mouth, and my mouth was so dry and empty and sore; I gasped in air.

He said, 'Tell me how to end this. I don't care any more, I'll even go back to Glen Parva, I don't care. I don't want things to be like this.'

I tried to speak, but my tongue felt oddly out of my control, as if it had swollen. I tried to swallow.

He said, 'If I tell them what happened to Danny, they'll have to listen to me. That's what I have to do, isn't it? Go out there and explain everything. That'll make it okay, won't it?'

He was looking at me as if he expected me to agree; as if he thought I would approve. There was a desperate edge to his words, though – I realized that he didn't believe them any more than I did. He wanted me to save him, to tell him how to get out of this, but I couldn't give him any glib assurances – there was nothing I could say. I felt cold.

He said, 'Tell me what really happened with my dad.'

'I told you already,' I said. 'I never even met him.'

'No,' he said. 'I mean the truth.' I raised my gaze to meet his. He said, 'You can't carry a secret like that around for ever. Those things eat you up. You should tell me everything. You'll feel better, I promise.'

I forced myself to laugh. 'There's nothing to tell.'

'Yes, there is.' His voice was quiet, level, with an almost dreamlike quality to it. Like he was hypnotized; or like I was. He said, 'I figured out why you punched me when I was a kid. It wasn't my fault. It wasn't even your fault, not really. I mean, you were in pieces – I'm surprised nobody else spotted it. But I never made the connection, so why would anyone else? You were in that state because of what you did to my dad, weren't you?'

'No,' I whispered, barely audible. But he was making me think about that night again; about the heavy rain, so heavy it washed down the windscreen and overwhelmed the wipers, and about the way the street lights flared and danced in the distortion, and about leaning forward over the wheel, trying to see the road. 'I went to the café but he never came,' I said.

He said, 'It was you. I know it was you. It's written all over your face. You were losing it before he died, I know that, but I've had time to think about it since. You were stressed out before, but you were a wreck afterwards.'

I wanted to stop him saying those things. My hands pulled at the bindings around my wrists, but I couldn't get free. 'I don't want to think about back then. I was sick, I couldn't cope, but it has nothing to do with your dad.'

'Tell me what happened the day he died.'

'Nothing,' I said, but I couldn't stop myself remembering. I couldn't stop myself remembering pulling into the car park, getting out of the car, sheltering under my umbrella as I locked the door. I hadn't heard him approach me over the hiss of the rain falling; it had given me a jolt when he said my name. I stretched out my hand in greeting but he just stood there, hands wedged into his jacket pockets, rain streaming down over his woolly hat and onto his face, running off his nose, off his chin. He didn't seem to notice the rain. Before I had thought what to say, he started to talk. Those cold eyes looking at me; hard eyes, a hard expression, a mean little man. He was telling me that I had no right to interfere, that I was causing trouble, that he wouldn't let me destroy his family. I tried to say that I just wanted to talk, that I was looking for a way to resolve the situation, that I didn't want to destroy his family, but he had his fists clenched at his sides and I could see that he wasn't listening.

I said now, 'Sean, your father was a very unpleasant man, but I didn't kill him.'

'How the fuck do you know what he was like? You said you never met him.'

'Okay,' I said. 'Okay, so I did meet him. In the car park. But I didn't kill him.'

Sean frowned, trying to think that through.

I said, 'I thought you were going to end this now? Go out there and tell them everything you think you know about me? Well, go on, then. Tell them what you think happened to Danny.'

'No,' he said. 'No, I want to know about my dad. I want to know why you killed him.'

'I didn't,' I said. 'Don't be absurd.'

'But if you saw him in the car park, why wait for him in the café? It doesn't make sense.'

The coffee had been too milky, too weak, I remembered that much. Sitting there chain-smoking; I drank three cups of coffee before I felt even slightly calm. 'Your dad wound me up,' I said. 'The things he said – he was poison, Sean. He really shook me up. I went there to calm down.'

'After you knocked him down.'

'No,' I said. 'I left him in the car park.'

I had seen him stop at the car park entrance. He was wet through, the rain pounding down on him, but he had stopped and turned and leered back at me. The car park was edged by a knee-high trim, a single-barred metal fence running around the tarmac square – he could have stepped over it, but he was waiting for me to exit first. In his expression, I saw all the contempt, all the mistrust and loathing that made me hate my job, that made me hate the people I worked with and the estates I visited. I started the engine but as I eased out towards the exit I was filled with a bright burn of anger that made me grip the wheel hard, clench my jaw. He was laughing at me – I couldn't stand to see the laughter twisting his cruel face. I felt the emotions like a surge of energy through my whole body. He was laughing, and there was nothing I could do about it, and in that moment I felt the car move forwards, and I jammed my foot down on the accelerator.

I had only caught him with a slight blow. A tap, nothing more. I swung the wheel, slid on the slick tarmac, headed out onto the road. I twisted my body to look behind me and saw him lying as a dark huddle on the pavement. A slight blow and he had been thrown clear of the car park, right over that little fence.

I said, 'I didn't kill him,' because I couldn't have done, not that easily, not when I hadn't meant to.

Sean said, 'Didn't anyone see the damage to your car?'

'There wasn't any,' I said. I had been surprised by that. Not a broken headlight, not even a dent or a scratch. Then I realized what I had said. I realized that I was in the caravan still, that Sean was there, that he had heard my words.

I said, 'There wasn't any damage because it wasn't me,' but I knew it was already too late.

Sean let out a long breath. I couldn't read his expression. I didn't want to. He said, 'You have to tell people.'

'No. There's nothing to tell.'

'Then I'll tell them,' he said. 'I'll tell them that you left him there to die. You mowed him down and left him to die like an animal, like a fucking animal.'

And he would do it. There was no point appealing to him, no point telling him that it wouldn't change anything. I couldn't let him go out there and tell them what he thought he knew. His father – Danny. . . . He could destroy everything, and I couldn't let him do that. I twisted my hands, working them against the loosening material, but he didn't notice.

'I went back for you,' he said. 'I brought you in here, checked you were okay, when I could have got away. I did that for you, but you left my dad to die in the street. How could you do that? How could you live with that?'

He was starting to move away from me; I had to act. I pulled my hands free of their binding, forced myself to move, forced myself to grab the knife off the mattress with both hands. A spasm of pain ran down my arm from my damaged shoulder; nerve-endings tingled and numbed, but I couldn't stop now. He realized what I was doing, turned back, reached his hands out towards the knife. My fingers closed around the handle a moment before his hands closed over mine. I tried to pull the knife away from him.

'No,' he said. 'I don't want to hurt you.'

But he already had hurt me. I remembered the car hitting me; remembered Sean striking me across the back of the head, and that long plunge down into unconsciousness. I thought about Dave outside, and Alex with Louise, and Colin's hand over his face after I had hit him. I couldn't allow Sean to destroy what was left of my life – he couldn't get away with hurting me. I held onto the knife; he was trying to break my grip, twisting my fingers, but I held on. He was so strong, so much stronger than me, but I couldn't let him win. My shoulder burned; I could feel every bruise, every cut across my body, and the strain of muscles, and the oxygen in my lungs, and the blood in my veins. He was strong, but I had strength, too. His knees dug into the mattress; he was above me, trying to get the knife away from me, and I couldn't allow that. I pushed the knife up towards him and the tip of the blade wavered close to his body, snagging on his loose T-shirt.

'Don't do this,' he said, 'I don't want to hurt you,' but I knew he was lying, I knew because he'd hurt me before, and now he could destroy me.

He tried again to jerk the knife out of my grip, and I felt the heat of the blade against my fingers, slicing into my soft flesh. I saw my blood on my hands, bright red smears, and I pictured his flesh cut through, and streaks of blood on his pale skin. The pain sharpened; he was forcing the blade into the palm of my hand, trying to make me drop the knife. I jerked away from him but didn't release my grip, because I couldn't relax my fingers; I needed to feel their pressure against the smooth knife handle.

He was leaning over me, closer to me, closer to the knife, and I felt it press against his chest. I felt the resistance of his flesh, the solidity pushing against the tip of the blade. He was fighting me but I was stronger; I realized that I had always been stronger. I plunged the knife up, up to where I thought his heart was. The blade punched through his clothing, through his skin, into the firm mass of his body. I didn't hear him cry out; I couldn't hear anything over my own breath, and the roar of blood inside my head, and the volume of my own voice. It took all my strength, everything I had to force that blade in.

My eyes were closed – I didn't want to see anything. But I stabbed him again, and a third time – I couldn't stop myself repeating the action. I could feel something hitting me; heavy drops of hot liquid, and then a gush that splashed onto my chest, my neck, my face. Sean's hands scrabbled against me, fingers finding my eyes, my mouth; I tasted his blood, tasted it as his fingers forced my lips open.

I thought I heard him trying to suck in breath, but I couldn't be sure. Then he seemed to slump; I sensed him falling before the blunt end of the knife handle hit me hard on the breastbone, and his weight pushed me down into the mattress, expelling the air from my lungs. I tried to breathe but he was so heavy, his weight engulfing me, and the knife handle had me pinned, its blade sinking deeper into his flesh. I needed air – I couldn't breathe. I opened my eyes and saw a haze of red, and I couldn't tell if it was blood or if I was suffocating, and I could feel pools of liquid, pools of his blood on me, soaking through my clothes and onto my skin, running out to the edges of my body, streaming down my sides and collecting against the mattress. I wanted to scream but I couldn't even breathe. I wanted to move but I was pinned down by his weight, by the knife handle connecting his chest to mine.

I closed my eyes again. I could feel my heart thumping beneath the knife handle, and the pull of my lungs as I sucked precious air down. Every muscle, every tendon, every joint burned with the effort of breathing. I could feel every part of my body anchored by his weight, and his head lolled against my neck. I could taste the bitter metallic flavour of his blood in my mouth. I wanted to move – I needed to move – but I was trapped.

I kept my eyes closed even when there were people around me. I didn't open my eyes when the weight was lifted off me, or when I heard Dave speaking to me, softly, or when they helped me to sit up and wrapped a blanket around my shoulders. Dave held me tight as he talked to me, held me so tight that I felt as if our bodies were merging, our molecules combining, and I didn't want him to ever let me go. He was telling me that I was safe now, Sean couldn't hurt me now, and it hadn't been my fault, I had only been defending myself, and he was right, he was right. I let Dave hold me tight, let him say that he wasn't going to leave me, and I needed to hear those words, I needed those words to block everything else out. I was thinking about being unconscious, about that dizzying fall towards the shop floor and the comfort, the warmth of the darkness that had greeted me. Sean could have done anything he wanted while I was lying there, just as he could have during the night, when he had put me on the bed and waited with me while the police gathered outside. He could have done anything, but he didn't. I could feel the impact of the knife handle on my breastbone, long after he had gone. I couldn't feel anything apart from the heat of the bruise that was growing there.

Thirty-three

Dave followed me into the through-lounge and put the cardboard box he was carrying down on the carpet. I set mine down next to his and we both straightened up. It was a warm day, the start of summer, and there was a gloss of sweat on his face. I laughed and reached up to kiss him quickly on the lips.

'You look hot,' I said.

He grinned and moved in closer to me, his hands running to my waist. 'Not as hot as you,' he said.

I laughed again and pushed him away. 'Come on. We've got to get your stuff upstairs before people start arriving.'

'We've got ages yet,' he said, but turned to go back outside. 'This should be the last trip.'

I followed him back into the street. The air was thick with the summer heat. I could hear the tinny sound of distant stereos, and car engines, and I could taste exhaust fumes in the air. The sky was cloudless; perfect barbecue weather. Dave had his car boot open and started loading items into my arms – I pretended to stagger under the weight and he laughed and said, 'Nearly done.'

'We deserve a nice cold beer after this,' I said.

I took the armful of items into my house – our house – and dropped them onto the sofa. I could see Dave through the window, trying to lock the boot without dropping the things clutched under his other arm. I could have gone back to help him, but I stood there at the window and watched him instead. Until that moment, I had never quite been sure that things were going to work out between us. At first, I thought he was only staying around me out of guilt – I had thought that about Alex, and Colin, and all our other friends, too. But as time went by, I realized that I was the one feeling the guilt; and I was the one person who didn't deserve to feel any. Dave had made me see that.

I went into the kitchen and fetched two small bottles of beer from the fridge. I opened them both and took them back into the through-lounge just as Dave put down the last of his stuff. I handed him one of the bottles and held mine up. He touched his bottle against mine and smiled.

'Welcome to our house,' I said.

'Thank you,' he said, and took a sip of beer.

I sipped mine too. The chilled liquid made me shiver after the stickiness of the day. Dave took another swig from the bottle, then put it on the mantelpiece and started to collect together the items I'd dropped onto the sofa.

'Here, let me.'

'No, no,' he said. 'You must be tired. They'll be here soon. Go and get ready, I'll deal with this.'

Taking the bottle of beer upstairs with me, I went into the bathroom. I closed the door, put my beer down on the windowsill and took my T-shirt off. I leaned over the bath and washed my hair with the shower attachment, working the suds into my roots. The water ran warm across my neck as I rinsed the suds out. Then I wrapped a towel around my head and ran myself a hot bath, dropping in some of the aromatherapy oils that people from the office had bought for me while I was signed off work. The scent was slightly sickly, too sweet, but when I got into the bath and lay back and closed my eyes, the steam and the oils did have a strangely soothing effect.

I lay there for a long time, feeling my skin soften and wrinkle. When the water started to cool, I opened my eyes and looked down at my body. I still had stiffness in my shoulder and knees sometimes, and it had taken a long time for most of the cuts and bruises to fade from my skin. I looked at my hand, at the soft pad of flesh below my thumb. There was a scar there, a zig-zag of hard white tissue that I could feel when I ran my fingers over it. Defence wounds, the doctors had said – I'd been trying to stop Sean stabbing me, of course I had cuts on my hands. Sometimes, Dave would catch me looking at the scar, or running my fingers over it, and he would take my hand and raise it to his lips. A sign of my bravery, Dave called it, as he kissed the snake of ridged tissue; gentle lips touching the only mark left by the experience.

Wrapping a towel around me, I went back into the bedroom. The bed was still unmade; I smoothed the duvet before opening my wardrobe and laying out the outfit I'd decided to wear for the barbecue. Dave had told me not to worry about it – it was just our friends, after all – but I wanted to make an effort, now that the marks from my injuries had finally faded. I felt that this was a new beginning; the start of my new life, and Dave was always going to be there with me.

The bedroom door was closed and I could hear Dave coming up and down the stairs, putting his things in the spare room to sort out later. I suddenly wanted him to come into the bedroom, to find me still wrapped in my towel and start to unwrap me; I wanted him to be unable to resist, to be overwhelmed. I imagined that, and people arriving, people coming upstairs to look for us and realizing – I imagined Alex's expression if he burst in on us. I nearly called out to Dave but I felt slightly sleepy from the hot bath and the oils, and before I summoned the energy I heard him going down the stairs again.

I dried myself slowly and got dressed, pausing to take sips from my beer. Now that the barbecue was approaching, I felt nervous. I wasn't sure why – after all, I'd seen all of my friends at various times since, and even before I was out of hospital Alex and Dave had explained to them what had happened. I was still in hospital when the inquests were held, and the media had been all over the story for a couple of weeks, trying to get into the ward to interview me, wanting to hear about the kidnap from the victim herself. They paid a lot of money to Gary Adams for his account of the neighbours from hell, and several papers ran photos of Katie Adams with her children huddled around her, next to a small photo of the Metcalfe house, boarded up. I didn't read everything that was printed; I just wanted to get back to work and put it all behind me.

I heard Dave calling me from downstairs. I went to the bedroom door and opened it a little. 'What?'

'Colin's here. And Alex and Louise.'

'I'll be right down,' I said.

I went back to the mirror and brushed my hair through, looking at my reflection. Soon everyone would be downstairs, and even if we had officially called it Dave's moving-in party, everyone knew what this really was. I wondered whether maybe I should make a speech, try to explain, but I knew they would never understand. Even people like Alex and Colin – even they wouldn't understand, and I knew I would never be able to articulate it. But it was like Colin had said, in that previous life, sitting in Alex's back yard with a beer in our hands. You had to get on with it or get out, and I had no intention of getting out.

Even after everything had happened, even when the nightmares were still making me wake, covered in sweat that felt like his blood, shaking and struggling for breath; even then, I knew I couldn't give in. One wrong word, one slip and I could undo everything I had achieved, and I was still needed – Sean's desperate appeals for my help showed me that. I had given that family a great gift – a chance at a new life, free of the violent husband, the vindictive father. I had given them what they needed, but they didn't recognize what was good for them. Sean hadn't realized – and it was my fault that I hadn't managed to save him. I hadn't even saved Danny, but their sacrifice did have meaning, I could see that now. I hadn't saved them, but they had saved me. I had been hurtling down the same self-destructive path that I'd been trying to pull Sean back from, but they had saved me from that. I didn't have to deny things to myself any more – I knew that I was needed, that there were more people who needed my help. People who weren't able to make decisions on their own – I saw it so often; every time I went into one of their mean little houses, and sat on their second-hand furniture drinking cheap tea, and talked to their snotty, scrawny children, and heard all their whining excuses. They needed me to take charge, just as Sean had needed me, just as Danny had. They needed me to find solutions to their problems, however hard those solutions turned out to be. I wasn't going to hide from my responsibilities. Other people – Alex, Colin – might hold back, might allow a situation to drift, but I wasn't one to give in so easily, not when I knew what needed to be done, not when I had already come so close to losing everything.

When I woke with nightmares, Dave woke, too, and held me tight, moulding his body around mine as I waited for my breathing to calm. He would brush my hair with his hand, and snuggle in closer, and then I would listen to his breathing as he drifted back to sleep.

Dave told me it would all take time, I had to allow myself time.

It had taken me a while to get used to the way people spoke when they were around me – the hushed, level tones, as if any loud noise, any kind of emotion might trigger off bad memories, might be too much to cope with. And people didn't complain in my presence any more – even when I could see that something was tearing at their insides, even when they could barely keep their anger or frustration or upset in check, if I asked how they were they just put on a brave sort of smile and said, 'Oh well, mustn't grumble.' I had the feeling that they were embarrassed that their suffering, their problems were never going to be big enough to match the things I'd been through. I wanted to tell them that it was ridiculous, that this wasn't a competition to find out who had suffered the most. But then, I knew they wouldn't understand that. They would just think I was being even braver, and that would make them feel even worse, but what was brave about it?

'It's how you're coping with it,' Dave had told me

when I tried to talk to him about it. 'You seem so together about it all. So strong.'

I had laughed and said, 'What, did they expect me to go to pieces?'

He hadn't replied immediately, and I realized that was exactly what people had expected – they had all thought I wouldn't cope. I said, 'I've changed.'

'I know you have,' Dave said. 'You're so much stronger now.'

I rubbed my hair with the towel, thinking about that. It wasn't strength; I knew that now. None of this was about being strong, or being able to cope. It was about being hard, about not being affected, about not letting anything get in the way when I knew I was doing the right thing. It was about courage, yes; the courage to push on, no matter what the obstacles.

I ran the brush through my hair one last time, straightened my dress and opened the bedroom door. I could hear voices and laughter from downstairs. A CD started playing – 'Sunny Afternoon' by The Kinks, one of my favourites. I wondered whether Dave had chosen that track especially; a way to call me downstairs. I stood at the top of the stairs and listened to the song right to the end, and I could hear my friends having a good time, waiting for me to join them.